City of Ash

Also by Megan Chance

Prima Donna

The Spiritualist

An Inconvenient Wife

Susannah Morrow

City of Ash

A Novel

MEGAN CHANCE

Broadway Paperbacks / New York

BROADWAY

This is a work of fiction. Names, characters, places, and incidents either are the product of the author's imagination or are used fictitiously. Any resemblance to actual persons, living or dead, events, or locales is entirely coincidental.

Published in the United States by Broadway Paperbacks,
an imprint of the Crown Publishing Group,
a division of Random House, Inc., New York.
www.crownpublishing.com

Library of Congress Cataloging-in-Publication Data
Chance, Megan.
City of ash: a novel / Megan Chance.
p. cm.
1. Great Fire, Seattle, Wash., 1889—Fiction. I. Title.
PS3553.H2663C58 2011
813'.54—dc22 2011001060

ISBN 978-0-307-46103-2
eISBN 978-0-307-46104-9

Printed in the United States of America

BOOK DESIGN BY BARBARA STURMAN
COVER DESIGN BY KYLE KOLKER
COVER PHOTOGRAPHS: (WOMEN) © GETTY IMAGES;
(SEATTLE) © UNIVERSITY OF WASHINGTON

2 4 6 8 10 9 7 5 3 1

First Edition

To Lynn Corbat, Beth Johnson,

Peggy Lanzafame, and Pat O'Malley,

for all the years of laughter, friendship, and support.

This one's for you.

Leave the fire ashes, what survives is gold.

—Robert Browning, from *Rabbi ben Ezra*

City of Ash

Chapter One

Geneva

Chicago, 1888

I remember very well the night that changed everything, although of course I could not know it then. One could not tell at the start that it would be different from any other night, because even the lavish display of Louise Berkstad's ballroom could not disguise the fact that the same faces wandered among the vases of blooming night jasmine perfuming the air, nor that the same musicians played the same tunes beneath a ceiling painted deep blue and spangled with stars of phosphorescent paint, nor that the same matrons with their judging glances —my grandmother included—sat pretending not to gossip beside the huge stone fountain dripping into a "pond" decorated with moss and lily pads sprinkled with gold dust.

I was twenty-three and self-assured in that way only favored daughters could be, the heiress to Stratford Mining, who was fondly chastised for racing carriages in the park and forgiven for flirting too obviously with boys at dances. My father encouraged my high spirits. He was my first and best audience; he laughed when people worried over the way I pushed at convention and said, "Let the young be young. As long as it doesn't interfere with my business, I don't see the harm."

I was conversing with artists and philosophers at his suppers before I was fourteen. By fifteen, I served as his hostess along with my grandmother, my mother having died when I was nine. At eighteen, he made me the trustee of his art patronage, which was extensive—my father loved art as I did; portraits of him hung above nearly every mantel in our house, and he had a room devoted to sculpture: classical nudes, Grecian beauties, muscled Roman youths. And though I had no artistic talent of my own, I did have a talent for introducing artists to the society that would support them. By the time I was twenty-one, I had gained a reputation for taste and originality that belonged to a woman twice my age. I thought I knew everything.

There's the challenge fate loves best, isn't it? I was ripe for a fall and so . . . the apple.

Nathan Langley was the scion of an old society family that had lost everything in the crash of Jay Cooke & Company. His father had committed suicide; his mother died soon after. Everyone knew she'd ended her days in an asylum, though her son refused to speak of it. Nathan had been forced to go into trade, and he proved to be good at business—something society never quite forgives, preferring destitute gentility to ambition, but Nathan had enough of a pedigree that we could afford to be gracious.

I had known him for some time, though we had never been formally introduced. Rather to say, I knew *of* him. He was older than I, and off to a university in Boston before I was out of short skirts. By the time he returned to Chicago, I was fully grown, and as aware of my own charms as a woman could be. He was sandy haired, blue eyed, finely muscled in the way that meant he worked at it. And he had the advantage of not being one of the feckless, spoiled, and barely grown young men of my circle. He was someone new. Someone . . . intriguing.

He seemed equally intrigued. "Ginny Stratford," he said, eyeing my décolletage with a practiced eye as we danced. "How you have grown."

"I could say the same for you," I said.

He leaned close to whisper, "How well we look together. Look at how they watch us."

"It's because they're afraid I'll do something outrageous," I teased.

"Ah yes. I've heard rumors about you."

"Interesting ones, I hope."

"Interesting." He laughed—I liked his smile, his straight white teeth. "Yes, I should say they are at least that."

"You shouldn't believe everything you hear," I told him.

"No? Oh now, that is a pity." He pulled me closer than was proper, and I let him. "Don't tell me you're as staid and traditional as the other girls in this room after all."

"Would you be disappointed if it were true?"

"Devastated," he said

I laughed. "So tell me, Mr. Langley, which is the most interesting rumor you've heard?"

"Hmmm . . . which one? There were so many," he teased. "I think it must be that you were the muse for that poem of Jonathan Hastings's. I can't remember the name of it."

"*Lilith in the Garden,*" I said. "And that happens to be true." What was true as well was that I'd lost my virtue to Hastings when I was eighteen, in the guest room of my father's house while Papa waited tea for him in the parlor.

Nathan Langley raised his eyebrow at me as if he'd guessed that as well. "Well, then, I suppose I should read it."

"If you like."

"Yes, I should like. I wonder what secrets are to be found within it?"

"I have no secrets, Mr. Langley. Ask anyone."

"I beg to disagree. I rather think you have a great many secrets, Miss Stratford." His smile said that he wished to be one of them, and I felt a little shiver of the kind I'd never felt before.

He was not anyone's choice for me, which is why he became the choice I made for myself. But it was more than that. Nathan was as impatient with social niceties as I. That night I danced with him three times, much to the dismay of my grandmother, who shook her head at me from where she sat talking with her friends. I would have danced with him again but for the fact that my card was nearly full before I'd met him. I was . . . entranced by him, I suppose. By the things he said, by the way he talked to me, as if I were an experienced woman—which I was not, Jonathan Hastings notwithstanding, as it was only the one time, and not as I'd dreamed passion would be. The way Nathan looked at me was the way a man looked at a woman he wanted, and it made me realize how badly the other men I'd known compared. My experience with Jonathan Hastings had been quick and soon over. I had thought it love, but I'd been too young to understand how to be a lover, and he had not bothered to teach me. And here was Nathan Langley, who it seemed increasingly did wish to teach me . . . something. He made me feel as no one else had ever done.

Our first kiss was in the night garden at a soiree celebrating the newest sculpture by one of my father's artists, a man of great talent though little grace and charm, whom I'd managed, with no small effort, to make the most coveted guest of the season.

"Tell me why you like his *Leda,*" Nathan said and then listened with an intensity I'd never known as I spoke of sublimity and the purity of love, and when I asked him what he'd thought of it, he looked at me consideringly and said,

"It reminded me of you."

"Why do you say that?"

"Sublime," he whispered, his gaze never leaving my face, falling to my lips. "Pure love. I never look at you that I don't want to lose myself in you."

How easily I fell. How well he knew what to say, how to win me. When he kissed me that night, I felt the impatience in him, a roughness that frightened and excited me at the same time. I would have lain with him there in the grass if he hadn't stopped, breathless but not apologizing, instead saying, "Dear God, the things we could do to each other . . ."

When he asked me to marry him, I did not hesitate. I wanted him too badly. Fortunately, my father liked him. Because Nathan was a good businessman, Papa readily folded him into Stratford Mining, where he became, very quickly, indispensable.

I was blissfully happy. I was in love and in a state of heightened desire that had me reaching for Nathan whenever he was in the room. Society called us lovebirds and twittered nervously around us, and both Nathan and I laughed at it. I felt myself ridiculously lucky—what other woman had a husband who was so fine a lover, who listened so intently to everything she said? Nathan said I had a mind unlike any woman's; he told me how thoughtful were my opinions, how I'd opened up worlds for him.

It was not unusual for us to stay awake into the wee hours of the morning, making love and talking over some philosophy or another. Oh, there were little annoyances, of course, as there are in every marriage. Nathan had a temper, I learned, and he was easily irritated. There were arguments, mostly over my behavior, I admit. I was spending too much time hobnobbing with disreputable artists, or this writer or that actor was a fool, how did I not see it, or it was unseemly for a married woman to debate philosophy in little cafés into the wee hours of the morning.

I was uneasy at the comments, but I attributed them to his exhaustion—by the time we'd been married three years, he had become my father's most trusted adviser, and Papa began to talk of the possibility of Nathan entering politics, as it would be of great benefit for Stratford Mining to have a voice in government. Nathan was very busy now. He was often out late. His comments about my behavior became more pointed, sometimes now accompanied by tempers that left no object safe—a vase, a shoe brush, a little bisque statuette. But it wasn't until Emily Dentridge's ball that I became worried.

Nathan was working late, and so he meant to meet me there. By the time he arrived, dinner was over, and I was playing cards with Ambrose Rivers—who was Chicago's most notorious art critic and my dear friend—and Miles Ashby, a painter Papa had lately taken a liking to. I had always enjoyed gambling, and I was winning. Nathan came into the parlor just as Ashby fell to his knees before me, bowing in mock supplication, laying his head in my lap. We were all a little drunk by then, and he made me laugh.

I didn't see Nathan until he was upon me. He grasped my arm; I didn't see how angry he was until we were in the carriage, when he turned on me with a furious, "What the hell did you think you were doing? Did you not see how everyone was staring?"

I was taken aback. "I cannot help it that people watch me, Nathan."

His voice was tight. "Of course you can. You encourage it with your behavior."

"There was nothing wrong in—"

"Playing cards? Having Ashby swoon over you like a schoolboy?"

"He doesn't swoon. We're friends—"

"You will end the friendship tomorrow."

"I will not! Why should I?"

His gaze was burning. "Because I forbid you to continue to see him."

I was startled. He had never before been so vehement. "Forbid me? You can't forbid me."

"I can and I will," he snapped. "People are talking, Geneva, and I won't have it."

I thought he couldn't mean it. I thought he was only tired. It turned out that I was required to do nothing in any case; Miles Ashby left for New York City within the week. He'd secured a patron there, he told me, and he was anxious to work on a new commission.

In the months that followed, things only deteriorated between my husband and me. We made love infrequently now, and when we did there were times when he was very rough, when I had the vague sense that he was punishing me.

I admit I was unhappy. I was unused to being ignored and dismissed, and we were both so angry. I missed the man I'd married. I looked for ways to bring him back to me, for ways to help him. I thought that if I could aid him with his languishing political career, he would turn to me again. I would help him the way I'd helped my father. Nathan needed the influence of important people, and so I decided to start a salon, a weekly meeting of artists and intellectuals. Papa was ambivalent about the idea, but not forbidding. Nathan, who I thought would understand my purpose, said, "Stop wasting your time and money on idiotic painters and actors too self-absorbed to see past their own noses. They can do nothing for me."

He was wrong, and I knew it, so I went ahead with the salon. I was certain he would come to see its value. At first, it seemed he was right. Chicago society was upended and confused. They hated it, though no one would say so overtly; the Stratford name and money were not something to offend. I cultivated the salon carefully, courting my guests assiduously—divine actors and creamy prima donnas and luscious tenors, poets, and philosophers and artists of all kinds. They moved among vases of orchids and sideboards set with champagne and wine and absinthe. I crowded candles onto every surface, as talk seemed to flow so much more naturally in candlelight that flickered with every breath and movement. Gradually it began to have the influence I'd hoped for. Within a year, my salon became the most talked about in Chicago.

The man I'd begun it for would have nothing to do with it. Nathan refused to attend; he berated it at every opportunity. When I told him I'd done it for him, he said, "Don't lie to yourself or to me. You did it for yourself, Ginny. You're the most spoiled woman I've ever known. I asked you not to do it. But God forbid you ever do anything I ask. Did you never once think of how it might look?"

"There's nothing wrong in it."

"People think you a step above a whore," he said brutally.

I felt myself pale. "That isn't true."

"Isn't it? You should hear the rumors I hear."

"I don't believe you."

He threw a wineglass across the room so the wine stained the wallpaper. I was afraid, and there was something in his eyes that disturbed me, that reminded me of the rumors about his mother, but I was too angry myself to heed it. He said, "You *will* do as I say," and I screamed at him that I would do as I wished, whatever anyone else thought of it. Nathan grabbed me then. I thought he might hurt me. For a moment we stood staring at each other, and then it changed, it twisted. Anger into passion. He kissed me, and I bit his lip until it bled. It became the most passionate interlude we'd had in months, and I was afraid of myself, of how I urged him on—this anger was better than nothing, after all.

That night of passion changed nothing; in fact, we grew further apart. Nathan became more and more entangled with my father, who adored him, and more and more distant from me. When I tried to tell Papa how Nathan and I were growing away from each other, he said impatiently, "It's time you grew up, Ginny. You've had your run. Best to settle down now. Nathan knows what's best."

The comment stung; my father's criticism was so rare I had no defense for it. I tried to do as he counseled—to be a loving wife—but Nathan ignored my overtures. For months at a time, he refused to touch me. I was lonely. I missed the passion between us so dreadfully that I sometimes cried myself to sleep, listening to the clank of the scotch decanter in my husband's adjoining room. I did not know what to do, and Nathan seemed not to care. By our fourth anniversary, the passion that had been between us was gone.

As I lay in bed alone, night after night, I began to suspect that Nathan had used me. For my money, for my father's influence. He was ambitious, after all, and without means until he'd met me. How quickly he'd changed once we'd taken vows. And our talks about art and philosophy . . . had he ever once ventured his own opinion, or only agreed with mine? I had been a fool. I had made a terrible mistake. My salons became my solace. I told myself I must learn to be content with this half life. After all, I had chosen it.

Then . . . then there came Marat.

Jean-Claude Marat. It was a Thursday in January when he first entered my parlor with Ambrose Rivers. I knew who Marat was only because Ambrose had told me the famous French sculptor would be coming. But for that, I never would have recognized him; he was young to have garnered such a reputation for genius. I'd expected a bearded man in middle age. Vivacious, yes; brilliant, of course, but *tested.* The man who came to the salon that night was not that, and it was not just the fact that he could be no older than my own age of twenty-eight. Though snow fell in great drifts outside my door, his dark blond hair was gold streaked, as if he'd been in the sun, and he was, frankly, beautiful. There wasn't a woman there who didn't notice him. His smile took me aback—of all the men I'd met, I'd only been so affected by a personality one other time, when I'd first seen Nathan.

Marat reminded me of everything I'd once had, everything I'd lost. He made me realize what a prisoner I'd become, how unhappy I was. Nathan ignored me—even worse, he was contemptuous of everything I believed in. Marat had that combination of intellect and poetry and passion that had once been my husband, and he was taken with me. I had missed that kind of admiration. I began to feel alive again. He made me see that there were other men, men who accepted me as I was, who *wanted* me as I was.

Jean-Claude Marat was in truth everything that Nathan had pretended to be. When my father asked me whom he should commission to sculpt a bust of himself for the newly built Harriet Stratford Wing of Mercy Hospital—my father's endowment in my late mother's name—I didn't hesitate to give him Claude's name.

I went to every sitting. I sat quietly and watched as Claude sketched and chatted amiably with Papa. Soon I was bending over his shoulder as he sculpted Papa's head in clay, his fingers working so quickly I could barely grasp the movements, forming a nose where before there had been only a lump; a bold, quick thumb drag, and suddenly there was an eyebrow. When the sittings were done, Papa would have luncheon served, and often he would be too busy to stay, and so Claude and I lingered over duck or lobster salad and wine and talked.

I was starved for the passion Nathan had kindled and withheld. When Claude said to me one day, half drunk, at my salon, "I would like to sculpt you, my sweet Ginny," I saw the opportunity I hadn't realized I'd been waiting for.

A scandal. The one thing Nathan would never tolerate.

I knew it would work. I wanted to end my marriage. Divorce was not a choice; it was nearly impossible to attain, and Nathan would surely fight it. My father would be devastated, my grandmother horrified. Most important, I had no cause to offer any judge. Unhappiness was not an acceptable reason. Women in many marriages were unhappy; should the world set them all free?

Marriage had taken from me what control I had over my own life. My only choice now was to try to control Nathan, and Marat presented me with the one thing I knew my husband could never ignore. To pose for a statue meant for a very public display—the exhibition at the Art Institute of Chicago—would be so scandalous Nathan would never forgive it. He would leave me. I would be free. My father would understand in time, as would the rest of society. I had done worse things, after all, and been forgiven.

Someday I would tell my father the truth. He might even admire my cunning, particularly when I told him how cruel Nathan could be.

So I agreed to pose. I met Claude each afternoon in his rooms, sitting for hours while he sketched me. It was to be Andromeda on the rocks awaiting the sea serpent, just at the moment when she saw Perseus for the first time, and I knew it would be brilliant. I must pose from life for it, of course, but Claude and I were friends and nothing more, though I did not miss the way his eyes burned when he looked at me. I even encouraged it, stretching and preening upon the fur rug he'd spread on the floor for me to lie upon. I liked the attention; it felt forever since I'd had it. He called me *ma muse américaine,* and I liked that name. I liked it very much.

The room was scented with absinthe and the metallic earthy tang of clay and the perfume of our bodies in sun and close quarters. He moved from sketching to clay, his fingers covered in slurry, white where it dried at his knuckles, smeared upon his cheek. Clay gave way to marble. I began to take form beneath his hands, a reverse Galatea, Pygmalion turning me from flesh into stone. I began to feel a growing excitement. Soon. Soon it would be displayed, and I would be free.

I knew there was gossip, of course, but I ignored it. Claude and I must spend a great deal of time together, and people noticed. It was part of my plan. I waited for Nathan to notice too, to say something. He did not. And I was so absorbed by my own intentions that I was blind to all else.

I was naive, and so I misjudged everything.

The sculpture *Andromeda Chained to the Rocks* was taken to the Art Institute of Chicago. The opening night, Nathan and I arrived fashionably late, and I was nervous with excitement and anticipation.

The electric lights blared, from somewhere came the sound of a small orchestra, talk, laughter. The first of my set that I came upon was Mrs. Steven Bentham—I smiled at her, and her expression froze; she turned away from me so violently I was startled. I looked at Nathan, whose own expression had gone grim. "Shall we see what you've done this time?"

I had never been cut like this before. Not one after another, cut after cut. My closest friend, Anna Lowe, widened her eyes in horror when she saw me and moved swiftly away. I had not expected this, and I faltered, uncertain. Nathan put his hand over mine, his fingers squeezing cruelly tight as he led me steadily into the main gallery. There was a crowd gathered at the center, a scandalized silence around one sculpture. They looked up as we approached. I felt their disapproval and anger as I took in Claude's masterpiece. Scaled to life, every sinew and muscle delineated, every curve and curl, in the expression desire and longing. I had not expected it to look so much like me, and yet it was me made divine, manacles about the wrists, staked out in chains, the arch of a back, breasts thrust, hair curling about a nipple, a raised knee, the splash of waves upon the rocks. It was a beautiful thing—but no one could see how beautiful it was.

Nathan simmered in a way I recognized too well. My father was there, but as I went to him, he made a gesture, and suddenly Nathan was hurrying me out of the gallery. The whispers vibrated in the air. Nathan bundled me into the carriage and stared out the window at the falling snow. I was unsettled. I began to feel sick. This had not turned out as I'd hoped. I'd meant only to alienate Nathan, not my friends. But they had turned from me, and Nathan was still here—why was he still here? Why did he say nothing? I couldn't bear his silence. I forced myself to say, "Nathan—"

He slammed his fist against the carriage wall so violently I jumped and shrank back. When we pulled to a stop before my father's house, my childhood home, I was grateful. My father would understand. He would soothe society and help me with Nathan. This could still end as I'd intended.

We had just hurried up the snow-slicked walk when there came the sound of my father's carriage. He and my grandmother got out, and then they were in the foyer beside us, and we gave up our cloaks and scarves and hats in silence. My grandmother's face was drawn and white—she'd aged ten years in an hour. But it was the disappointment on Papa's face that startled me. It was unexpected and impossible. I realized suddenly what they believed, what everyone must believe. I'd thought only of the scandal of posing, not of what an unclothed sculpture said about me and Claude. They thought there'd been an affair.

"Oh no," I began. "You don't understand—"

My father pointed to the parlor. "Wait in there, Geneva, while your husband and I discuss what is to be done." The forbidding cast of his face made me swallow my objection; with the habit of obedience and adoration, I went into the darkened parlor while the three of them went down the hall to Papa's study.

When they finally sent for me, what felt like hours later, I was stiff with dread. The study was too bright after the parlor and the dim hallway, electric light illuminating everything too well: my grandmother's pink scalp beneath her thinning white hair, the fleshiness beginning to show on my husband's face, the brown age spots at my father's temples. My grandmother sat in a burgundy-striped chair by the fire, erect and regal. Nathan sat on the matching settee, elbows on his knees, hands clasped between them. Handsome Nathan, his uninjured fingers flexing and unflexing while the other hand was wrapped in a bandage. He looked up at me with reddened eyes—no anger now, but a calculation that made me even more anxious.

My father stood, half leaning against the expanse of his polished rosewood desk. His eyes, so often laughing, were not laughing now but inestimably sad, as if he'd borne a mortal hurt. "Sit down, Geneva," he said tiredly.

I perched myself on the very edge of the nearest chair and folded my hands in my lap. "It's not what you think," I said quickly. "I would never . . . Claude and I are friends and nothing more."

"Oh, please, Geneva," my grandmother said sharply. "Surely you don't think us fools."

"But it's true. I only posed for him—" Her look made me swallow the rest. I felt guilty in the wake of it, and ashamed, and that made me angry. There had been no affair; there was no reason to feel guilty. "You must believe me."

"You've put us in an untenable position." How stern my grandmother sounded.

I felt the urge to comfort her, to comfort them all. "Yes, of course, but surely it can be mended? Once everyone knows the truth—"

"Robert Montgomery withdrew his offer to partner with Stratford Mining tonight," Papa broke in. "He said he does not wish his company to be associated with debauchery."

"Debauchery?" Suddenly I was afraid. If there was one thing my father valued above me, it was Stratford Mining. "You cannot be serious."

"This is no trifling matter, Geneva. Your behavior has affected my business. You've embarrassed your husband and your family. Your lack of discretion—"

"I tell you there was no indiscretion. And you have a room full of nudes just like that one. You told me it was art. It *is* art."

"For God's sake, Geneva, you've exposed yourself needlessly to ridicule and shame, and not just yourself, but your husband. How is Nathan to feel now that the whole world knows you were Marat's . . . mistress?"

My eyes filled with tears. I could not look at Nathan or my father. "I was not his mistress," I insisted. "It was not an affair. We are friends only."

Papa said, "I need someone to oversee the acquisition of a coal mine in Seattle. Nathan has suggested he do so, and that the two of you go there. Which is very generous of him, considering. Therefore the two of you will be leaving for Washington Territory in the morning."

It took effort to understand him. I managed, "Washington Territory? I . . . forgive me, but I don't understand."

"Marat has left the city," Nathan said tonelessly. "He at least realizes how this looks."

Papa said, "I've told you this before: you're a married woman, and it's time you act like a wife. Your husband is good enough to forgive you and to sacrifice his own happiness on your behalf. You will go to Seattle with him until such time as things are forgotten and you can return."

Grandmother said, "It won't be forever, you know. Something else will take the place of this scandal, and memories fade with time. I should say only two or three years."

This was not what I'd expected, not what I'd wanted at all. Why wasn't Nathan threatening to leave me? "Two or three years? You must be joking. Why should I go? I've done nothing wrong!"

Nathan sighed. "I'd hoped it wouldn't come to this, but I've spoken to Dr. Robertson at Bloomfield Estates—"

"The asylum?"

"A place to rest," he corrected, and there was that calculation again that frightened me. I remembered his mother. Of course he would know all about asylums. "We've all seen how unbalanced you've been recently. The doctor agrees . . . he is quite certain you will do very well at Bloomfield."

I could not believe the words. "Nathan, no. You know I'm not the least bit mad. I only posed. I meant to . . . it wasn't what you think. It wasn't what anyone thinks."

Nathan looked away. Desperately I looked to my father.

"You've suffered a derangement of the senses, Ginny," Papa said gently. "It's affected us all. No one would say we were wrong to send you there."

Grandmother said, "You are not yourself, my dear."

"We can have you installed at Bloomfield within the hour," Papa said, and this time it was his expression that shamed and frightened me. "Or will you choose Seattle?"

They were silent. Watching me. Waiting.

There was no choice, and I knew it. I had been naive and foolish. How had I not seen that the collusion of society and marriage and family would keep me firmly in my place?

The answer came to me quickly. Because I'd been too self-assured. Because I'd thought I was invincible.

I looked down at the floor, the convoluted pattern in the carpet, twisting vines and leaves, and said, "Yes. I'll go to Seattle with Nathan."

My father let out his breath. "Very well."

"Perhaps you could look at it as an opportunity to make a new start," Grandmother suggested.

I glanced at Nathan, and he met my gaze, and I thought of all the ways I'd loved him. A new start. Yes, perhaps that was what we both needed. To be away from all these things that had come between us. To somehow find each other again.

Papa said, "In Seattle, you will do as Nathan directs, Geneva. I rely on him, as you know, and he has suffered much for you. I expect you to behave dutifully and honorably. I want them to view the Stratford name with respect. This is the only time I will suffer a business setback on your account. Do you understand?"

"Yes, Papa. I understand."

He said in a voice sadder than I'd ever heard, "I have never before been ashamed of you."

The next morning, my father directed our servants to pack up our things, to close up the house. By three that afternoon, Nathan and I were on our way to Seattle, Washington Territory, sitting together and silently on a train that whisked us away from Chicago and everything I knew.

Chapter Two

Beatrice

SEATTLE, WASHINGTON TERRITORY, 1888

There are three rules to remember in theater. Three rules you learn when you're a nobody in the corps de ballet wearing flesh-colored stockings and not much else. Rule one: Don't be late; Rule two: Know your lines; and Rule three: Never trust a manager or another actor.

Sometimes it doesn't matter how well you know something. Sometimes you can fool yourself into thinking the rules don't apply to you—at least not then, not at that moment.

I met Stella Bernardi on my one night off from performing

at the Regal Theater. She was in Seattle as part of a touring company booked at the Palace, and I was only there because my company needed an actress to play the traveling lady line, and Lucius Greene, our manager, had said, "Go on over to Langford's, my dear, and see if you can't persuade some ambitious young lovely to join us."

I noticed Stella right away. She was playing a trouser part that night, but she did it with style, and Lucius had always liked style. So when the show was over, I went backstage and waited outside the dressing room door until she came out. She was pretty, which always helped, and blond. She would be a good foil for me, who was her opposite in coloring, and match our current leading lady, Arabella Smith, and I was certain Lucius would think so too. When I proposed that she come to the Regal to audition, she was smart enough to see that it was an upward move.

Lucius liked her. After she won the line, he pulled me aside and stroked the waxed ends of his large brown mustache and said, "Well done, sweet Bea. I shall remember this," and I was ambitious enough myself to be glad. There's no better currency than a favor owed by a manager—if you could trust him to remember it, and with Lucius, you usually could.

I'd been at the Regal three years. I'd come to Seattle with the rest of a touring company from New York, expecting to debut *Rip van Winkle* at a theater whose name I can't remember now because the advance man had got into a fight with the theater manager, and we ended up stranded with no money and nowhere to play and no way to get back either. Two of us had got on with Lucius's company at the Regal, myself and Brody Townshend, who was sixteen then and a pretty boy with almost no ambition. The only reason he was still onstage at all was that he'd discovered women liked an actor, and fucking was all he cared about. God knew I'd never met a man who didn't practically live for sex, and Brody was the worst of them when it came to that. Some nights there was a crowd of girls waiting for him to come out the backstage door, and once or twice I'd seen him leave with two or three at a time. He was nineteen now, and he'd boasted to me that he'd probably had more than two hundred women, and I didn't doubt it.

The Regal Theater was one of the most popular houses in Seattle, although it wasn't luxurious. There were ten boxes for society, and the parquet had been fitted with decent seats that had wire cages beneath to store your hat, but it was small, with maybe only four hundred seats, and it was built of green lumber, so it weathered badly. The narrow stairs to the gallery were crooked and pitched, and half the time someone up there was swooning from the heat or the gas fumes that settled up near the ceiling because there was no ventilation—which you might think would be a blessing in the winter, but it was only cold and damp and wet then, and no pleasanter. In fact, there was no time of the year when the Regal was comfortable, but people loved it just the same, as much because of its location—sited exactly between the St. Charles Hotel and the Occidental, so we got not just society but everyone else as well—as because of the bill of fare.

Lucius Greene had turned the theater into the best melodrama house in the city. The Regal was a favorite with the "gallery gods," the newsboys and miners and lumbermen who paid their ten cents for the worst seats in the balcony and thought it entitled them to an opinion on everything. They hooted and whistled and clapped their way through the crashing spectacles Lucius thought up, learning the songs by the second night a play was performed, shouting tunelessly along with whoever was onstage and sometimes so loud you couldn't hear yourself, and society loved it too. There was no one who didn't love a spectacle, and Lucius was a genius when it came to knowing what would please a crowd.

He was a fair enough manager too, though like all of them he was always looking for a way to make a profit and didn't necessarily care who he had to step on to do it. And he wasn't one of those who expected favors from his actresses either, which already made him better than three-quarters of the managers I'd worked for. He liked to think of his company as a family, and so, because Stella was a stranger to Seattle, he made me responsible for her.

Another favor he owed me, and I added it to his tally. Stella clung to me like a barnacle. I got her a room on the floor below, and Stella got into the habit of coming upstairs to my room after the performances, when we were both giddy and flushed and it was hard to be alone after the noise of the audiences and the crowded halls backstage full of admirers. I had a fondness for candy, and she for absinthe, and that was how we spent whatever extra money we had, which was never much. I'd buy a little packet of hard candy, and as we never had sugar, we'd melt a cherry or orange lozenge in water to add to the absinthe, and sometimes we were still drinking near dawn.

Stupid, I know. But I thought she couldn't harm me. I'd been the first soubrette of the company for two years now, the next to move up to the leading line when Arabella moved on—and I was working on that too, believe me. For months, I'd been feeding Arabella's vanity, taking every opportunity to hint that she was better than the leading lady of a small Seattle stock company, and that her future might best be played upon other stages. I suppose the mistake I made was in thinking that Stella was green and believing I had enough currency banked with Lucius to protect myself. Too cocky, my pa would have said, and he would have been right.

Even Brody didn't know anything about where I was from or what I thought, but Stella got my life story out of me before I knew it, how I'd grown up in the theater and loved everything about it, how my father had been a set painter, and my mother a seamstress, and how I'd left my New York City home at fifteen to go onstage and traveled around so much since that when my parents moved they couldn't find me to tell, so I had no idea where they were or whether they were even alive. She told me her parents were farmers in Ohio who'd stopped speaking to her when she took up the stage, and that she'd bedded more managers than she could remember, even though she was only twenty-two.

That should have told me. If I'd been listening, it would have. But Stella's eyes sparkled, and she had this way of leaning close, as if she were about to entrust you with something she'd never told another living soul. We laughed about the company's heavy, Aloysius Metairie, and the boys who waited for him after the show, and our "first old lady," Mrs. Chace, who waddled about the stage gasping her lines; and for a while Stella was in love with Jackson Wheeler, who was our leading man and who never had a lack of admirers, and it fell to me to talk her out of him, because Jack was nearly as bad as Brody when it came to women.

"You want to fall in love, fall in love with one of those rich men who send you flowers," I told her as we sprawled on the frayed settee in my room, red velvet so worn there was no nap left. "At least then when it's over, you'll have something more than a broken heart."

It was good advice, though I'd never taken it myself. But Stella didn't love acting the way I did, and she didn't have a deep talent. So when she began an affair with Richard Welling, who owned a portion of one of Seattle's sawmills, I was glad, even though I didn't see her as often, because she was busy with him after the performances. It was the best step for her.

It wasn't until Stella had been with us for six months that Arabella began to believe the things I told her. She drew in the crowds, who loved her for her sparkling wit and flashing eyes, even though the wit was written by other people and when she was offstage her eyes were dull and stupid as a cow's. Arabella began not showing up for rehearsals, which Lucius could not abide, and insisting on special treatment. She was hinting around that she was ready to begin a turn as a star.

I was twenty-eight; I'd been an actress for thirteen years. In the three years I'd been at the Regal, I'd worked hard to make myself as steady as any manager could have wanted. I'd collected a trunkful of costumes. I knew more than two hundred parts, half of them leads. When Arabella left, I would be ready to step into her shoes. The truth was that I was desperate to step into them. I was getting old; there wouldn't be many other chances for me, and I knew it, unless I managed somehow to get enough money to start a company of my own—and I could count on one hand the actresses I knew who had, and I wasn't likely to be one of them. If I meant to be a leading lady, if I meant to be a star, it must be soon, or I would be destined to playing seconds, and then old ladies and heavies, for the rest of my career.

I'd dreamed of acting since I was six years old, watching rehearsals while my father painted sets in the background. I'd studied actors and actresses as if I could inhale their tricks, as if my own muscles could hold their memories. To act was all I'd ever wanted, and I knew I was good enough for the juicy lead parts, the star turns. I knew I was not meant to linger in obscurity. I loved it too much for that—surely God wouldn't have given me this passion if he meant not to honor it. But my climb had taken longer than I'd anticipated; too many missteps and compromises, too often fucking managers who never had any intention of moving me up, or actors who had less power than I'd thought.

I'd grown up around the theater, so it wasn't as if I didn't know the methods everyone used to get ahead. The first time I'd used one myself was when I was a member of the corps de ballet at Niblo's, when I waxed the soles of Marie Denbroeder's slippers so she couldn't keep her feet onstage. It wasn't as bad as it sounds, and she'd tried to get me out of the way first by putting an emetic in my coffee so I'd been unable to move more than a couple steps from a chamber pot. So I waxed her slippers, and she fell down four times that night and burst into tears, and she was gone the next day and I was kept on. I didn't feel the least bit guilty for it either, as she would have thrown me to the wolves if she'd got the chance.

It was just the way things were. It was expected, you know, that an actress would fuck the manager or the lead actor to get a better part, and damn if the managers and actors didn't use that to their advantage. The worst of them played actresses off each other, so you not only had to fuck them, you had to be better at it than the next girl. And as much as I hated to admit it, talent didn't count for much; you could quote every line from *School for Scandal* or cry waterworks on cue, and it mattered less than how pretty you were, or what you were willing to do, or how many costumes you had. There were times when I'd almost given up, but I couldn't do it. I just couldn't walk away. It was too much a part of me for that.

What you learned quickly enough was not to trust anyone, that you had to make your own success, that you were a fool if you counted on anyone to help. I knew that in my bones. But when Stella Bernardi came along and acted as if she could hardly cross the street without me . . . well, I thought I knew all the tricks. I thought I was an expert at playing the game. But Stella had a trick I didn't know, and she understood how to play me. I fancied myself a kind of mentor to her, as pathetic as that sounds. She asked my advice, and I thought what a fool she was for trusting me, and I meant to protect her from herself—*and* prove I was worthy of her trust too and that's even more pathetic, I know—and so I was honest with her. I thought I was building up a cache of goodwill, but all I was doing was putting blinders on.

One night we were both staring out my window at the moon rising high in the sky, half obscured by the smoke from the mills and the steamers that always hazed the harbor beyond. We shoved up beside each other and rested our elbows on the narrow sill, and leaned out to smell the city—the tang of tar and the rotting sulfur scent of the tideflats at low tide, smoke and the odor of garbage and manure in the streets, and always, always, the stink of wet sawdust.

"Do you really think Arabella will leave?" she asked me, swirling the pale green cloud of absinthe in the glass we shared.

"I'd say it's certain she will," I told her. "She's blinded by the limelight."

"And then *you* will take her place."

"I hope so. I think so. Yes."

"Lucius will move you up. You've been around so long. The rest of the company can't help but take your side."

I laughed. "Maybe. Brody will. Jack will never commit to anything unless it advances him, and Aloys is pragmatic. He won't take sides until he's certain."

"Mrs. Chace then. Mr. Galloway surely."

"They'll follow wherever Aloys leads. And they're lazy. They like things to be easy."

"Then me," she said, lifting the glass, taking a sip. "I'll take your side."

"You're sweet." I stared out at the night sky, the wisps of smoke drifting across the moon. Below, a carriage made its slow and thudding way through the mud, the horses' heads dropped low, as if their day had been a long one. "I hardly dare to think it's going to happen. Every year that passes and I . . . I'm starting to feel old, Stella. These other girls I see coming along . . . they're so young and pretty. I don't know. I think this might be my last chance."

She tilted her head to look at me. "You can't truly believe that. You're still so pretty yourself. And you don't look old at all."

"But I am. Twenty-eight. It's old to be a lead."

"No, it isn't. Look at Mary Anderson. Or Clara Morris. They'll be playing leads until they're dead."

"But they got the leading line younger than I did. Maybe I don't have the talent."

"Don't be silly. You're the best in the company, and we all know it." Her hand came down to cover mine. "You'll be the lead, and I'll step into your shoes. Hopefully I won't slip right out of them."

I laughed then, and she said, "I mean it, Bea. You'll see I'm right. When Arabella leaves, Lucius will choose you. He has to."

I had smiled and thought maybe it was good that I had a friend, that maybe trusting someone for a change wasn't going to turn out badly.

It was only a month later, when we were rehearsing Lucius's "new" play—which had been stolen outright from Augustin Daly, though Lucius added some new songs—that Arabella stepped to center stage and announced, "In two weeks, I shall perform my last with this company. I have been asked to go on tour, and I have decided to accept the challenge."

We clapped and hooted and kissed her, tendering our congratulations, even as we were all secretly glad she was going, myself more than anyone. That night Stella and I drank a toast in the dressing room we shared. "To the leading lady!" she'd said, and I laughed and gulped down the wine, and after the performance we went to Arabella's farewell supper at the restaurant on the corner and then to a saloon after, and we all got very drunk.

But though my head was pounding the next morning, I woke and went to first call. I would be damned if I would miss Lucius calling my name for the lead. I wanted to savor the moment, no matter the pain. I wanted to hear everyone's congratulations; I had worked so hard for them. And too, there would be Stella's rise to celebrate as well. My handing off to her the first soubrette.

I went downstairs and knocked on Stella's door, but there was no answer; she must have gone already. That was odd, but I told myself she'd probably had some errand to run before she went to the theater. I went outside, where the morning was so bright it felt as if the sun were burning right through my eyes. It was midmorning, and the boardwalks were busy, wagons and drays splashing mud as they barreled down streets whose planked surfaces sank and rotted in the wet. It was a morning I wanted to fix into my head, the morning my dreams came true.

The Regal was only a few blocks from my hotel, so in no time at all I was there, hurrying through the back door into the dead, burnt-out air of the theater, my eyes adjusting to the dim gaslight, so I nearly tripped down the dark and narrow stairs leading to the below-stage warren of dressing rooms and storage and Lucius's office. At the bottom of the stairs, to the right, was the darkness under the stage where loomed the prop carriage and bigger sets that rose or descended through the traps in the stage floor; to the left was the greenroom. The door was open; I heard voices and stepped inside.

The greenroom was furnished with several cushioned seats and chairs, all in various colors and various stages of disrepair. A three-foot-long wavery mirror hung on one wall, and good—and bad—notices were pinned and fluttering here and there. The call box was to one side of the door—just now it held only Lucius's orders to appear at first call this morning and a formal good wishes proclamation for Arabella. Along with the familiar smell of gas lingering in an unwindowed room, the greenroom had a constantly moldy smell from the carpets. Aloysius claimed they'd once been abandoned in a swamp and Lucius had got them for almost nothing, and though I didn't know if that was true, the smell was right.

William Galloway, the company's "first old man," was there, finishing off a pastry while Aloysius read the newspaper, and Brody lay back on one of the settees, picking at his nails with a penknife. He was singing some tuneless song, and Aloys threw him an irritated glance before he rose and put aside the paper to give me a kiss. His dark mustache and Vandyke beard were soft against my cheek. "Darling, thank God you're here. Now perhaps the boy will mind his manners."

Brody grinned and sat up, shoving the knife into his pocket. "Bea, thank God you're here," he said in perfect mockery of Aloys. "You've saved me once again from the old man's pontificating."

"Perhaps he wouldn't pontificate if you didn't provoke him so," I said with a smile, forgetting my headache.

"Exactly as I've told him again and again." Aloys reseated himself. "But look at you, darling, why, you're blooming as a rose. Dare I take it to mean you have some foreknowledge of today's events?"

"I couldn't say," I said. "You know I'm not privy to Lucius's secrets."

Brody guffawed. Aloys only smiled.

Our "first old woman," Mrs. Maryann Chace, sauntered in, huffing and puffing, and Mr. Galloway licked the last of the pastry's glaze from his fingers and said, "At least Lucius isn't bringing in some new girl. No need to get used to Bea."

"Good God, I *hope* so!" Mrs. Chace said. "It's so *jarring* to adjust to something new. Change is so enervating. Why, I vow, each time a new day begins, it requires all my stamina to accommodate it."

"Where's Jack?" Aloys asked, taking his watch from his pocket. "It's half past already."

" 'Too swift arrives as tardy as too slow.' " Jackson, handsome as ever, his blond hair oiled and smooth, curling at his pockmarked jaw, stepped through the door tapping his cane, a new affectation, against the doorjamb. Jack glanced about the room until his dark eyes fell on me. He made a little bow, flourishing his cape like a melodrama villain. "Ah, there she is! 'A daughter of the gods, divinely tall and most divinely fair.' Shall we prostrate ourselves before our new queen Bea?"

Now I laughed. "What assumptions you all make! I'm certain Lucius will have something to say about it."

"What can he say, except to anoint you in Arabella's place?"

"It'll be good for you, Wheeler," Brody put in. "You're always bitching about kissing Arabella. Now you shall have Bea to kiss instead."

Jack rubbed his chin and gave me a lecherous wink. "Softer lips than that wrinkled old hag's, I'll warrant."

"That's not what you said two days ago," Brody teased. "Bella was 'radiant'—isn't that what you said? I remember now: 'I shall miss you as the sun misses the moon.' "

Jackson sighed heavily and sat down, crossing his legs, resting his cane against the chair's arm. "Come, come, you know I am the basest hypocrite. Like any drone I have no choice but to pursue the new queen."

"And I thought you loved me for myself," I teased.

"I do, my dear, I do. But you must admit you've grown more attractive with your new crown." Jack inclined his hand toward me. "Come now, Queen Bea, and give us a kiss for joy."

I stepped over to him, and he unfolded his legs, gesturing for me to sit upon his lap, which I did, and then I leaned forward and quite mischievously gave him a long and lingering kiss. When I pulled away, Jack wrapped his arm about my waist and jerked me into his chest, saying, "My queen! Ah, take me now that I might die happy!"

The room filled with laughter.

"What's this! Roman orgies in the greenroom? Please, children, I shall be collecting forfeits if you break rule number five!"

It was Lucius's voice. I looked over my shoulder to see him sweep in, clad in a dark blue coat I'd never seen before, and a bronze-checked vest that glimmered in the gaslight. His face was ruddy, as if he'd come from a distance, though his office was just down the hall. Behind him came Marcus Geary, our prompter, a man who resembled nothing so much as a little monkey, and behind him, Stella.

There was something strange about that, you know, but I only thought it fleetingly, because she was beaming as she came in; of course she was—she was to be promoted as well. I took myself off Jack's lap and smiled at her, and she ducked her gaze shyly.

Geary shuffled papers, the parts for the next play, and my excitement and anticipation rose. I imagined Lucius would start us off with something we hadn't done in a while, something to showcase my skills, and I wondered which gown I would wear on my opening night, the old, deep blue satin with its bit of lace? Or perhaps, with the extra money I would make now, I could buy some new costume. I'd seen a green in a nearby secondhand store that I thought might work—

Lucius cleared his throat. He seemed flustered. "Are we all here? Ah, good, good. Well, as you must expect, I have something to announce. Tomorrow we shall start rehearsals for *The Wickedness of Saints,* a new adaptation by myself, of course, to celebrate our new leading lady—"

I tensed, waiting.

"—Mrs. Stella Bernardi!"

His words fell on silence. There was this wretched, terrible moment when I tried to find my name in the sounds and couldn't, and Stella flushed an unbecoming red, and Lucius cleared his throat again.

"What? Have we no congratulations?"

Suddenly Jack was up, pushing past me, and the others were murmuring platitudes. It was only then that I realized what she'd done. It was only then that I felt her betrayal, and I was so angry and sick it was all I could do to keep from rushing across the room to claw her eyes out. And the worst part was that I should have known better. I *did* know better. What a fool I was. I had never broken one of the three rules without regretting it, but some people just get what they deserve, and that morning, I was one of them.

"Mr. Welling has graciously agreed to fund the building of a new set," Lucius said with a nervous smile, glancing at me, then away again quickly. "And I agreed with his choice for leading lady."

"I am so grateful Lucius put his trust in me," Stella gushed. "It shall be difficult to fill Arabella's shoes, of course, but I trust I will not slip out of them."

Every ounce of love I'd felt for her disappeared.

"I think you will all find something familiar in your parts," Lucius said. "Our honorable heroine—"

"Why have Stella play so against type?" I asked loudly enough that they all went quiet. "She'd be so much better as Judas; at least there's a part she knows."

Stella's smile was sickly sweet. "You know you shouldn't frown so, Bea. It only makes those wrinkles on your forehead deeper."

I would have launched myself at her if Jack had not stepped just that moment in front of me.

"Children, children," Lucius said. "Let's avoid a row, shall we? Metairie, perhaps you would be so kind as to take our sweet Bea to luncheon after rehearsal. Have the bill sent to me."

Aloysius inclined his head in agreement. He took my arm, which would have been comforting had I been inclined to be comforted, which I wasn't. All I could think was how stupid I'd been, how wretchedly I'd mistaken her. I hated her, but I hated myself more, and when Aloys whispered in my ear, "Her paramour is paying the production costs, darling. One can't fault her for playing her cards well," it was all I could do to keep from crying.

Later Lucius shrugged and said, "Come, Bea, the part of the wounded doesn't become you. Welling was insistent—what could I say?"

"That you had another in mind for the lead. I've worked hard for this, Lucius."

"So you have. But she has worked equally hard, eh?" Lucius smiled. "A theater is always in need of money, my dear, as well you know. And I have given you the juiciest of the supporting roles. You shall chew well on it, I think."

What was I to do? Where should I go? There was only one other troupe in town, and their leading lady was well established and not going anywhere soon, nor was their second. I had no hope of overthrowing either of them, and I hadn't the funds to start my own company. And to do anything else . . . to be anything else . . . what else was I made for?

Brody said, "Might as well make the best of it, Bea. My guess is Stella ain't long for the Regal. She's got finer things in mind." He gave me his bright, teasing smile. "And you ain't an old hag yet. You maybe got a few months left afore you're too well done."

He was right, of course. I had no choice but to settle in.

But I'd learned my lesson too, the lesson I thought I'd already known. Friends were for people who had nothing to lose. And now that Stella wasn't my friend . . .

Well . . . let's just say I knew just what to do to get what I wanted.

Chapter Three

Geneva

I had not known what to expect from the town Nathan and I were now to call home. Nathan himself knew little about Seattle, and what he did know he had been reluctant to speak of during the long journey, saying only, "There's a town there, Ginny, and society, of a sort. We'll do well enough, I think, if they haven't heard of your scandal."

My scandal. As if it were underlined and italicized, tagging along like an unwelcome but apt nickname, a definition one could neither escape nor explain without embarrassment. I began to feel as if it were somehow emblazoned across my forehead, the first thing people saw when they looked at me.

Beyond comments like that, Nathan seemed content to silence. His temper had been mercifully absent—the only evidence of his earlier rage was the healing scab on his hand. In a way, I preferred his anger—something I was used to. The punishment of his silence was worse.

There had been plenty of time to reflect upon things on the journey west. I'd thought myself accustomed to my banishment; as we passed each mean little station and wild landscape and tiny town, I had been at first horrified and then, gradually, accepting. I tried not to think of Claude or my ill-conceived plans. I had failed, and I must be a good wife now and try to salvage my marriage, to act with dignity and restraint. I could not risk Papa's further displeasure. If I ever had a moment of doubt of my ability to do so, all I had to remember was how much more my miscalculation might have cost me, of Bloomfield Estates.

And surely . . . there had once been so much passion between Nathan and me—it could not *all* have been a lie. It must be possible to find it again. But Nathan had little to say to me and seemingly no interest in starting over, and I knew it was up to me to prove to him—and my father—that I could be the wife he needed here. I had no other choice after all. If I could not do so, my life would be unbearable. I vowed to be at my most charming. I vowed to make Seattle love me.

But when Nathan escorted me down the wet and slippery steamer ramp to a town knee-deep in mud and tidal stink, my resolve wavered in the face of a crushing disappointment. Seattle was astonishing in the depth of its plainness. The elegance of Chicago was gone; I'd seen only one block of brick buildings, the rest were all wood, some painted, most not. Boardwalks ramped up and down to meet doorways that had been built without regard to one another, some six feet off the ground and some only three. Puddles beneath pilings, sagging awnings, streets paved with wooden planks that sank into the mud or warped and split, horses and people splashed with mud. Hollowed-out logs that served as sewer and water pipes, elevated on stanchions, snaked past saloon windows.

There were signs of modernity in the midst of the ugliness. Telegraph wires stretched over everything, looping from pole to pole, and when Nathan told me there were telephones too, I hadn't believed him. I was amazed to see electric streetlamps. But those things were far more the exception than the rule. Instead of my bright streets lined with shops and well-dressed, well-bred women, there were too many men dressed in coarse trousers and collars open to show their underwear and Indian women camped on the street corners, stinking of rotting fish, selling clams and baskets and speaking some odd sort of patois I didn't recognize.

I felt out of place in my military-styled traveling suit of deep plum; I'd seen not a single other woman of my class as Nathan helped the driver load our trunks onto the back of the carriage. Even that had been a mean thing, shabby seats and springs so stiff Nathan and I were jounced from one side to another as we made our way to our new home.

"I shall have our own carriage sent for," Nathan informed me; it was the most he'd said to me in an hour.

In that moment, I missed Chicago and my life there wretchedly. "Dear God," I murmured, looking out the window, seeing nothing but blurred buildings past the gauze of rain. "How does anyone survive here?"

We had barely arrived at the house we'd leased when we discovered the scandal *had* followed me here. As if blown by the wind or deposited by birds flying overhead. As isolated as Seattle was, it was only a steamer journey away from San Francisco and with a vibrant trade between them. There was even a newspaper with a society page waiting on the table for us when we arrived, as if someone had set it there helpfully.

> ARRIVING TODAY, Mr. and Mrs. Nathan Langley, late of Chicago. Mr. Langley has been given charge of the newly formed Stratford-Brown Mining, and is a well-respected businessman. After the divine Mrs. Langley's recent brush with scandal (dare we mention Marat's latest *Andromeda*? Yes, we dare!) one hopes she will restrain herself in her newly adopted home. Thankfully Seattle society has not yet found debauchery to its taste, and we trust our most respectable matrons will take Mrs. Langley firmly in hand.

Nathan stood staring at the paper in his hands, his face pale, and I crossed a parlor too sparsely decorated for my taste and still, *still,* in 1888, lit by gas. I meant to touch him, but he flinched before I could, and I let my hand fall again and said softly, "I'm sorry, Nathan. But I will overcome it. I promise. They'll see nothing untoward in my behavior tonight."

He gave a short nod and said only, "You'd best get dressed."

We'd been invited to a welcoming supper hosted by Emery Brown, who owned the Brown part of the new Stratford-Brown Mining, and with whom Nathan would be working, and although I was tired from the last leg of our journey, I was also anxious to meet those who would be my new friends. I took care with my appearance, wearing one of my best Worth gowns, a lovely deep blue embroidered with butterflies in golds and burgundies, its skirt draped and caught up over a bustle that ended in a train. I'd had matching hairpins made—butterflies of sapphires and rubies. No one could fault my elegance at least. They would recognize the Stratford breeding in my bones.

It was not far to go. Only four blocks until our carriage was before a home that was small by Chicago standards. Like ours, it was on a hill overlooking the city and surrounded by other houses, one of which was very large, and a vacant lot. There was a stable in the back and a cow beyond in a fenced enclosure. The pathway was unpaved; my slippers, which had been dyed to match the gown, were filthy by the time we reached the front door.

At least they had servants, I thought, as a woman in an apron opened the door and ushered us inside. I'd been afraid Mr. Brown's wife might answer herself. She took our cloaks and Nathan's hat and said, "The other guests are waiting for you."

We were the last to arrive. Apparently, fashionably late in Chicago was only late in Seattle. Something to make up for already. Mrs. Brown, a diminutive woman in a rather plain brown silk, whose only decoration was the cameo brooch at her collar and the dangling pearls at her ears, eyed me suspiciously as we were introduced, but she was coolly pleasant.

"I do hope you enjoy your time in Seattle," she said, her gaze dipping to my very low décolletage—it was the fashion in Chicago, but I was dismayed to find no one here wore anything even half so low. I was scandalous already, and through no fault of my own, and I saw Nathan's jaw tighten.

But I smiled my best smile and said, "I expect to like it very much," and was pleased when she seemed a little impressed, as if she'd expected terrible manners and coarseness from a woman as notorious as I. "How happy Mr. Langley and I were to be invited to your home this evening. We are quite the strangers here, I'm afraid."

It prodded her into courtesy. She took Nathan and me about the room, introducing us. The party was more intimate than I'd expected—only twenty, and most of them were disappointingly undistinguishable. Not an artist or writer or even a sea captain among them. It reminded me of my grandmother's suppers, which were so dull and boring I'd learned to escape them as often as I could, and these people might have been her contemporaries, not in age but in demeanor. There wasn't a woman there who didn't look askance at my gown, nor a man who didn't eye it surreptitiously, though everyone was polite enough, and my smile was beginning to wear as we went in to supper.

The dining room was small, with barely enough room to house the table. Mrs. Brown had decorated it prettily with evergreens and red ribbon, and candles burned brightly in a simple candelabrum of highly polished silver. The plates were simple as well, a plain white bordered with green.

Nathan was seated near Mr. Brown, and I nearer Mrs. Brown at the other end. At least Seattle adhered to the basic society rules; no man sat next to his wife. On one side of me was Mr. Thomas Porter, a tall, exceedingly thin man who also worked in the mining company offices, and on the other Major Shields, who looked to be a man who enjoyed himself. I found myself leading the conversation, as both men seemed incapable of it—as tired as I was, I tried to be witty and charming, yet neither seemed interested in clever little bons mots and philosophizing. Instead the conversation turned to politics and the possibility of impending statehood.

"There will be plenty of positions for good and honest men," declared the major. "Men who wish to lead us into a new century."

Mr. Porter leaned forward. "We have too few men with such ambitions. I wish to God the city council would do something with all these vagrants in the hills. Transients everywhere."

"There are worse problems to contend with." The major took a sip of his wine. "What about you, Langley? Have you political aspirations?"

Nathan looked up. "I should think the new company will take most of my efforts, at least in the beginning. But I don't rule out the possibility of government service."

"Excellent news," said Mr. Brown, glancing unsubtlely at me. "Of course, circumspection is the order of the day in this city, as you've no doubt heard."

I felt myself flush.

Nathan's smile thinned. "Yes, of course. Well, I dislike

making decisions precipitously. I expect it will take some time simply to become used to the rain."

The rest at the table laughed. "Oh, I think you will find it not so bad as that," said Major Shields's wife. "We're in the worst of it now, but the summers will prove delightful for it."

The conversation went on in much the same vein for three more courses, all meant, said Mrs. Brown, to showcase Seattle's bounty: a heavy salmon pie, oyster stew, and a dessert of jellied cream flavored with red currants. As we finished the last bites, Mrs. Brown rose, saying, "Shall we leave the gentlemen to their cigars, ladies?"

It was a custom I hated and one I never adhered to in my own home, having long ago asserted that the men saved the more interesting conversation for after dinner. Many of my friends in Chicago had followed my lead. But I remembered my father's admonitions and my resolve, so I restrained my tongue and followed the other women demurely into a parlor hardly big enough to accommodate us all. The furniture was pleasant enough, if all machine made and Jacobean in design, though there was a lovely rosewood table inlaid with ivory and set with a delicate opaline vase from which emerged the thin stems of two wax roses. A few paintings decorated the walls, mostly landscapes by artists I had no familiarity with.

We milled about, some finding a chair, a few standing by the window that overlooked the street and darkness grayed by rain. Mrs. Brown poured tea from a graceful silver tea service. She handed a cup to a woman who sat on the chair opposite—Mrs. Porter, I remembered—and glanced at me.

"Mrs. Langley, please, come talk with us awhile." She patted the space beside her on the settee; when I went to it, she handed me a cup of tea as well.

"You're living at the old Post place, I hear," Mrs. Porter said to me.

"I do hope it's to your liking," Mrs. Brown interjected. "I wish we could have done more, but with such short notice . . . well, you understand."

The censure was in her words. I did not mistake it; I was an expert myself at scolds hidden in graciousness. "I think it remarkable that you managed to accomplish what you did," I said courteously. "I could not have hoped for better."

"We are not lacking the more graceful aspects of life in Seattle. There are many shops downtown. If you're looking for something in particular, I do hope you'll look to me for guidance." Again, the quick eyeing of my bodice. "We don't lack excellent seamstresses either. I would be pleased to recommend one."

"Is there one trained in the French style?"

"French? Like the one you wear now?"

"Yes. It's a Worth," I said.

"It's quite beautiful," Mrs. Porter said. "Is it the fashion in Chicago?"

"Oh yes."

Mrs. Brown sighed. "You must realize, Mrs. Langley, that Seattle is not Chicago. As beautiful as the gown is, I think you'll find that here you won't have need for such . . . immoderation. We much prefer simple elegance."

I forced an answering smile. "Thank you, Mrs. Brown. I shall remember that."

"I understand you held a salon in Chicago." Mrs. Porter offered this carefully, as if fearful of the landscape.

There was a whisper, a titter, from somewhere over my shoulder. Someone else laughed. I was meant to hear both, but I ignored them completely. I grasped gratefully at the subject. "Yes. It was quite renowned. You must tell me, as I have no idea: Do authors ever visit Seattle? Or artists? My Thursday evenings had quite a following among actors as well."

It was too much, too fast; I knew it the moment Mrs. Brown said, "I'm afraid no one would be much interested in a salon of that kind."

This place would require patience, I realized. It was my own fault; I could not blame them for wanting to see evidence of my humility. Still, I could not help my disappointment. I struggled to keep my smile. "Of course," I said finally.

We lapsed into an uncomfortable silence that lasted until someone said, "Did you see the new shipment of cloth at Schwabacher's?" and they joined together in palpable relief to speak of silks and worsteds, and I drank my tea in silence.

It was only later, when Nathan stopped at the doorway of the parlor to say he was fetching our coats, that Mrs. Brown said to me in a low voice, "I feel it only fair to warn you, Mrs. Langley, that there are those here who do not welcome your arrival. In fact"—a pause, as if it troubled her to say it—"there are some who have said already they won't receive you." Here she looked at me helplessly.

"I understand," I said softly, taking pity on her, wondering what it had cost her to host this supper, to introduce me to a society that had already measured me and found me wanting. "Thank you for being so forthright, Mrs. Brown. I am grateful."

Again, that short, firm nod, as if she had dispensed with a difficult duty and was back to the usual nonsense again. "I've promised my husband to help you get along until you settle yourself."

"I shall not trouble you unduly," I promised, and I knew I was not imagining the relief in her expression.

That night, I sat at the dressing table brushing my hair, thinking over the evening, which had been a disappointment, though, if nothing else, I'd gained a good idea of what I was up against. The furnishings, the clothing, the food, the talk . . . Those who passed for society in Seattle would barely have reached the lower rungs of the social ladder in Chicago. But I was at their mercy, and I saw my task clearly. They were so afraid of any indiscretion that they would band together to keep me out unless I showed myself above reproach in every way. I could win them over eventually, I knew, though it would take every ounce of my charm to do so.

Just now, the thought made me weary. I stared into the mirror, which was old and wavery, flecked with spots, my reflection hard to see, nothing but the dark shadow of my hair, my eyes like black dots, and suddenly I was thinking of my last salon, the one before the exhibition had turned everything so impossible. I thought of Ambrose laughing, flushed as he drained his glass. Charles Furth saying, *"Yes, of course, Rivers, but I wonder sometimes if the world slows to a crawl for you alone. The rest of us see things in motion, details escape us. Which is why Gauguin's vision is truer than Millais's. Do you not agree, my dear Ginny?"* And my answer, as Claude stood beside me, smiling, *"The world moves in slow, does it not, Charles? I think it is we who move too fast. You cannot fault Ambrose for moving with the world."* Furth's laughter. *"She is your devotee as ever, Rivers. You've armored her with your Pre-Raphaelites and none of the rest of us can make a dent."* The candlelight flickering, sending dancing shadows upon the walls, glancing across the fat rubies encircling my wrist.

A movement in the mirror took me from the memory; I looked over my shoulder to see Nathan enter my bedroom.

"They were kind tonight," he said quietly. "Didn't you think so?"

I sighed and turned back to brushing my hair. "Was it kindness, do you think? I would venture to call it something else. I received a lecture on behavior along with my tea. When I mentioned to Mrs. Brown the possibility of starting a salon—"

"Good God, Ginny, you didn't."

"Don't worry. Mrs. Brown made it quite clear how unacceptable they would find it."

"And you intend to heed her?" He sounded wary.

"Oh, but of course," I said with a bitter laugh. "For now, at least. I have promised to make a new start, and I shall."

"You have no one to blame for that but yourself."

I closed my eyes.

"I know it's not what you're accustomed to," he said. "But these are good people."

"I suppose next you'll tell me that Major Shields's snorting into his tea is an endearing habit."

"It's a young city. They haven't had time to learn to be pretentious."

"You think them as backward as I."

"Perhaps. But there's something to be said for those who act instead of merely talking about it. Here, they're too busy building a city to natter on about the subtleties of a brushstroke. In any case, I should think you would like the idea of leading them into the future."

"It will be like dragging a cow."

"So one must go slowly." Nathan considered me in the mirror. "Slowly, Ginny. We've a chance to mold this city, you know."

"Mold it?"

"Which is not the same as stomping it into submission. I see real opportunity here."

"Yes indeed. All that political talk. Do you mean to pursue it instead of only talking about it as you did in Chicago?"

"You don't know what you're saying, Ginny," he said bluntly, and I saw the quick flare of anger in his eyes. "If you paid half the attention to me that you do to your artists, you'd know that I had intended to run for a city council position in Chicago. Your father and I had already put things in motion."

I could not have been more surprised had he told me he was a frog-prince. "You never told me of this."

"It required careful study of the landscape first. By the time I decided for certain, you were otherwise engaged."

I felt myself flush. "I see."

"It was one of the reasons to come here. What with statehood on the horizon, the opportunities are legion."

I was surprised again, that he had been so farsighted. "This was no sudden move then. How long have you been planning to come here?"

"Since it became clear that my political career in Chicago had an impossible liability."

"Which was what?"

"My wife, whom the whole city knew spread her legs for Jean-Claude Marat."

In his words I heard the depth of his resentment and anger. "I've told you there was no affair. How often must I say it before you believe me?"

He made an impatient gesture. "My opinion doesn't matter. Everyone believes you did, which makes it true enough."

"It matters to *me* what you believe," I said.

"Does it?"

"Yes, of course."

He looked at me thoughtfully, an expression that made me uncomfortable, before he said, "I hope in time to start a political career here, Ginny. It will depend upon you, of course. They'll need to accept you."

"They'll need to accept me," I repeated quietly. I was so disappointed that he had offered me no reassurance, I could not keep myself from saying, "I wonder that you don't send me away. It would be so much more convenient."

"You refused Bloomfield."

"I don't mean an asylum. I mean . . . to the Continent, perhaps."

His smile was thin. "Ah yes, no doubt you'd like that. But what would that avail me? There would only be rumors that you've run after him, or that you're cavorting with some other poor artist in Paris. It would hardly do my career any good. When one cannot control one's wife, et cetera, et cetera. . . ."

How far we were from each other. I despaired that it could ever be otherwise. "You look at me as if you cannot stand the sight of me."

He shrugged. "Do you wonder at it? But you could be quite an asset to me, Ginny, if you do as you say and make the fresh start you promise. You're beautiful and clever. You could be the best hostess this city has ever seen. You bring a fortune with you."

"My fortune." I laughed shortly. "Sometimes I think that's the only reason you married me."

"It has become the reason I keep you," he said, and the bitterness in his voice was unmistakable.

I turned to look at him, trying to ignore how much I believed that to be true. "Nathan, don't you remember how we once were? Do you remember how we talked the night away? How we made love—"

"While you flirted with every artist and writer who came into view?"

I said bitterly, "I missed you. You've ignored me for months and months."

"Yes, of course it was my fault," he said. "By all means, blame me. It was not as if you had anything to do with it."

"Make a new start," my grandmother had said. And my father: *"Nathan knows what's best."* I could not fight him over the past, not if I meant to salvage anything at all. I closed my eyes. "I'm sorry, Nathan," I said softly, a whisper.

He made a sound of dismissal. "It's too late for that, Ginny. I no longer care about your regret—if you truly feel any. What I care about is atonement. Can you be the wife I need you to be here? After what you've seen tonight, can you keep your promise?"

I met his gaze and nodded. "Yes, I think I can do that."

"Good," he said, and left me.

Chapter Four

But it turned out that the promise I'd made Nathan was even less easily kept than I'd anticipated. Nathan went to the office and I sat about the house, waiting for the society women of Seattle to pay their calls, and when they did not, I remembered Mrs. Brown's words about those who did not intend to receive me. I'd thought she must be overstating their reluctance; I could not imagine the women of this outpost would truly spurn the daughter of Stratford Mining, especially if they were made to realize that I was on my best behavior.

But the invitations did not come. Oh, Mrs. Brown was as good as she'd promised to be. Those first weeks, she took us to other suppers, other dances—two public affairs, with drunken merchants and their coarse wives hoping to elevate themselves socially and Nathan greeting some of the business owners as if they were old friends.

"You've the charm of a natural politician," Emery Brown told him with a laugh. I was unused to being in eclipse, and it didn't matter how I smiled, or what I said, I was given a humoring smile in return, dismissive words, and slowly I came to realize that everyone here meant to keep me firmly in my place, in Nathan's shadow.

But I accepted it. My father was quick to remind me of my duty with every letter.

> *I understand you are finding life to be somewhat difficult there, but it is to be your home now, and*

> *you must put what happened in Chicago behind you. Please make an effort to be circumspect, Ginny. There are several business dealings of mine that would not tolerate your further transgressions. Your grandmother has spent these last weeks bearing down upon doors that are suddenly closed to her—your bad behavior has cost us all. Please consider that your grandmother is seventy-six this year, far too old to reinvent herself in society.*

My father's admonition hurt—I was afraid I had irrevocably lost the man I'd so adored. I was determined to atone. I told myself that Papa had never managed to stay angry with me for long, and if I were careful, I would be restored to his good graces quickly, no matter the state of my marriage, which looked to become no better. I kept my letters to him chatty and optimistic, but the truth was just the opposite. Nathan remained so firmly distant that any true reconciliation seemed impossible. He spent hardly any time with me and joined the newly established Rainier Club, which kept him away many nights, hobnobbing among the men he'd made his friends, "Important Men" he called them, men who could help him in our newfound home. I languished in our parlor with only the maid for company. I thought of my salons, of the famous and notorious, of every night filled with something new and outrageous, something to make me laugh or think, and I found myself keeping the maid with conversation, her "yes, ma'am, it is quite cold" instead of *"Hand, heart, or head, Ginny? Which is it that makes art true? And don't say all three. That's too easy. . . ."*

I was drowning in memories, in the chatter of my past life, and I knew I would languish there if I didn't push a little harder. Perhaps Seattle matrons *were* waiting for me to make the first move. I decided to hold a dinner of my own. I invited the Browns and the Porters, of course; but also Mr. Orion Denny, whose father had been one of the founders of Seattle, and his wife, Narcissa; and Henry Yesler, the owner of the sawmill, whose late wife, Sarah, had been rumored to be a spiritualist, so I thought he would not mind my notoriety. I also sent invitations to the Wilcoxes and the Gatzerts, whom Nathan told me were important. It was to be a small, intimate dinner, and I wished very much for someone from my salons—a writer or actor or artist or two; there was no one better than an actor for making conversation. I checked the papers assiduously for any visiting luminary. There were none, and I supposed that was best. I meant to do as Nathan suggested and start slow. I did not want to alarm them. After I proved to them how congenial I could be, I would provide a philosopher or two. Then perhaps I would hold a ball.

I planned for that dinner like a general. My trunks had finally arrived from Chicago, and I went through them with a critical eye, the petticoats and underthings, the satin and lace corsets in a rainbow of colors, traveling suits and morning gowns, furs and cloaks. I kept boxed the newest Worth gowns, bejeweled and beautiful, instead pulling out those I had not worn for two seasons or more, those with higher necklines and smaller bustles and modest lace inserts that seemed more in kind to those I'd seen at the Browns' dinner. I filled the dining room with my own plate, elaborate, gold-trimmed. I decorated expansively with expensive gewgaws to remind them of my status—if charm would not do, I was willing to resort to bribery of a kind. I went over menu after menu with the cook until I finally wore her into tackling some of my favorite French dishes, and I had wine sent from our cellar in Chicago.

And I hardly had time for a breath before the declinations began to arrive.

Mr. and Mrs. Orion Denny, along with Mr. Yesler, regretted to say they would be out of town. Mrs. Wilcox's refusal was a simple "I will not be attending," as was the Gatzerts'. Half my dinner party gone before they'd set foot through the door. There were only the Browns and the Porters left, and though their husbands were smiling when my maid showed them into the parlor that night, Mrs. Brown and Mrs. Porter looked pained, as if they'd been told they were going to the opera and been dragged to a bawdy melodrama instead.

I was on my best behavior. I smiled so that it felt my face

might break. I offered wine and sherry. I said nothing when they picked at the unfamiliar French dishes and Mrs. Porter finally put her fork down with a "Sweetbreads, you say? How . . . unusual." Instead I thought of how much Ambrose Rivers had adored sweetbreads, and I wanted to cry at how I missed him.

When the men withdrew to Nathan's study for cigars, I led Mrs. Porter and Mrs. Brown to the parlor, bowing obediently to tradition. The women looked with studied disinterest at all my careful arrangements, and I saw Mrs. Brown discreetly turn a small but exquisitely sculptured nude so she would not have to look at its naked breasts. It had been a gift from the sculptor who'd made it, *"a small token of my gratitude, my dear Ginny, for all you've done,"* a man so talented it seemed nothing coarse could come from his hands, and here was Mrs. Brown, refusing even to look at it.

I bit back any comment and instead smiled and offered them both tea, and Mrs. Porter said, "A lovely dinner, Mrs. Langley," and Mrs. Brown echoed the sentiment, and I said, as casually as I could,

"Unfortunately we were missing half the party. I hope next time to pick a better date."

They glanced at each other.

Mrs. Brown said, "I hear your husband has joined the Rainier Club."

"Yes indeed. He seems to quite like it. He's been there nearly every evening."

"They do get involved with their cigars and their talk."

"So I've heard," I said. "I assume your husbands are often there as well?"

"Oh yes," Mrs. Porter said.

"Then you must be as bored as I. Tell me, how do you spend your evenings? I've looked through the newspaper, but I've seen nothing but phrenologists and temperance lecturers at the Lyceum. Oh, and a cat trained to pick up a bottle and carry it offstage."

Mrs. Brown smiled thinly. "There are plays, of course. At the Regal and the Palace. But we don't go often."

"No opera?"

"Now and again at Frye's." Mrs. Porter looked a bit uncomfortable. "Nothing like what you're used to, I imagine."

"Oh, it seems it's been so long since I've been entertained, I imagine I could get used to anything. Even, I suppose, a trained cat."

Mrs. Brown's smile took on a pitying quality. "Our charity work manages to fill the empty hours and then some, Mrs. Langley, though I doubt that would interest you."

"Charity work? I used to do some of that as well. My father financed a wing for Mercy Hospital," I said. "And I helped him organize the financing for the Chicago Art Institute. And the artist studios, of course. They had such need for them, you couldn't imagine. Why, Miles Ashby was working out of a shed! Can you imagine? A genius such as that! He said it was often so cold his paints would freeze before he could use them."

"I see." Mrs. Porter's expression was so purely blank it could have been a slab of untouched marble. "Who is Miles Ashby?"

I laughed; for a moment I thought she was teasing. When I realized she wasn't, I managed, "Why . . . you mean you haven't heard of him?"

"No," she said. "Unfortunately, we've more pressing concerns than artist studios here. The Relief Society has never been so overwhelmed. Orphans starving, women beaten, men who cannot feed their families . . . I'm sure you can imagine."

I felt myself flush with embarrassment and felt a stab of anger for it, which I quickly tamped. "It is true I was more concerned in Chicago with my father's art patronage. But what better help can we offer the world than to support those who give us truth and beauty?"

Mrs. Porter said, "I myself believe that truth and beauty are better appreciated on a full stomach. The starving and downtrodden must rather concern themselves with surviving. What good are artists if there is no population to see them?"

Again my anger flared. I reminded myself of what I wanted: a fresh start, friends, though I knew already that Mrs. Porter was unlikely to be one. Still, she was here. She had attended a pariah's dinner, and she was willing to be seen with me, and regardless of the fact that it was no doubt because of her husband's position in Stratford-Brown Mining, she was an ally when I had too few. I forced myself to say, "Why, I've never looked at it quite that way before. Do you suppose . . . could the society use my help?"

Her glance to Mrs. Brown was quick and a bit panicked. Mrs. Brown said smoothly, "We should hate to impose, Mrs. Langley—"

"No, not at all," I said quickly, and sincerely. Such charity work was not what I had in mind, but it was a start. At last here was something I might do, a way to fit in. And Nathan would be pleased at it—he could find no fault with homeless women and orphans. "And you did say the society was quite overwhelmed. I'd hate to have it be so, when I'm here and quite at liberty."

They looked at each other. Mrs. Brown cleared her throat. "We would love to have you, Mrs. Langley, you understand, but unfortunately Mrs. Porter and I are not the ones who decide such things."

"Who is?"

Mrs. Porter said, "Mrs. Wilcox and Mrs. Gatzert."

The two women who had, in unison, declined my invitation to supper.

"Oh," I said. "Oh, I see."

Mrs. Brown took a deep breath. "Yes."

"Well, then, when is Mrs. Wilcox's calling day?"

Mrs. Porter's glance was faintly pitying. "Before you go calling, Mrs. Langley, I wonder if you should ask yourself just how strong is your desire to ladle out soup to the downtrodden."

"You don't think me capable of such feeling?"

"Mrs. Wilcox is unlikely to receive you," Mrs. Brown said bluntly. "She has stated publicly that she won't."

"Mrs. Gatzert then. Mrs. Denny."

There was silence.

A little desperately, I said, "They cannot mean to snub me forever."

"I think you'll find they have impressive staying power," Mrs. Porter said quietly.

"I mean to make Seattle my home. What must I do to convince you I am not what the rumors make me?"

Mrs. Brown said, "Are the rumors true?"

"I suppose . . . some of them."

"You see the difficulty?" Mrs. Porter asked.

And I did. Very well. They wished me drowning in shame, humbled and contrite, and they could not know that the evidence of those things was the very fact that I was here now, that I had held this dinner, that I volunteered for charity work, that I was so desperate for friendship I was willing to offer myself for Mrs. Wilcox's consumption. Public self-flagellation would have suited them, I realized. But my pride was all I had left. I would not give them that.

The problem was that it was the only thing they wanted.

"Yes, I understand," I told Mrs. Porter softly. "But I have to try, don't I?"

But trying was easier said than done. As the weeks passed, I began to feel as if I were disappearing. My favorite days became the ones where the city was socked in with fog, because on those days there was no world beyond the one in my parlor, and it was strangely comforting to think there was nothing to miss. I read a great deal. Poe and Hawthorne, Whitman and Coleridge and Browning. The world inside my head took on vibrant life and melodrama. But as far as the world outside . . . I felt myself wrapped in cotton, a dull automaton.

My father's letters continued, now touched with concern, as I could no longer keep to my promises to be cheerful, and I'm afraid my loneliness crept into every missive.

> *I am grown worried about you, Geneva. Nathan tells me you are quite despondent. Surely there is some social life there to please you? Are there no plays or operas to go to?*

Yes, there were, but I dared not go alone here as I had in Chicago, not after the promises I'd made my husband and my father, and Nathan claimed to be too busy. But then, one morning in February, as I sat at the table, playing with a piece of toast and sipping coffee and wondering what I should do with the day, Nathan laid something at my elbow. I glanced over without interest until I saw they were tickets. Tickets to the Regal Theater to see *Black Jack, or, the Bandit King of the Border.*

I glanced up at my husband, who seated himself and poured coffee into one of the fine china cups I'd had shipped from Chicago. "Do you mean for us to go?"

"Why else would I have tickets?" he asked irritably. "Robert Wesley gave them to me last night. You've seemed so despondent, I thought you might enjoy it."

"Oh, I should love to!"

He shrugged. "It's only a mellie, but I didn't think that would matter. God knows we've seen enough of them."

"You mean to escort me?"

"Yes, of course. Why, did you have someone else in mind?" He glanced around. "You haven't some artist hiding in the woodwork, do you?"

A lump rose in my throat, a quick and bitter longing. "Don't be absurd."

He took a final sip of his coffee and rose. "We will be attending Judge Burke's supper after. I shall send the carriage for you."

I was ready long before the carriage came, dressed in one of my most modest gowns, a pale blue silk that I wore with a lace fichu to cover the expanse below my collarbone, and sapphire earrings that were only droplets compared to the huge square dangling ones I'd worn at our first supper here. It had been some time since Nathan had the time or inclination to attend a play with me, and I dared to hope it meant something more, an indication that he cared, that he too wished not to be so estranged. I planned to be on my best behavior.

The Regal Theater was very small and not the least bit elegant; it looked as if it might crumple to the ground in the merest breeze. I went through the side door leading to the box seats and found Nathan waiting for me at the bottom of the dark and narrow stairs, impatiently taking his watch from his vest pocket to check the time.

Mr. and Mrs. Brown were waiting for us in the box, as well as six or seven strangers. There was the loud thumping from those in the gallery above, and a general commotion in the parquet below. A small orchestra tuned their instruments in the pit; a boy with a basket called, "Lozenges! Buy your lozenges afore the show starts!" The theater was dim and cold, the smell of gas heavy from the footlights ringing the stage and those set in tin sconces about the walls, but the seats were padded, and the curtain was heavy blue velvet to match the blue and gold decor, a large gas chandelier hung imposingly above—trappings of elegance that only served to send the meanness of everything else into relief.

As we took our seats, Mr. Brown leaned forward to say, "I'm so glad you could come with us tonight."

Nathan said, "Ginny has always enjoyed the theater. Do you know this play?"

Mr. Brown shook his head. His wife said, "Mr. Greene's company can be counted on for the most diverting entertainment, if not always the most elevated."

The gasolier above dimmed, the crowd went quieter but not quiet, not until the orchestra began to play, and even then the gallery above was never silent, whistling and catcalling even as the deep blue curtains slid open to reveal a desert mountain setting, and the play began.

Mrs. Brown was right; it was not edifying, but it was energizing and quick, full of action and brilliant stunts—the bandit swinging across the stage on a rope, he and his henchman dashing up a narrow pathway on horseback to toss a blond-haired damsel—clearly a crowd favorite, given the stomping of feet and shouting at her entrance—into a mountain ravine, a daring rescue by the equally blond hero over the same. I was enraptured from the first moment Black Jack told of his intentions in a rollicking song that had those in the gallery singing along, shouting the chorus: "She will be mine, mine, mine or die a thousand times!" And when Sweet Polly's dark-haired sister entreated the hero not to forget his duty, her song took up residence in my head, and I was still humming it when the play ended in fireworks and startled cries.

I did not want to leave. The time had passed too quickly; how I had missed this! It was nothing compared to the theater I'd seen in Chicago. It was coarse and mean, but it accentuated my loss; I could barely smile my good-byes to the Browns when my husband led me to the carriage.

It was pouring again, spattering and spitting on the carriage roof. The window sweated against the cold and wet, impossible to see out as we made our way to Judge Burke's, the haloed streetlamps only a suggestion of light. I could not see Nathan's face.

"Did you enjoy it?" I asked him.

There was a pause; I had the sense he had only just heard me, that his mind was somewhere far away. "Enjoy it? Why, yes. Yes, I did. Did you?"

I could not contain myself. "I would love to see it again. How long does it run?"

"I've no idea," he said. "Why, did you see an actor you fancied?"

I was stung. How little it took to bring the shame and humiliation rising again. "That's unfair, Nathan."

The carriage stopped. He sighed. "Yes, it was. Forgive me. Now here we are. Judge Burke is trying to broker a deal between Seattle and the Northern Pacific Railroad, and he is most certain to figure prominently in the change to statehood. My future could very well be in his hands."

"Don't worry," I said. "I won't embarrass you."

He gave me a weary look and offered his arm as our driver opened the door to let us out. There were a few carriages already waiting, and a wagon or two as well. Lights shone invitingly from the windows, and Nathan and I hurried toward them through the rain. We were shown into the parlor, where a short, stocky man with a mustache and the look of the florid Irish about him, and his taller wife, held court.

Nathan led me to them without hesitation. "Judge Burke, Mrs. Burke, may I present my wife, Geneva Langley."

The judge peered at me as if it were hard for him to focus in the dim light. "I'm happy to meet you, Mrs. Langley. I must say I've heard a great deal about you."

"Nothing too bad, I hope."

His wife's smile was hardly there. "Your husband has assured us all that is in the past."

"Indeed it is. In fact, I've thought a great deal about joining the Ladies Relief Society I've heard so much about."

"The Relief Society?" Judge Burke looked faintly bored.

"Well, then, you will want to speak to Sarah Wilcox." He pointed through the crowd, and I looked in that direction to see an older woman dressed completely in black. "She was one of the founders of the Society, along with Mrs. Gatzert. She can present you to the others."

Mrs. Burke's expression seemed strained. "Of course you must speak to her."

But she did not offer an introduction, I noticed, and just then two others came into the parlor, and Nathan and I were dismissed as Mrs. Burke and her husband went to greet the newcomers.

"What is this about a relief society?" Nathan asked me in a low voice. "You've never shown any interest in such things before."

"I've never needed to. But as it seems to be the entry into the hearts of the women here, I thought it would be best to join."

"Well." His expression was surprised, his tone reluctantly impressed. "I'm surprised."

"Did you think me too small to change?"

"Not too small. Too . . . invested."

"Invested in what?"

"In your little rebellions."

I felt the uncomfortable ring of truth. "I think I shall go mad if I must spend another day staring out the window."

Nathan let out his breath. "Well, good. Good. I'm glad to see you mean to be the asset I need, Ginny."

Just then I saw Mrs. Wilcox across the room, her gray hair perfectly swept up in a clasp of black feathers, the jet beads at her ears matching the cape she wore over her shoulders. She was speaking with some other woman and a gray-haired man.

"There she is," I said to Nathan. "The dragon herself. Shall I go and introduce myself?"

He took a drink from a passing servant and said mildly, "You know best, I imagine."

"Very well, I shall," I said, though my nerves were taut. Foolish—I was Geneva Stratford Langley, after all—what had I to be afraid of? How difficult was it to just walk up to her, introduce myself, and mention the Relief Society? I started across the room toward her. I knew that not only was Nathan watching me, but others were too—my step was purposeful enough that they must wonder as to its destination.

I was only a few steps away from her when a woman I didn't recognize tapped her on the shoulder. I saw Mrs. Wilcox catch sight of me. For one moment, she met my gaze, for a moment, she held it. Obvious. Deadly.

And then, quite deliberately and with a lethal flamboyance, Mrs. Sarah Wilcox turned her back on me and walked away.

Suddenly I was back in the exhibition hall, with my closest friends turning away from me and talk like confetti in the air. I heard the quick whispers. I heard someone laugh. I faltered and came to a stop, feeling heat move into my face. Humiliated.

I turned quickly, struggling to keep my composure, looking back to my husband, who drank his sherry with a frown, trying to hide his embarrassment and consternation, and I thought of Chicago, of home, of my door thrown open to welcome guests, the gifts they pressed into my hands, the kisses on my cheek, and I thought how stupid I'd been. How stupid and ridiculous, to throw it all away.

Chapter Five

Beatrice

I first saw him during our performance of *Black Jack, or, the Bandit King of the Border.* He was sitting in the boxes, next to a woman in pale blue. Faces in the theater were easy to see because the houselights were never turned down all the way, and I was no different from Lucius or the others in the company when it came to keeping an eye on who was in the boxes. The most important people in any city always had those tickets, which were the most expensive. So I noted them. While Stella screamed her stupid voice hoarse, I watched them from the wings. The woman clapped furiously and leaned forward as if she could breathe in the show. He was more reserved, but the strange thing was that I felt his gaze whenever I was onstage, and I knew he wasn't watching Stella or Aloysius or Jack. He was watching me.

I saw the opportunity, of course I did. And I knew I was going to take it if it was offered and tried not to think of it as compromising. I'd never taken a patron because it was too close in my mind to being a whore. But Stella had taught me a lesson. All those years of hoping my talent could move me ahead, of doing what was expected, had got me nowhere. Lucius had said it was pure business, and I took that to heart now. So I played to the man in the box, and the next morning, there was a bouquet of flowers delivered to the theater for me. Nothing too fancy, mostly carnations with a few roses, but they were pretty, and as it was usually Stella—or *La* Stella, as they were calling her now—who got flowers, I was surprised and pleased. There was no card, but I knew who they were from.

I set them on the table in the dressing room and left them there. When I came back that afternoon to get ready for the performance, the smell of roses was so strong in that airless little space I had to keep the door ajar to breathe.

"Who sent these?" Susan Jenks—our new traveling lady, who'd taken over Stella's old line—asked me as she came inside. "Pretty."

"They are," I agreed, feeling another little stab of pleasure. "I got them this morning. There wasn't a card."

"A secret admirer! Do you have any idea who?"

"None," I told her, a lie, but she didn't ask any more questions.

I looked for him that night, in vain, it turned out, because he wasn't there. Nor the next night, nor the next. I'd decided he was probably a visitor to town, and I'd never see him again, and there went *that* opportunity, which was disappointing, you know, but I was a little relieved at it too. I wasn't meant to go that route after all. When the flowers withered I threw them in the refuse pile out back and forgot about him.

I didn't see him again until the party for Aloysius's birthday. No reason for a party was ever too small for the company, so we gathered at the saloon on the corner—even some of the set builders and supernumeraries came, and we ended up taking the place over, drinking lager and whiskey, and of course Stella was there with her damned absinthe while half the theater people crowded around her. I'll admit, she did look elegant, performing her little absinthe ritual, the water, the sugar, the slotted spoon. Her motions were smooth and theatrical, as if she were on her own personal stage, and I thought: *she's not long for us,* and wondered why I thought it. She'd only been the lead for a few months; surely she couldn't already be thinking of starting her own tour as a star. But the more I looked at her, the more I thought that was just what she meant to do.

I'd told myself to settle in, exactly as Brody had said. Watch and wait. Play the game and try not to think too hard about the passing time. But now I leaned against the bar and sipped at my beer and watched Stella and my impatience and hunger rose. That very moment, the man who'd sent me the flowers came into the saloon.

The lady wasn't with him. He was with a bearded, spectacled gentleman, and they both wore expensive suits and vests and sparkling watch chains. The two of them fairly stank of money. I saw Stella catch the scent too, though she hardly needed riches now; she still had Welling for her protector. But her sharp little chin came up quick as a weasel's; even from where I stood I could see her nose twitch.

Neither of them did more than glance at her. Instead they came to the bar near where I stood. The man had light brown hair that was just short of blond, and it shone with pomade or macassar, and he was handsome, better looking close up than I'd seen at a distance. He didn't look at me, didn't even glance in my direction, but you know, I felt that he knew exactly where I was, that I was even the reason he was there.

They both ordered whiskey and leaned on the bar, facing each other, to talk. The blond man's back was to me; he was only a foot away. The place was noisy and crowded, heavy with smoke. I couldn't hear a thing they were saying. But I stood there and drank my beer. I wondered if he would follow me if I left. I thought of Aloysius's words: *"Her paramour is paying the production costs, darling. One can't fault her for playing her cards well."*

The tailoring of his suit was perfect. His boots were so darkly shined a person could lose themselves looking into them. All I had to do was tap him on the shoulder, bump into him, flirt with him a little. But before I could, Brody spun up to the bar, nearly falling against it. "Another whiskey for me, and one for my good friend, Aloys!" He thumped his hand down hard enough on the notched, stained wood that I felt it shudder against my back. He turned to me. "Come and join us, Bea. There's an extra chair now Lucius is gone."

I glanced at the table where he sat with Aloysius and two loud girls and a man who looked at Aloys as if he might gulp him for dinner and said, "I don't think I'm drunk enough for your table."

He laughed. "Then order another beer."

"I think I will," I said, drinking the rest of the mug and turning to order another, but before I could say anything, the man beside me called, "Another beer for the lady." I heard him quite clearly, and when I turned to look at him, I realized his friend was gone—whether for good or just to visit the privy in the back, I had no idea.

He smiled at me, and it made his cheeks dimple. His eyes were dark blue.

"Thank you," I said as the bartender put the beer in front of me.

"My pleasure," he said, and then, "You're Mrs. Wilkes. I saw you in *Black Jack*."

Now it was my turn to smile. "You have the advantage of me, I'm afraid."

"Nathan Langley," he told me. He paused to sip his whiskey. "You're very good, you know. I'm surprised you're not the lead."

He was heaven sent. Just dropped into my lap like a present. I saw the way he looked at me, his eyes lingering at my breasts, my mouth. His tie was the finest silk, the buttons on his vest were horn. His cologne was something fresh and citrusy—whatever it was, it smelled expensive. His nails were trimmed and his hands clean and smooth. "You're very kind," I said.

"Just telling the truth. You can act rings around the little blonde. Why aren't you?"

"Those decisions are made by the manager, I'm afraid."

"Well, he has no eye at all, then."

He was discerning too, which was even better. I leaned back against the bar again, thrusting out my breasts, and saw how his gaze followed my motion. "I shall tell him that, sir, but he tends not to listen to me."

He smiled and took another sip of whiskey. "Does your husband not lobby on your behalf?"

"Oh, I've no husband, sir. The Mrs. is only a courtesy. It's meant to keep people from confusing actresses with whores." Which seemed a stupid point to make just then.

His smile widened. "That's good to know."

Just then the bearded man returned, and Nathan Langley turned back to him as if we hadn't been talking, and I felt a swift disappointment and desperation too that made me drink too heavily of my beer.

But Mama had always said I was too hasty, and I tempered that impatience in me now. Rich men like to think they're doing the chasing, I'd heard, and I was reassured when I looked up into the boxes the following night and saw him there, this time without any woman seated next to him. I felt a little flutter of triumph.

Backstage that night was crowded. *A New Way to Pay Old Debts* was always popular, and it was a Saturday night besides, so the house tended to be sold out in any case. Lucius was swelling like a cock of the walk, almost preening, slapping Jack on the shoulder and kissing Stella, so receipts were good. I had to fight to get through the crowd waiting at Stella's dressing room, and the whole time I was looking for Nathan Langley. Outside the dressing room I shared with Susan, there were a few young miners waiting for her, and one or two admirers for me, wanting to hand me a single rose or a daisy, but none of them was Nathan

Langley, and I was so anxious for the sight of him that when I saw someone lurking in the shadows near the dressing room door, my heart jumped; I thought it might be him, but when I got closer I saw it was only a man wearing a frock coat about twenty years out of date, with dark hair that was unfashionably long and eyes pale enough to be strange in the half-light. He was attractive; perhaps another time I might have looked at him again, but he was not Nathan Langley, and I knew by his dress that he was too poor to take Langley's place, and when he stepped forward to say, "Mrs. Wilkes," I pretended not to hear him and went into my dressing room, closing the door hard behind me.

I plunked the flowers into a vase and unbuttoned my gown so fiercely one of the buttons came loose. I told myself not to hope for Langley, but now that I'd decided I would take him, I couldn't help it, and when there was a knock on the door, I nearly tripped over myself to answer it. And there was Nathan Langley, holding a posy of carnations and a pink box with a ribbon.

I smiled like he was the Second Coming. "Mr. Langley! How lovely to see you."

"I brought these for you," he said, handing me the flowers, holding out the box. "Candied fruit. It's French. I thought you might enjoy it."

"You are so sweet," I said. I took the box and put it on the dressing table, and then lifted out the flowers I'd put in the vase, laying them aside, not wanting them to spoil the look of the artfully arranged bouquet he'd brought me, wanting him to see how I favored it. I turned to face him. My costume was still unbuttoned halfway down the bodice; his gaze went to what could be seen of my corset, my breasts, half exposed now.

"I'm gratified you came to the Regal again, Mr. Langley," I said. "Did you enjoy the play?"

"I've never liked *Old Debts* much. I came to see you."

How boldly he said it, as if there could be no doubt that I would find such a statement flattering, and in fact, I did. "You make me blush, sir."

He smiled; he looked up at me from beneath his lashes, bedroom eyes, and I thought how easy it would be to fuck him. He was nothing like Stella's Richard Welling, jowly and given to fat.

He said, "Let me take you to supper."

Very bold indeed—not the words, but the way he said them. Low and heavy, as if what he meant to say was, *"Let me take you to bed,"* and, again, had no doubt of the outcome of such a question. I was sure Nathan Langley was a man who got what he wanted, and just now there was no confusion: what he wanted was me. Why, I had no idea. But I was an actress, and, like all my fellows, superstitious, and when fate threw something at me, I knew better than to refuse it. Luck had finally decided it was my turn, and it was about time.

He waited outside while I dressed and took off my makeup. I put on a cloak and took up the candy—if I left it, Susan would eat it all—and then Nathan Langley helped me into his carriage, which waited brazenly out front: a big, shiny black brougham with gold scrolling on the door and a fancy coat of arms. I'd never been inside a carriage so fine. Leather seats so padded one sank into them, and a curtain with fringe over the window—which he didn't lower—and a brazier at our feet that sent out a steady warmth. He was a gentleman; he attempted nothing for the few blocks to our destination, a café just below Mill Street, not yet into the worst part of town. I was impressed by that, by the fact that he didn't seem to care if we were seen. The café was full with after-theater patrons, mostly men. He ordered something in French that turned out to be salmon baked in a pie, with a rich sauce, delicious, and he didn't eat but only watched me, and I had a moment where I thought he was like that witch in *Hansel and Gretel,* fattening me up to gobble me down.

And the truth was that I did my own fattening. When he asked me about the theater, I told him Stella had stolen the lead from me months ago, and that Lucius was prone to choose money over talent—all little hints, and he listened and I saw the calculation in his eyes and thought that we both knew what we wanted from each other. All this talk was nothing but negotiation.

After supper, he had the driver take us to my hotel. When the carriage stopped before it, Nathan said, "You know, I've always had a wish to invest in the theater."

I answered, "I can arrange for you to speak to Lucius if you like."

He glanced out the window at my door, darkened now, and said lightly, "I do hope your landlady keeps a respectable house."

"Respectable enough. But she's willing to overlook some things as long as the rent is paid."

"Shall I walk you to the door?"

"I would feel much safer if you did. In fact, if you wouldn't mind it, I would be most grateful for an escort to my room."

How politely he nodded his assent. How easily we played out the fiction, our own melodrama with a standard act two seduction.

The front door was unlocked as always; Nathan Langley followed quietly behind as I led him up the stairs, open on one side as an atrium with skylights in the roof and relights all along the wall that let in the faint glow from the streetlights to slant across the floor. One landing, one cross to the next set of stairs. Now that I was actually doing what I'd never thought I'd do, I was nervous, second-guessing myself. *You don't need this, Bea.* But I thought of Stella and what I wanted, and it was too late to refuse in any case.

He was very close behind me, his hand nearly touching mine along the railing as I led him up the third flight of stairs, to the top floor, where my room was. He wasn't shy; as I slipped my key in the lock, he settled his hands upon my hips, pulling me back, pressing hard up against me, so I could feel him against my bustleless backside. His mouth was at my ear, sliding to the joining of my neck and shoulder. When I opened the door, he pushed me inside so hard I nearly fell. I looked at him over my shoulder; my room was dim, not dark—the curtains were open to let in the light from the street, and he was almost white in their glow. He had the box of candy beneath his arm and he threw it onto the dresser, where it landed and slid, and then he said hoarsely, "For God's sake, take off your clothes."

Not even the semblance of a seduction now. In a way it was a relief. No prettiness, only the raw transaction. I did as he asked. He watched as I unbuttoned my bodice, as I slid my dress off, and then the one petticoat I wore, and in the dim light I knew he couldn't see how patched and gray it was, nor the roughness of my corset and chemise. I took them off and let them fall, one thing after another, drawers last, and when I bent to take off my stockings and my boots he told me in a rough voice to leave them on.

He jerked off his coat and laid it aside, and then his vest. He bade me come to him with a quick motion of his hand, and when I did, he shoved his hand into my hair to anchor me and kissed me, and then he had me against the wall and unfastened his trousers and fucked me that way. I moaned and cried out as if I liked it, and when he pulled out to spend himself against me I was relieved it was over.

Except it wasn't. He was breathing heavily still, and he pulled me to the bed, and told me to make him hard again, and then we did it once more, and when he finally left with a "I shall see you again tomorrow night," I was exhausted; I could hardly bring myself to take off my boots and my stockings before I crawled into bed.

I heard his carriage below, the shout to the driver, the close of the door, and then the wheels and horses' hooves. It must have been near to 2:00 A.M. And as I drifted into sleep, I wondered when he would speak to Lucius about investing in the Regal and hoped it would be soon.

The next afternoon, when I arrived at the theater to get ready for the performance, Lucius stopped me in the hallway on the way to my dressing room. "Ah, here she is now, my beauteous Helen. 'Twas this the face that launched a thousand ships?' "

"Please don't speak in riddles, Lucius, I'm late already."

"We have a new investor, thanks to your charm, my dear," he said with a smile. "A most lucrative admirer."

I was relieved; I had not realized how tight was my stomach, nor how afraid I was that I had judged wrongly, until he said the words.

I saw Nathan in the box that night, and after the performance he came to my dressing room. As I stepped out, I saw that the man in the old frock coat was there again. He took a step forward as if he meant to say something to me, but Nathan Langley took my arm to propel me to his carriage, and the man stepped back again. I meant to smile at him—I was not such a fool as to disparage the few admirers I had, no matter how poverty-stricken, but just then Nathan whispered some obscenity in my ear, and I forgot all about him.

There was no pretense this time, no supper, no pretty seduction. Nathan drove me directly to my room and came up, and he barely said two words to me, but at least this time he took off his clothes. Afterward I lay in bed and watched him as he finished dressing.

"I've spoken to your manager and taken up a third share in the costs this season. He seemed happy enough. I shall be happy to invest in your future, Mrs. Wilkes, as long as we continue this . . . understanding. Is that acceptable to you?"

I hadn't expected it to be so boldly stated, but you know, it was best just to look at it head-on so there would be no misunderstandings. "Yes. It's acceptable."

"Good. I won't be here tomorrow night; I've other obligations."

I wasn't sure what to say. I settled on "I'll miss you."

He laughed shortly, reaching to the dresser, to the box of candied fruit I hadn't yet had time to open. He threw it to the bed; it landed just to the right of my hip. "Appease yourself with comfits, Mrs. Wilkes. These are very fine."

Then he left. I lay back with a sigh and was relieved that I would have a break from him tomorrow. The sex was as tiresome as sex had ever been, though he seemed to like it, and I supposed that was the point.

I stretched, my hand came into contact with the box of sweets, and I took it up and untied the ribbon, lifting the lid to find glacéed fruit, luscious figs, and dense and glistening cherries and apricots. I picked up one of the apricots, and it was plump and sleek, sticky with syrup, sheering smooth as butter when I bit into it. I nearly swooned at the taste of it; I'd never eaten anything so good, not ever. God, those apricots alone were almost a good enough reason to spread my legs for Nathan Langley.

Almost. I thought of Stella Bernardi, stirring the louche of her absinthe with a languidly elegant hand. She would be gone within months, or I missed my guess completely. And then it would be my turn at last. All I must do was continue to keep Nathan Langley happy. And perhaps it would not be so very long either. Perhaps . . . I tried to remember if I had told Stella what I'd done to Arabella before her, how I'd fed Bella's vanity with dissatisfaction, and then I realized that even if I had, Stella had enough vanity of her own not to remember it. After all, she'd been manipulating me even then. How clever she thought herself! She would never suspect that she could be prey to any one of my tricks. Which, of course, made her especially vulnerable.

I lifted my arm, appraising the small bruise upon my wrist where Nathan had held me too hard. It was not so bad, and it would fade quickly. And it was worth it. It was all worth it now. My dreams were coming true at last.

Chapter Six

Geneva

Frye's Opera House was the most opulent theater in town, with its great domed roof, green plush seats, and gas-flame chandeliers. It was not as elegant as McVicker's Theater in Chicago, but even I was impressed by its grandeur. Nathan and I were there to watch *East Lynne,* a play I'd already seen a dozen times or more, but which I loved—as did everyone else. Even Mrs. Wilcox attended. The famous Mrs. Ethel Brown played the Lady Isabel Severn Mount, and Seattle was like every city in its need to be recognized for having the taste to appreciate such a lauded talent.

At the intermission, Nathan and I went into the salon for refreshments. I saw Mrs. Wilcox across the room, but I had learned my lesson, and I did not venture near. When Nathan returned with lemonade, he brought also another couple trailing in his wake.

"Darling, may I introduce Robert Stebbing and his wife," my husband said as he handed me a cup of rather warm lemonade. He gave me the look that meant these people were important to him. "Mr. Stebbing is on the city council."

"How pleased I am to meet you both," I said.

Robert Stebbing nodded stiffly; he was rather an officious little man with dark and receding hair and a receding chin as well. His wife, however, was slim and lovely, and she wore a gown with a mulberry stripe that immediately marked her as one of the more fashionable in the city. I was ready to like her, but as she stepped forward I saw the look in her eyes that said she had been trapped into this introduction, and I was disappointed once again, swept through by loneliness. Four months in Seattle, and I had not yet found a single woman I could call a friend, and it looked as if Catherine Stebbing would not be changing that.

We exchanged boring small talk until Nathan said, "Tell me, Stebbing, what role is the city council playing in this push to statehood?"

Stebbing turned to him. "Have you an interest in politics, Langley?"

"I dabble," Nathan said humbly. "I find I'm fascinated by a city where such things are not hopelessly corrupt."

How easily he spoke, how well he managed them, while I felt uncharacteristically ill at ease.

Stebbing said, "I welcome it. Too many don't find it at all interesting, you know. But a fledgling government always has need of men with certain . . . resources."

Nathan said, "If there's any way I could be of service . . ."

Mr. Stebbing looked thoughtful. He turned to his wife and said, "My dear, we really must invite the Langleys to our ball."

"A ball?" Nathan asked politely.

Reluctantly, Mrs. Stebbing nodded. "Next week. It's a small thing, really, in celebration of spring. Of course I'll send an invitation 'round. I do hope you can make time in your schedule on such short notice."

Her tone said that she wished no such thing, but I was willing to take any tidbit, no matter how small. "Oh, I'm certain we can fit it in."

Her answering smile was sour. "How wonderful."

That night in the carriage, Nathan said, "You must try to do better, Ginny."

"I *am* trying," I said. "But they all look at me as if I'm the devil himself. Mrs. Wilcox's cut—"

"Try harder. Perhaps you should pay a call on her."

"Don't be ridiculous, Nathan. She wouldn't admit me. It would only be one more humiliation. Haven't I been humiliated enough?"

"We've all had to make sacrifices. It wouldn't hurt for you to be more repentant."

"More repentant? What should I do? Genuflect in the streets?" I stared out the carriage window at the passing streetlamps and whispered miserably, "I've done everything I can to appear contrite. It's not enough for them."

"To *appear* contrite," he repeated. "Perhaps that's the problem. Perhaps we all recognize that you don't truly mean it."

Bitterly, I said, "I do mean it. But they would not be happy until I was whipped and pilloried before their eyes."

He was quiet. The carriage jostled over the roads, the lights passed over his face and then fell into darkness, and I could not see his expression.

"These people . . . They don't want to like me, and so they won't. I haven't met anyone who even cares to make the attempt."

"Remember who you are, Geneva," he said impatiently. "Use your charm."

"They seem immune to it. Perhaps they'll never forgive me. What would you do then, Nathan?"

"Let's hope it doesn't come to that, shall we?" he said.

The invitation to the Stebbings' spring ball came the next afternoon. Two days later, Nathan told me that the territorial governor had telegraphed his intention to be in Seattle on that date, and that he would also be at the Stebbings' ball. Suddenly the occasion was much more than a simple supper with dancing to follow, and my behavior was to be more important than ever—if that were possible.

The night of the ball, I was nervous; not only was the territorial governor to be there, but also the Dennys. They had refused my dinner invitation, but I had not yet seen them in company, and I still had some hope that they might find me acceptable. I dressed with considerable care, trying to look dignified without looking severe, in a washed silk gown of deep topaz.

The carriage ride was silent, but when we pulled to a stop before the Stebbings', Nathan said, "Remember what you must do, Geneva."

As if I didn't think about it nearly every moment.

We were ushered quickly in, not the last to arrive, but still later than most. Governor Semple held court in the parlor. He was just now surrounded by several people, Mr. Stebbing among them. Nathan made no attempt to have me introduced to the governor but got me a glass of sherry and became immediately embroiled in some conversation about city politics. I listened until there was no more sherry in my glass, and then I caught sight of Mrs. Stebbing speaking with a woman who I thought might be Mrs. Denny. I put the glass aside and started in that direction, but a man I'd never seen before stepped in my way so suddenly I nearly fell into him. He caught my arm to steady me.

"Please excuse me!" he said with a jovial smile. His dark hair was cut short; a bushy mustache covered his upper lip. "Tell me I didn't step on you."

"Not at all," I told him.

"Thank God for that. I was searching for my wife when the tide apparently shifted. Now, I fear, she's lost."

"One would think it not easy to do in a house so small," I said.

"Small, yes, but every inch seems to be filled." He gave me a slight bow. "I don't think we've met. Let me amend the error. James Reading."

I offered my hand. "Geneva Langley."

He looked surprised. "Ah! So you're the beauteous Mrs. Langley. The talk of the town, I hear."

"I hope to live long enough that such a thing is no longer true."

"I hope you come from a long-lived line then," he said. His smile was charming, broad and even.

I laughed; he was the closest thing I'd yet found to someone of my own kind. "Where do you come from, Mr. Reading? Please tell me you're not just a visitor here."

"My wife and I are residents, much to my dismay. Came up from San Francisco three years ago."

"Three years? How have you managed to survive so long?"

"Bourbon, mostly," he said, and then, when I laughed again, "society tolerates me well enough. It helps that I'm with the water company. No one wants to die of thirst."

"I don't believe that's possible to do in this town. Surely all one has to do is go outside and open one's mouth."

Just then a little woman in russet pushed up beside us, wrapping her hands around Mr. Reading's arm. "Mr. Reading, there you are! I'd quite lost you in the crowd." Her fine dark eyes shifted to me. "Tell me you haven't been boring this lovely lady."

"On the contrary!" I exclaimed.

Mr. Reading said, "Mrs. Langley has been keeping me entertained while I searched for you. Mrs. Langley, this is my wife, Martha Reading."

Mrs. Reading gave me a friendly look. "I'm certain she's too well bred to complain of you. Please, Mrs. Langley, you really must feel free to scold him for all his theater talk. He's really most single-minded."

"We have not yet broached the topic of the theater, madam," Mr. Reading said with mock outrage. "But I assume you share my love of it, Mrs. Langley, given the talk."

"Oh yes. I would go every night if I could. Do you attend often, Mr. Reading? Are you a critic? Apart from your water duties?"

"A critic? Good Lord, no, no. An actor, morelike."

"A *temporary* actor," Mrs. Reading corrected. "James has taken up with the Willis troupe at the Palace just now. He's hired them to act with him in *Julius Caesar*."

I said, "I'm afraid I don't understand. You hired them to act with you?"

Mr. Reading nodded. "To tutor me in acting. I'd always fancied the stage, but unfortunately, the siren call of business—and my father—was too difficult to ignore. The Willis troupe has been kind to give me an opportunity to fulfill a lifelong dream."

"For a fee," Mrs. Reading put in.

"Well, yes, yes. But they've been most obliging. I shall be playing Brutus at the Palace in a few weeks. I would be most gratified if you would come, Mrs. Langley."

I'd never heard of such a thing. Even in Chicago, no one I knew had gone slumming with an acting troupe. I admired Mr. Reading immensely for it and was intrigued as well. "I would be delighted to attend, Mr. Reading."

Mrs. Reading said, "How nice for you, James! But you mustn't be too kind, Mrs. Langley. I fear only that would dissuade him from continuing on."

I laughed. "I feel I should praise you for the attempt alone."

"As long as you're honest, ma'am. God knows there's little enough of that in the world. Now that you've seen fit to grace our little town, Mrs. Langley, I do hope you mean to turn it on its ear."

I shook my head reluctantly. "I've been warned I should not."

He leaned close, lowering his voice to whisper, "One should not allow dragons like Mrs. Wilcox to get the best of one, you know."

"Unfortunately that seems a difficult undertaking. I am a stranger here, and I wish not to be. It means I must follow more shoulds than I like."

Mrs. Reading sighed. "It is a pity Mrs. Wilcox has so much influence. *I* find you delightful."

"Tell me, Mrs. Langley—is it true what they say, that you kept a quite famous salon in Chicago?" Mr. Reading asked.

Wistfully, I said, "It was very well attended."

"Do you intend to continue it here?"

"No, I think not. Much as I wish it otherwise."

"You should not let them stop you," he said. "They control too much of the city as it is."

Mrs. Reading leaned forward, her plump face etched with compassion. "He's right, I'm afraid. Do you know, Mrs. Langley—and

I mean this in the best possible way, you understand—I believe it would be best if you not try to placate those who cannot be pleased and simply . . . be as you are."

Her kindness, the sentiment, the hope she raised . . . I remembered Nathan's words from the other night. *Remember who you are, Geneva.* Though he had not meant it the same way. I said simply, "I wish I could."

"You will consider the salon, then?" Mr. Reading asked.

"Assuming I did start it, Mr. Reading, who would even attend?"

Mr. Reading said, "We would. And I am quite certain there are others who would welcome the opportunity."

"Welcome what opportunity, my dear?" Nathan was suddenly at my shoulder. He said hello to the Readings, then leaned close to say, "They're calling us to dinner. This way."

"It was a pleasure to meet you both," I said to Mr. and Mrs. Reading before Nathan led me away, and it was the most sincere thing I'd said in weeks. The few moments I'd spent in their company had been like breathing again. As we went to the dining room, Nathan said, "Ginny, there are twenty people here at least it would be better for you to meet. Trust you to land in a conversation with James Reading."

I glanced at him. "He isn't . . . inappropriate?"

"Inappropriate? No. But he is unconventional. People were watching. It can't have done you good."

"Do you know he's paid a troupe to rehearse a play with him? He's always wanted to be an actor."

"He's a laughingstock, is what he is," Nathan said shortly. "The perfect example of what happens to a fool and his money."

"Perhaps." I could not help sounding wistful. "But it's a clever idea. I don't know why I never thought to do it myself when I was in Chicago."

He gave me a look that made me wish I'd said nothing. In fact, I wished James Reading had never told me of it. Because all I heard the rest of the night was his laughter, and the things he'd said danced in my head, and I knew I was not done with them, and was afraid of myself, of the things I wanted, of everything I could no longer have.

Chapter Seven

The next morning, Nathan seemed strangely thoughtful. We sat silently at breakfast, but his gaze rested on me now and again as if something troubled him, and finally I put down my coffee and said, "Was it so bad last night, do you think? I . . . I didn't realize the Readings were . . . well, I didn't realize. It's a pity, you know. They're the first people I've met here that I actually enjoy."

"I had a visit from a playwright yesterday afternoon," Nathan said abruptly.

I blinked in confusion. "A . . . what?"

"A playwright. I had not wanted to mention it last night, what with the ball, and the governor, but yes, a playwright came to my office. DeWitt, I think his name was. Yes, that was it. Sebastian DeWitt. Have you heard of him?"

"Sebastian DeWitt? No, I don't think so. Why ever did a playwright come to see you?"

"Because I've invested in the Regal Theater."

I stared at him in surprise. "You invested in a theater?"

"I was looking for opportunities, and the Regal was suggested to me. It's a popular theater and a good return for my money."

"And that's all you care about, the money," I said bitterly.

He gave me an impatient look. "Your father doesn't buy art just because he likes it, Ginny. It's also a good investment."

"He's not quite so mercenary as that. And unlike you, he doesn't care what people think."

"Don't deceive yourself. And people understand a good investment, art or no." He sighed. "In any case, I thought you'd be pleased. It *is* art, of a sort."

"I thought you cared nothing for art anymore."

"It's not that I care nothing for it so much as I care nothing for how foolish you make yourself over it."

"You once thought my enthusiasm fascinating."

"I once thought toy soldiers so as well. But eventually one must put aside childish things."

I was wounded. But I reminded myself of my purpose, my vows, and I managed to keep my voice even as I said, "Why are you telling me all this, Nathan? What has your theater to do with me?"

"The playwright," he said. "I mentioned him for a reason. He came to me with a play he wanted me to buy. Apparently the manager at the Regal is interested but has no ready cash."

"And you do."

Nathan nodded. "DeWitt did his research, I'll give him that. Few enough people know of my involvement there."

Carefully, because I wasn't certain what Nathan wanted from me, I said, "A play. How interesting."

"Yes. Interesting." My husband's tone was dry. "And if it proves to make money, it would be more interesting still. I thought perhaps you would take a look at it. You have an incomparable eye for this sort of thing, and I'm too busy just now to read it. I need you to advise me whether my money would be well spent."

I felt a surge of excitement. Still, I was cautious. "Why, yes, of course. You know I'd be more than happy to read it."

"It could be drivel," Nathan warned.

"Even so. It's something better than sitting here staring out the windows all day."

A quick glance, though he made no comment. "I've invited him to dinner here tonight to discuss it."

A playwright. To dinner. "Tonight? Oh . . . then . . . well, I've so much to do—"

"Try to contain yourself, Ginny," Nathan said. "Remember what I need from you. This isn't an invitation to return to your Chicago ways. I thought you would enjoy this, and I value your opinion when it comes to art. I'm trusting you won't embarrass me. He's poor as a church mouse, and he could use a good tailor. Just your kind, so don't think I haven't considered whether it would be wise for you to meet him at all."

He'd worded it just precisely enough that I was ashamed. "Nathan, please. Have I not been on my best behavior these last months? Have I done anything the least bit untoward? Deliberately, I mean."

Nathan hesitated. "Perhaps this is a mistake."

"How could it be? It's only dinner, isn't it? You'll be there, and I'll meet him and read his play and tell you what I think. No one can complain of it."

He considered me, and finally he nodded and put aside the newspaper. "Very well. I'll be home at my usual time. I've told him to come at seven." He rose, tossing his napkin to his chair. "Don't make a pet of him, Ginny."

"I won't," I promised.

Once Nathan left for the office, I was in a flurry of anticipation. I told myself that any playwright of worth wouldn't be in Seattle. I told myself I would be lucky if he had a shred of talent. This could simply be a waste of time, one more pedestrian poet angling for a patron. I had known some like that in Chicago. Poor intellects, worse conversationalists. Only opportunists. Why should I think this Sebastian DeWitt would be anything different?

Still, I called in the cook and changed the menu for the evening. Still, I spent some time considering what would be the best gown to wear. This was no member of Seattle society; there was no need for the more sedate fashions they required. And so I chose one of my favorites, an off-the-shoulder gown in burgundy silk, with a low décolletage, heavy with gold and black embroidery. I wore rubies like plump tears and was satisfied with how their color set off my pale skin and dark eyes. If nothing else, I would measure this man by his reaction to my appearance. I smiled a little as I remembered all the little gallantries, men stumbling over themselves vying for my favor. Was it so bad to admit how much I missed the attention?

I was ready far too early, and all the rest was impatience. I paced, I tried to read, I watched the clock and its slow count of the seconds. I checked the table settings; I went into the kitchen to be certain the cook was not spoiling the beef bourguignon and that the Nesselrode pudding was chilling. I checked the decanters in the parlor—all full: sherry, port, bourbon, and scotch. A bottle of absinthe, for which I had the maid bring ice water and sugar.

I expected Nathan by six; by six-thirty, he still had not returned home. I stared out the window over the haphazard lay of the city as the sun set, the Olympic mountains on the other side of the Sound fading into deep blue shadows against pink and gold and then disappearing altogether into the empty darkness beyond the haze of the streetlamps. I wondered if he'd forgotten. I wondered if perhaps the dinner had been canceled and he'd neglected to tell me. Six-forty-five, and twilight, and still no Nathan. Then, promptly at seven, there was a knock on the door. Sebastian DeWitt. I felt a little stab of excitement, and worry too, because I could not imagine Nathan meant for me to receive him alone.

But I'd received far more important men alone, and there was the maid, and . . . I hated that I must think of this. For God's sake, I intended nothing untoward; what did it matter?

Still, as I heard Bonnie go to the door, murmured talk, I crossed my arms and stared out the window, willing Nathan's carriage—this was unlike him, to be so late. An hour past his usual time. Undoubtedly something had happened to keep him.

I heard the footsteps down the hall, the pause at the parlor.

Bonnie said, "Mr. DeWitt, ma'am."

I turned from the window, and when I saw the man standing behind her, I forgot Nathan and everything else.

Sebastian DeWitt was a lean, clean-shaven man with longish dark hair and pale eyes. He was attractive in an underfed way, but more important, he had that muse-driven confidence I recognized. I'd seen it enough in those who'd come to my salon, and his frock coat, which was not in fashion and very worn, only emphasized it. He reminded me immediately of Claude; he had that air about him, whether studied or not, that said art was the only thing that mattered. I was fascinated by him already.

I smiled and held out my hands. "Mr. DeWitt! You are very welcome."

He came forward, taking one of my hands. His fingers were marked with faded ink stains, as if he'd tried vainly to wash them away. He had a heavy leather satchel over one shoulder, as worn as his coat. But his thick hair was neatly combed and shining, and his smile was compelling and confident. "Mrs. Langley. It's a pleasure to meet you."

"Unfortunately, my husband's been delayed," I said. "But I

expect him shortly. We shall just have to carry on without him for a time. Would you care for a drink before dinner? I've sherry, or something stronger. There's absinthe, if you like."

"No absinthe," he said. His voice was smooth, an actor's voice, perfectly pitched. "But I will have some bourbon, if you have it."

I motioned for him to sit as I poured the bourbon. It seemed forever since I'd entertained someone like him, and the fact that I liked his look, that he reminded me so sharply of Claude—oh, not his features so much, though there was that same aesthetic about him, but his air, his manner. . . . I bit my lip, trying to harness my thoughts, my reaction.

I turned back to him. His fingers were warm against mine when he took the glass, and he gulped a little hastily, as if he too were nervous, which reassured me. There was a great deal at stake for him, I remembered, and I sat down beside him on the settee and adopted the air of the accomplished hostess I was and said, "My husband tells me you've written a play."

"Yes." His fingers rested lightly on the satchel.

"What is it about?"

"Revenge. Hauntings. Ghosts and a villain. A heroine attempting valiantly to save her sister and her honor."

"Revenge? How exciting. I've always loved revenge tales. *Macbeth* is one of my favorites."

"You have a bloody sensibility, then?" he asked.

"Shall I tell you a secret, Mr. DeWitt?" I asked, leaning closer.

He smiled a little warily. "Only if you can afford to have it told."

"You're a poor keeper of secrets?"

"I'm a writer, ma'am," he said. "All secrets end up betrayed by my pen, I'm afraid. I seem incapable of stopping it. I wouldn't trust me with anything you hold dear."

"Oh, this is but a small one. And most could discern it, I think, if they looked closely enough."

"A secret hidden in plain sight. A 'Purloined Letter,' perhaps?"

"You're familiar with Mr. Poe!" I said in delight.

He gave me a curious look. "Isn't everyone?"

"Oh, you'd be surprised how many are not." And then,

because I couldn't help myself, because I liked him so much already, and that drew from me an intimacy I knew better than to risk, I said, "I'd warrant that none of my 'betters' here have read him."

A lifted dark brow. "Your betters?"

"The women who spend their hours working for the Relief Society."

"You sound disparaging, Mrs. Langley. You have no interest in charitable pursuits?"

I had revealed too much, I knew, but his presence was heady. We were heading toward a conversation I knew I would enjoy, the kind of talk I had missed, and he was exactly the kind of artist I most liked. So few minutes, and already it was like being in my salon again. I could almost feel the heat of the gathered candles and hear the talk in the air. "It seems rather that they have no interest in me."

"Ah. Your reputation preceded you, I imagine."

"My . . . reputation?"

"Forgive me, I should not have mentioned it."

"Does my reputation trouble you, Mr. DeWitt?" I asked sharply.

"I should not have mentioned it," he said again, gently. He smiled. His lips were very full. I was taken by them, unable to look away until he said, "You still haven't told me your secret."

The talk of my reputation had put me off balance. Hastily I tried to regain myself. "My secret? Oh . . . oh, well. It . . . it's nothing really. Only that I confess I have a rather unseemly fondness for melodramas. And spectacle."

"Your bloody sensibility," he noted.

"Indeed. My father despaired of it when I was young. I think even Nathan finds it rather appalling."

"Does he?" Mr. DeWitt took another sip of his drink. "Well, that's unfortunate. I imagine he won't care for *Penelope Justis,* then, and I was rather hoping he would like it enough to buy it."

"Fortunately for us, he won't be making the decision," I said. "He's left it to me."

"To you?"

"Between the two of us, Mr. DeWitt, Nathan has many talents, but he wouldn't know a good drama if it sat upon him."

He laughed. "Perhaps this isn't a good drama."

"You don't think that," I said.

He met my gaze, his smile faded in seriousness. "No," he agreed. "I don't think it."

"I much prefer confidence in a writer," I said. "Or in any artist, frankly. Otherwise, how is it possible to persist in one's vision? One must often stand alone among the slings and arrows of the world."

"You sound as one who knows."

"I've known many, many artists," I said. "Since you know of my . . . reputation, perhaps you've also heard that I held a rather famous salon in Chicago. I've hosted writers, artists, actors, intellects of all kinds."

DeWitt said lightly, "How intimidating."

But I saw to my satisfaction that he was not the least bit so. I said with a smile, "May I see the play?"

He set his drink on the side table and fumbled with the bag over his shoulder, undoing the buckle holding it closed, flipping it open. He took out a sheaf of papers bound with an old and rather twisted ribbon, and handed it to me.

I glanced down. His handwriting was flourished and looped, yet easy to read. As confident as I'd thought him. That was a good sign. None of that cramped writing that said a man wished his thoughts to be inscrutable. *"Penelope Justis,"* I read aloud. *"Or Revenge of the Spirit."* I glanced up with a smile. "Why, the title alone makes me shiver, Mr. DeWitt."

I turned the page. The first line: *It is the saddest and most familiar story in the world* . . . I scanned the page, past the summary, to the first lines, which took place at a funeral in an ancient graveyard, afraid he would not be what I hoped he was. After only a few minutes I knew; after several I realized he was all I'd wanted him to be and more. I looked up—oh, how casual he wanted to be, and yet I saw his anxiety in the tight set of his jaw.

"Mr. DeWitt," I said, "this is wonderful. And I am stunned to find an artist of your caliber in this town."

His eyes glittered in appreciation. "You can tell that from reading only a few lines?"

"I'm rather a connoisseur of plays. I've seen more than you can imagine. Some many times. And this . . . well, I can't say I'm surprised. I knew you'd be talented the moment you walked through the door. It simply shines from you."

"I would rather have thought poverty shone from me."

I laughed. "You remind me of someone, sir. And that man was very talented indeed."

"Perhaps I'm nothing like him at all."

"Oh, I think you are more like than unlike. Shall I make a guess?"

He shrugged. "As you wish."

I tilted my head to observe him. "You haven't had a good meal in some time."

"Unfortunately, I should think that obvious."

"There are days where you get so lost in your writing you forget the time. You forget to sleep. When the muse comes upon you, you hear nothing and see nothing else."

A bemused expression. "I'll give you that one."

I laid my finger against his cuff, a little flirtation I could not help and one I did not think he'd mind. "You've written other plays. None successful. Perhaps . . . not even performed?"

"Two were."

"They didn't take the world by storm."

An inclined head, an acknowledgment.

"And now you wonder if you'll ever make a success of it. You've never cared for patrons or critics, but now you think it's time you should. You heard of my reputation, and you thought I could perhaps help you. When you discovered my husband had invested in the Regal, you saw an opportunity."

"Mostly correct," he said.

"What of it was wrong?"

"I knew of your husband before I knew of you."

"Really?" It was the first thing he'd said that I didn't believe, but artists were sometimes prickly when it came to such things. They didn't like to admit to such calculation; art should be pure, blessed by the muses, a communication with God. I let

Mr. DeWitt keep to his fiction. "Well, you've happened upon providence then, haven't you, Mr. DeWitt? I've been waiting for someone like you."

"Have you?"

"I'd begun to despair that there was anyone worth conversing with in this town. But now I've found not just you, but another lovely couple who have more to talk about than the weather. It makes me wish to start my salon again."

"You're a collector, then?"

"A collector?" I laughed. "I do own some art, but it's my father who has the galleries—"

"I meant a collector of people," he said.

"Oh." I was taken aback. "Well, yes. Yes, I suppose so. Though the way you make it sound . . . I assure you I had artists knocking on my door, hoping to make my acquaintance. I had no need to go out looking for them."

"I didn't mean that to be disparaging," he hurried to say. "It's only that I've known some for whom such things are a measure of prestige rather than real interest."

"Yes, I've known people like that as well. But I promise you I am not one of them. I lived for those salons, Mr. DeWitt. I miss them terribly. The conversations we had. . . ." I took a deep breath, remembering. "I think I would give anything for such a conversation again."

He studied me; it was not an unpleasant feeling. Dear God, how I had missed this. This simple flirtation, the flare of attraction, like minds, magnetized. "You're very courageous, Mrs. Langley. Or very foolish. I can't decide."

"Perhaps a little of both. I confess that there have been times when I've been very, very foolish. I suffer sometimes from an excess of passion."

"Like most artists, I think."

"Well, I wouldn't claim to be that. Though I admit I do have one talent."

"And what's that?"

"I'm very good at helping to bring talented men out of obscurity."

"Only men?"

"Thus far," I said. "Women artists are much rarer, don't you find?"

"Rare indeed," he agreed. "Though not extinct, I think."

"I should like to meet one," I said. "I think it must be difficult to tread such a different road when all the world really wants from its women are children and domestic bliss." I heard how wistful I sounded suddenly, how pensive.

"You sound as if you understand," he said softly.

I met his gaze. "Of course I do. Passion from women is unwelcome, Mr. DeWitt. In Seattle, even more so."

"Perhaps you mistake it. Perhaps the city might thank you for bringing it a new vision."

I laughed. "You *are* idealistic, but I like that."

There was a movement at the parlor door. I glanced up to see Nathan standing there—I had not even heard him come in, and I felt guilty of a sudden, stupidly so, because there was nothing to feel guilty over. My finger was still on DeWitt's cuff; I snatched it back and rose in a flurry and pretended not to feel the flush that heated my cheeks.

"Nathan," I said, too enthusiastically, and he looked at me as if he knew it. "How late you are. Mr. DeWitt and I were just talking about his new play."

Nathan's smile was thin. "Hello, darling." He came fully into the parlor, and Dewitt stood to shake his hand. "DeWitt, how good of you to come. I apologize for my tardiness. I was unavoidably detained. I do hope my wife has been diverting in my absence."

"Very much so," Sebastian DeWitt said smoothly. "Her compliments have quite restored my faith."

"Compliments?"

"I read the beginning of the play," I said eagerly. "Mr. DeWitt is very talented. I should think you'd be a fool to let him go."

Nathan raised a brow. "Is that so? Well, then, perhaps we have something to celebrate this evening."

The three of us went into the dining room, and Bonnie poured wine and brought around a creamy bisque, and Nathan said, "Where do you come from, Mr. DeWitt?"

DeWitt paused in spooning up soup. "San Francisco."

"Really? I would have thought there was a bigger market for playwrights there. What brings you here?"

DeWitt's smile was grim. "Disaster, I'm afraid. Two poorly received plays and opportunities lost." He glanced at me. "The idea that perhaps it was time to stop tilting at windmills."

Nathan blinked. "Tilting at windmills?"

"*Don Quixote,*" I said. "You remember, Nathan."

"Ah yes. The mad Spaniard. Tilting at windmills, you say? That's my wife, sir, always looking to inspire, to collect the best butterflies—careful, now, or you'll find yourself caught in her net as well." He took a large sip of wine.

DeWitt said quietly, "I imagine sometimes there's an advantage to being caught."

"Sometimes," Nathan agreed. His voice softened oddly. "Sometimes one cannot see the beauty right away, and it needs some study to find it."

Something passed between them, something I didn't quite understand, and Sebastian DeWitt nodded. "Like a rare jewel."

"Yes," Nathan said. He raised his glass to me. "And none rarer than that sitting here at my table. You think she's a beauty now? Why, six years ago, Ginny was the rarest of jewels herself. The first time I saw her, in fact, she was wearing nearly the same color she has on this evening. When she came into that ballroom, I thought . . . well, she was not quite an angel, you know, but sometimes a man prefers a little wickedness, doesn't he?"

DeWitt said, "The world needs both devil and angel, Mr. Langley. I'm not averse myself to exploring both sides."

Nathan laughed. "A man after my own heart! Do you hear that, Ginny?"

Nathan was more the man I'd married than I had seen in some time. I did not know what made him that way except perhaps for Mr. DeWitt, whose charm had similarly affected me. I was too relieved at it to question. I teased, "I find it a bit disheartening to know that I am no longer the 'rare jewel' I was."

"Well, my dear, now I can see the flaws in the stone—that's my only reason. As you no doubt can see mine. But flaws often make a thing more precious, and you have evolved to something different, if no less fine."

"Like a well-loved treasure," put in Mr. DeWitt.

I smiled. "You *are* a writer, I see, to so easily make a compliment of an insult."

"It was not intended as an insult," Nathan protested. "But, DeWitt, I thank you just the same. I begin to see how you might make my deficiencies more tolerable to my wife."

"My goal would be to elevate you in her eyes," DeWitt said.

Nathan leaned back in his chair. "Ah well, good luck with that. But such is marriage, I think. I tell you what, DeWitt. You are an exemplary dinner companion, and such efforts deserve a reward. As my wife tells me you've talent as well, I will speak to Greene tomorrow and tell him I've bought him a play that requires production immediately. Will fifty dollars be recompense enough?"

Sebastian DeWitt had a wonderful smile. "It's very generous."

"Oh for goodness' sake, don't say that," I said quickly. "You reveal your hand. Better to hem and haw so he'll raise the price."

Nathan said wryly, "You see how well she works to my disadvantage? In any case, fifty is my best price. But you would do well to heed her in other ways, DeWitt; God knows she's milked genius out of lesser men. In fact, I daresay she could do you some good, don't you think so, Ginny? What say you—shall we make you Mr. DeWitt's patron saint?"

I stared at my husband in surprise. Only this morning he'd warned me not to make a pet of this man, and now here he was, looking for all the world as if it was exactly what he wished me to do. I did not quite believe it, and my good humor fled in sudden suspicion. I knew him well enough to know how quickly this could turn. But he would not like me questioning him in front of Mr. DeWitt, and I'd already pushed things a bit too far this evening, and so I said, "I'd be happy to try."

"Good," Nathan said with a smile. "Let my wife serve as my proxy then, DeWitt. She has the advantage when it comes to this patronage business. She knows better how it all works."

Sebastian DeWitt nodded. I did not think I was imagining the light in his eyes when he turned to me. "I cannot adequately convey my gratitude. To both of you."

"You've done it all yourself, you know. We've simply recognized your genius," I said.

Nathan grabbed up his wine. "Well, then, it's settled. Shall we have a toast? To the future—may it serve us all well."

After Sebastian DeWitt took his leave, Nathan and I stood together in the parlor, staring awkwardly at each other. Nathan reached for the glass of port he'd been nursing since dinner.

"Well," he said. "I thought that went well, didn't you?"

Echoes of the words he'd said to me that first night in Seattle, after the Browns' welcoming dinner, and I was uncertain. The entire dinner had felt odd. I had not known what to make of Nathan's mood then and had less idea now. I said, "He was very . . . personable."

"Yes indeed."

I told myself to be silent, to leave things be. But I could not. "Nathan, it was kind of you to make me your proxy, but I cannot think you meant to do it."

"Why not? You said he was talented."

"Not twelve hours before, you warned me not to make a pet of him."

"And I still caution you not to do so."

"But I cannot understand why you wish me to have anything to do with him at all. Not after all your warnings and all your talk about atonement and reparation—"

He held up his hand. Obediently, I went quiet.

"Tonight I watched you with him before you realized I was there," he said softly.

I went still and wary. I thought of what he must have seen, my smiles and laughter, the way I'd flirted, and I cursed myself inwardly. I saw no sign of anger in my husband's expression, but that was odder still; I knew better than to think it wasn't there. "I'm sorry. He was the first person I've met who reminded me of what I was in Chicago, and I'm afraid I—"

"I don't want your apology, Ginny."

"No. I understand. It's penance you want."

"Not that either. I was reminded tonight of something I'd forgotten. I'd forgotten . . . how beautiful you are. How . . . charming." His voice was soft, his eyes glittered in a way I had not seen for some time.

I stared at him.

He went on, "I admit I've taken satisfaction from your misery. Seattle has seemed a proper penance. But I did not realize society would spurn you as it has. I've begun to doubt it will ever accept you, and tonight I realized I no longer take pleasure from your unhappiness. Perhaps . . . perhaps these last months have been enough."

"Enough?" I whispered.

"I've spent years trying to make you into something you're not, instead of enjoying what you are, as I once did. All that foolishness with the salon . . . I could not admit to myself that you were right. It was influential; it could have helped. I should have embraced it, especially as it made you so obviously happy. But I was too angry, and stubborn." He met my gaze. "Perhaps I am equally responsible for what happened with . . . Marat. I should not have neglected you as I did. And for that I *am* sorry."

They were the words I'd been waiting months for. Years, even, if I was honest with myself. "Nathan, I—"

"Please, let me finish. You have gone too far, over and over again, Ginny. But I realize also that I could be less . . . restrictive. I have thought lately that perhaps we can come to some sort of compromise."

"I would like nothing better," I said honestly.

He smiled—a smile I had not seen for so long. He met my gaze, and something passed between us, some understanding I had thought never to experience with my husband again.

He said, "I want you to be happy."

It was what I wanted him to say. I wanted to believe he still loved me, that he wanted back what we had lost, that my suspicions of him had been wrong. In that moment, I *did* believe it.

"Take DeWitt as your cause *du jour,*" he went on. "Let me worry about what will help or hurt my career."

I did not know what to say. I managed, "Thank you."

Nathan smiled. "You're very welcome, my dear."

Chapter Eight

Beatrice

Nathan collapsed upon me with a final groan, breathing hard, sweating. I wished he would get off me; he was heavy, and there was a bruise on my hip from how hard he'd held me that hurt like the devil. He'd been rough tonight, as if he were stewing about something and taking his anger out on me, or maybe it *was* me he was angry with, though I didn't know what the hell I'd done. All I knew was that he'd been here three nights in a row, and I was tired and I wasn't getting lines learned as long as he insisted on seeing me after every show.

I heaved a little, just enough to hint that I might like to breathe, and he made a sound deep in his throat and leveled himself onto his elbows—which meant the bone of his hip pressed hard enough into my bruise that it brought tears to my eyes.

He didn't seem to notice. Instead his hand went to one of the hairpins he'd given me, his latest gift, which he'd made me wear and then wasted no time in loosening from my hair. It dangled near my ear, and he pulled it free; the sapphires and rubies caught the light from the oil lamp on the bedside table, and he dangled it so the butterfly wings seemed to dance. "I like the way they look on you."

He dropped the pin to the table and rose. I pulled the other one from my hair and laid it beside its partner. They were pretty things, and obviously expensive, and I liked them, just as I liked the other gifts he'd given me, but Stella was still at the Regal, and I was still the first soubrette, and though I never missed a chance to compliment Stella or tell her she belonged on better stages, she seemed determined to stay, and I was beginning to wonder if I'd made a mistake, if French candied fruit and pretty hairpins might be all I ever got from Nathan Langley.

He went to the window, open now to let in the night air, though there wasn't any breeze and the only thing that came in was dust. He looked lost in thought, and I wondered if it had something to do with the way he'd been tonight, and the sheer fury he'd put into fucking, and that made me ask, "Did I do something to displease you?"

He glanced at me as if he'd forgotten I was there. "Displease me? No, of course not, why do you ask?"

Now I wished I hadn't said anything. "I don't know. You seemed . . . distracted." A pretty way to put it.

"Did I?" He looked back out the window again. "Yes, I suppose I am. My wife, you know."

No, I didn't know. And I didn't want to. All I knew about Mrs. Langley was that she had dark hair and wore pale blue to see *Black Jack,* and even that was too much information as far as I was concerned. But that he'd even mentioned her was strange; he never had before.

I didn't know what to say, whether to ignore his words or pretend he hadn't said anything, but I didn't have to decide, because he laughed and said, "She needs a firm hand. That's what I told everyone when I married her. That all she needed was a firm hand."

Well, what the hell was I supposed to say to that? I mean, here I was, splayed upon coarse sheets with *his* seed drying sticky on my stomach, and he was talking about his wife's misbehavior. I settled on "Did she?"

He spoke as if he hadn't heard me. "I thought, moving here, things could be different. I thought. . . . But it's obvious they'll never accept her, and she'll never change. Now she's taken on some new *artist*—you should see the way she fawns over him. Christ, she practically had him there on the dining table. She's so damn predictable. She'll have the whole city talking within days."

"Why don't you tell her to stop?" I asked.

He laughed again, and it was mean and unpleasant, and it

made me think of how he'd fucked me tonight. "Oh, I'm long past telling her to stop. But, believe me, this time I'll have what *I* want—" He stopped himself, pressing his lips together in a self-satisfied little smile that made my skin crawl. "Well, let's not speak of her."

That was a relief. "I wasn't."

"No, you weren't, were you?" He smiled at me. "Poor Bea. What kind of a gentleman am I, to talk of my wife when I've you there waiting for me? But I think I've something to make up for it."

I saw the way he looked at me and I had to swallow my dismay, because I knew that look and I knew that I wouldn't get out of spreading my legs for him again tonight. But still I played the part he'd given me; I gave him as hopeful a look as I could manage, one that said I liked nothing better than to have him heaving about on top of me, though what I really wanted was for him to leave and let me go to sleep.

He said, "Don't you want to know what it is?"

I leveled myself up on my elbows and waggled my fingers at him and said in my best lascivious voice, "Why don't you come and show me?"

His expression creased in irritation. "We've something to celebrate."

That was different. I frowned and sagged back to the bed. "Celebrate what?"

"Your ascension. What else?"

Not so fast, Bea. Maybe he doesn't mean what you think. "My ascension? But . . . Stella—"

"La Stella's leaving. Off to San Francisco in two weeks."

My heart raced. "She is? How do you know? She didn't say anything to me."

"I wasn't aware you were confidantes. It was Greene who told me, this morning. He's moving you to lead."

I had waited for those words so long that now I couldn't believe he was saying them. "He's said nothing—"

"No doubt he will tomorrow."

I tempered my excitement. It wasn't that I doubted Nathan, but I did doubt Lucius, who would say anything to get what he wanted. And you know, he'd betrayed me before and probably would again and I knew better than to believe something before I heard it from his lips.

Nathan frowned at me. "I thought you'd be happy. Isn't this what you wanted?"

"Yes of course. But . . . are you certain?"

"You don't trust my word?"

"It's only that Lucius has promised things before—"

"But he has never promised them to *me,*" Nathan said.

I wasn't imagining his irritation. Nathan *was* a powerful man. Lucius would not dare go against him. "Yes, of course. It's . . . I can hardly believe it. To be the lead . . . I've been working for this for so long."

"All your dreams come true," he said wryly. "There's to be a new play too, to introduce you as the Regal's leading lady."

"A new play?" Oh, that was clearly too much. Too much to hope for, too much altogether.

Nathan nodded. "I paid dearly enough for it, so I hope you like it."

"Oh, how could I not?" I couldn't help my smile. I saw when it took him aback, when he looked at me as if he'd never quite seen me before, his interest piqued once again. His gaze slid to my breasts and downward.

I was so happy I didn't care when he stepped over to kneel on the bed, or when he took his cock in his hand and pulled me toward him, pushing me down, his fingers digging hard into my shoulder. "I'm glad it pleases you. Now why don't you show me how grateful you are?"

The next morning, I woke and washed in a hurry. I didn't bother with breakfast; instead I opened a box of glacéed fruit and took out one of the apricots I hoarded. Nathan brought the candy often now that he knew how I loved it, but I'd lived too long pinching and saving, and though I never denied myself the figs or the cherries whose taut skin popped beneath my teeth, I saved my favorite apricots for last.

Now I treated myself to one—no cutting it in pieces to savor and save, but the whole thing, in celebration. I licked the syrup from my fingers and told myself it wasn't too hasty to celebrate, but you know, the doubt I'd managed to get past last night sneaked back, and I was nervous. I knew Lucius much better than did Nathan, and I didn't trust him. But Nathan had been so certain. And the news about the new play . . . if Nathan had paid for it, he would want me in it. It was that simple. Even Lucius couldn't wiggle out of that.

As I made my way to the Regal, I wondered what the play was about, what it would require costumewise. Whatever money didn't go to room and board went to my costumes, and I had a decent enough selection for lead roles. A cheap blue satin gown that could be made to look expensive if you dressed it up with the bit of lace I'd salvaged from a secondhand store (not too tattered, and as gaslight made everything look yellow, its age didn't matter). Another gown of pale yellow I'd embroidered myself with rosebuds about the neckline and trim that was perfect for innocent ingenues. I had a bustle I wore only onstage to keep it nice, and a dressing gown a friend had given me when she gave up acting, and that I'd dyed to hide the tea and food stains. There was a piece of white flannel I'd embroidered with little black tails so it looked like ermine, for royalty. I had a few other things: trousers and a waistcoat and a man's shirt for when I'd had to play trouser roles and two simple calicos and an apron. The bulk of it, however, I'd been gathering in anticipation of today. No one in the company was more prepared than I to be whatever the part called for.

I took a deep, full breath of dusty air and lifted my face to the sky, which was grayed by the clouds of ash from the forest fires in the hills above the city that came, as always, with the late spring, but my mood was so good I didn't see anything but blue.

When I got to the Regal, I opened the back door and stepped into the still, close darkness. It was hot, and the fumes from the gaslights and fresh paint and glue made my eyes burn. I heard the sounds of the carpenters building new sets above, and Aloysius chanting his lines in his dressing room below, his voice deep and perfectly villainous, as befitted the part he was to play tonight.

Stella's favorite play, *Divorce*—stolen wholesale from Augustin Daly this time, not that Lucius gave a damn about that—because it showcased her ability to cry, and Stella had never met a broad gesture she didn't like.

I took the stairs to the stage, coming out from the wings to see Brody sitting on the edge of the proscenium, licking his fingers as he finished off an apple. Behind him the painters were putting the last touches on a flat.

"Hiya, Bea," Brody said, flipping back his dark hair in that way that made most women swoon. "Lucius is looking for you."

Again, I felt that little jump of joy in my chest. "Where is he?"

"Dunno. In his office maybe."

I tried not to show my excitement and went back down the stairs to Lucius's office, knocking on the door, calling through it, "Lucius? Brody said you were looking for me."

"Sweet Bea," he boomed from inside. "Was there never a lovelier flower? Come in, come in, my dear. I've been waiting for you."

I turned the knob and stepped in. Lucius's office was cluttered as the rest of backstage, littered with scripts and promptbooks, bits of costume, a dress dummy, props. He sat behind his desk, leaning back in his chair, his broad, florid face red with the heat, his mustache drooping.

At his side stood a man I recognized: pale eyes, old frock coat, the same man who had been nearly a constant presence in the hallway outside my dressing room the last weeks, though I had never spoken to him.

"Oh, forgive me," I said. "I didn't realize there was someone—"

"My dear Bea," Lucius said. "I'd like you to meet Sebastian DeWitt. I've just bought his newest play. Genius, my dear, simply genius! Even Harrigan couldn't do better than this. A heroine of most uncommon virtue, an ingenious villain, revenge . . . my God, we'll have them cheering in the aisle!"

"Mrs. Wilkes," DeWitt said, stepping forward. "It's a pleasure to meet you."

The frock coat suffered in the light. Cuffs and collar well worn, almost white at the elbows. A collarless shirt, no tie. A scuffed leather bag was slung over his shoulder. But now I saw too what I hadn't seen in the darkness of backstage. He had a truly lovely face, sharply planed, almost aristocratic, and beneath heavy dark brows were those light-colored eyes that regarded me with that same uncomfortably intense interest that had caught my attention at my dressing room door. His thick hair was a beautiful color, a rich dark brown with red woven all through it, long enough to brush his shoulders. That he was penniless was obvious. That he was a writer, more obvious still—his fingers were dappled with ink stains. You could have men like him for a dime a dozen, and they'd thank you for it, because that was still more money than they made in a year.

But, penniless or not, this was the man who had written the new play Nathan had spoken of. I gave Sebastian DeWitt my best smile and said, "The pleasure's all mine, Mr. DeWitt. I hope you've written songs too. You can't forget the songs."

"I've written lyrics, but I'm no musician, Mrs. Wilkes."

"I'll take care of the music," Lucius said, waving his hand dismissively. "The important thing is, Bea, this will be our first production without Mrs. Bernardi. La Stella's leaving for better lit climes. She's been offered a star turn."

Here it was. I tried to pretend I knew nothing, because now I saw that Lucius was nearly bursting with trying to hold it in, and I could be generous and not ruin his pleasure at telling me. "She's going? Finally?"

Lucius leaned forward, planting his elbows on the desk, steepling his fingers. "I've already spoken to Langley. He forestalled the need for Mr. DeWitt to shop his play elsewhere by providing me with a ready influx of cash."

I could hardly stand my impatience. "Lucius, please. Just say it. Am I the lead or not?"

"Now, now, child. Such impatience!"

DeWitt smiled. "She fits the part."

"What part?" I asked, snappish with anticipation. "Lucius, I swear I'll throttle you if you—"

"Ah, Mr. DeWitt, have you ever witnessed such a churlish temper in one so fair?" Lucius sat back with such a flourish he sent the many watch chains crossing his ample girth to shaking.

"Both Langley and DeWitt here seem convinced only you could play this part, and as I find myself in need of a new leading lady . . . well, it seems the line belongs to you. Congratulations, my dear—may your star burn as brightly as Stella's has."

I couldn't help my squeal; it had been held in too long. I nearly threw myself across the desk to embrace him. "Thank you. Thank you so much, Lucius. You won't regret it, I promise it."

"Oh, I've no doubt I shall at some point," he said with a heavy sigh, though he laughed and kissed me before he halfheartedly pushed me away. "Don't forget to thank DeWitt."

I looked at the playwright over my shoulder. "Would you like a kiss too?"

He said, "Only if you mean it. But you should know: I wrote the part for you."

That startled me. I turned fully to face him. "For me?"

He gave a short nod. "As they say: 'two stars keep not their motion in one sphere.' You've been eclipsed by La Stella 'til now. I thought you should have the limelight for a change."

Imagine someone's given you your heart's desire. Now imagine they've said: *oh, and here's something to top it that in all your dreams you never even thought might be possible,* and you'll have a good idea of how I felt at that moment. I'd had admirers before, of course, but Sebastian DeWitt was much more than that. I'd never before snared a playwright enamored enough to write a play for me. I knew no one who had, though of course I'd heard of it happening. But to stars, people like Edwin Forrest or Clara Morris. Not to actresses like me, in second-rate companies. I leaped back through my memory, trying to figure out if I'd ever been rude to him—but no, I'd smiled at him, hadn't I? Yes, of course I had.

I couldn't think of what to say. "I—I'm flattered, Mr. DeWitt, truly I am. I . . . I'm sorry, I know you've meant to speak to me before now, but I . . . I didn't realize. . . ."

He shrugged. "I wasn't forward enough. And you've been busy with other . . . admirers."

"Admirers that keep the cash flowing into the coffers, don't forget," Lucius said. "Couldn't have bought the play without

Langley, you know. My sweet Bea, you've done doubly well. Better than Stella and Arabella both."

"I feel stunned," I said with a laugh. "I hardly know what to make of all of it."

"Oh, I feel sure it will come to you soon enough," Lucius said wryly. "We'll begin rehearsals in three days. Mustn't make Stella feel as if we're rushing her out, you know. Now go on. You've a performance to prepare for."

I went to the door and stopped, turning to look back at him. "What kind of a part is it, Lucius? An ingenue? Royalty? I need to know for costuming."

Lucius waved his hand dismissively. "Take DeWitt with you. He can explain it."

Obediently Sebastian DeWitt followed me out into the hallway, closing Lucius's door behind us, and I'll admit I was nervous and there was a part of me that believed I might ruin everything if I said the wrong thing. His gaze came to mine; he had the oddest color eyes. I couldn't decide if they were gray or blue.

He said, "You know you're even more beautiful offstage."

That set me at ease. Flirtation was second nature. I laughed. "You've been around actors all your life, I can tell that already. You know just what to say."

He grinned. "In this case, it happens to be true."

"But a waste of your time to say it. You had my attention already."

"In my experience, flattery is never wasted."

"Ah. Well, then, how am I to judge how sincere you are? How do I stand in comparison to all the other subjects of your compliments? Do you write a play for every pretty actress you see?"

"You're the first."

"Am I really? Should I believe you?"

"Why shouldn't you?"

"Because you seem a clever enough fellow to know it's what I want to hear."

"Well, then, I'll leave you to determine my veracity," he said. "Quiz me all you like, and see if you find the answer."

He was amusing; I liked him, though of course I had plenty

of reason to. "But I don't know you well enough to tell if you're lying or not. That could take months."

"I'm at your disposal, Mrs. Wilkes," he said, smiling again. "I have months, if you require it."

"You'd be my own personal playwright, then?"

"I suppose that depends upon the payment." Again, his eyes caught mine.

I saw his desire. I heard what he didn't say. But even if there hadn't been Nathan to consider, I wasn't going to fuck Sebastian DeWitt—at least not until he proved himself. Selling a single play did not a success make, and he looked just the type to think sex and love were the same thing, and I didn't need that kind of trouble, at least not from someone who looked as if he rarely managed to afford a meal.

But I could keep him happy enough without that, I knew, at least for a time, so I smiled to ease the change in subject and said, "Tell me about this play."

"It's called *Penelope Justis, or Revenge of the Spirit*. It's a drama. That is, it *was* a drama."

"Was?"

"I think Greene has some changes in mind."

"Lucius loves a spectacle."

DeWitt winced. "Yes, I've gathered so." A sigh. "Well, I shall do what he requires."

I didn't think I imagined his reluctance. An *artist,* on top of everything else. How well I knew the kind. I managed to keep from sighing myself. "Well, you're lucky it's Lucius. He always knows what an audience wants. Is this your first play?"

"I've written one or two others. Unfortunately, they weren't great successes. But I've high hopes for this one. I've never been so directly inspired." Again, a challenging glance. "You seem made for melodramas, Mrs. Wilkes."

"Really? Do I seem such a mewling innocent?"

"Oh, hardly."

"Is that an insult or another of your compliments?"

"I only meant that I see a kind of . . . purity . . . in you."

"Purity?"

"Which is not the same as innocence. Or chastity," he said wryly. "My Penelope has that quality too. Your Mrs. Bernardi would make a hash of her. But you've more subtlety than that."

"Yes, well, Stella's fond of playing to the gallery."

"And she's very young."

I wasn't sure whether or not to be offended. I settled on not being so and said, "I don't want to talk about Stella. Tell me more about your play."

"I'll do better than that." He flipped open his bag, reaching inside to pull out a sheaf of papers, which he handed to me. I saw the title written upon the front page in a hand that was at the same time scrawling and easy to read.

"This is it?" I asked.

He nodded. "Greene already has one he's having copied."

"I'll read it tonight and have this back to you tomorrow," I told him.

He smiled at me. "I don't want it back. I copied it out for you, Mrs. Wilkes."

It was very thick. It would have been an effort to make an extra one for me—the entire play, not just the scenes I was in, as our prompter Marcus Geary would do. I looked at him in surprise.

DeWitt leaned over me, thumbing through the pages I held. "I've made notes for you here and there that aren't in Greene's copy. A few things . . . not many, but they'll help you understand."

"Prompting cues?" I asked.

"Character cues," he said, and then his voice deepened and went soft. "There's no reason you couldn't be brilliant in this, Mrs. Wilkes. If you'd care to try."

I could not help but stare at him. Suddenly I didn't know what to make of him. I hardly knew what to say.

He didn't wait for me to say anything. He reached into his pocket and drew out a battered tin watch, glancing at the time. "I'm off, I'm afraid," he said, giving me a quick smile. "You can tell me if you have questions at the rehearsal."

"You . . . you'll be at the rehearsals?"

"Cutting and rewriting at Greene's request."

He said good-bye, and then he was gone, striding down the hall, his frock coat flapping.

As it turned out, I couldn't read *Penelope Justis* right away, much as I wanted to. There was that morning's rehearsal to attend, and then a crisis over a set, so that some scenes of *Divorce* had to be reblocked before curtain call, and then it was too late; I had to dress and put on makeup for the show. I put the script in my costume trunk and tried not to think about it—because there would be no time tonight either, as I saw Nathan watching from one of the boxes when I delivered my final lines. I resigned myself to putting off *Penelope* until tomorrow.

Nathan did not like to be kept waiting, and so I didn't delay or loiter about with the others as I made my way to my dressing room after the show. Susan Jenks was already there, taking up the one mirror.

"Where are you off to in such a hurry tonight?" I asked her.

Susan smiled. "Tommy's waiting for me."

Her latest conquest. A miner who spent most of his wages on whiskey.

"Why do you waste your time on men like that?" I asked, turning to her to undo the buttons up my back. "He'll never be able to help you."

"But he fucks like God's own angel," she said with a grin, making quick work of my gown. "And I guess I don't need him to do more, if the rumors I hear are true."

"What rumors?"

She gave me a sly look. "Why, that I'll be first soubrette before the end of the week."

I tried to keep a straight face. "You will? Do you mean to kill me off then?"

"Don't tease, Bea. Everyone already knows Stella's leaving and you're to have the lead."

"Has Lucius said something?"

"He doesn't have to. Stella's been hinting about San Francisco all week. Didn't you hear her at rehearsal today? 'I shan't have to stand a prop boy's insolence where *I'm* going.' "

Susan mocked Stella's style perfectly. I couldn't help but laugh.

"How long before Lucius tells us?" she asked me.

"I think tomorrow," I said. "But pretend to be surprised, will you, please? I don't want him thinking I said anything."

Susan threw her arms around me. "Oh, I'm so glad! And not just for you either. It'll be nice to have a leading lady who can act."

I thought of Sebastian DeWitt. *"There's no reason you couldn't be brilliant in this. . . ."* I glanced anxiously at my trunk.

But just then there was a curt knock on the door. "Mrs. Wilkes? Mr. Langley's waiting." The voice of Nathan's driver.

I sighed and called back, "I'll only be a minute!"

Susan laughed and twirled to the door, waving at me before she went out, and quickly I changed and put up my own hair, angling the butterfly hairpins, two above one ear. They sparkled in the gaslight, the jewels trembling as if they were alive. Nathan's driver was outside the door, and I found myself looking past him for Mr. DeWitt. But he wasn't lurking in the shadows as he'd done nearly every night the last weeks. I followed the driver to where Nathan waited, at the top of the stairs leading to backstage, looking impatient and mildly annoyed.

"There you are," he said. His glance swept me approvingly, and then he shook out something he'd had folded over his arm—a cloak of fine blue wool, a beautiful thing that he put about my shoulders. "Perfect," he said, standing back to look at me while I preened in the cloak—I had never had anything so fine, and with it and the hairpins I felt as grand as Pauline in *Lady of Lyons*. His driver opened the carriage door and helped me inside. And then Nathan climbed in, and we started off.

"Did Greene move you up?" he asked.

"Yes," I said. "As soon as Stella leaves."

"Excellent," he said, sitting back. "You no longer doubt me, then?"

"I never did," I told him.

"He gave you the new play too, I take it?"

"Yes. I met the playwright."

"Ah." A pause. A passing streetlight shone through the open

window, momentarily illuminating his face. "I understood him to be talented."

"Wherever did you find him?"

"He went to your Mr. Greene," Nathan said. "Apparently he knew of our . . . relationship and thought I might be willing to fund a new production."

"How clever of him."

"Indeed." Nathan lapsed into silence. When we got back to my room, he watched me undress and had me put on the cloak again so I was naked beneath it, and he wouldn't let me take down my hair, and then he took me as if he meant to punish me. But when it was over, he was laughing, as if at some private joke. I don't think he even said good-bye before he went out the door, and I lay there in the darkness, feeling uneasy and wondering what the hell that had been about, what game we'd been playing for his pleasure, what play we'd acted that I didn't know the script.

Chapter Nine

Geneva

It was two weeks after my dinner with Sebastian DeWitt that I saw the notice in the newspaper for James Reading's *Julius Caesar* at the Palace. I remembered how he had begged me to come see him. *"I assume you share my love of theater."*

When Nathan came down to breakfast, I held the newspaper out to him. "Do you remember Mr. Reading's play?"

He looked blank for a moment, then he glanced down at the page and said, "Oh yes."

"I would like to go. I promised him I would."

Nathan adjusted his cuff and looked thoughtful, and I waited, schooling myself. Since our talk in his office, we had circled each other cautiously. But I'd seen nothing in my husband to make me think he regretted the things he'd said. And now he did nothing to contradict them.

"I suppose your going can harm nothing. But I've other commitments. Why don't you see if DeWitt will escort you?"

I was disappointed—not at the thought of Mr. DeWitt as an escort, but because I'd hoped Nathan would come; I wanted his company. It would be the truest measure of my sense that we were working toward reconciliation, although perhaps it was enough that he wasn't thinking of appearances. In Chicago, I had often gone to theaters or dances without Nathan, escorted by Ambrose or one of my other friends. But this was Seattle, and there was still Stratford Mining to consider.

"Do you think that would be wise?" I asked.

Nathan frowned. "You don't want to?"

"I didn't say that. I just thought . . . there are people who might find it objectionable."

"I've told you to let me worry about that. And I've no interest in watching Reading cavort about the stage. No one will find anything amiss unless you choose to disrobe in the box. Which I assume you won't."

"Of course not."

A smile. "Well, thank God for that. I'll get the tickets and send a note to DeWitt."

"If you're certain."

"I am. Come, Ginny, how many times must I say it? Go and enjoy yourself. Take the playwright. There, at least, is someone you can talk to."

I did want to see Sebastian DeWitt again. I had thought of him often in the time since our dinner, and I'd invited him to lunch twice—invitations he had declined very nicely, saying that as much as he would enjoy it, his work precluded a midday break. That was something I understood. It was my own fault that I was so unengaged during the day; most people were not. I hoped he would not decline an evening engagement.

He did not. Whether it was because his evenings were freer or because Nathan had tendered the invitation, I didn't know. When he showed up at my door, still wearing the lamentable frock coat—I really must find him a tailor—I didn't care what had brought him. Only that he was here.

I could not help my smile of delight when Bonnie ushered him into the parlor. "Mr. DeWitt, I *am* glad you could escort me this evening."

His smile was arresting. "I'm happy to be of service, Mrs. Langley." A little bow. "I believe our carriage awaits."

I called for my blue cloak, and there was a moment of confusion when it could not be found and I must wear the black, but that was the only thing that marred the perfection of going to the theater with Sebastian DeWitt. I warned myself to be careful—I liked him perhaps too much, and I did not want to risk my reconciliation with Nathan. Still, when I took DeWitt's arm, I could not restrain a heady little shiver of pure joy. When he gave me a sideways glance, I laughed.

"Is something funny?" he asked.

I shook my head. "It's only that I'm so glad to be going tonight."

"Oh yes—your love of blood and spectacle."

"My love of anything different from my parlor," I corrected. "I warn you, Mr. DeWitt, tonight might be excruciating. I have no idea whether Mr. Reading can act."

"I can't imagine he could be worse than other actors I've seen," DeWitt said as we went outside and he helped me into the carriage.

"Except that James Reading is no actor."

"Perhaps we'll be lucky. Perhaps it's his hidden talent."

I settled onto the seat. When he sat across from me, and the door closed, I said, "You say that as if everyone has one."

"Don't they?"

"I don't think I do. Or if so, it's hidden very, very deep."

"Perhaps I meant to say that everyone has a talent. In some it's hidden. In others, it's obvious for anyone to see."

"And what would mine be?"

"Why, you've told me yourself. You shine a light on men's vision."

"Ah yes." I settled back again, smiling. "I had thought you might say I harbored a talent for embroidery."

"I said your talent was obvious. If you've one for embroidery, I've yet to see it."

"I did try a footstool cover once. Truly wretched, and uncomfortable as well. One could not put one's foot upon it without being gouged by knots."

Sebastian DeWitt laughed. The passing light striped his features, bringing out the sharp planes of his face. "Remind me never to ask you to embroider my handkerchiefs."

"I expect you would leave that task for a wife," I said, unable to resist probing. "Or, perhaps, a sweetheart?"

"I've neither, more's the pity." He sounded truly dismayed.

"I imagine it's not for lack of opportunity."

"One look at my coat, and women run screaming," he said wryly. "I can't blame them, really. I imagine most of them prefer to eat."

"Then they don't find you as charming as I do," I said. "And they're shortsighted as well. Your future is very bright, Mr. DeWitt. Has *Penelope* begun rehearsing yet?"

"Not yet. Mrs. Bernardi is leaving the company, and Greene prefers to introduce the play with a new leading lady."

"Oh, I'm glad. You know, I think Mrs. Bernardi is rather . . . too broad. *Penelope* needs a greater talent."

"My thoughts exactly," DeWitt agreed.

The carriage pulled to a stop; I glanced out the window to see we were before the Palace Theater. "I suppose it's time to discover if acting is Mr. Reading's hidden talent."

The Palace had a better pedigree than the Regal, but it was not nearly as grand as Frye's Opera House. Sebastian DeWitt was every inch the gentleman as we went up the stairs to our seats in the lower tier of boxes. I saw one or two people glance our way, no doubt noting the disparity between my gown of deep plum silk and his frayed frock coat. As we took our seats, I saw the flash of opera glasses turning toward us.

"Look how they all stare," I said to him in a low voice.

"They can't help but wonder why the lovely Mrs. Langley is hobnobbing with a peasant."

I laughed. "Is that what you are?"

"Oh, I come from humble enough stock, madam. I think you would turn up your nose at me if you passed me on the street."

"I am convinced I would not." I turned, unable to resist touching him, and tapped my finger to his lapel. "We really must get you a finer coat, Mr. DeWitt. One more befitting of your new rank."

"As your escort?"

"As America's new Shakespeare."

He laughed, flashing white teeth, pure amusement. "A compliment I've no doubt you will rethink once *Julius Caesar* ends, and you remember what genius it is."

"Perhaps not, with Mr. Reading acting Brutus."

"Perhaps not," he agreed with a smile.

The orchestra began to play; the crimson velvet curtain swished aside to reveal a Roman street and village, and I was plunged into the story, despite the fact that Caesar wore a doublet that had seen better days and Marc Antony a frock coat and James Reading was often so softly spoken as to go unheard.

Even so, I was held rapt, as I always was. By the beginning of the fourth act, as Brutus defended himself against Cassius—"Did not great Julius bleed for justice's sake?"—I was leaning forward, caught completely. When Brutus committed suicide at the end, I did not see James Reading lay himself gently upon the stage floor as if afraid of bruising himself, but Brutus falling insensate. And when the company bowed to the hoots and jeers of the gallery above and the polite applause of the boxes, I stood and clapped loudly.

"You are an actor's favorite audience," Mr. DeWitt said as we rose to leave. "Enthusiastic and uncritical."

"My friend Ambrose Rivers often said so," I told him. "He used to say I would be useless as a reviewer, as I found the grossest actors on par with the best. But that's not really true, you know. It's only that I'm willing to overlook everything else if the story is a good one."

"Then you are precious indeed," he said, guiding me into the throng making its way to the stairs.

Right in front of the Stebbings. Mrs. Stebbing glanced at Sebastian DeWitt and then to me, giving me a polite, cold smile.

"Ah, Mrs. Langley," said Mr. Stebbing as we moved into the crowd beside them. "Your husband said you would be here this evening."

"Yes indeed. I wouldn't miss it." I introduced DeWitt to them, noting the slight widening of Mrs. Stebbing's nostrils, as if she smelled something rotten. "Mr. DeWitt is a playwright of quite astonishing talent."

"Mrs. Langley is very kind," DeWitt said modestly.

Mrs. Stebbing said, "Is she?" And then, suspiciously, to me, "Wherever did you meet a *playwright*?"

The implication was there quite clearly, that I'd gone slumming into one of the worse neighborhoods and stumbled upon him, and I smiled and said, "My husband introduced us. Nathan is invested in the Regal Theater."

"Then he has the power to hire Reading should he decide to make acting his occupation," Mr. Stebbing said. "Which is good, because I fear otherwise no one would have him."

We laughed. I said, "I think him very brave to try it, but I do think he should not relinquish his job at the water company."

Mr. Stebbing winked. "Luckily, he's an amusing fellow. We mean to go backstage to offer our congratulations. Will you join us?"

I turned to Sebastian DeWitt. "Do you mind?"

"Not at all," he said.

We followed the Stebbings down the stairs to the hall that led to the parquet. Mr. Stebbing had a commanding presence; the crowd parted for us as we bucked them to go back inside, past the rows of seats and those patrons still making their leisurely way out, the musicians putting away their instruments, programs littering the floor beneath our steps. When we reached the short flight leading to the stage, Mr. Stebbing went up as if he owned them, despite the fact that the stage was crowded with men rushing about, moving sets, taking up props, one sweeping away the detritus the audience had thrown in either appreciation or mockery.

I had known many actors, but I had never been backstage before, and now I felt as if I'd entered an unknown land. Of course it was all illusion; I'd known that, but the buildings that had looked so large and substantial from the box were nothing but painted wooden flats, and the backdrop of a Roman street was coarse and undetailed now with proximity. We plunged into the darkness of the wings, a dozen or more ropes snaking up the walls, a bulky table tangled with gas tubing, the prompter's high stool and podium. Down another set of stairs and then into a narrow hallway crowded with people. It was so hot and close it was hard to breathe, and my corset felt much too tight, my hands sweating in my fine kid gloves.

Beyond the waiting admirers there was an open door through which I heard James Reading's voice.

". . . Do you think so? I'm flattered, truly I am."

We went inside. The dressing room was small. There was a mirror, a dressing table littered with pots of rouge and powder. Reading turned to us, throwing up his hands in delight. "Ah, my dear Stebbing, your presence humbles me. And Catherine!" His face crinkled with obvious delight. "And Mrs. Langley! How kind of you to come!"

"I've brought my friend, Mr. DeWitt," I said. "He's a playwright, Mr. Reading, so you must be kind to him, else he'll write you as a villain in his next play."

"Well, then, I shall be my most genial self!" Reading said, shaking DeWitt's hand. "I am gratified beyond measure to see you all."

"We could not let you linger in obscurity, could we, man?" Mr. Stebbing said, shaking Reading's hand, clapping him on the back. "Orion and Narcissa Denny were here too."

"Both of them? Well, excellent, excellent! How did you all enjoy the play?"

"Delightful," Mrs. Stebbing said.

"And you, Mrs. Langley? I'm afire for your opinion, you know."

"I enjoyed it very much," I told him.

Reading had on a dressing gown now, but the soft leather boots he'd worn onstage were still on his feet. His costume—a blue silk doublet—hung on a hook near the door, brushing my shoulder. Not silk at all, but broadcloth, the cloak only a very heavy and stiff brown serge that had been painted or dyed to look like leather.

"How funny," I said. "It looks nothing here as it does upon the stage."

Reading turned from Mr. Stebbing. "Not at all," he agreed. "You'd be amazed at the secrets I've learned about the theater, Mrs. Langley. No doubt you know them all already, Mr. DeWitt, but for me it's a most singular experience. It's been the most exciting thing I've done."

Stebbing said, "More exciting than climbing Mount Rainier?"

"Oh, by far," Reading said enthusiastically.

Stebbing laughed. "A dusty backstage better than incomparable glaciers?"

"I'm quite serious." James Reading's gaze came to me. "Mrs. Langley, I can see your fascination from where I stand! Have you ever given thought to trying this yourself?"

Mrs. Stebbing frowned. "Goodness, James, you can't mean to suggest that Mrs. Langley take a turn upon the stage?"

"Why not? She seems a braver soul than most." Mr. Reading wiped at his face, smearing kohl. "It takes little imagination to see her treading the boards. But I suppose you've already got her well tied up with charity work, eh, Catherine? Ah well, I suppose we actors must sacrifice that little orphans might have succor."

"I'm afraid the orphans must do without me," I said. "My task now is to make certain Seattle sees what a talent they have in Mr. DeWitt."

"A poor trade, I've told her," DeWitt said with a pained smile.

"We could certainly use some talent in this city," Mr. Reading said. "Don't you agree, Catherine?"

"As long as it's not of the lowering kind," Mrs. Stebbing said stiffly, glancing at DeWitt.

It pricked at me, but I managed to say politely, "Not all of us have the eye to appreciate the difference, it's true. I do think it takes a superior mind. Most genius was disparaged in its early days. Why, even Shakespeare was thought to be common once."

She frowned, as if uncertain she heard an insult.

I turned to Mr. Reading. "Sir, I thank you for a most diverting evening. I am grateful for the invitation; I will not soon forget your presence upon the stage."

He laughed, and the talk turned to other things, and Sebastian DeWitt and I made our good-byes and left. But once we were in the carriage, I found I was loathe to say good-bye to DeWitt, not so soon. The play and his company had worked a kind of magic; I wanted to prolong the evening, and it occurred to me once again that it was dangerous—there were things about him that reminded me too well of Claude, and I was a little afraid of that.

But these last months had been too miserable to give up what little joy I found now, and Sebastian DeWitt was not Jean-Claude Marat. Nathan said he wanted me to be happy, and I knew better now the boundaries I dared not cross.

"Oh, I've no wish to go home yet," I told him. "Is there a place around here you know? A little café, perhaps?"

Quietly, he said, "Are you certain that's wise, Mrs. Langley?"

"Wise? How do you mean?"

"Your friends find me disreputable."

"They aren't my friends. Well, Mr. Reading is, but not the Stebbings. Not really."

"Still, I can't think you'd care to have your reputation blemished by having a drink in a café with a playwright."

I leaned forward to touch his hand. "You're very kind to worry, but I fear my reputation is already blemished beyond repair."

"Your husband—"

"My husband asked me to help make you and your play a success. That's what I'm doing. If you like, think of it as a business meeting."

"Mrs. Langley—"

"Have you another obligation this evening, Mr. DeWitt?"

He paused. Then he shook his head.

"Then I insist you have a glass of . . . beer with me. Or absinthe—oh, no, you don't like it. Beer then."

He sighed. "There's a café a block or so from here. It's not in the best part of town."

"Then the fewer eyes there are to see us. And if you're worried for my safety, why, you're here to protect me, are you not?"

He knocked on the roof of the carriage, and when the driver called down, I told him, "We're going to a café, John. On—" I looked to Mr. DeWitt.

"Commercial and Main," he provided.

"—Commercial and Main." I sat back, unable to keep from laughing as the carriage started off again. "Oh, you look so dour, Mr. DeWitt."

"Your husband asked me to escort you to a play."

"You're worried he might revoke his patronage if he learns where else you've taken me?"

He looked uncomfortable. He glanced out the window.

"Believe me, Mr. DeWitt, my husband is no doubt at the Rainier Club right now, talking about mining contracts and what-have-you and drinking and smoking cigars. I assure you he won't be back until quite late. He'll never know. And even if he does discover where we've been, I'll tell him I insisted. Your position is quite safe."

DeWitt looked at me, and there was an expression in his eyes—pity, was it? I could not see well enough in the dark, but I thought that was it.

"You've no need to pity me," I said. "Nathan and I . . . we have not rubbed well together for some time. But I hope that will change. I have reason to believe it might."

DeWitt looked as if he might say something, but then he glanced back out the window, and the carriage came to a stop. "Here we are. I hope you don't find it too rough."

"Don't you mean colorful?" I asked.

The place was small, tucked between a saddlery and a grocer. The lights glowed from tiny windows, and inside was dim and close. In the corner a man played a fiddle, not very well. The room was heavy with smoke and talk and laughter. At one table a man who looked familiar, though I could not place him, glanced up with interest, and I felt a tremor of anxiety that I quickly quelled.

I glanced away again, dismissing him, as DeWitt unerringly led me to the only empty table, in the opposite corner from the fiddler. As we sat, he leaned forward to ask, "Do you really want a beer, Mrs. Langley?"

"Is that what you're having?"

"There's not much else to choose from, I'm afraid."

"Then a beer it is."

He rose and went to the bar to get it, and I thought too late that I should have given him the money to do so, but then he was back, carrying two glasses that were foaming over his hands, and I did not want to embarrass him by offering to repay him. He set them on the table and wiped his fingers ruefully on his coat as he sat down again.

"Not the best beer in the city, but it's not too bad," he said.

I picked up the glass, which slipped a little in my gloved hands, and took a sip. "There was better lager in Chicago. But then there were more Germans there."

"Did you drink a lot of beer in Chicago?"

"Does that shock you?"

"No more than anything else about you."

"There was a café that sold fried fish and beer," I said, remembering it wistfully. "I spent many a delightful hour there. They let the artists draw on the walls, and there were charcoal sketches everywhere. Caricatures, mostly. There was even one of me."

"Was there?"

"Yes. Huge eyes and a long nose, with these puffy lips." I pushed mine out in a pout. "I miss it, even though they were barbarians, really. Shouting at the owner to bring them more fish while they threw the bones on the floor and talked of socialism and Hegel."

"You'll not find any of that here."

"Really? Where do the actors spend their hours? And surely you're not the only playwright in town. Where are your fellows?"

His smile was wry. "Unfortunately, I seem to be a nearly extinct species. Only the one of me."

I took another sip of the beer. "What do you do with your evenings, then?"

"Drink beer with my betters in little cafés."

"I refuse to allow you to think of me that way. You're a writer, Mr. DeWitt, where is your egalitarian spirit?"

"Too busy trying to make a living."

"Well, you shan't have to worry about that any longer. I forbid you to, in fact." Another sip. "You didn't answer my question."

"I see plays."

"Every night? Is there that much variety in town?"

"I tend to stay to one house."

"Which one?"

"The Regal."

"Ah, my husband's theater." I frowned. "It seems so strange to say that, you know. He's never shown so much interest in theater."

DeWitt looked down into his beer. "Perhaps he's found something new in it."

"He's realized there's money to be made," I said with a laugh. "He has an instinct for finance. It's why my father loves him."

"Your father?"

"Maynard Stratford, of Stratford Mining." Then, at the sudden lift of his gaze. "I see you know the name."

"Doesn't everyone?"

"I imagine so. I'm his only child. With an inheritance from my mother on top of it."

"You are full of surprises, Mrs. Langley."

I leaned over the table, feeling a little warm and loose from the beer, which was nearly gone, liking the light in his eyes. "Do you like surprises, Mr. DeWitt?"

"Good ones. Who doesn't?"

"Am I a good one, do you think?" I should not be flirting this way, but I told myself it was harmless. We were only talking. I had no intention of more. I'd learned my lesson too well.

"I like you," he admitted. "More than I thought I would."

"More than you thought you would?" I prompted.

"I expected a bored society wife," he said.

"I have hated it here," I said heedlessly. "Until I met you and James Reading, I could hardly breathe. But now I think perhaps I can bear it after all. Still, I wish . . ."

"You wish what?" he prodded gently.

"I wish for the things I used to have. Foolish, I know, but I do. I wish to eat fish in cafés again and talk of socialism and Hegel. I wish to talk with men like you far into the night, until the stars go down and the sun comes up. And . . . I wish I could act upon a stage like James Reading."

He smiled. "I cannot think your husband would like that."

"No," I agreed. "And that's why I don't do it. Because of Nathan. And my father. I've promised them I'll behave."

"I think you'd best stop talking, Mrs. Langley. Remember what I told you. I can't keep secrets." His warm eyes belied his words.

"I'm not telling you one." I reached across the table for his hand, which laid flat upon it, and rested my fingers on his knuckles, liking the feel of him in my fingertips, even through my gloves. "I'm only saying what I feel."

"Honesty is a dangerous business."

"But I think you understand. I read *Penelope*. I know you understand a woman's heart."

"I can't hope to do that."

"But you do," I insisted. My glass was empty, but his was still half full. I picked it up and brought it to my lips, and he watched me without saying a word. Nor did he pull his hand from beneath mine. I drank and set it down again, and then I said, "How do you know such things? I want to quote Byron to you—'what woman told you this?' "

"None," he said with a little smile, a shake of his head. "I watch. If you observe carefully enough, you see things people wish to keep hidden. If you're lucky, you see into their souls. But really, I think perhaps men and women are not so different from each other in what they feel."

"Well spoken, sir," I said. "But I don't believe you. There *is* a woman you've watched—you must admit it. I see her all over this play."

I wondered what was going on behind those pale eyes; he gave nothing away. Then, finally, a smile.

"You have me, Mrs. Langley."

"I knew it," I said triumphantly. "Who is she? Not a sweetheart and not a wife, you said."

His smile faltered. "An actress. I've been watching her for some time."

"Then I envy her. For how well you know her."

"I'm not certain I do. I've barely spoken to her."

"I had a friend once who told me that muses were sometimes best when they were not intimates. That too much familiarity defiled the purity of inspiration."

"There might be something to that. Though I suppose it depends on the one being inspired."

"Yes," I said. "I don't believe it myself. Inspiration is so rare, I think, that an artist should grab it close and roll around in it."

He laughed out loud. "How very vivid."

I laughed with him. "Do you know, I think I'd like another beer."

He twisted his hand, still beneath mine, catching my fingers with his, a quick clasp, and then he rose, pulling me to my feet. "It's late, Mrs. Langley. Time to go."

I was disappointed, but of course he was right. "Let me take you home."

"No need. It's not far from here. An easy walk."

He tucked my hand into the crook of his arm and led me from the café and into the street, where dust and the constant and heavy low cloud of smoke obscured the stars. At the door to my carriage, he unhanded me and opened the door. John, half-asleep in the driver's seat, stirred and sat up.

I paused at the door, turning back to DeWitt. He was lovely there in the half-light, and I felt the danger of him and told myself once again that I was only doing what Nathan wanted. "When will I see you again?"

Gently, he said, "Soon enough. I like you, Mrs. Langley. I want no harm to come to you because of me."

It may have been the most beautiful thing anyone had ever said to me. I did not know what to say in response.

He took my hand and kissed it. I felt the warm press of his mouth through the kid of my gloves; when he released my hand,

I felt a shaft of longing that made me curl my fingers into my palm.

"Good night, Mrs. Langley," he said.

He helped me into the carriage and closed the door and stepped back, slapping the side with his palm so we were off, and I sat back against the seats, staring out the window until he was nothing but a shadow against wooden buildings, and then gone altogether.

I sighed, and then I thought of *Penelope Justis* and how well Sebastian DeWitt understood the things that constrained women, their hopes and their desires. I thought of the things I'd told him I wanted. To have my life back, to eat fish and talk late into the night, to stare into his eyes, to act upon a stage. Impossible things. Nathan wanted me to be happy, yes, but I was no fool to think there were no limits in that. Claude had taught me that. My father and Nathan and society had hammered it home. For me . . . for any woman . . . satisfaction could only be taken in half measures. And all my wishes otherwise, no matter how ardently felt, were as nothing.

Chapter Ten

Beatrice

Sebastian DeWitt's play began like a dozen others:

It is the saddest and most familiar story in the world, a beautiful and innocent young girl out walking happens upon a handsome young man who

> pretends to be something he is not. Despite the warnings of the townspeople, Florence Justis falls in love with Barnabus Cadsworth. He is worse than untrue; he is insincere. He promises to marry her, and she believes him and falls victim to his seduction. Then, abandoned and in a most desperate circumstance, too ashamed to confess her humiliation to her loving family, she drowns herself in a well.
>
> The story begins with a funeral.

But that beginning was misleading; by the time the first scene ended, I knew I was reading something different, and I loved every moment of it, the haunting by the betrayed Florence's spirit and Penelope's strength of purpose in attempting to save her other sister, Delia, from Barnabus Cadsworth's clutches. It was a vengeance melodrama, a grieving family bent on justice, a rich, spoiled villain used to getting whatever he wanted, yes, all seen a hundred times, but the twist DeWitt put on it was something fine; what a mind he had! First there was the servant girl's plan to turn the villain mad by degrees, then there was Penelope's taking greater risks and putting herself in greater and greater danger to keep sweet Delia from Florence's fate. . . .

And the characters were some of the best I'd ever read: the villain, Barnabus Cadsworth, had more depth than the usual melodrama villains, and it was a part that would showcase Aloysius's tragedian abilities perfectly; the twin roles of the younger sister Delia and the scheming servant Marjory were ones Susan would relish not just because they were so much bigger than anything she'd played before, but also because Marjory Hart was both loving and devious, and that was an actor's favorite meat. There was Mrs. Cadsworth, the villain's mother, who would give Mrs. Chace a more active part than she'd had in years. And of course the hero, Marjory's brother, Keefe, who had all of Jackson's favorite traits: good looks and stunts to show off his prowess. Jack would find Keefe Hart irresistible.

And there was Penelope Justis herself. I knew the moment I read her first lines that she would be the role to make my career, and that I'd no doubt still be playing her into my dotage, and it wasn't just because of the sheer beauty of her tragic death soliloquy. The audience would fall in love with her. So pure of heart, so *good*, but impulsive, and so angry at the villain's mistreatment of her elder sister that she fell thoughtlessly into Marjory's fatal plan.

I could not put the script down but found myself mouthing the lines into the night, bending close to see Sebastian DeWitt's penciled comments. He understood the character so well, and I knew what he'd told me was true—if I followed his comments, if I became Penelope Justis instead of simply bending her to my usual bag of tricks, I would make an unparalleled success of this role.

Thankfully, Nathan had not seen fit to visit me the last two nights, so after performances, I'd had the hours to myself to learn as many lines as I could. Lucius was a tyrant when it came to rehearsals; our first, scheduled for ten this morning, would be the only one where he allowed us to work with the script. After that, he'd levy forfeits, which I couldn't afford.

So I worked until the early hours, sighing when I finally set the script aside to get some sleep. But the play would not leave me, and when the morning came fully on, I was still awake. I was too excited to be tired. I washed and dressed, and ate a candied fig and two cherries, and that morning I didn't waste time worrying that no amount of scrubbing could rid the kohl from the fine lines forming at the corners of my eyes. I was about to embark upon the role of my life, at long last, and I wanted to grab Sebastian DeWitt and kiss him for it.

When I got to the stage, the others were already there. Aloys and Brody running lines—Brody was playing Barnabus Cadsworth's servant as well as the reverend and several other minor roles—and Mrs. Chace waving her fan about her florid face. Mr. Galloway, who would play both my father and the elder Mr. Cadsworth, ate a pear while Lucius and Marcus Geary conferred near the script table. Susan sat on a riser, swinging her legs like a little girl as she memorized her part, her lips moving fast and silently.

The carpenters were already working on the sets; the theater was filled with the sounds of hammering and sawing, and painters perched on scaffolding before a huge drop of sized muslin, filling it with the broad outlines of what looked like a cottage garden.

Jack leaned back against a flat. When I went over to him, he winked and said, "I see we have a passionate kiss in act one, sweeting."

"Is that so? I didn't notice."

"Liar. I shall endeavor to make it pleasing for you. God knows you've been waiting for it long enough."

I smiled and pressed myself teasingly against him. "Stick your tongue in my mouth, Jack, and I'll cut it off."

He laughed. "One wonders that Lucius could even think of casting you as such a sweet innocent."

"It's who you know, Jack."

" 'Truer words, et cetera, et cetera.' . . . I wonder where I could find a rich protector of my own?"

"Try the Rainier Club," I said.

Jack gave me a wry smile. "I had thought rather a patron*ess*. Or better yet, a besotted playwright along the lines of your Mr. DeWitt. But of the opposite sex, of course. How clever you were to have found him."

Jack's gaze slid toward the seats in the parquet. I followed it to see Sebastian DeWitt coming down the aisle between them.

"He's been watching you for months, you know," Jack told me. "We were beginning to wonder whether we should call the police. Or . . . whether perhaps he was the father of your secret child."

I laughed. "A secret child? You couldn't give me a long-lost brother instead?"

"My dear, that kind of brotherly affection is against the law—or if it isn't, it should be."

We both watched DeWitt bound up the stairs to the stage. His glance came to me—immediately and intensely—and he said, "Good morning, Mrs. Wilkes," as if I were the only one in the room before he went to the script table, pulling his satchel off his shoulder.

"Good morning to you too, DeWitt," Jack mocked in an aside.

Then he looked at me. "What's that on your cheeks, my sweet? A blush? How damning."

"You know me better than that," I whispered back. "For God's sake, Jack, look at his coat."

"Not rich enough for you, eh? Well, he's moving up in the world. I hear Lucius paid him fifty for the script."

"Really? So much?"

Jack smiled. "Another benefit to having a rich patron. How lucky you are, darling. One man rich in coins and another rich in words."

"And I mean to keep them both happy," I said.

"What a faithless heart! I almost feel sorry for your hapless playwright, that he doesn't know you better."

"But of course you'd never do the same."

"Oh, never." Jack laughed and chucked me under the chin.

Lucius called out, "Now that our playwright is here, children, we can begin. Act one, scene one. The funeral, my dears. Places, please."

For the next three hours, I was hardly aware of DeWitt or anything but the play. It was obvious that the others felt as I did about *Penelope Justis,* one could see it in the way they said their lines, their little flourishes and the relish in their voices, even though no one ever acted fully during a rehearsal. They were all laughing and talking as they left—not that common an occurrence, either, as rehearsals were dull and boring and none of us liked them. Even Lucius seemed pleased, though one would not know it by the way he'd had Mr. DeWitt furiously cutting and recrafting lines. The script table was littered with pages spattered with ink, and DeWitt was still scratching away when I walked over to the table.

He didn't look up as I approached. He held up his hand, silencing me when I started to speak, which was a little irritating, you know, but I waited obediently until he wrote the last words. He put the pen aside and looked up, blinking as if he'd just waked from some dream. He smiled. "What can I do for you, Mrs. Wilkes? Have you a line you dislike or a scene that requires tightening?"

"I think it's perfect," I said.

His smile widened. "Do you?"

"Lucius is always very hard on playwrights, you know. You shouldn't take it to mean he doesn't like it."

"He has a funny way of showing it." DeWitt leaned back in his chair, rubbing rather absently at a large ink stain on his forefinger. "He's changed it already so much I hardly recognize it. He's added a waterfall for you to plunge over. But never fear, you'll be rescued by the daring Keefe."

I thought I heard a little resentment. I'd seen it before; Lucius's venality making mincemeat of a poet's soul. But DeWitt should have expected it; he'd sold the play, after all; he couldn't imagine it would stay pristine.

He said, "Well, at least he's paid for it, which is more than anyone's done before."

"I doubt he'll need to change it very much. Your words work beautifully as they are. I admit I was surprised."

"You didn't think me capable of it?" His gaze was disconcertingly direct. His eyes looked gray today.

"No, not that. It's just . . . you seem to understand a woman's heart so well. Or Penelope's heart, in any case. I've rarely played a character I liked better."

"I'm gratified to hear it."

"And your cues for me are brilliant, though I think I'll have to work very hard to capture Penelope as you've written her."

"You're very talented, Mrs. Wilkes. I expect you'll have no trouble at all, but I'll be happy to work with you if it would help."

I'll be happy to work with you. It was clear he meant something else entirely. I was not misreading the challenge there, or his desire. I bit back the retort that was my first instinct and reminded myself that I meant to keep him happy. So I smiled at him instead. "I'll be sure to let you know if I feel the necessity."

"Please do," he said. He held my gaze for a moment more and then dropped it. He capped the inkwell and gathered up his pens, shoving them all into his satchel. "Shall I walk you back to your hotel, Mrs. Wilkes?"

"Oh, there's no need. It's broad daylight. I'm safe enough."

"Who escorts you at night?"

"Lately I don't often need an escort."

"Of course." He picked up the scattered papers, seemingly heedless of their order, and tapped them on the tabletop to even them. "But surely you don't see Langley every night? Ah—forgive me. It's none of my business."

"No, it isn't."

"I'm only concerned for your safety. What of the nights you're alone? Who walks with you then?"

"Sometimes Aloys," I said. "Or Brody. But not always."

"Will you promise me something? Promise me that if you find yourself walking alone at night, you'll ask for me."

"That's absurd, Mr. DeWitt. How will I find you to ask?"

"I'm always here, Mrs. Wilkes. All you need to do is look around."

"But that's ridiculous. You can't come to the Regal every night."

He put the papers into his bag carefully and put the leather flap down. "Why not? Like any writer, I follow my inspiration. Just now, it resides here."

"I'm certain you could find it in other places as well."

His smile was wry. "I wish it were so. I can think of several places I'd rather it be. Unfortunately, at present, my inspiration doesn't seem inclined to follow my wishes."

"Perhaps because it has other . . . obligations."

"Perhaps so." He shook back his hair and took up the strap of his bag, slinging it over his shoulder. "Let me walk you home, Mrs. Wilkes."

"I'm not going home just now. I . . . I thought I'd do some embroidery. On a new costume. In my dressing room." It was a bald lie. Lucius hadn't yet given me the raise I'd earn as lead, and so there wasn't money to buy another gown at the secondhand shop, and I couldn't embroider a nonexistent dress. But DeWitt's longing made me vaguely uncomfortable, and I did not want to have to refuse outright what he so obviously wanted. Though neither did I want to anger him.

"Then I'll see you tonight."

"Tonight?"

"After the performance." He smiled. "In the event you need an escort home. Good-bye, Mrs. Wilkes."

I watched him go down the stage steps and make his way down the aisle. He did not look back, and I had the disconcerting sense that keeping Sebastian DeWitt happy might not be as easy as I'd thought.

He was there that night, just as he'd promised he would be. When I left the stage and went to change, he was lingering in the shadows, and I smiled at him, but Nathan had been in his box tonight, which meant I only had a few minutes to change.

I was taking off my makeup when Susan flounced in, saying, "You coming to the Pitcher with us?"

The Broken Pitcher was the saloon where I'd first met Nathan, and tonight was Stella's last night. She was leaving tomorrow for San Francisco. No one would think it odd if I didn't go—we weren't exactly friends, after all, but I might have gone if I hadn't had Nathan to tend. When I said as much to Susan, she said, "Bring him along. Hell, he'd probably enjoy himself."

I didn't think he would, and he wasn't a patient man besides. I didn't imagine Nathan Langley would take well to delaying his fuck so I could have a beer. But when I came out of my dressing room, and he was standing there, looking elegant in his perfect coat and vest, his hair shining in the half-light of backstage, I found myself saying, "Tonight's Stella's farewell party. Everyone's going to the Broken Pitcher."

"Does that mean you'd like to attend as well?" he asked.

"If you don't want to . . ."

He glanced into the shadows. "I see DeWitt loitering about, as usual. Is he going?"

"I don't know." I looked over my shoulder. "Mr. DeWitt, are you coming to the Pitcher tonight?"

He emerged from the shadows like some demon king, glancing at Nathan. "I hadn't decided."

To my surprise, Nathan said to him, "Come along then, and it won't be a complete waste of time. I have something to discuss with you."

That surprised me even more, you know, because, beyond the play he'd bought for me, I didn't think Nathan had much to do with the mechanics of the production, or that he knew DeWitt well enough to have anything to discuss, and he didn't seem the kind of patron to trouble much with the *art*. It made me a bit uncomfortable to think of them in the same room, and how I'd have to somehow please them both, and I was just thinking the whole thing was more trouble than it was worth when DeWitt said, "I'm at your beck and call, Mr. Langley, as always."

Nathan said, "Come along then. You can ride in my carriage."

And that was even more uncomfortable. We went to the carriage, and Nathan handed me in and sat beside me, very close—not that he could do otherwise in such a small space—and Sebastian DeWitt sat opposite me, his knees brushing my skirts, and looked at me with those strange eyes, and even though his desire was banked, I felt it.

We'd barely started before Nathan said to DeWitt, "Enjoy the occasional beer, do you?"

It was the kind of stupid, casual comment men often made to each other, and I rolled my eyes as I stared out the window and waited for Sebastian DeWitt to make some stupid comment back, when he said instead,

"You heard."

"The whole city heard. It's all anyone's talking about."

People were talking about Sebastian DeWitt having a beer? I frowned and looked back at Nathan, who ignored me.

DeWitt said, "It was nothing, just—"

"Just a beer, I know," Nathan said. He was smiling. "Drinking. Talking. You know, Mr. DeWitt, you may be one of the best investments I've ever made."

I was confused, and it was clear DeWitt was as well. His gaze met mine for a moment before he looked back at Nathan. "It won't happen again."

"Now, now, Mr. DeWitt, do you want to be a famous playwright or not?"

"Not at someone else's expense," DeWitt said.

"No one's paying any price." Nathan leaned forward reassuringly—or as reassuringly as that smile could make him, which wasn't much. "You're gaining quite a name around town, which is exactly what we want. Why, think what it will do when your play finally debuts. Every seat will be full. And with society, no less, which can hardly serve you ill."

Now he had my attention. "Society? But the Regal gets society all the time."

Nathan didn't look at me. His gaze was focused on Sebastian DeWitt. "Not like this, my dear. When I say the seats will be full, I meant not just one or two coming for an occasional evening's entertainment, but people like the Dennys. Governor Semple. How will it feel, do you think, to know the most powerful people in the city are watching you?"

I glanced at DeWitt, whose expression had gone very still.

"Lucius would be over the moon," I said.

"Perhaps he would even give you a raise, my dear," Nathan said. "And from everything I hear, this play—what is it called again?"

"*Penelope Justis,*" DeWitt answered.

"Yes, this *Penelope Justis*—I've heard it's a masterpiece."

"It is nearly that," I said, quietly now, because there were undercurrents here I didn't understand, and I didn't like the way Sebastian DeWitt looked, as if he might be sick.

"If it is, it's because the actors will make it so," he said.

"Mr. DeWitt is too modest," I said.

"So I hear." Again, Nathan smiled. "How easily you make the world fall in love with you, Mr. DeWitt. Why, you're a veritable talent in many, many ways, aren't you? Do you know, I think I should like to see one talent in particular put to use."

They stared at each other, and I had this nasty sense that they were fighting some kind of duel, only with words and meanings that weren't what they seemed to be, and I wished I hadn't decided to go to the Broken Pitcher after all. Because then Nathan and I would already be in my room, and he'd be thinking of nothing but getting my clothes off, and this baiting of Sebastian DeWitt—if that's what it was—wouldn't be happening, and I wouldn't be feeling as if I somehow needed to come to his rescue when I couldn't even see if he was in trouble.

"I think you misunderstand me," DeWitt said quietly. "My interests lie in a different direction."

"Do they?" Nathan looked surprised. "How fascinating. But should you want to change your mind . . . well, you have my permission. In fact, I encourage it."

DeWitt glanced at me. "Let's not speak of this now."

"Of course," Nathan said smoothly. "There's no need to speak of it again. So long as we understand each other."

"We do," DeWitt said shortly.

"Well, I don't," I said, because I couldn't help myself, and then I wished I hadn't said anything when Nathan put his arm around my shoulders and let his hand dangle to caress my breast. I saw how DeWitt's gaze snapped there, and I had to resist the urge to bat Nathan away.

"It's business, my dear. Nothing for you to concern yourself with." Nathan's voice was forceful, and a little needling too, I thought, as if he noticed the way DeWitt was looking at us.

DeWitt slid his gaze to the window. We came to a stop, and I was never so glad to get out of a carriage in my life. Whatever this game was, I didn't want any part of it; I had enough trouble keeping the players straight in my own.

DeWitt was the first out, and he strode to the door of the Broken Pitcher without waiting for Nathan and me, which was a relief, and Nathan took my arm as if I were a lady he was escorting to some fancy dress ball instead of just into a tavern where the only dancing was when some drunk took it into his head to reel to the tune of a tone-deaf fiddler.

Most of the others were already there. Aloys and Brody and Jack and Stella and Mrs. Chace gathered around tables they'd pushed together, and Stella laughed and hung on Jack, and I could tell she'd already had one or two drinks by the way her cheeks were flushed, though she couldn't have been there long. DeWitt went to the bar, and Nathan went to get me a beer, and it was all I could do to keep from looking at them to see if they were talking again.

"There you are, Bea!" Brody motioned me over to the table, and when I went to him, he said to me in a low voice, "Stella says she's playing at the Elysium next."

"There's an appropriate name," I said, "as she'll no doubt put them to sleep."

We both laughed, and then Jack made some sally and Stella gave him a wet kiss and spilled her drink all over her breasts, which set Jack wiping furiously with a handkerchief, and I forgot about Nathan and DeWitt for a time, except to see that they weren't together. Nathan lounged against the bar, looking for all the world like an indulgent, rich prince, and DeWitt sat watching the way he always did. I liked the way they both had their eyes on me, and I was half aware of putting on a show for them, laughing prettily, flirting with Jack and Aloys, cocking my hip just so as I leaned against the table.

Brody said, "Well, why don't you leave again tomorrow, Stella, an' we can have another party."

Stella pursed her mouth in a pretty little moue I'd seen her practice a hundred times before the mirror. "Then I'd be late for my *debut*"— a quick, feline glance at me—"and that would be *unforgivable.* They tell me the theater is already sold out, and subscriptions are up ten percent."

"They go up ten percent at the Palace when Johnny Langford books that cat who can carry a bottle," I said. "So you're in good company."

Jack laughed, and she boxed his ears, but he was drunk, and that only made him laugh some more, and for the next hour and a half, we were as bosom friends, joking and laughing and singing at the top of our voices, and Aloysius and I acted out the scene from *Baron Rudolph* where Rudolph comes home drunk and his wife leaves him, and it was so affecting I saw tears in the eyes of bar patrons who might have thought it was real—because they were as drunk as most of us were, and when I cried out, "You shall never see your son again!" some man at the bar jerked to his feet as if he might come at me, and shouted, "You cruel bitch! You can't do that to the man!"

Nathan stirred from his place against the bar and said something to him. I don't know what it was, but it calmed the man down enough that he just cried piteously into his beer. I glanced at Sebastian DeWitt, who was watching me with this thoughtful little expression. Then Nathan came over and took my arm and whispered, "What a good show, my dear," and I knew he had delayed as long as he was going to, and I forgot about DeWitt.

I said my good-byes, and Nathan took me out to the carriage and back to my room, and after he'd had me—no gentleness this time either, and there was that anger again that I didn't understand—he rolled off me and onto his back and said, "Do you and your friends do such things often?"

It took me a moment to know what he was talking about. "Oh, you mean the play. Now and again. When we feel like having fun."

"It doesn't bother you that people think it's real?"

I shrugged. "Not really."

"Well, it was very clever," he said in this thoughtful way that made me a little uncomfortable. He rose and began to dress.

I said, "Should I expect you tomorrow night?"

"I don't know," he said. "I imagine not. I should tend to my wife."

"Tend to her? Is she ill?"

He laughed shortly. "More so than she realizes, I think."

I had no idea what the hell that meant, and I didn't care either, and I fell silent as he finished dressing. When he went to the door, he was laughing again, low and quiet beneath his breath, the way he'd done the night he'd made me wear the cloak, and this time I asked, "What's so funny?"

"I was just thinking of you and your fellows tonight."

"I'm glad we amused you."

Nathan's hand was on the doorknob, and he turned and smiled at me. "Oh, you did. You don't know how much."

And then he was gone, and I was left wondering if there was some way to end things with Nathan Langley without losing everything he'd given me, because I was discovering that I really didn't like him at all.

Chapter Eleven

Geneva

My evening with Sebastian DeWitt had left me with more than thoughts that leaped often and regularly to the stage; it had also left me with a slight cold, and one that settled into my throat.

Nathan eyed me dispassionately when I complained and said, "Did you enjoy the café, at least?"

I looked at him in surprise. "The café?"

"It was the talk of the Relief Society, I hear," he said wryly. "You should have been a bit more circumspect, darling. Did you not see John Barrister sitting at the table next to yours?"

John Barrister. I vaguely remembered seeing a man I recognized, though I still could not have put this name to him. Nathan did not seem upset, but I rushed to say, "It was nothing. Mr. DeWitt and I had a beer, that's all. We discussed his play. There was nothing wrong in it. I cannot help small minds that would see something untoward in my every action. And you *did* tell me to guide Mr. DeWitt."

Nathan eyed me thoughtfully. "So I did. But you must be a bit more careful, my dear. Slowly, remember."

I looked studiously down into my tea. "Yes, of course. I'm sorry. I was too . . . enthusiastic."

"Your usual flaw," Nathan said with a smile. "Well, no harm's done this time, I think."

The charm of the old Nathan, with none of the anger, and though I should have been relieved, I was still wary. But before

I could speak, I was racked by a paroxysm of coughing. When it was over, I found Nathan watching me with concern.

"Perhaps you should send for Dr. Berry—"

I waved the comment away. "He'll only prescribe hot tea and honey, which is what I'm drinking already. I'm perfectly well, Nathan. Better than I've been in some time, in fact."

He rose and crossed the parlor to me, leaning down to kiss me lightly on the top of my head. "Good."

The kiss surprised me, and filled me with hope too. I was reminded suddenly of a time when Nathan and I had sat together in my father's parlor, and he had laughed delightedly at some joke, his hand brushing lightly against mine—such a small touch, but it had raised a desire so strong in me that I had wanted nothing more than to sweep him into some darkened alcove, to feel his body against mine, to touch his skin . . . how much I'd wanted him once.

Almost desperately, I grabbed at Nathan's hand as he stepped away. "Do you think you might attend the theater with me one night? I should like it very much. Perhaps something at the Regal, now that you've a stake in its success."

He disentangled my fingers from his, not ungently. "I'm quite busy with the new firm." Then, at my obvious disappointment, "I'll try, Ginny. But that's the most I can promise, unfortunately."

I felt a rush of relief, a little joy.

Nathan said, just before he left, "Take care of that cough, Ginny, or I'll have the doctor here after all."

Beatrice

Off with you all," Lucius said, waving us away. "We've rehearsed enough today. Back at four, children."

We all scattered, but for Mr. DeWitt, who was busy scribbling Lucius's last changes, and though I should have gone on—I must do some errands before I had to be back again—I waited. I'd been thinking over that conversation between Sebastian DeWitt and Nathan Langley, and it bothered me in ways I couldn't explain, and I hoped DeWitt might tell me what it had been about. Or that's what I told myself anyway, as I stood at the edge of the apron watching him gather everything up—pen nibs and ink, and papers. When he'd shoved them all into his bag and buckled it and looked up, he seemed surprised to see me there.

"Is there something I can do for you, Mrs. Wilkes?" he asked politely.

Well, I couldn't just say "What were you and Nathan talking about last night?" because he'd just tell me it was none of my business, which it wasn't. So I scrambled for something else, and landed on, "I've a few questions about your notes on Penelope. I'd thought, if you had a moment. . . ."

"I'm at your disposal, as always," he said.

So easy. As if he had nothing better to do, and suddenly I was curious. "Surely you can't always be at my disposal, Mr. DeWitt. Haven't you other places to go? Other things to do?"

"None so pressing they can't be put off."

"Really? What do you *do* all day?"

He smiled. "Mrs. Wilkes, I'm like you. I eat, breathe, and sleep the theater."

"My father used to warn me about theater people," I mused. "He said they were all selfish. I think he was very on the mark."

"I'll endeavor to be different then."

"I'm not certain you can. Certainly I cannot."

He put his satchel over his shoulder and came toward me, a slow walk, an amused expression. "You don't give yourself enough credit. I imagine you could be generous enough if you tried."

"I think you have me confused with your imaginary Penelope, Mr. DeWitt. I think it only fair to warn you that we are not the same."

"In my mind you are. There are hidden depths in Penelope, you know, just as there are in you."

"You see, that's why I need you. I've not seen those depths. In Penelope, I mean."

"You're not paying enough attention, then." He was very close, more than I felt comfortable with.

I took a step back. "No one spends more time learning lines than I."

He stepped forward. "Lines are not the only things that matter. You have more talent than that, Mrs. Wilkes. I knew it the first time I saw you in *Lady of Lyons*. Do you know what I thought then?"

"That I needed a better dress to play the upper class?"

He smiled and shook his head. "I thought: there's a woman who loves her craft. But she's a little afraid of it too."

I frowned. "Afraid of it?"

"Afraid to invest too much in it. As if you had once, and been disappointed, and meant not to be disappointed again."

I stared at him, too surprised to say anything.

"Am I right? What was it, Mrs. Wilkes? What made you lose faith in your talent? Too many unscrupulous managers? An actor or two who promised you a step up the ladder if you came to bed, and then never delivered? Or was it losing too many parts to favorites who don't know the meaning of subtlety?"

It was as if he were reading my life. I felt as if I were an open book to him, which wasn't a good feeling, you know, because it meant I was vulnerable, and I'd spent too long trying not to be, and he was practically a stranger, and in a profession where one couldn't even trust one's friends, a stranger—especially a charming one—was more than dangerous. *Time to walk away, Bea*. But I didn't. Instead, I heard myself saying like a fool, "All of those things."

"You know you'll never move higher if you don't unlearn those lessons," Sebastian DeWitt said gently. "If you don't have confidence in your talent, you'll never transcend the material. There are actors who can do that, Mrs. Wilkes. I think you could be one of them."

Oh, he was clever. Pandering to my vanity, to the arrogance every actor had. "Why do you say that? What do you see?"

"You *were* Pauline in *Lady of Lyons*. You played the upper class as if you were born to it. And when you cried, those were real tears."

"Stella can cry on cue too," I said dismissively. "Any actor worth his salt can."

"But *you* felt them. Tell me—have you ever considered giving up acting?"

I was wounded. "You think I should?"

He shook his head. "There's a point to be made. Have you?"

"About a hundred times," I said drily.

"What stopped you?"

I sighed. "I don't know. I didn't want to be a shopgirl."

"It was more than that, wasn't it?"

"I couldn't do it," I said honestly. "To be onstage . . . it was all I ever thought about. I loved it. I love it still."

"And if you were never a star?"

"I don't know. I suppose . . . I'll still be here playing old ladies 'til I die."

"So I thought."

I laughed a little. "It's pathetic, really, when you think about it."

He didn't even smile. "It's passion, Mrs. Wilkes, and too few people ever feel it. You owe it to yourself to nurture it. It's why you're here."

How strange he was, how fervently he spoke. I'd met hundreds of actors and playwrights, but I'd never known anyone like him. "How am I to do that?"

"Run your lines with me," he urged in a low voice that went through me the way my teeth went through those candied apricots, sheering just that smooth, and my breath went all jumpy and short. "You're very good at tricks. I can help you to let the truth show instead."

He had me off balance again. *This one you should run from,* and damn but wasn't *that* the truth I should be listening to. Still, he knew just what to say. He knew what would hook me. The thought of being better grabbed tight, and I found myself saying, "All right. When?"

"How about now?"

"We can go to my hotel," I heard myself say. "It's—"

"Foster's. I know."

"How do you know that?"

He smiled. "Shall we go?"

And that was how I ended up taking him back to my room. There, he opened the window and let in the afternoon, and my thin and faded muslin curtains fluttered in the little breeze and the air smelled like horse manure and piss and sawdust and smoke with that lilt of salt mud. Sebastian DeWitt took off his coat and sat on that faded red settee and I sat on my bed and ran lines with him.

And that was all it was, just that simple, except that he made me laugh out loud once or twice when he spoke Marjory's lines in this breathless, little high-pitched voice, and once, as he spoke Keefe, he leaped from the settee and raised his hand over me as if he held the knife that Keefe nearly plunged into Penny's breast before he realized who she was, and it was such a sudden movement I gasped and fell back with a startled little scream, and he smiled with satisfaction and said, "Perfect!" and I liked pleasing him much more than I should.

By the time we reached act four, he was lounging on the end of my bed while I sat at the head. I spoke the last lines of the scene: "I would do anything you asked of me, my love—anything at all," and when I said the words it was as if I'd become Penelope

Justis, and he was Keefe Hart, and he looked up at me just at that moment and the breeze stirred his hair and I was caught by his eyes. I mean, I was *caught,* you know, when I'd always thought that was just a stupid saying, and I don't know what I might have done or said, but suddenly there was a loud and blistering curse from someone in the street below, and it cut the moment dead, and Sebastian DeWitt laughed and looked away, and I laughed too, but I was thinking *What the hell are you doing?* I felt how much I liked him as this purely dangerous thing. He reminded me of everything I wanted, everything the years had taken away from me, and I forgot how hard those things were to have and to hold on to. With him, I was just Beatrice Wilkes, who loved acting more than anything in the world.

But that was the lie. That Bea was long gone, and DeWitt was right when he said I was afraid to have her back. I *was* afraid, and with good reason. I couldn't afford to be that person again.

"It's—it's getting late," I said when we'd done laughing. "I need to think about getting back to the theater."

DeWitt nodded and rose, stretching his arms over his head so his untucked shirt rose high on his thighs, as casually and intimately as if we were lovers, and I had to look away at the image *that* brought into my head.

He went to the window and looked out and said mildly, "I've been thinking . . . I know someone. Someone who can help us both."

"Help us both do what?"

"Show the world what we can really do." He didn't turn from the window, and he spoke the way someone might speak of God. "If you can make Penelope Justis come alive the way I saw today, this woman could take us very far."

"*Woman?*" I was suddenly jealous, and don't think I didn't know how stupid *that* was.

He nodded, turning now to look at me. "It's her gift—to bring artists out of obscurity."

And maybe she had other gifts as well. Ones that made him talk like that. "I don't imagine she would care to do much for me, Mr. DeWitt. But you . . . no doubt that's a different story."

He smiled and went to his coat, getting more wrinkled and

disreputable-looking by the minute where he'd thrown it haphazardly on the settee. "Leave that to me. Just remember what's at stake, Mrs. Wilkes. That's all I ask. Give me something to work with."

He went to the door, and I was suddenly, stupidly afraid I wouldn't see him again. "Wait, Mr. DeWitt. Do you . . . could we do this again, do you think? Run lines, I mean."

"As I said before: whenever you want, Mrs. Wilkes. You've only to ask." He gave me this beautiful seductive smile that said he was hoping for something more than just running lines, and I was so flustered both at the smile and at the way it dropped through me that I could do nothing but sit there and watch him close the door.

Chapter Twelve

Geneva

Over the next few days, my cough worsened; it required that I stay home from two functions, which was probably a fortuitous occurrence, as it would lessen the gossip about my late-night café visit with Sebastian DeWitt. It also meant I could not see him, as I most certainly would have done otherwise, which I regretted. It even occasioned a letter from my father alluding to my "illness," though it seemed so out of character for my father to concern himself over a small cough that I supposed it could have been his newest way of referring to the scandal in Chicago, as if it were some disease I'd managed, against all odds, to recover from. It was just like Papa to label something unpleasant with euphemisms until he came to believe them true. Years from now, I suspected, Papa would frown at any mention of Marat and say, "Wasn't that when you had the cholera, Ginny?"

Nathan was more solicitous and kind than he'd been in years, and I no longer doubted he truly meant the words he'd spoken the night of our dinner with Sebastian DeWitt. One morning, as we breakfasted together, he said, "Robert Stebbing said the most astonishing thing to me last night—he said that James Reading had suggested you try acting."

Reading's suggestion had nagged at me since *Julius Caesar*, but I hadn't dared mention it, and now I treaded carefully. "Yes, he did. He said it was the most exciting thing he'd ever done. Better even than climbing Mount Rainier."

Nathan laughed. "Of course Reading would say that."

"He was quite sincere, Nathan." I coughed delicately into my napkin.

His gaze became sharp. "I do think it's time Dr. Berry took a look at you."

"Don't be foolish. It's getting better every day."

"You won't be able to attend the Memorial Day parade if you aren't recovered, and—"

"I pooh-poohed Mr. Reading's idea, of course, but . . . I admit it's tempting."

"—as it is the inaugural parade, I think we should be there." Nathan stopped and frowned. "You admit that what is tempting?"

"James Reading's idea that I should take to the stage."

Nathan looked surprised. "You're taking it seriously?"

"Of course not. But . . . there's no doubt it would help make the play a great success. The Stebbings and the Dennys *did* come to see Mr. Reading in *Julius Caesar*."

"Not to put too fine a point on it, Ginny, but Reading is a man."

I tried to smile. "I realize that. I wasn't suggesting I do the same. It's only that the part of Penelope haunts me. I've thought of little else since I read it."

"Penelope?"

"From Mr. DeWitt's play. Don't you remember? *Penelope*

Justis. I think I could do it well, with Mr. DeWitt's help, of course, and with that and your connections at the Regal—"

"Reading's a laughingstock, as I think I've already told you."

I shrugged, attempting a casualness I didn't feel. "Yes, of course. Still, it didn't keep society from flocking to the theater. I can't help but think how much it would help Mr. DeWitt. People would come just for the gossip, but they'd be swept away by his words. You and I could be responsible for introducing an American Shakespeare."

"Yes, but at what cost?"

"How can it be more than I've already paid? You've said it yourself, Nathan. They hate me. They will never accept me. In one sense, that could be an asset. My notoriety means the play would earn a fortune. But I understand. Neither you nor Papa could like it, and I've promised to be good—" I had to stop to cough. When I looked up again, I saw how carefully Nathan was watching me.

"I want Berry to see you. I'll bring him by this afternoon."

I ignored that. "I want to help you, Nathan. You must believe I do."

He sighed. "As usual, Ginny, you go too far."

I had not realized how much I'd hoped for him to agree. I was so disappointed I could not look at him.

He said quietly, "I do want you to be happy, Ginny, but this—"

I glanced up, my hopes flaring again. Nathan looked troubled. "Slowly, remember? Slowly."

But all I heard was the *maybe* he did not have to say.

I'd forgotten about the doctor, but of course Nathan had not, and that afternoon, he was home early from work, Dr. Walter Berry in tow.

Dr. Berry was nearly as wide as he was tall, the buttonholes of his vest strained so it looked like a breath might pop the buttons loose to go rolling across the floor. He was gray and balding, with muttonchops and a thick mustache, as if to make up for what wasn't on his head, and round spectacles perching on a rather bulbous nose.

"My cough is really so much better," I protested. "I hardly notice it at all."

"Whatever possessed you to go out so late in the evening, Mrs. Langley?" he asked, peering into my face as if he were searching for the secrets of the Egyptians.

"An enjoyable play," I told him. "Good company."

"My wife often has trouble remembering that things have consequences," Nathan put in.

I looked at him over Dr. Berry's head. "Lately I've been such a recluse that it seemed impossible to consider them."

Dr. Berry took my wrist, feeling for my pulse, which obliged by fluttering and leaping. He frowned and looked at me. "Have you been nervous recently, Mrs. Langley?"

"I've recently moved to a new town, Doctor. I admit there are times I've been anxious."

"Have you taken laudanum?"

I shook my head.

The doctor sat back and considered me. "You might want to try a few drops in the evening to quiet your nerves, and also for your cough. In fact, I consider it quite necessary."

"Well, for the cough I will oblige you," I said. "But I'm already feeling so much better."

"You must not overdo it, Mrs. Langley. Rest is the best prescription."

"I'm afraid I won't have much time for rest these next months."

The doctor frowned. "You should curtail your charity work and your functions, madam, or I cannot guarantee a good outcome."

"But I've so much to do. And I've spent so many months already resting. I vow I'm quite tired of it."

"My wife was very active in the arts when we were in Chicago," Nathan said smoothly. "And she has hoped to do the same here."

Dr. Berry's frown intensified. "I cannot advise it."

Before I could respond, Nathan said with a smile, "She's discovered a new playwright, doctor, and I'm afraid there's no gainsaying my wife when she discovers new talent. The rage to present it to the world is quite . . . unstoppable. I myself am only grateful that her despondency these last months has seemingly passed."

"I see." The doctor put his stethoscope in his black bag and took out a small brown bottle. The laudanum he'd spoken of. He handed it to me and rose. "Well, Mrs. Langley, my advice remains the same. Rest."

"I appreciate your concern, Doctor. I do. But activity is the best remedy for a restless mind, is it not?" I waited while Nathan showed him to the door. I heard their low murmurs, the clap of one man's hand upon another's shoulder, and then the door closing, and Nathan's footsteps back to the parlor.

"Are you reassured as to my health?" I asked.

"I only wanted to be certain the cough was not something worse," Nathan said. "And as you aren't as ill as I'd feared, I've a surprise for you."

"A surprise?" I gave him a wary look.

"I spoke to Greene today. He would be delighted to have you join his company for the production of *Penelope Justis*."

I stared at him uncomprehendingly. I could not possibly have heard him correctly.

He frowned. "Did you not hear me, Ginny?"

"You . . . you want me to take to the stage?"

"Well, no, I don't want it," he said. "But as you seem to have your heart set upon it—"

"But what about Papa? And . . . you said it was too fast," I said.

"I changed my mind. You're right about the financial benefit, and Reading did it, after all, why not you? Perhaps his support will bring in the rest of society, as you said. And I'll deal with your father. He did put you into my hands, and as this is my decision, he can't complain."

"But . . . what of your concerns? Your political career. Appearances?"

He smiled grimly. "What I'm more concerned with now is money. In this town, it matters more than what society thinks, and there's no business leader who doesn't respect it. Make me a fortune with this play, Ginny, and I'll be looking at a city council seat before the end of the year." He frowned. "I did think you'd be happy at the news. If you're not, I can tell Greene to—"

"No!" I jumped from the settee, rushing into his arms. His reasons seemed good enough, whatever else had moved him, I had no wish to protest. Nathan had used me before to gain what he wanted, and this at least was what I yearned for. I took it in the spirit of a gift, a promise, the compromise he'd spoken of. "Oh thank you, Nathan! You cannot know how glad this makes me."

"Oh, I've some idea," he said, holding me briefly before he let me go. "You're to meet Mr. Greene the day after tomorrow. Nine-thirty A.M."

"Does Mr. DeWitt know?"

"I've no idea."

"I hope I can do it justice. Certainly I can do better than that wretched blonde who was in *Black Jack*. Don't you think?"

Nathan moved away from me and toward the decanters on the sideboard. "Oh, I've no doubt that you will simply overwhelm them."

Beatrice

We'd been rehearsing *Penelope Justis* for a week when Brody waylaid me as I went to dress for that night's performance. "Lucius is looking for you. He's in his office."

I sighed. Whatever it was Lucius wanted, I wasn't in the mood to hear it. I was tired; Nathan had come twice this last week and kept me up late, and the other nights I'd spent memorizing lines for more than just *Penelope Justis,* because we were also doing *The Last Days of Pompeii,* and though we'd done it often, I'd never before played the Grecian slave girl.

I made my way down the narrow, obstacled hall toward his office and knocked on the door. "Lucius? It's Bea. Brody said you wanted to see me?"

There was a moment of silence, and then Lucius said, "Come in," in a rather labored voice that was unlike him.

At his desk, Lucius looked as tired as I felt, his hair standing on end as if he'd run his hands through it. There were none of his usual bad puns or references to honeybees. He only looked at me consideringly, which made me nervous, you know, because Lucius was always so full of bluster that it was his quiet you had to beware of.

He said, "I'm making a change to *Penelope*."

I frowned. "All right. But why tell me? Where's Mr. DeWitt?"

"It's not in the writing, Bea. I'm making a change in the casting. Miss Jenks will go to Delia and the traveling parts. You'll be playing Marjory."

"Marjory?" I stared at him in disbelief. "You're joking!"

"Alas, I'm not."

"It's that bitch Stella, isn't it? She wants to come back, doesn't she? Well, she can't have Penelope!" I slapped my hands flat upon his desk. Papers poufed and fell. "What happened? Did her tour fall apart? Let her go someplace else then! She can't have Penny! She's mine! She was written for *me*!"

"Bea." Lucius put up his hand. "It's not Stella."

"Then who?"

"Langley came to me this morning."

I was bewildered. "What has he to do with it?"

"It appears he'd prefer someone else in the part."

It was as if he were speaking some foreign language. I'd just seen Nathan the night before last, and he'd said nothing of this. There couldn't be another actress he'd taken a fancy to—he'd fucked me into the early hours just as he always did and told me he'd see me later in the week. I'd seen nothing different in him. I was confused; none of it made sense. "Nathan doesn't want me to play Penelope? But . . . he's the one who bought the play for me."

Lucius squirmed. "Yes, well, it appears he's changed his mind. He's asked that we tutor his wife in the theatrical arts. And he wants her to play Penelope."

"His *wife*?"

"Apparently Mrs. Langley has a hankering to set her foot upon the stage."

"Let her go somewhere else then! Why didn't you say no?"

"Does anyone ever say no to Nathan Langley, I wonder? Do you?"

"I don't believe this."

"He paid me five hundred dollars to have her here. Should I have turned it down?"

"Yes, that's exactly what you should have done!"

"Why, when I've leaped to implement his every other suggestion?" Lucius gave me a bitter smile. "And you were happy enough to take advantage of it a few days ago."

"God *damn* you for a faithless swine, Lucius! You can't do this to me!"

"It's not me doing this to you, my darling. It's your paramour. He's most convincing."

"You could have given her another part."

"Langley said this one. He bought it, after all. He can decide who plays it."

"Mr. DeWitt will never stand for this."

"DeWitt will do what I tell him," Lucius said wearily. "Just as you will. Go home, Bea. Learn Marjory's lines. If you see Susan, send her to me."

"Lucius . . ." I was pleading now. "Lucius, you can't. This was to be my debut. I've waited for this so long. . . ."

"It's only a few weeks, and then you'll have your debut."

A few weeks. Anything could happen in a few weeks, and given Lucius's nature and Nathan's damned inconsistency, it no doubt would.

Lucius waved his hand at me in dismissal. "I am sorry, my dear. But I've no doubt you'll recover. If you're angry, have it out with your lover and not with me."

I went, but only because I was afraid of what I would say if I stayed. I hated Nathan for paying off Lucius to bring his wife here. I hated the silly wife whose whim had cost me the part I meant to be brilliant in. I hated Lucius for his grasping disloyalty.

And I hated how helpless I was. There was not one thing I

could do other than leave the troupe, which was no choice at all. If I had my own company . . . *but you don't, do you? And it's only a few weeks.* Only a few weeks.

It was small consolation. When Susan came into the dressing room later, she was as downcast as I. "We'll make her life a misery, Bea. She won't want to stay beyond a first rehearsal."

I smiled wanly at her and let her chatter away about Mrs. Langley and Lucius's perfidity and the unfairness of it all, and though it helped that she was miserable too, it didn't help enough. When I heard my cue at the beginning of the second act and went onstage, I saw Nathan sitting in the box, and my anger erupted so quickly and fiercely it was all I could do to stay in character.

When the play was over, I nearly ripped off my gown. I scrubbed the powder and rouge and kohl from my face so hard I reddened my skin. I dressed quickly. I had no intention of waiting for Nathan. I stepped out the door, slamming it behind me, and nearly barreled into Sebastian DeWitt, who was waiting on the other side.

He caught my arm. "Mrs. Wilkes, if I might have a word. . . ."

I said, "Did Lucius tell you?"

"Yes." He looked miserable. "I'm sorry."

"I take that to mean you didn't fight for me," I said bitterly.

"It wouldn't have mattered if I had. Langley bought the play. I can't just take it back."

"Yes, of course." I jerked from his hold. "It would have cost you fifty dollars."

"Yes, there is that," he said.

"To stand by one's principles is often costly."

"A pretty thought, coming from you." He glanced down the hall and then leaned close to whisper, "Here comes our benefactor now. How much were your principles worth, Mrs. Wilkes? What did Langley pay for them?"

I nearly snapped at him again. I remembered just in time that he wasn't the one I was angry with. It wasn't DeWitt's fault that Nathan had kowtowed to his wife, just as it wasn't his fault that Lucius would have sold his own mother for ready cash. Then I saw Nathan, striding down the hallway with all that *aplomb,* just so composed and rich, and I wanted to throw something. Instead I spun on my heel and pushed past the other backdoor Johnnies lingering in the hall, hurrying in the other direction, toward the stairs on the opposite side of the stage.

Nathan was on me in moments. He jerked me around to face him. "Come," he said, his voice smooth, brooking no argument. "My driver's waiting."

"I'm not going anywhere with you tonight."

He smiled, but I saw the force behind it. "I can either take you down that hallway kicking and screaming, or you'll come with me as if you want to. Your choice."

He grabbed my arm and led me back down the hallway. I could not make myself look at DeWitt as we passed; I pretended he didn't exist. I went with Nathan up the stairs to the back door. The carriage was waiting.

When we started off, I said, "I only came with you to keep from embarrassing my friends. You can leave me at my door. I don't want you to come up."

"Don't be unreasonable."

"We had an agreement," I said angrily. "You told me the part was mine."

"I'll buy you another play."

"This one was written for *me*."

Nathan shrugged. "I'll ask DeWitt to write another one for you. A better one. You'd like that, wouldn't you?"

My eyes went blurry with disappointment and frustration. I thought of running lines in my room with Sebastian DeWitt, the way he'd spoken of passion. "You don't understand. I waited so long for this. And I was going to be . . . I was going to be brilliant."

"Geneva won't stand in the way of that. It's only a few weeks. After that, believe me, we won't have to worry about her again." Nathan reached for a box. I knew before he handed it to me what it would be. He smiled. "There now, my dear. Forgive me?"

And my anger burst over me again. Before I knew what I was doing or could tell myself I was the worst of idiots for doing it, I shoved the box back at him. "I don't want your damned candy."

Just then the carriage stopped before my building. I opened

the door without waiting for the driver, and I was out before Nathan had a chance to stop me. I was inside the door of the hotel and halfway up the first flight of stairs before I heard him cursing behind me, before I realized he'd followed me, and then, suddenly, I was frightened. I picked up my skirts and began to run up the stairs, thinking I could make it to my door and inside before he got to me, but he was so damn fast, and he didn't have a corset or skirts to hold him back either.

He reached me before I was halfway up the second flight. He didn't say anything; just wrapped his hand around my arm to slow me, and then he propelled me up those steps. I didn't struggle—there was no point. When we got to my door, he nearly threw me inside and locked the door behind us.

The last few days had been hot, and my room was sweltering, in spite of the fact that I'd left the window open. I was sweating already as I stumbled against the bed and turned to face him. I was breathing hard, and the damned tears were back. "Leave me alone! Go home to your wife. She's the one who has something to thank you for." Stupid, very stupid, but I was so angry. "When she's gone, you can come back."

I knew before the words were out of my mouth that I'd made a mistake—not that I hadn't known what was coming for me the second he'd followed me up those stairs, and you'd think I would have been smart enough to keep my mouth shut.

Nathan was on me in two steps, gripping my wrist, twisting it back so I couldn't fight, so I had to fall on the bed, where he wanted me.

I heard myself pleading, "Nathan, please," but he pulled up my skirts and tore off my drawers, shoving his knee between my legs. The look in his eyes frightened me. When I fought him, he slapped me, not hard, but it stunned me, and in that moment he jammed himself into me.

His breath was hot on my face. I tried to buck him off, but he said, "That's right, you little whore, fight me," and I saw it excited him and that was when I went still. I lay there and my face stung and he just kept pounding away, rougher than he'd ever been, almost as if he hated me as much as I hated him just then.

When he collapsed on me, I didn't even give him a second. I pushed at him. "Get off me, you son of a bitch."

But, you know, he was so much bigger. I couldn't budge him. It was as if he didn't feel me or hear me, and I had the sense that he meant to show me he would have his own will or none. He lay there for a moment more, guising his control over me in lovemaking. He kissed my jaw and stroked my hair. His hand ran over my bare hip.

I was not going to give in. But he just kept touching me, kissing me, urging me, murmuring, "Come, little puss, don't be angry," and really all I wanted was for him to be gone, and so I sighed and turned my face so he could kiss me properly, and it was only then, after he'd ravaged my mouth and I thought with dismay that he meant to fuck me again, that he got off me.

He fastened the trousers he had not even taken off, and I lay there and turned my face so I didn't have to look at him.

"It won't be for long, you know. A few weeks—maybe less. No one will even see the damn thing. Ginny's stupid whim, but it won't get her where she expects." He laughed meanly. "You'll have it back soon enough."

"Go to hell," I said.

His voice went tight. "I'll commission a new play from DeWitt. One even better than this one."

I heard him reach for something, the box of candy I'd left on the bureau. He laid it on the bed so my fingers brushed it. "Here, take an apricot. I know how much you love them. I'll have my driver bring up the other box. I'll see you never lack for them. I'll fill this room with them, if that's what you wish."

"Go away, Nathan," I managed. "Please just go away."

"As you wish. I'll see you tomorrow then."

I was stunned—and relieved—when he said nothing more, when it seemed he would do what I asked. I heard him open the door and go out. I waited until his footsteps were gone.

Then I pulled myself up and pushed my skirt back down over my legs, and sat against the headboard and ran my fingers over my face. If he'd left a bruise, I would kill him. It was too damn hard to cover with makeup. I glanced at the box of glacéed fruit, and its pretty pink cover mocked me as if to say: this is what you traded for, apricots plumped in syrup, and along with that I heard Sebastian DeWitt's words: *"How much were your principles worth, Mrs. Wilkes? What did Langley pay for them?"* and I grabbed the box, meaning to throw it against the wall.

But I didn't. Instead, I pulled out one of those gleaming, glistening apricots and shoved the whole damn thing into my mouth.

Chapter Thirteen

Geneva

I dressed to go to the Regal Theater with a thrill of excitement. I had awakened early that morning, still not believing I was truly to take my place upon that stage, to speak Sebastian DeWitt's sublime words. I'd half expected Nathan to come to my room this morning and laugh it all away as some joke. But as I'd watched the sun come up, my mind presented vision after vision of what might await me there, how the other actors would greet me, how I would end the day with new friends. I wrote a letter to my father about the play and my hopes for Sebastian DeWitt, sprinkling in a few comments about Nathan's kindness, but even that did not take long. By the time I put the finishing touches to my toilette, my nerves were prickling with agitation. The minutes were moving too slowly; I was afraid to be too early, afraid to be late.

There was a soft knock on my door. Bonnie called from the hallway, "Ma'am, Mr. DeWitt's come calling."

The sound of his name was a pleasant little shock. I had not expected him. I glanced at the clock—it was a little before nine. Early for any sort of visit, but he must know by now about my acting experiment. No doubt he was as excited as I.

I glanced about for the butterfly hairpins—they would go well with the watered bronze silk of my gown, and I wanted the extra sparkle to reflect my joy, but I could find them nowhere, and finally I substituted pins with diamond and citron and went downstairs to meet Mr. DeWitt.

He turned from the window when I said, "Mr. DeWitt, what a pleasure to see you this morning."

He did not smile, which took me aback a bit, but then I decided he must be restraining his own excitement, and I went to him, holding out my hands. He took my fingers in his, and a smile did touch his lips then, and I was reassured.

"Would you like some tea?" I asked. "Although I am rather in a rush. I'm to be at the theater at nine-thirty."

"Yes, I know. I understand you're to act in *Penelope*."

I laughed. "Indeed yes. I hope you are as thrilled as I."

"Have you discussed this with your husband?"

"Of course. Nathan can't help but see the advantage."

"What advantage is that?"

"Why, we both think it will bring society out in force to see your play."

"They won't be coming to see my play," he said. "They'll be coming to see you."

"Yes," I agreed. "But what does it matter what brings them there? They won't be able to deny your genius. What better way to introduce you to the world?"

He seemed uncertain. In fact, his whole manner was a bit odd, not at all what I'd hoped.

I went on, "I've always wanted to try my hand at acting. Do you remember the other night?"

"You wanted to act in a play," he said. "Eat fish and speak of socialism."

"You *do* remember!" I said with delight.

He looked away, obviously uncomfortable, and that was what finally stabbed through my happiness and made me pause.

"Is something wrong, Mr. DeWitt?"

His gaze was direct. "I'm surprised your husband arranged for this, Mrs. Langley, and I can't believe he's thought it through completely. In fact, I've come today to ask you to reconsider."

It took a moment for his words to fully register, and when they did I frowned at him. "You're concerned for my reputation, no doubt. Please let me reassure you that I have little reputation to lose."

He shook his head impatiently. "The other actors—"

"Oh, I know I haven't their experience, and I don't wonder that you might think I haven't the skill to play Penelope. But I understand her so well, Mr. DeWitt. Truly. And you could help me, couldn't you, if you think I'm going in a wrong direction? I know I could do it."

"You may be right. That's not the reason I ask you to withdraw."

I was confused. "Then what is your reason? I would have thought you would be happy at such an opportunity—"

"I appreciate your intention. I do. But . . ." He paused. "I thought you said your talent was in bringing artists to light."

"Yes, of course. But I suppose it's possible to have more than one talent, isn't it? I mean to find out if acting might be another."

Again the quick glance away. "The play is already in production, and has been so for a week at least. You won't endear yourself to the other actors by coming in this way."

"Ah," I said quietly. "Now I see. You think it would offend them."

"Perhaps . . . some of them."

"You mean the blonde already holds the part. But how can she possibly do your words justice?"

"Fortunately, Stella Bernardi has left the Regal."

"Oh good. Then there's nothing to worry about, is there? As far as the others go, I believe you underestimate me. I've charmed Sarah Bernhardt. Edwin Booth was a guest at my home each time he was in Chicago. I don't think a Seattle company . . . well, I suspect we will all be friends quite quickly. We'll be drinking wine together by the end of the week, I promise you."

"Mrs. Langley, this play isn't just an opportunity for you—"

"I realize that. I've already told you; it's not for my benefit that I do this, but yours. And I vow I'll be on my best behavior, if that's what worries you. I will win them over, you know."

"I've no doubt of that, but—"

"I won't embarrass you, Mr. DeWitt. I value your friendship. I would never do anything to harm it."

That made him pause. He considered me with those strange eyes for a moment, and then he sighed and smiled—not so broad as he could, or had, but enough that I suddenly realized how tight was my stomach, how much his approval meant to me already. "I value your friendship as well, Mrs. Langley."

His words warmed me. "Do you think . . . might I ask you a favor, Mr. DeWitt, in the true spirit of friendship? Will you come with me to meet Mr. Greene this morning, if you've no other obligations? I confess I'm a bit nervous. It would comfort me to have you there."

"As it happens, I was on my way there myself. For rehearsal. I'm making revisions."

"Revisions? But it's quite brilliant as it is. Surely Mr. Greene can't want to change too much."

He made a face. "I imagine that remains to be seen."

"I cannot think how discouraging that must be, to have your words be at the mercy of lesser men. I've always thought criticism to be the bane of artists."

"I should say it was reality instead. And necessity."

"In any case, the play is perfect as it is."

"Perfection too is in the eye of the beholder." He held out his arm. "Shall we go then? You don't want to be late."

I placed my hand in the crook of his arm, and together we went to the waiting carriage. With him beside me, my nerves quieted. We spoke of small things on the journey to the theater. I think he saw how strung tight I was and thought to put me at ease. But when the carriage finally pulled up in front of the theater, my nerves flared again. I was almost giddy. "Oh, I can hardly believe I mean to do this!"

He said, "I can hardly believe it myself."

We went in through the parquet door, which led to the back of the theater, into rows of empty seats, cast into darkness. But on the stage, the footlights were lit, and men shouted back and forth to one another as they painstakingly painted a canvas backdrop suspended from hooks. A backdrop for *my* play, I realized, and felt that stabbing little thrill of excitement again that caught my breath and made me cough a little—the lingering residue of my cold—and Sebastian DeWitt stopped and looked over his shoulder. "Greene will be waiting for you," he said. "This way."

He led me down the aisle between the seats, and up the few steps to the stage, and then ducked behind the curtains flanking it. I followed. The backstage was in near darkness, barely held within the periphery of the lamps onstage, and the heavy curtains did their part to keep out the light as well. Dim shapes of props and sets loomed before me as Mr. DeWitt took my arm and led me to the stairs, narrow and falling into shadow, with a light glowing at the bottom.

They ended in a hall, musty, dim, dusty, and narrow, with doors lining either side and scenery and props leaning against the walls and creating a confusion of obstacles. I could not imagine there was an office down here, but Mr. DeWitt was not the least hesitant, and finally we came to it. There was a key box on one side and a row of narrow boxes with names scratched beneath each on the other, and on the door was painted in black: LUCIUS GREENE, MANAGER.

Mr. DeWitt knocked sharply on the door. "Greene? It's Sebastian DeWitt. With Mrs. Langley."

"Come in, come in!" The voice came from the depths of the office, and it was booming and welcoming.

Mr. DeWitt opened the door and stepped aside to let me precede him, and I was face-to-face with the manager of the Regal Theater.

He was dressed rather flamboyantly, in a coat of an earthy reddish color and a satin vest of purple. His thick brown hair stood up on his head, and his mustache was waxed at the tips, and everything about him, even the way he moved, was theatrical, as if he'd been nursed not on mother's milk but on the very essence of the stage instead.

Mr. DeWitt introduced us, and I smiled and said, "Mr. Greene, I am very pleased to meet you."

"And I you, madam." Mr. Greene came around the edge of

the desk, nearly colliding with a dressmaker's dummy clad in a red satin cape. He reached for my hand and made a little bow over it. "As I told your husband, Mrs. Langley, I had thought that the leading role would fit you, but now that I've seen you I must say I'm overwhelmed at how perfect it is! Do you not think so, DeWitt?"

"She looks the part indeed," said Mr. DeWitt smoothly.

Mr. Greene fumbled with the papers on his desk, pulling forth a sheaf bound with a tie. "Ah, here it is." He handed it to me. "*Penelope Justis, or Revenge of the Spirit.* A spectacle to end all spectacles! That is the script—well, not in its entirety, you understand, but the pages containing your lines."

"I shall devote my evening to them," I told him.

"Just so, just so. The rest of the company has been rehearsing for a week or so, but you should have no trouble catching up. We will need you here every morning at ten, Mrs. Langley, for the next few weeks."

I nodded, trying to contain my excitement. "I look forward to the challenge, Mr. Greene, but I do hope you all will be kind."

"Mrs. Langley has enthusiasm rather than experience, you realize," Mr. DeWitt told Mr. Greene.

"Yes, of course, of course," Mr. Greene said quickly. "Our company is delighted to host her." He took a rather ornate watch from his pocket. "In fact, they should be gathered now for rehearsal. Will you come and meet them, Mrs. Langley?"

"Oh yes. Yes indeed." I could hardly wait to make them my friends.

"You've a few hours to work with us, I hope. Time is of the essence in the theater."

This, I had not expected. I glanced at Sebastian DeWitt, who raised a brow and said, "She's barely looked at the script."

Mr. Greene led the way from his office. "No matter, no matter. My dear Mrs. Langley, you shall work from the book as long as you like. As long as you know the lines by the night of our performance, I shall have no complaints."

I nodded, and Mr. DeWitt and I followed him to the stage.

"Children! Children!" boomed Mr. Greene as we stepped upon it to see a group of people milling about. At Mr. Greene's words, they quieted and looked up, some of them looking past him to me, their gazes curious. "Here is our most special guest, whom I mentioned to you all yesterday. Mrs. Nathan Langley, who will be playing Penelope Justis from this point on. I know you will greet her with open arms, and we will all be a merry family!"

I stepped forward. "Good morning to you all. Thank you so much for this opportunity. I'm so pleased to meet you, and I trust we shall become great friends."

There was a pause. It was uncomfortable and puzzling; I had the distinct sense they were waiting for something. One or two of them looked to a woman with hair as dark as mine, loosely coiled at the nape of her neck, pin-straight strands escaping. She had pale skin, and she was trim and neat, clad in brown broadcloth. She met my glance; I was taken aback by the venom in her dark eyes.

"Perhaps you could be the first to welcome Mrs. Langley, Bea," said Mr. Greene, and even on such short acquaintance, I recognized his tone; there was no brooking the request.

The woman smiled, showing even white teeth, incisors a bit too long, but her smile was about as welcoming as that of an attacking dog. She sauntered forward—saucy, no, more than that, insolent—and held out a limp hand. "Mrs. Langley. I'm Beatrice Wilkes. I'll be playing . . . your servant. Marjory."

She did not like me; that was clear, and I had no idea why. But I took her hand and smiled and said, "I saw you in *Black Jack*. You were Sweet Polly's sister. You have a lovely singing voice."

She nodded as if the compliment were no more than expected and wearying at that, and stepped back, and I saw the way she looked at Mr. Greene—again with a bit of insolence, and I wondered why he didn't chastise her, but then the others came forward as if they'd been waiting for her to make the first overture, and I found myself overwhelmed with names and faces, some of which I remembered from *Black Jack*. Mr. Wheeler, for example, and Mr. Metairie, who had made such a superb villain, and Mrs. Chace, who was so corpulent it was difficult to forget her figure upon the stage. The others were kind, though more reserved than I hoped. I told myself it didn't matter. This was only our first meeting. I would do my best to win their affection. I was confident that soon we would find ourselves gathered together after rehearsal to discuss art and philosophy over a few glasses of wine.

"Shall we begin then, children?" Mr. Greene called out. "Act one, scene one, for Mrs. Langley."

Mr. DeWitt touched my arm and leaned close to whisper, "Courage, Mrs. Langley," as if he knew how quickly my nervousness had bloomed again, and then he and Mr. Greene and Mr. Geary went to the table set to the side of the stage. The others spread out. Mrs. Chace sat laboriously on a riser; Mr. Metairie and the young man whose name I could not remember sat on a settee just off to the side, and Mr. Wheeler sighed and lay down on the floor near the edge of the stage, spreading out his legs and closing his eyes as if he meant to go to sleep.

"We'll start with Penelope's entrance, stage right, upstage," Mr. Geary said.

The right side of the stage nearest the audience, I supposed, and I crossed to go there.

"Stage right," Mr. Geary corrected with a gesture.

"Oh." I paused. "It's quite the opposite then."

From the floor, Mr. Wheeler laughed.

"Stage directions are as you look at the audience, madam," Mr. Geary explained patiently.

"Perhaps you should give her a primer, Lucius," said Mrs. Wilkes. "So we aren't all wasting our time."

"An excellent idea," said Mr. Greene acidly. "Perhaps you'd care to be her tutor, my dear, and show Mrs. Langley the blocking for this scene?"

Mrs. Wilkes clamped her lips together tightly. Rigidly, she pointed toward the back wall of the stage. "*That* is upstage, Mrs. Langley." She marched to the spot. "We're at the funeral of your dear sister Florence. I don't imagine even you will find it too difficult to pretend to listen to a sermon."

I chose to ignore her rudeness. I was determined to make this woman my friend—of all of them, I knew she and Mr. Metairie were the most talented, and therefore the most worthy of my attention. I went to where she stood and smiled. "Thank you, Mrs. Wilkes."

"And now"—Geary rapped his hand upon the table—"Townshend, the line is yours."

The young man barely glanced up from where he sat on the settee with Mr. Metairie. " 'Ashes to ashes, dust to—' "

"It *is* to be a waterfall, right, Lucius?" yelled a man from behind the curtain. "Not a stream?"

" '—dust,' " Mr. Townshend went on. " 'In sure and certain hope of the Resurrection into eternal life.' "

"Not a stream," Mr. Greene called back. "A quite large waterfall."

"Twenty feet up good enough?"

"Mr. Townshend has given you your cue, Mrs. Langley," Mr. Geary said above the noise. "The next line is yours."

The next line. I fumbled with the script; the pages slipped apart, some of them falling to the floor. I bent to retrieve them and heard Mrs. Wilkes's loud sigh of exasperation, and she said, "Mrs. Langley, the line is: 'My poor dear sister, struck down in the bloom of youth!' "

It was the way she said it, with assurance and theatrical intonations—a quite different voice from her usual—as if she'd practiced it many times, that gave me pause. I remembered what Sebastian DeWitt had said, how the company had already been rehearsing the play for some days, how my coming might offend them. Suddenly I felt uneasy.

I picked up the pages and rose. " 'My dear sister, struck down so young.' "

" 'My *poor dear* sister, struck down in the *bloom of youth*,' " Mrs. Wilkes corrected impatiently.

Mr. Galloway said, " 'How could my dear girl be gone?' "

I glanced down at the pages in my hand. I could not find the words Mr. Galloway said anywhere.

"You say: 'How fragile she was! How well she believed Barnabus Cadsworth's lies,' " Mrs. Wilkes filled in.

I looked at her. A suspicion began to grow in my mind. I tried to smile. "You know the lines so well."

Mr. Geary threw up his hands in exasperation. "Please, Mrs. Langley—"

Mrs. Wilkes's eyes narrowed. "Yes, of course I do. This is how I make a living, Mrs. Langley." She spoke as if I could not hope to understand, and her contempt for me colored every syllable.

"Children!" Mr. Greene said. "Your line, Bea."

" 'Miss Penny,' " said Mrs. Wilkes, but this time in a simpering voice—Marjory's no doubt—" 'do not grieve so. She is gone to a better place.' "

The line dropped into silence. I glanced down again at the pages, shuffling through them. "They're out of order. Please, if you'll give me just a moment to right them—"

" 'Oh, Marjory, I pray heaven loves her as well as we have,' " went on Mrs. Wilkes, not missing a pause, the tempered voice she'd used before, and then she dropped again into the simpering voice, " 'I am sure of it, miss, and the little unborn child too.' " Then again to the Penelope voice, " 'Did he know of it, do you think? Did he know of the child he got on my sister before he abandoned her?' "

Miss Jenks burst into laughter. From the floor, Mr. Wheeler said, "Perhaps we should do *Jekyll and Hyde* next, Lucius. Bea would be sheer perfection in the role."

"I only asked for a moment," I said to Mrs. Wilkes. I was angry now, though I made an effort to speak politely.

"I'd hoped to get through the scene in less than two hours," she said coolly.

Mr. DeWitt said, "Greene, perhaps it would be better to give Mrs. Langley a chance to study the script before you throw her to the wolves."

"I had not thought the landscape so infested," Mr. Greene said drily. "But I think DeWitt is right. Mrs. Langley, please come and sit down. Here, we have a chair just for you. As for the rest . . . we'll go to act two, scene one, where Barnabus vows to take the sweet Delia as his own."

I was more than grateful, both for Mr. DeWitt's suggestion and to deliver myself from my proximity to Mrs. Wilkes before I lost my temper. This was not what I'd wanted or intended. I retreated to the table. When Mr. Greene turned his attention back to the rehearsal, I leaned to whisper to Mr. DeWitt, "Thank you for coming to my rescue."

He nodded. "I had told you they might not welcome you."

"I did not imagine they would be quite so. . . ." I let my words trail off, alarmed to find that my eyes had filled with tears.

Mr. DeWitt's hand covered mine, a gentle squeeze. "They'll learn to like you as much as I do, Mrs. Langley."

"I wonder."

"They will," he whispered. "Don't let her disconcert you."

I glanced at the actors who had made my first foray among them so difficult—at Mrs. Wilkes especially, and I found myself saying quietly, "You said the company had been rehearsing this play for a week. Who had the part of Penelope before me?"

Mr. DeWitt paused. Then he said, "I think you must already know."

He was right; I did know. It was clear that Mrs. Wilkes had had the part before me, and that she'd thought to keep it. I understood why she disliked me. I understood why she was angry, and as Sebastian DeWitt went back to his pen, I glanced up to see her staring at me, her eyes like cold little stones, and I wondered how I would ever make this up to her.

I was already at dinner when Nathan returned home that evening.

"Forgive my tardiness, my dear," he said, pouring a glass of wine and taking roast onto his plate.

I told him, "Mr. Greene insisted I attend a rehearsal today."

"Ah yes. The theater. I'd forgotten. How was it—as scintillating as you'd hoped?"

I took a sip of wine. "I'm afraid I stumbled a bit. I had not thought . . . the part of Penelope had already been given to someone else. A Mrs. Wilkes. Do you know her?"

"Mrs. Wilkes. I know of her, of course."

"She was quite angry."

He shrugged. "She'll adjust, I imagine. Greene won't tolerate it otherwise, regardless of what right she feels she has to the role."

"What right she has to it? What do you mean?"

"DeWitt wrote it for her, I understand."

My appetite left me completely. I put down my fork. "Mr. DeWitt wrote *Penelope Justis* for Beatrice Wilkes?"

Nathan glanced up. "I believe so. Is something wrong?"

"Dear God, he said nothing of that. I hadn't realized . . ." I could not help my distress. "Why didn't he tell me she was the muse he'd spoken of?"

"Why would he?" Nathan frowned. "What does it matter?"

I barely heard him. "That explains everything."

"Everything? What happened?"

"Nothing. At least nothing that isn't completely understandable."

"Should I say something to Greene?"

"Please don't. I'll find a way to make it up to Mrs. Wilkes. Perhaps I'll buy her a gift."

Nathan paused in taking a bite. "I've heard she has a sweet tooth."

"Oh, I think something useful instead. She can't make much money at the Regal, and she's certainly not a star. If I could think of a way to help her . . ."

Nathan made a noncommittal sound.

I picked up my wine again. Beatrice Wilkes was Sebastian DeWitt's muse. I'd thought her the most talented of the company, but still, she was so . . . common. Nothing as I'd imagined the actress who'd inspired such divine words to be. Shouldn't muses be so much more vibrant and charismatic? I saw none of that in her, but perhaps. . . . No sweetheart or wife, he'd told me. Still . . .

As casually as I could, I said, "Are they lovers, do you think—she and Mr. DeWitt?"

Nathan said, "Oh, I hardly think so. She's an actress, isn't she? Aren't they all looking for rich patrons? He can't make enough money to interest her."

"I must admit I'd be surprised. She doesn't seem his sort."

"Hmmm. Well, she must have a charm you're blind to."

"I suppose."

Nathan said, "By the way, at the club today, a friend of mine expressed some interest in your theater experiment. He'd thought of trying such a thing himself. Reading seems to have started an epidemic. I told him he might watch a rehearsal."

I blinked at the change in subject. "You should have him speak to James Reading."

"Oh, I will. But he may wish to speak to you as well."

"Is he important?"

Nathan smiled. "Exceedingly so." He pulled his watch from his vest pocket and glanced at it, then pushed back his chair and rose, throwing his napkin down, leaving his dinner half-eaten. "Now you must forgive me, but I've an appointment. I shall be out quite late, I think. Don't wait up."

Chapter Fourteen

Beatrice

I was still angry when it came time to go to rehearsal the next morning, and tired as hell because I'd been up late studying the rest of Marjory's lines. There were fewer than I'd had as Penelope, of course, but still it took hours. By the time I went to bed, I was beginning to like the idea that I was playing the woman who put Penelope Justis into the hands of the villainous Barnabus Cadsworth, even if she didn't mean to. Now, if only the waterfall he dropped her from was real. . . .

Fortunately, Nathan hadn't shown up last night—I wasn't sure what I would have done if he had. After the performance, I'd found the box of candy I'd left in his carriage in my dressing room, along with some American Beauty roses—pricey things, those, and lovely, even if they had no scent—but no note, which was just as well, as I didn't want to forgive him yet, as stupid as that was, and I knew it, but I couldn't help it. His wife had been as insufferable as I could have predicted. I'd spent the entire rehearsal wondering if she knew about me and her husband, and I'd finally decided she didn't and toyed with the idea of telling her. Nathan hadn't said *not* to tell her, though what man wanted his wife to know about his mistress? It seemed stupid on his part, actually, to put us in the same room together. It would serve him right if I told her everything. But then I remembered how Nathan had slapped me, and I didn't want that either; I didn't want him angrier with me than he was already. He was a rich man, and he already had Lucius on his side, and to go against him directly was suicidal. But I wanted my revenge as well—on both of the Langleys, and I didn't need it to be explosive to be satisfying. I could be subtle enough if I tried.

When I showed up for rehearsal at ten, the scene painters were still working on the backdrop. The prompt table had been dragged out; now it was placed downstage near the footlights. There were three chairs, two of them spindly and the last one, which I recognized from Lucius's office, I knew was meant for Mrs. Langley. There was always a chair for a star, whenever we worked with one, but seeing that chair there for her . . . it made me angry all over again, so when Sebastian DeWitt appeared behind me suddenly with his "Good morning, Mrs. Wilkes," I snapped, "It's too damn hot to be a good morning—or don't you sweat like the rest of us?"

"'A serpent's tongue hid by a flowery face.'" Aloys fanned himself with a folded *Post-Intelligencer*. "What is it, Bea? Can't resist stinging such a pretty bud this morning?"

I sighed and smiled my best at Mr. DeWitt, who, thankfully, seemed stunned by it. "Forgive me. I'm not myself this morning."

Jackson said, "Who is? It is dreadfully hot."

"I fear I should quite shrivel up and blow away," Mrs. Chace said, plopping herself down on the edge of the stage, already red-faced, her grayed strawberry blond hair tumbling from its pins as if she'd walked twenty miles instead of a block and a half to get here.

"You've a bit more shriveling to go before that might happen, milady," Jackson said.

Brody chortled; it turned into a snort.

Mrs. Chace glared at him. She wiped her neck with her handkerchief. "Well, I feel quite *evaporated.*"

Mr. DeWitt went to the prop table and began laying out his pencils and pens. His fingers were already black with ink, as early as it was. Mr. Geary strutted onto the stage. "Are we quite ready, ladies and gentlemen? Where is our star?"

"Not here yet," Susan said.

"Maybe she'll send a maid to fill in for her," Brody said.

"We've got Bea for that. After all, she's Mrs. Langley's proxy in other ways." Jack guffawed.

In irritation, I said, "We can't start without her. She has lines on nearly every page. I don't know about the rest of you, but I've better things to do than wait around for someone who thinks she's a star when she hasn't a lick of. . . ." I trailed off as Jackson put his finger to his lips and shook his head, and then I heard Lucius's booming voice behind me.

"What 'better things' might that be, my dear? Have you decided against accepting the part of Marjory?"

I turned to see him emerging from the wings, Mrs. Langley behind him. "You'd fine any one of us for being this late."

"But Mrs. Langley hasn't signed a contract, and thus she has no idea of the rules, which are more precisely meant for actors who can't remember their place." Lucius smiled, but his eyes were fierce. I looked away—of course I did. Lucius was a money-grubbing toad, but I was here by his sufferance, and I should have known to expect nothing more. I was the fool who'd trusted him. And it wasn't really him I was angry with anyway.

"I *am* sorry. There was an accident on the road." Mrs. Langley came forward.

Said sincerely enough, though she had that infuriating society way about her that made me angry just on principle.

Lucius strode to the table. "Well, then, the day whiles away. Shall we begin?"

Mrs. Langley followed him. She took off her hat and reached

into her bag to pull out the script pages, though the rest of us had been off book for days now, and I waited for Lucius to tell her she couldn't use it. Of course he didn't, the hypocrite, just as he wouldn't fine her either—and no lack of contract had ever stopped him before, whatever he said.

Lucius called out the scene. The rehearsal was what all rehearsals were: studied exercises in chaos, but Mrs. Langley's inexperience forced us to rehearse scenes four or five times. I was torn between resenting that she was ruining the part I would have been so brilliant in, and taking delight in how she stumbled about the stage, in how stiffly she read the lines. At any other time, I would have found it amusing. Today, it only made me angrier.

Though Mrs. Langley could not know it, she was the victim of the company's merciless guying. There had never been so much stumbling, flubbing lines, or crossing up stage right and stage left. All meant to keep her confused. It didn't seem to faze her, actually; she had this smiling dignity that would have cowed lesser actors. But my fellows were bent on taking their revenge for me, and she didn't manage to guilt them into behaving. Lucius sat there simmering, but you know, what could he do when the whole company was in revolt?

"I do not think I can speak this line," Mrs. Chace called out, plopping herself down beside me where I sat on the edge of the stage. "I simply refuse to say it. Mrs. Cadsworth would never be so cruel as to not let Penelope rest!"

"She is a villain, madam," DeWitt said in exasperation.

"Still she is, in her heart, kind. I insist you rewrite the line. I shall say instead something like: 'My dear Miss Justis, you are weary. You must sit a spell.' And I shall say it standing to your left, Mrs. Langley."

DeWitt said, "She means to get Penny to her son before Keefe discovers them."

Mrs. Chace said, "Perhaps an accident could delay Keefe."

"There is no accident."

"It would erode a great deal of the tension, my dear, if you took time to rest during what is in essence a kidnapping," Aloys pointed out. "Speed is imperative. I am after all hoping not to be discovered as I wait to meet you. I cannot pace about the street forever without rousing suspicion."

"I cannot say it," Mrs. Chace said stubbornly.

"I'll be happy to take the line," I put in. "Perhaps Marjory could be secretly working against Penny."

Brody laughed beneath his hand.

DeWitt's sigh was loud and long-suffering. "It needs to be Mrs. Cadsworth's line. Marjory is racing back to tell Keefe what has happened. She cannot both be trying to find her brother and in town."

I gave him a bright look. "Perhaps you should rewrite it then. We could put a song in between, and no one would notice she was in two places at the same time."

"A brilliant idea, Bea," said Jackson. "That is exactly what you should do, DeWitt."

DeWitt jammed his face into his hands, threading his fingers through his hair. Mrs. Langley looked uncertain.

Lucius glared at me. "Shall we continue with the play as DeWitt wrote it, please?"

I shrugged. "Perhaps you should ask Mr. Langley's advice, Lucius. He's so good at *casting,* after all. Who knows but that he might be good at plotting as well?"

Mrs. Langley frowned.

Jackson whistled low between his teeth.

"Put away your stinger, Bea," Lucius said sourly. "Unless you're inclined to pay a forfeit, you will continue with the play as it is written."

I feigned offense. "You've allowed us to make suggestions before."

"Yes, when they were honest ones," he said. "Now carry on."

I knew when I'd pushed him far enough. I turned away and caught Jackson's eye. He winked at me, and I couldn't help smiling. But I didn't do anything else to stall the rehearsal. I didn't need to. Mrs. Langley's inexperience was doing enough all by itself.

She consistently moved to the wrong places; she was wedded to the script and spoke haltingly, her line readings all wrong—

twice Brody laughed out loud. Three times she walked right into stagehands moving things about, and once she stumbled into the backdrop so the painters complained—fortunately for her, the real painting was going on above, and she smudged nothing. By the time rehearsal was over, the rest of us only had two hours before we had to be back again.

When Lucius finally excused us, Mrs. Langley looked near tears. She spoke to no one as she shoved her script back into her matching bag and repinned her hat to her head, and no one spoke to her. At least, no one did until Sebastian DeWitt stepped up to her. I couldn't hear what they said, but she turned to him with a relieved smile and put her hand on his arm, and I realized with a little start that he was comforting her. *My* playwright, comforting the woman who'd made such a mess of the play he'd written for *me,* the woman who'd stolen it from both of us.

And that was when I put it together. Nathan's talking about his wife fawning over some artist. DeWitt saying he knew someone who could help us. It was her: Geneva Langley, and I was filled with a jealousy I didn't know what to do with—because why the hell should I be jealous? But I was, and when he smiled down at her and I saw how proprietary was her hand on his arm, I knew they were lovers. I thought of him in my room, running lines, the way he'd stretched, the thoughts I'd had, and I hated her more than ever.

When DeWitt turned away from her again, her smile was still there. He passed me as he left, and his voice was cold when he said, "Good afternoon, Mrs. Wilkes," and he was gone before I could reply.

I watched him go with dismay, feeling sick to my stomach, which, you know, wasn't a feeling I liked, and it didn't get any better when I turned to see Mrs. Langley suddenly beside me, holding a package wrapped in white paper, tied with a ribbon. "Mrs. Wilkes," she said. "I feel I must apologize."

"Apologize?"

"I didn't understand how disruptive my presence would be, or that Penelope was to be your part."

I stared wordlessly at her.

She smiled and held out the package to me. "I feel terrible

about it. I would like to amend the error. I hope you'll accept this as a token of my regret."

I glanced down at the package in her hand. It was rectangular and flat, the same size and shape as the boxes of candied fruit Nathan gave me, and it suddenly seemed so ridiculous, the same gift from both of them, that I could not prevent the bubble of laughter from coming up my throat. I choked it short.

She gave me a bewildered little frown. "Mrs. Wilkes?"

"Forgive me," I said bitterly. "Keep it for yourself, Mrs. Langley. I'm afraid I've grown tired of Parisian candy."

Her frown deepened. "Oh, it's not candy, Mrs. Wilkes."

She pushed it toward me insistently, and I found myself taking it, pulling at the ribbon, sliding my thumb beneath the white paper. The ribbon and the paper fell; what was beneath it was a blue patterned box. Inside were sheets of paper. Creamy, thick writing paper of the best quality, tied into place with a thin satin ribbon.

She said, "I thought you might have need of something nice."

Something nice. It brought my anger back like a flood, and I wanted to hurt her, to watch her flinch. It was all I could do to say in a flat voice, "Who do you imagine I would write to?"

She went still. I threw the box down onto a riser and walked into the wings, away from her and her useless gift, the stupid apology she'd offered as if it solved anything, and I hated her and the life that told her I might have need of fine writing paper when it was all I could do just to pay my rent, when the best meals I ate were at her husband's pleasure, where her mere whim could take everything I had away.

The Last Days of Pompeii was well received; it was a favorite, after all, with all its sulfurous smoke and spectacle. The hall by the greenroom was crowded as I pushed my way through it to the dressing room I still shared with Susan because Geneva Langley would be using Stella's old one.

Susan was wiping off her makeup with a towel, her brown hair tumbling down her back. She glanced at me in the mirror. "A good house tonight."

I nodded, grabbing at the pins that held the elaborate hairstyle

Lucius had determined was best for a Greek slave who'd once been a princess—ha! "They'll always come to *Pompeii*."

Susan said, "I didn't see your Mr. Langley in the crowd."

"No." I didn't want to think about "my" Nathan Langley. Or any Langley, for that matter. I took up a towel to wipe at my own makeup, threw it aside and undid the gold-painted laces binding the drape I wore, standing nearly naked before I grabbed my chemise from the hook and pulled it on, shaking my hair free. I reached for my corset.

There was a knock on the door.

"Who is it?" I called impatiently, hoping it wasn't Nathan's driver. I wanted no visitors. I was tired and dispirited, and I meant to go home.

"Sebastian." A pause. "DeWitt."

Susan threw me a knowing glance, which did not help at all. I remembered this morning, Mrs. Langley smiling at him, the chill of his good-bye to me, my belief that they were lovers, and I wondered if he'd come tonight to tell me he'd decided to take her side. *Now there's good work, Bea, to lose both the lead and the playwright before you've had them two weeks.*

"Come in," I called, and if I sounded nervous, well, I had good reason to be.

The door opened. He stepped inside, took in my state of undress, then, like any real playwright—not those who pretended to it, but those who'd spent their fair share of time about the stage—ignored it.

"Close the door," I said, pulling closed the hooks of my corset. And then I couldn't help testing just how close Mrs. Langley held him. "As long as you're here, you can tighten my laces." I turned my back to him so he could.

"How is the hallway, Mr. DeWitt?" Susan asked. She twisted on the bench, allowing her dressing gown to fall open a bit too obviously. "Is it quite crowded this evening?"

"It seems so." I felt his fingers at my back as he obediently, and with unexpected skill, tightened my laces.

"I think I'll go out and look for Tommy." Susan rose, winking at me as she did so. She flounced out of the room, leaving DeWitt and me alone.

I stepped away from him to get my dress and pulled it on. "Did you want something, Mr. DeWitt?" I hit the *want* as coyly as I could and hoped like hell he would flirt back. But instead he looked so damned serious.

"I wanted to speak with you."

I went to the mirror, grabbing up my brush. "About what?"

"I wanted to let you know that Langley commissioned me to write another play for you."

I was surprised, first that Nathan had done what he'd promised and sccond that he'd done it so quickly.

I set my brush down. "He did?"

"This afternoon. Summoned me to his office."

Quickly I coiled my long hair and pinned it up. "What did he say about it?"

"That I was to write a play. The only thing that mattered to him was that you were to have the main part."

"Hmmm. Did he already pay you?"

DeWitt regarded me steadily. "Yes. He's a generous patron. For both of us, it seems."

"Indeed." And then I couldn't help myself, or keep the acid from my voice when I said, "How well you've played things, Mr. DeWitt. You have both Langleys in your pocket already. Nathan tells me his wife is quite *taken* with you. And I don't think he means as a patron."

DeWitt said nothing.

I glanced at him in the mirror. His face was expressionless. "Is he wrong?"

"I don't know why he would tell you that. I don't know what he means by it." He frowned. "I think he . . . intends something."

I didn't give a damn about Nathan's intentions regarding his wife. "Perhaps he's only angry that his wife has a lover."

"I don't think it would make him angry."

"What do you mean?"

DeWitt shrugged. "You were in the carriage with us that night. You heard him."

I remembered that strange conversation. The one I'd been so curious about before Sebastian DeWitt's talk of passion swept it from my head. "I heard him say a great deal I didn't understand."

"He so much as told me he wants me to have an affair with his wife."

"Really? When did he say that? You must have misheard him." I thought of how Nathan had spoken of his wife's infatuation. "Believe me, I don't think he likes the idea at all."

DeWitt seemed puzzled. "How . . . interesting."

I went back to pinning up my hair. "So are you?"

"Am I what?"

"Having an affair with Mrs. Langley?"

Now a faint smile, as if he were laughing at me, which irritated me more than a little. "Not that it's any of your concern, but no."

"Why not?"

His gaze was on me, and I thought he would say some little flirtation then, *because I'm waiting for you* or something like Jack would say, and I waited for it, I wanted it, which was stupid, but I was as vain as the next woman, and I knew—whether Sebastian DeWitt did or not—that Mrs. Langley wanted him, and would have him too, if she could manage it.

But DeWitt only said, "In any case, I only stopped by to tell you about the play."

His change of subject was firm. Very well, there'd be nothing more from him, and in a way I was relieved. I didn't want to talk or even think about the Langleys anymore.

"When will you start writing it?"

"When the revisions to *Penelope* are done. Or perhaps sooner, if I can manage an hour here or there."

"Will it be another part like Penny?"

"I don't know yet."

"I think I should like that. Someone honorable, but strong willed too. Though no sisters. I think they detract too much attention from the heroine."

"Do you?"

"You're a talented playwright, Mr. DeWitt, as I believe I've said before. You could probably do much better than writing mellies."

"You're a talented actress, Mrs. Wilkes, as I've said before." He met my tone word for word. "And you could probably do better than playing naive heroines overly concerned with their virtue."

I frowned. "Write me something better then."

"What would you suggest?"

I swiveled on the bench to face him. "I've already told you. Someone honorable. Someone kind."

"Do you think you could play someone so out of character?"

His expression was so bland, it took me a moment to realize I'd been insulted, and by him—the man whose gaze followed me about likc a shadow in search of the sun, the man who'd sat on the end of my bed and told me that he wanted to help me follow my passion. I said stiffly, "I'm not sure I take your meaning."

He shrugged. "I think perhaps those ingenues and virtuous wives are too pale for you. You know you've the makings of a superb villainess. In fact, I'm rewriting Penny to reflect it. You've quite a cruel streak."

"A cruel streak?"

"You don't think it's cruel, what you did in rehearsal today?"

"It was a prank, nothing more. And she deserved it. She took Penelope from me."

"You're her husband's mistress."

"What has that to do with anything? She doesn't know it."

"Not yet. But if you keep on as you did today, she soon will."

"Perhaps she *should* know. Then she'd realize he's really to blame for all this."

"Oh?" He raised a dark brow at me. "You had no part in it? You didn't pursue her husband? He's quite a coup for a second-line actress, you know. Or did that never enter your mind? He's rich. He's handsome—"

"He pursued me first."

"You could have said no."

"Oh yes," I said sarcastically. "That is just what I should have done. Refuse a rich man who wants to invest in the theater where I work, and become a stepping-stone for people like Stella Bernardi. Besides, it's not as if I *want* him, you know. It's a sacrifice for me—"

"To fuck him?"

It sounded so crude coming from him, so calculating, and it

made me angry. "How dare you judge me for it! It *is* a sacrifice. You can't think I *enjoy* it!"

"Why not? Isn't he a good lover?"

"Is any man?"

"You would know that better than I."

"He's like all the rest of them," I said dismissively. "I would rather be doing almost anything else than endure it."

"Really? Then no wonder you were so ruthless to poor Mrs. Langley. All that work of servicing her husband, and what do you have to show for it?"

Warily, I said, "Exactly."

"I should think you might feel pity for her instead."

"Pity? For someone as rich as she is?"

"So she has money. But she's also married to him, and she's 'endured' him far longer than you have."

His words caught me off guard. Such a thing had never occurred to me, and I found myself faltering. "It's not all my fault. The others dislike her too."

"They dislike her on your behalf. They follow your lead. Come, Mrs. Wilkes, you know you're in the wrong."

"Don't mistake me. I am not your damned Penelope Justis."

"Yes, I see that now."

I glared at him.

"I want you to remember something," he said. "That woman I told you about—the one who could help us both? I was speaking of Mrs. Langley. I can't lobby in your favor if you won't at least try to be pleasant."

"I don't think it's me she means to help," I said nastily.

"I can't imagine why." He went to the door, and I was glad. I waited for him to leave.

But he turned just before he opened it and said, "Mrs. Wilkes—"

"What?" I snapped.

"If you'd rather be doing something else when a man's in bed with you, perhaps you've never found the right lover."

With that, he went out the door. It thudded shut behind him.

I threw my brush at it. I fucking hated playwrights. Trust them to always know exactly how to get in the last word.

Chapter Fifteen

Geneva

By the time the carriage dropped me before the theater the next morning, I thought I knew most of my lines well enough. I'd stayed up late into the night studying, determined to win whatever grudging respect the company might offer. It seemed obvious that impressing Mrs. Wilkes was a lost cause—and I did not let myself think of the very expensive notepaper she'd tossed aside as if it had no more worth than one of the printed broadsheets that adorned every telegraph pole in the city—but I had hopes of impressing the man who had made her his muse. Now I understood what Sebastian DeWitt had been trying to tell me that day in the parlor, and I wanted to prove to him that I was worthy of Penelope Justis—and yes, even more worthy than the woman who embodied the character for him.

When I stepped onstage, Mr. DeWitt glanced up from the table and gave me a reassuring smile. "Ah—here you are. Good morning, Mrs. Langley."

"Good morning." I was thrilled by his smile, but my own faltered as I looked at the others, their expressions all variations on a theme of dismissal and dislike.

Lucius Greene looked up from where he was conferring with a carpenter over some drawing, and twirled his wrist at me, a broad and overly theatrical gesture. "There have been some script changes this morning, Mrs. Langley. Mr. Geary has your pages copied out."

I looked at Mr. DeWitt in alarm. All my effort for naught. "Script changes?"

"It couldn't be helped," he said. "But as you'll see, it affects everyone."

It was true; it seemed everyone had pages they were studying. I would not be the only one this morning. Still, I had wanted so to impress them. I had wanted to impress *him*.

I said quietly, "I had learned all the lines."

He glanced up again, obviously surprised. "You did? How long did that take you?"

"The better part of the night, I'm afraid. I told you I meant to do your play justice."

He smiled.

I said, "You didn't tell me you wrote it for *her*."

His smile died; he glanced to where she stood. "It hardly matters."

"I wish you had said something."

"What difference would it have made?"

I did not know what to say to that—he made me want to speak the truth, and the truth was that it would have made none at all. I had wanted to help him, yes, but I had also wanted this play for myself, and it was as Nathan said, she could have it back when I was done with it. It wasn't as if I meant to keep it. I felt disconcerted and guilty. I glanced down at the pages in my hand. "Well, I hope Mr. Greene has not ruined it."

"Not all of the changes are of Greene's design. Some are my own."

"Yours? But why?"

Again, a glance toward Mrs. Wilkes, as if he could not help himself. "I've decided Penelope has a more . . . cunning nature."

"Oh? Do I detect some disillusionment?"

"Let's just say I've had an epiphany," he said with a small and rather curious smile.

"I cannot help but say that I'm glad to hear it. You're no ordinary man, Mr. DeWitt. You deserve a muse who understands that."

This was too much; I knew it by the way his expression

tightened. He was not ready to hear criticism of her, no matter how well earned.

"She's been treated as unfairly as you have, Mrs. Langley." His voice was very soft. "You may want to keep that in mind."

I felt his censure like a little burn.

Mr. Geary shouted, "Act one, scene three! Places, everyone!"

Mr. DeWitt picked up his pen and looked back at his papers. "Your cue, Mrs. Langley."

It was the scene where the servant, Marjory, reveals to Penelope her devious plan: to dissuade Barnabus from seducing the young Delia by calling up the spirit of Florence, the older sister he'd wronged, and therefore nudging him toward madness.

It was also a scene for only two characters: Penelope and Marjory—or in this case, myself and Mrs. Wilkes.

I went to center stage with as much dignity as I could muster. Mrs. Wilkes stood there already, frowning at the pages in her hand—a relief, I had to admit. I'd half expected her to have them memorized already. Mr. Greene brought a chair.

"For Penelope," he told me, and I sat obediently. "The fireplace is there—" He gestured vaguely before me. "Marjory is building up the fire for her mistress."

Mrs. Wilkes went to the nonexistent fireplace, going down onto her knees before it, muttering beneath her breath something about "a familiar position" though I didn't hear all of it. It was no doubt some crude insult leveled at me, and I was still attempting to decipher it when I realized she'd delivered her line and was staring at me with undisguised contempt.

"The words are in front of you, I believe," she said. "Or do you intend that the prompter should act your part?"

"Forgive me," I said, flustered and disliking that I'd allowed myself to be so. "I was momentarily distracted."

"There are many more distractions onstage. How will you manage then?"

I ignored her and glanced down at the pages, finding my lines. "'As if any fire could warm me now. I am cold clear into my heart, and I think I shall be as long as Barnabus Cadsworth walks this earth.'"

"'The Cadsworths live a long time, miss. 'Tis in their blood. I should hate to see you cold forever.'"

"Take her hand there, Bea," interrupted Mr. Greene. "Twist a bit so you're kneeling at her side. You're trying to comfort her. Your relationship is closer than master and servant."

Mrs. Wilkes turned, flopping her hand out stiffly. Reluctantly, I took it.

DeWitt said, "Ladies—"

"What?" Mrs. Wilkes snapped.

I was startled by her temper, but Mr. DeWitt seemed unmoved. "Just that it looks awkward. They do love each other. They're much more like sisters."

She said, "Have you such familiarity with the upper class, Mr. DeWitt, that you know such a thing to be possible? I doubt Mrs. Langley would allow such familiarity from a servant."

"It doesn't matter what Mrs. Langley would do," DeWitt said. "It only matters what Penelope would do."

"I agree," I said. "Penny does not look upon Marjory as a servant. After all, she is in love with Marjory's brother."

"Which also seems odd, don't you think?" Mrs. Wilkes asked. "A well-born woman like Penelope having an affair with her stableboy?"

"Mr. DeWitt has written it extraordinarily well," I defended. "He is hardly just her stableboy. Penelope and Keefe were raised together. It seems a purer sort of love to my eyes."

"Really? You think it so? In my experience, when the upper class mingles with the lower, they're only slumming."

I thought of Claude, of the artists I knew who came from poor families. "I'd prefer to think the feelings more exalted than that."

She gave me a slow, steady look. "You think lust an exalted feeling?"

I refused to give her the satisfaction of reacting to her crude word choice. Firmly, I said, "In some cases, it can be, depending on the circumstance."

"The circumstance. I see. How very convenient."

"Bea!" Mr. Greene said sharply. "Might we press ahead?"

She ignored him. "I suppose you're rich enough to make circumstances as exalted as you want them to be, aren't you, Mrs. Langley? How lovely you and your husband must find it, to be able to make the world whatever you like. It's not a stableboy coupling with his lady, but pure love. How wonderfully transcendent. Why, you could perceive anything in such a light. A patron and a writer, for example. Or a rich man—and his mistress."

She met my gaze boldly, and there was something reckless in her eyes that reminded me of . . . of me.

The others went still. I felt the change in the air, a hovering expectation.

I heard again the words she'd said yesterday—"*Your husband's so good at casting*"—and suddenly, with no more than that, everything fell into place, the little disparate things that had troubled me. Nathan's investment in the Regal. The ease of his arrangement with Mr. Greene. His buying *Penelope Justis* to begin with, and his knowledge that Sebastian DeWitt had written it for her.

"I've heard she has a sweet tooth."

Mrs. Wilkes was my husband's mistress.

I choked back my rage and pain and humiliation. I would not display it here, not in front of them. I would not give her the satisfaction. Instead, I said, as calmly as I could, "Shall we proceed?" and took great satisfaction at her puzzled frown. She'd thought to disarm me; well, she could not unsettle me, not outwardly, not with my generations of good breeding, stiff composure, unruffled dignity.

I felt the relief of the company, as if they'd taken a deep breath in unison. With a wary look, she read her next line.

How I got through the rest of that scene with her, I do not know. I only know that when I got to the last lines, the new ones, I understood them; I knew exactly how to say them, how to infuse each word with chilly anger. " 'I tell you this, God: whatever your will, I shall not rest easy in't! I shall have my vengeance on Barnabus Cadsworth. I shall catch him in the web I weave and strangle him with my strings. I shall not rest until he repents for the death of my sister.' "

The company went quiet as if someone had cracked a whip over them. I felt their stares. I saw Mr. DeWitt's startlement, Mr. Greene's puzzled frown. But mostly I saw Mrs. Wilkes still.

Mr. Geary called for a break, and I tucked the script pages beneath my arm and made for backstage. I did not think I could bear to look at her another moment. I wanted to flee, to nurse my pride and my hurt in secret. Nathan had betrayed me, and I felt like a fool. How grateful I'd been for his offer of the theater, how pleased that he was becoming again the man I'd loved. My vision blurred, my disappointment overwhelmed me. I'd tried so hard since we'd come here, and I'd thought everything was going so well. I'd begun to hold hope for our marriage again, and all the time. . . . How it must amuse him to think of the two of us together. How entertained he must have been when I talked of buying her a gift. *"I've heard she has a sweet tooth,"* indeed. And as for the others . . . it was obvious they all knew too. Even Sebastian DeWitt, and that was the worst thing of all. He must have known. She was his muse, for God's sake—I could not imagine how he could bear to see her with Nathan. And yet he had not shared it with me. I had thought him a friend, and he had said nothing, had given not a single warning.

I wanted to leave. But then I heard them there, on the stage, laughing with one another, and Mr. Greene called, "Let's resume, children!" and I heard her say, "Wherever did Mrs. Langley get to? Do you think she might have run away?" There was scattered laughter.

I took a deep breath and blinked away my tears. I turned back to the stage, ready to continue. Through the curtains, I saw her standing onstage, self-assured, composed, her face so like mine, and I went cold and resolute. If what Mrs. Wilkes wanted was a war, I was more than ready to give her one.

I had been so angry that when Mr. DeWitt gestured for me to come to him at the end of rehearsal, I turned coldly away and hurried to my carriage. My hurt and disappointment were unbearable, and I did not want to speak to him or anyone else. But it seemed I had little choice, because when I arrived home, Mrs. Porter and Mrs. Brown were waiting.

I was surprised, but I told Bonnie to bring the tea, and then I composed myself and went to join the women in the parlor.

They sat silently, identical bookends, perched on the edges of the striped satin chairs, their gloved hands clasped primly in their laps. When I came inside, saying, "Mrs. Brown, Mrs. Porter, how lovely to see you," they both looked up at me with polite smiles.

Mrs. Porter said, "Mrs. Langley, this is not a social call. In fact, we've come on a . . . well, a mercy mission, as it were."

"A mercy mission?" I asked.

Mrs. Brown nodded shortly. She looked uncomfortable. "I—that is, *we* heard only yesterday that you were embarking upon a rather troubling enterprise."

"We're speaking of your intention to follow in Mr. Reading's footsteps," said Mrs. Porter bluntly. "We've heard you're actually rehearsing a play at the Regal. That you mean to . . . act . . . with them."

"Yes indeed," I said. "We've only just started, of course, but it's been a singular experience thus far."

"Mrs. Langley, surely you can't mean to proceed!"

Mrs. Brown said, "My dear, my husband has asked that I introduce you to society and make certain you're getting on, and I have tried to do so. But you must understand . . . people are talking."

"People have always talked about me, Mrs. Brown," I said.

"Yes indeed. That *is* the problem, Mrs. Langley, or don't you see it? May I be blunt?"

I met her gaze. "Please."

"Your past has made things very difficult. You must understand that if you continue with this . . . this . . . escapade . . . Well, people already believe you to be reckless and possibly . . . unbalanced. I am very much afraid that this will convince them that you are much more than that."

"I see," I said. "Thank you for your candor."

"And, if I might say more, well, your relationship with that *writer*—"

"You mean Mr. DeWitt?"

"Yes, *him.* And to be seen in public. At the play and then at that . . . that *saloon*—"

"It was a café, I believe."

"—drinking *beer.* You must see how it looks."

"Mr. DeWitt is a friend of mine," I said, putting aside my irritation with him. "And he is the most talented playwright I've seen in years. I expect he'll be a frequent visitor to my home from now on. I'll be happy to send you tickets to the show so you can see his talent for yourself."

They both looked at me in blank-eyed horror.

Then, recovering herself, Mrs. Brown said, "You mean to continue to see him?"

"Yes indeed, I mean to continue to see him."

"Your reputation—"

"Had you delved more deeply into the rumors, you would have discovered that I don't allow anyone to dictate my friendships. But I understand. And I'm willing to forgive you both for your misstep."

"I thought we had discussed this," Mrs. Brown said in a quiet, almost strangled voice. "This city will not tolerate another scandal from you, Mrs. Langley. We will not be forgiving of another . . . dalliance."

"I had not thought you forgiving of the first one," I said, meeting her gaze.

"You must understand—if you continue this . . . relationship . . . with Mr. DeWitt, we will have no choice but to . . . well, you will not be welcome in our homes."

"I see."

Mrs. Brown nodded and stood. "We weren't certain you understood the consequences. We thought, if you knew . . . well, surely you would not wish to impact your husband's bright future so negatively."

"You must have heard that it was my husband who introduced me to Mr. DeWitt. He even bought the play I'm performing."

Another quick glance between them. Mrs. Brown said, "We understand that this move across country cannot have been easy for you. Especially given the . . . trauma you've been through. And your husband is such a considerate man. We all think so—"

"Yes, indeed we do," put in Mrs. Porter, nodding vigorously.

"—and he no doubt wishes to do what he can to make your life here more pleasant for you. He cannot realize the effect this will have. We did not think you would wish him to make such an unknowing sacrifice."

I could not help but laugh. When the two women looked at me in surprise, I said, "My husband knows exactly what I am about, ladies. And I have no intention of reconsidering either acting at the Regal Theater or my relationship with Mr. DeWitt. But please know I won't hold your intolerance against you. In fact, I'll reserve tickets for both you and your husbands in the event that you change your minds. I'll be certain to send a notice 'round when the performance is scheduled."

Their mouths gaped; they looked at me as if I were mad, and I was laughing as they took their leave.

But once they were gone, I was back to Mrs. Wilkes and Nathan, and I did not think of Mrs. Brown or Mrs. Porter again.

When Nathan came home for dinner that night, I smiled at him at the same time I inwardly wished him to the devil. He sat down and said, "How was your day, darling?"

"Quite busy," I said calmly, taking a bite of pink salmon with sweet tomato figs, though I had no appetite. "Mrs. Brown and Mrs. Porter came by to tell me I was scandalizing the city."

Nathan's smile was thin. "Did they? And what did you tell them?"

"That I would reserve them tickets."

Nathan sighed. "No doubt they were horrified."

"Yes. And, of course, I was at rehearsal this morning."

"Did my friend Mr. Edwards come to watch?"

"Not yet."

"Ah." Nathan took a bite of his own fish. "How did it go today?"

"Badly, I'm afraid. Mrs. Wilkes is very angry with me over taking her part."

He took a forkful of fish. "Does that still trouble you? I thought you meant to buy her a gift."

I ignored that. "I really don't understand why Mr. Greene keeps her. She seems too coarse for a leading actress, don't you think?"

"I leave such things to him."

"You should pay more attention, Nathan. After all, you're investing in the theater. Surely you can't mean to just give Mr. Greene money without getting any say in return."

"I did get my say," he noted. "I told him to cast you."

"But I'm only a guest player. It hardly signifies. I think you should take a more active role. After all, if you could keep such arrogance as Mrs. Wilkes's from progressing, it could only do the company good."

"I thought you believed her talented."

I set down my fork. "She's been most offensive to me, Nathan. I'm surprised you would defend her."

"I'm not defending her."

"How much of an investment have you in the Regal? Is it enough for Mr. Greene to dismiss her if you asked it?"

My husband went very quiet. "Why would I have her dismissed?"

I gave him a cold smile. "To make your wife happy, for one thing. Or doesn't that matter to you any longer?"

"I care a great deal for your happiness, Ginny," he said—was I imagining the irony in his tone?—"as I believe I've told you quite recently."

"Then perhaps you could suggest to Mr. Greene that Mrs. Wilkes might be better served performing somewhere else."

"It's only been a few days. I feel certain it will work itself out."

As lightly as I could, I said, "Well, I don't demand that you have her let go, of course. But I should think it might ruin your political ambitions."

"What has one to do with the other?"

"I imagine it would be quite the scandal if it was discovered that the head of Stratford and Brown was having an affair with a second-rate actress."

I waited for his anger, tensing for a fist pounded on the table, a shattered glass. But he was silent, and uncertainly, I said,

"It would be a great relief to me if she were gone." I looked up at him.

And was taken aback by the concern in his eyes.

"Are you feeling quite well, Ginny? Shall I call the physician?"

I blinked at him. This was not what I'd expected. "Did you not hear what I said about Mrs. Wilkes?"

"Of course I did. It's what makes me think you're ill. Or delusional."

"I'm not delusional. Nathan, I demand—"

"I'm an investor in the company and nothing more," he said, as if trying to soothe a wild animal, and I saw the disingenuousness of it, the lie of his concern.

"I will not have that woman—"

"Are you certain she's being so offensive as you say? If you believe I'm having a relationship with her, it no doubt clouds your judgment."

"I am not imagining her behavior toward me."

"I'll speak to Mr. Greene and ask him to have her sheathe her claws, if you like."

"I want her gone."

He gave me a thoughtful look. "Ginny, I ask you to consider how unfair it would be to dismiss a woman purely on the basis of an unfounded suspicion."

He looked so unmoved, and yet I knew he was lying to me. I knew it—didn't I?

He rose, tossing his napkin to the table. "But I'm willing to think about it for your sake. I don't want you troubled, my dear. And perhaps her misbehavior is enough excuse. After all, you are Geneva Langley. Now, if you'll pardon me, I'm off."

I could not help myself. "To see her?"

He didn't even blink. "Good night, Geneva."

Chapter Sixteen

Beatrice

That night, when the performance was over, and we were all onstage taking our bows, a woman with tears in her eyes handed a pie across the footlights. She shouted something to me as I leaned to take it, but the noise was too loud and I couldn't hear her. As she could have given the pie to anyone and she chose me, I assumed it was mine, and I paraded off the stage with it while the others trailed like hungry puppies begging for scraps. I laughed and teased them, "Oh no! Don't think I'll share it! It smells like mincemeat!"

I couldn't have got rid of them then for anything. We all crowded into Jackson's dressing room, because it was the largest, though that only meant he had a settee and a chair next to his dressing table, and we were nearly on top of one another.

Jack produced a paper knife from his drawer, and I cut pieces for all of us. We stood about, shoving pieces of moist, rich pie heady with spice and sweetness into our mouths, laughing and heedless of our makeup and costumes or the people waiting in the hall outside—even Brody traded his entourage for pie.

"What'd you do for this, Bea?" Jack mumbled around a bite. "Give her a fortune in gold?"

"She was moved by my performance," I told him.

William Galloway laughed. "It couldn't be just that!"

I made a face at him.

"Perhaps she's another lonely wife wanting acting lessons," said Jack. "At last, a payment worth the trouble!"

"Even pie such as this isn't worth working with a lack of talent," Aloysius said.

Brody laughed. "So you say, Aloys, but look at you, acting with Mrs. Langley just because Lucius tells you to. Ain't no reward in it."

"Ah, but you know, I do think she has an instinct," Aloys said slowly. He didn't look at me as he said it, and I was glad. I didn't want to talk about Mrs. Langley.

Jack snorted. "An instinct? For what, pray tell?"

"She knows how to deliver a line." Aloys's dark gaze swept us. "Don't tell me I'm alone in thinking this. Surely the rest of you saw it as well. Bea, even you must admit it."

"She has more talent than I thought, there's no doubt of that," Mrs. Chace said, popping the last crumb of her pie into her mouth and swallowing noisily.

My appetite for the pie vanished. "That's hardly the same thing as being able to act," I said meanly. I dropped my piece back onto the plate.

Brody said eagerly, "Are you done with that? Can I have it?"

"Yes, I'm done," I said, and when he took it, shoving it into his mouth with all the grace of an animal, I left them. There was a small group waiting outside the door for Jack, and when they saw me, they began to babble and I heard bits and pieces of their praise as I pushed through them and stalked down the hall to my dressing room, taking down my hair as I went. It wasn't until I was inside, and the door was closed, and the smell of Susan's orange flower water was sickly in my nose, that I realized my heart was racing.

I took a deep breath and stared into the mirror, at my half-undone hair and my face beneath the powder, the garishness of my kohled eyes and reddened lips—a crumb of pie clinging to the rouge that I brushed quickly away. Alone, I could admit to myself that Aloysius's words bothered me. Mrs. Langley did have talent. And you know, I couldn't bear thinking that, thinking she might be better in my part than I would have been. And now that the others had smelled talent, it was only a matter of time before they lost their taste for baiting her.

Then there was the little tête-à-tête with my playwright this morning—oh no, I hadn't missed that at all, and I remembered his words about what Mrs. Langley could do for us, and how he intended to lobby for me. And here I was, doing my best these past days to convince him that perhaps I wasn't *worth* any of it—not his help or the new play he was writing for me, even if Nathan had commissioned it, and that was as stupid as the other stupid thing I'd done today, the thing I was really trying hard not to think about, the look I'd seen in Mrs. Langley's eyes when she'd finally got the hints I'd been throwing at her about me and her husband. I didn't know what she would do about it either, and when you added to it the fact that Nathan hadn't been to see me in days . . . well, I was an idiot every way I looked at it.

Susan came inside gingerly, looking as if she was afraid I might bite her, and I sighed and picked up the towel and wiped the makeup from my face.

"Aloys didn't mean it," she said quickly.

"Yes, he did."

"Well, so what? It don't mean he won't take your side."

I said stiffly, "He's his own man; he can do what he likes."

She took the pins from her own hair, dropping them in a scatter onto the table. "What harm does it do to admit she can read a line?"

"None at all." I gave her the bench as I unbuttoned my costume, stepping out of it and then stowing it inside my trunk, laying it neatly so it wouldn't wrinkle—as if it were the finest silk instead of secondhand satin spotted all over the bodice with grease. When I closed the lid, Susan said, "She's not as good as you are, Bea."

I nodded and pulled on my calico, and then I went out the door without even a good-bye.

I buttoned my bodice as I made my way past those waiting to see the other players, and up the stairs to the back door, and then I was outside into a night whose air was thick with dust. It wasn't until then that I realized my hair was bouncing around my shoulders and I'd left my hairpins back in the dressing room, but I wouldn't go back despite how vulnerable it made me feel.

With my hair down like this I might be mistaken for a whore—more so than usual, anyway—and that made my nightly walk home even more frightening than it already was.

There were streetlamps all the way along to the hotel, but walking home alone late at night was still something I'd never got used to. It terrified me, frankly, and the streetlamps somehow made it even worse. In darkness, I was as invisible to someone as they were to me, but in the lamplight, anyone hiding in the shadows might see me, and I would never know it. I'd made rules for myself: walk purposefully and without hesitation. Say nothing, even when spoken to. Stare straight ahead, but be aware every moment of the edges and what was behind. Never pass between two advancing men. Never take the inside of the walk when passing a stranger. Never pass an alley without stepping into the street to put the whole width of the walk between me and it. Never be afraid to take to the center of the street.

I was about halfway home when I began to hear the footsteps on the boardwalk across the street. I glanced over—a shadow clinging to the other shadows. The width of the street was between us; I told myself I was safe enough. No doubt it was some man making his way home—it wasn't as if the boardwalks were deserted, after all. But this was different, as if someone kept time to my pace. I felt as if I were being watched.

I sped my step; whoever it was kept carefully behind, but the distance between us never changed. A coincidence, I told myself, but I knew it wasn't. *Just get home, Bea.* I crossed the street to the next block, hurrying now, walking as fast as I could without running. And then, finally, I was at the boardinghouse. I jerked open the door and ran for the stairs.

When I was at my door, I fumbled with the key; finally I got it open and stumbled inside, locking it again, leaning against it, listening.

It took me a moment to realize he hadn't followed me, and then another to rush to my window, which I'd left open, and look to see if I could spot him. The street was empty below.

But then I glanced down the block. There, just coming out from the glow of the streetlamp, was a man—and I knew it was the same man who'd been following me, because I recognized him. In the lamplight, his hair glowed a dark, rich red. I knew his walk, though I would have sworn I did not. Sebastian DeWitt.

Geneva

They were laughing when I came in the next morning. Mrs. Wilkes and that handsome boy, Brody Townshend, and Mr. Wheeler, huddled together at the far corner of the stage, and at the sight of her my anger surged anew. I looked away with as unaffected an air as I could muster. I felt defeated, but I was damned if I would let her know that. I hoped that Nathan had managed to have a word with Mr. Greene—if nothing else, it would put her on notice that I was not to be trifled with, even if I could not help whatever reassurances Nathan whispered to her when they were alone in bed. I took some solace from the fact that I was still his wife, and he would not risk everything over a mistress, nor, I thought, would he take the risk that I might write of my unhappiness to my father. So perhaps any word Nathan might put to her via Mr. Greene would at least have some effect.

I went to the table where Sebastian DeWitt sat scribbling over scenes like a madman. He glanced up—a quick, distracted glance, a distracted smile—and then down again as if he hadn't really seen me, and I said in a low voice, "You didn't tell me."

He paused, and looked up again, his pen stilling. "Tell you what?" he asked blankly.

I glanced at the others. "About Mrs. Wilkes. And my husband."

"Ah." Now I had his attention. He sat back, letting his pen fall from his fingers. "What was I to say?"

"You let her humiliate me—"

"No. Your husband allowed that."

"How you leap to her defense! Just as Nathan did. I know she is your muse, Mr. DeWitt, but it would have been a kindness to say something."

Patiently, he said, "You would have hated her from the moment you met her."

"Instead of hating her now. Yes, how much worse that would have been."

"It gavc you a chance to like her, at least. And your husband *is* my patron, Mrs. Langley. I doubt he would have appreciated my telling you."

"I had not thought you part of that wretched men's club."

"I can't bite the hand that feeds me."

"What about my hand?"

He met my gaze. "I'm sorry for that."

I understood his reasons for not saying anything, but I was disappointed too. I had thought we were better friends. I could not resist saying, "Do you know, Mr. DeWitt, I admire your fortitude. Truthfully, I don't know how you do it."

He looked wary. "Do what?"

"Tolerate the fact that your muse is my husband's mistress."

A self-deprecating smile. "To have what I want requires sacrifice. I've reached a point in my life where I accept the necessity."

"I don't believe you've accepted it. I believe you hate it."

"Hating it doesn't make it disappear. There are ladders to climb even to heaven, Mrs. Langley." He reached down and picked up a few pages, lines crossed out and overwritten, and handed them to me. "Here, I've given you a ladder. Perhaps it will help you to forgive me."

I stared down at the pages. "What is this?"

Again the smile. "More changes."

"More?"

"Greene wishes more 'spectacle.' And I've cut Delia."

"You've cut Delia? Why?"

"Because it works better if Barnabus goes after Penelope. Especially as she is to become nearly his equal in villainy."

"But then—" He had made Penelope a greater and more

complex character, and I suspected he'd done it for me. *"I've given you a ladder."* I glanced quickly at Mrs. Wilkes. "You would have had to take the meat from Marjory. Your muse cannot like it."

"Question not the whims of playwrights, Mrs. Langley, lest you offend them into cutting your part," said a deep voice from behind me.

I looked over my shoulder to see—surprisingly—Aloysius Metairie, stroking his closely trimmed Vandyke beard.

"You speak as one with experience," I said, suspicious and not bothering to hide it.

"Sadly, aye." Mr. Metairie glanced down at the pages in my hand. "Our own playwright is very evenhanded, fortunately for you, despite certain other . . . circumstances. And with your quick intellect, madam, I expect you'll have the additional lines learned in no time."

"Well . . . thank you."

He smiled, his dark eyes twinkling. "Fear not, Mrs. Langley. I'm no Trojan horse." He touched my arm lightly and then moved away, back to where Mr. Galloway and Mrs. Chace stood chattering.

"Metairie makes a good champion," Mr. DeWitt said in a low voice.

I was puzzled. "Champion? But only yesterday—"

"He's the chief tragedian," he said pointedly, and when I looked uncomprehendingly at him, he explained, "The others follow him, not the other way 'round."

Mr. Geary shouted, "Act four, scene one. Places, everyone!"

Despite Mr. Metairie's and Mr. DeWitt's reassurance, I was wary. Mr. Greene sent me and Mr. Metairie climbing together to the top of a scaffold that would eventually become the cataract that emptied into a pool below. The platform was very narrow, and my bustle was a distinct disadvantage, both in allowing me to climb and in giving us enough room to stand together at the top. I was afraid even my slightest turn would send Mr. Metairie plunging twenty feet to the floor. He had his arm about my waist, holding me tightly, while Mr. Greene called up from below:

"The pool will be quite deep, Mrs. Langley. I assure you that you shan't injure yourself in falling."

"In falling?" I asked.

"You can swim, can't you, madam?"

I swallowed. It seemed very far down. "I am not a strong swimmer, no."

From where she stood near the wings, I saw Mrs. Wilkes lean close to whisper something to Mr. Wheeler, who laughed.

"Good enough!" Mr. Greene said. "All you need to do is struggle to the surface. Ah, I wish we had a horse that could plunge in with you. People love a horse. Add a horse, Mr. DeWitt."

"We haven't time to make the waterfall big enough for a horse, Lucius." The carpenter looked up from where he stood beside Mr. Greene. "We're falling behind as it is."

"If you recall the disaster in *Mazeppa,* Lucius, Jack was lucky to escape with a broken leg," Mr. Metairie said drolly from beside me.

"A mere anomaly," Mr. Wheeler called out. "I don't mind a horse, and I've no doubt Mrs. Langley is a skilled rider."

I could not suppress my shudder at the thought. "I'm afraid I haven't the skill to ride a horse up a . . . scaffold."

"There's not enough *time,* Lucius," the carpenter said again.

Mr. Greene sighed heavily. "Oh, very well. No horse. But . . . what about a dog, DeWitt? Perhaps Miss Justis could have a little dog? One that does tricks, perhaps?"

"We could get that spaniel we used in *Murder on the Cliff,*" said Mrs. Wilkes sweetly.

"It didn't bite that hard," said Brody Townshend, smiling. "I've barely got any scar."

"It's a bit late for that, isn't it, Lucius?" Mr. Metairie said. "The play is to be performed the week after next."

"Days still to get a dog," Mr. Greene said.

"Why not a little circus of dogs?" Mrs. Wilkes suggested.

Mr. Greene stroked his mustache. "Yes. Yes, a good idea! Last year Langford had that circus at the Palace. It did very well. Mrs. Langley, have you experience with dogs?"

We were very high up. I was feeling dizzy. "I—"

"I think a circus of dogs might lessen the suspense," Mr.

DeWitt interjected drily. "Barnabus means to seduce Penny, after all—very hard to do with dogs performing tricks all about."

"Ah, yes of course," Mr. Greene said. "A bit distracting. I see. Ah well, then, no dog circus. Carry on."

"So am I to throw Penelope to the pool, or simply lose hold of her?" Mr. Metairie asked.

Mr. Townshend offered, "Perhaps you could try it both ways. I guess with that bustle, she'd bounce right back."

Mrs. Wilkes laughed out loud. I looked down into her jeering face, and I could not stop myself from saying, "I do wish we could find a way to put Marjory in this scene. With all the changes, I'm quite worried that she's barely in the play now."

Beatrice Wilkes gave me exactly what I wanted. In her expression I saw a stunned and angry surprise. I smiled at her as coldly as I could and was rewarded with her gaping mouth, eyes narrowed to slits. It was the most perfect moment.

Chapter Seventeen

Beatrice

She was clever enough, I had to admit. An insult delivered with such smooth polish, and that bearing—what the hell did they do, breed for it? Just one more reason to dislike her, and don't think I didn't.

Susan stifled a laugh and looked away from me guiltily, and I thought, *there goes another one*. And then, to make it all worse, when Geary called for a scene change, Lucius grabbed my arm, stopping me. "No trifling with her today, Beatrice."

Not *Bea. Beatrice.* I frowned. "Of course not."

"One should not prick a sleeping lion."

"I fancy myself the lion in this case, Lucius, but never fear, I'll tread lightly today."

He nodded and let me go, and I looked across the stage at Jackson, raising my eyebrow in question. He only shrugged.

And then Mrs. Langley approached center stage to meet me, frosty as ice on a pump handle, and angry besides, in that way people are when they're thwarted, and I wished once again that I'd managed to keep quiet about my arrangement with her husband. I thought of the note I'd sent Nathan this morning begging for forgiveness—I couldn't go on being such a fool, after all—and hoped to hell I'd see him tonight.

"You seem distressed, Mrs. Wilkes," Mrs. Langley said.

"Why should I be distressed, Mrs. Langley?"

"I've no idea. It's only that you sighed so prettily. It was quite dramatic. But then, I suppose you know exactly what gives the best effect."

Cuttingly said, coldly too. And lowering, all at the same time. I felt like a barnacle beneath her boot. How did one master such a tone? "Ah, but I'm always looking for ways to perfect it. By studying society, for example, I've learned how to sound pompous and say nothing at the same time."

"Your line, Mrs. Langley," called Mr. Geary.

She ignored him. Her eyes narrowed. "How is it that you can get close enough to study society, Mrs. Wilkes, when you're kept so well outside it?"

"How can I help it? Society is always popping up where it's not welcome. Rather like a boil. Or a bedbug."

Mr. Geary said, "Can we begin, ladies, please? We're wasting time."

"A bedbug," she repeated. "Yes, I imagine you know all about those, Mrs. Wilkes."

Everything she thought about me was in those words, and I felt the heat in my face and spat back, "Even a bedbug might prefer a warm bed to a cold one, Mrs. Langley."

She looked as if I'd slapped her, and I felt a vicious little stab of satisfaction. She turned on her heel and strode to the edge of the stage. "Mr. Greene, may I have a word with you?"

"Yes, Lucius," I called out. "Run and speak with Mrs. Langley like a good little slave."

"Bea," Jackson warned.

Mrs. Langley looked over her shoulder at me. "I haven't any idea why you thought you could be leading lady, Mrs. Wilkes. You truly haven't the style."

"Why, how else? I'll copy yours. Or perhaps it would be wiser not to take someone like you as my example."

"Beatrice!" I heard the fury in Lucius's voice.

Jack winced. Brody whistled low through his teeth.

"I will not go onstage with her," Mrs. Langley said loudly.

"You won't have to," Lucius assured her quickly, and I wished to hell I'd shut up. Lucius glared at me. "Mrs. Wilkes, may I see you in my office?"

The stage went eerily quiet. Even the carpenters stopped working; on the scaffold, a painter's stilled brush dripped onto the oilcloth spread below. I felt them all looking at me.

I didn't look at the others. I tried not to think of the fact that Nathan Langley would no doubt take his wife's side. I squared my shoulders and said, regal as a queen, "As you wish, Mr. Greene," and followed him offstage. I didn't hazard a glance at Mrs. Langley, because I knew the smug satisfaction I would see on her face.

Down the stairs, down the hallway, and Lucius wrenched open the door to his office and ushered me sternly in, following after, closing the door with a near slam.

"What in the hell do you think you're doing?" he snapped—all geniality gone, flamboyance reduced to quick, angry gestures.

"Why don't you just say it? Why prolong it? She wants me gone, and you haven't the courage God gave a worm to go against her."

"Do not try me, Beatrice, or I will."

I laughed. "Don't pretend you might not. Don't forget, I know you, Lucius. Once she gets Nathan involved—"

"You don't know what you're talking about. Langley *is*

involved. Whatever you're doing to him must be damned good, because he doesn't want you gone. At least not yet."

"He said that?"

A short nod. "He told me this morning that she wanted you dismissed and he was considering it. But only considering it, mind you. So for now, I'm not letting you go." Lucius leaned forward. "But I'll take you off *Penelope*."

"Who will play Marjory?"

"I'll move Susan into the part. You're still with the company; you're just not doing this show. Do you understand me, Bea?"

I nodded, and then, to my horror, my eyes filled with tears. "Thank you, Lucius."

"Don't thank me," he said shortly, unmoved. "Who knows what the hell Langley will want tomorrow? If I were you, my dear, I'd fuck him tonight until he can't walk."

I wiped at my eyes. "Yes. Yes, I will."

He leaned back in his chair again and waved his hand at me. "That's all. Now get out. Be back at four. You're still on *Debts* tonight."

I didn't hesitate. I fled his office before he could change his mind. I was half blind with tears. I didn't see Sebastian DeWitt until I ran into him.

"Sorry," I said, pushing away. "I'm sorry. I didn't—"

"Steady," DeWitt said. His hands were on my arms, holding me out. "What happened? Are you all right?"

"I'm off *Penelope*," I told him.

"But Marjory—"

"Susan will play her." I tried to laugh, not very successfully. "Maybe you'd better trim the part more."

"He can't do this," he said in a low voice. "I wrote the play—"

"For me. Yes, I know. Everyone knows. It doesn't matter." I loosed myself from his grasp. "It's all right. I don't care."

"Let me walk you home."

"You have a rehearsal to see to." I pushed past him.

"Wait for me then. I'd like to speak to you."

"I can't." I only wanted to be away. I took the three steps to the back door and pushed on it. Light flooded in, along with dust. "Good-bye, Mr. DeWitt." I let the door slam shut behind me.

Lucius's advice rang in my ears. Hadn't I already known that Nathan Langley was the key to everything? I thought of my note, delivered by now, and prayed that he would heed it.

I had to wait two hours for his answer, pacing my room all the while until there was a knock on the door and I opened it to find some errand boy, and my hands were shaking as I paid him a penny for the envelope he carried. I tore open that envelope as if it were some damned edict from God—which in a way it was, you know—and when I read those words I felt such a flurry of relief I had to sit down.

Tonight. Wear the cloak and hairpins. We're going to dinner. N.

Geneva

When Mr. Greene returned, he said tersely, "The role of Marjory will now be played by Miss Jenks."

He excused us then, and I left quickly, not daring to glance at any of the others; I did not think I could hide my smile of victory, and I didn't want to try. I wanted to celebrate that she was gone without being made to feel guilty over it and without thinking of what Nathan might say when I returned home, or about the fact that I'd taken the play from the muse it had been written for. I deliberately did not search out Sebastian DeWitt.

But I'd no sooner stepped out the backstage door than my relief at escaping turned to trepidation. Because just outside, leaning against the building, was the man I'd been hoping to avoid.

Mr. DeWitt's cool glance flickered over me. "Mrs. Langley, I salute you for so efficiently ridding yourself of a thorn."

"She turned the rehearsals into a circus," I defended myself. "She would not even try. And surely I should not have been required to bear my husband's mistress."

Quite reasonably, he said, "Perhaps you should blame your husband for that, and not her."

"Perhaps I would have," I said acidly, "had she made any attempt at all to bear me. It was clear from the start that she wished me to perdition."

"I tried to warn you. What did you expect when you took her part?"

"I didn't *know*. In fact, I didn't know a great many things, any of which you could have told me." I took a deep breath. "I *am* sorry for your sake, Mr. DeWitt. I know you admire her. Though I admit I don't quite see her allure."

"You could learn something from watching her, you know," he said. "She's a very good actress. She has the potential to be exceptional."

"Well, she can sing," I said dismissively. "And I liked her in *Black Jack*, but as for more than that. . . . I mean no offense, you understand. I realize that one must make allowances for inspiration. No artist can dictate its source. But perhaps *you* could make allowances for the fact that you might not see her clearly."

"You're being patronizing, Mrs. Langley."

"I only mean—"

"You mean that Mrs. Wilkes isn't worthy of being my muse."

"I think you don't realize the depth of your talent, Mr. DeWitt. An artist such as yourself . . . perhaps you'd be better served by someone who can understand you."

"Yes, you said that before. I suppose you've someone in mind."

"In many circles, I am regarded as something of an inspiration myself."

"One cannot simply replace one muse with another."

I was stung, but I tried to hide it. "Of course I know that. I'm not suggesting it. I understand the rather . . . coarse . . . appeal of a woman like Mrs. Wilkes, and I imagine it has its satisfactions, but I'm speaking of something more elevated, something like—"

"The relationship you had with Marat."

"I was able to help him a great deal, Mr. DeWitt. Without me—"

"He would not have been so brilliant as he was?"

I foundered. "He would have been brilliant in any case. But I did introduce him to a society that appreciated him. My father's patronage secured him a great many commissions."

"I'm certain you brought his genius to light," he said quietly. "It's your gift, after all. But did you inspire him?"

"You should have seen *Andromeda,* Mr. DeWitt. It was . . . magnificent."

DeWitt nodded and stared off into the little view we had of the street, given that we stood in the narrow pass between two buildings. Carriages and wagons flashed into sight and then disappeared again. "Did you commission *Andromeda*?"

"No one did. It was an exhibition piece."

"Marat paid for the marble himself?"

"No, of course not. Have you any idea the cost of that much stone? And Claude was . . . well, he was a peasant, really. Money ran through his fingers."

"So you bought the stone for him?"

"I considered it essential. I wanted the world to discover him as I had."

"You and your husband are very generous patrons."

"Nathan had nothing to do with it. Claude's talent didn't matter to him, just as yours doesn't. He's financing you for *her,* Mr. DeWitt. He'll be happy to take credit for discovering you, though."

DeWitt smiled. "Discover me? As if I'm a bit of gold buried in quartz?"

"Yes, exactly. I assure you, you have no idea how heady it can be. It's intoxicating. When others realize that you've glimpsed the gold when they had already looked away . . . well, I lack the words to fully explain it. I don't know, of course, but I imagine it must feel very like creation. I thought I could put it aside when we came here. I thought I could be . . . different. But I miss it so terribly. It's like . . . I suppose it's an addiction, really."

He said gently, "Sometimes I think of writing that way too. If I could only stop . . . well, there's no point in thinking that. I can't stop. I'm like a moth beating its wings against a flame. As long as the fire is there, I can't fly away."

"The fire of inspiration?" I asked.

He shrugged. "For lack of a better word. But there are different types of fire."

"What do you mean?"

"For example, your husband pays me fifty dollars and asks me to write a play—well, money's a fire of one kind. I can be . . . inspired . . . to write whatever he wants. If he says to add a circus of dogs, why, I'm happy to do so. Tie the heroine to train tracks? As you wish, sir. And what good taste you have, if you don't mind my saying so. You've a wit beyond ages, sir; I've never worked for anyone so discerning."

I began to feel vaguely uncomfortable, though I could not say why.

"And then . . . then there's the kind of fire that seems to come from nowhere. It knocks you to the ground. Suddenly you can't sleep for the ideas racing through your brain. Your fingers itch for a pen, and you can imagine a thousand ways . . . well, it's like God is inside you. Perhaps it's a form of madness—I don't know. All I know is that it so rarely happens that you don't let go of it when it does. Not for anything, not for any amount of money. I'd rather starve than give it up."

He spoke so passionately; his eyes blazed, his face animated. And I began to feel this strange, disturbing awareness, a discomfiting sense that I was on the cusp of understanding something I wasn't certain I wished to know.

Still, I couldn't keep from asking, "That's what you feel for Mrs. Wilkes?"

He glanced at me, his expression quieting again. "Without her, there would be no Penelope Justis. It's the best work I've ever done, but I know . . . I can feel . . . it's only the beginning. I've never felt so . . . limitless. Believe me, I've no desire to question it. I don't know why she fires it, except . . . perhaps it's that something in me recognizes the passion in her. She feels it, you know. For acting. Though she tries to hide it."

I thought of Claude, of the mad flailing away at marble, chips flying, how, in the throes of creation, he seemed consumed by madness. How much pride I'd taken in being his muse. How exceptional I'd felt. And I missed that so dreadfully. I missed being important, being exceptional. I wanted. . . .

"It so rarely happens that you don't let go of it when it does. Not for anything, not for any amount of money. I'd rather starve than give it up."

But Claude had walked away without a backward glance. In his way, he had used me, just as Nathan had. I'd given him money and prestige, and he'd taken them and fled. He had not even said good-bye.

I looked at Mr. DeWitt, who was looking at me as if he saw something in my face that arrested him.

"Are you all right, Mrs. Langley?"

"Yes," I whispered, though I felt ill. It made me more honest than I would have been, than I should have been. "How I envy you, Mr. DeWitt."

"For what?"

"For what you have."

He sighed. "Mrs. Langley . . . what I did . . . not telling you . . . "

"You don't have to explain."

He met my gaze. "That morning, when I came to your house—I meant to tell you then. But you were so enthusiastic, and I didn't want to hurt you. I'm sorry."

My discomfort faded, along with my pain. The evidence of his concern was a restorative. "Thank you for caring, Mr. DeWitt. It . . . means a great deal to me."

He looked at me, and something fell between us, some understanding that I'd felt for few other people, and I smiled and said, "Will you come to lunch with me?"

"Your husband tells me there's been talk," he said. "The café—"

"Yes, I know."

"If we're seen together in a restaurant, it will be worse," he warned. "I don't want to cost you."

"My dear Mr. DeWitt, you are truly my only friend in this

town. Surely you won't abandon me to my lonely purgatory for fear of some ridiculous gossip?"

He smiled. "I suppose, when you put it that way—"

"Then lunch it is," I said.

Chapter Eighteen

Beatrice

That night I felt a flurry of anxiety. Though I thought Nathan's note meant he'd forgiven me, I wasn't quite certain. I hadn't seen him since I'd told him to leave me the hell alone, after all, and there was every chance he would still be angry, and I wasn't forgetting that slap or that strangeness in his eyes that had frightened me or the way he'd fucked me, either, and there was a part of me that wished he would leave me alone, even though I knew what that would cost me, and I couldn't afford it.

I went to the theater at four and put on my costume and did my hair and makeup for *Debts* beside a very quiet Susan. I knew she felt guilty about taking over Marjory, but I didn't feel like consoling her. I went onstage and searched the boxes as I delivered my lines, and there Nathan was, in his usual box, and I felt this terrified relief that almost made me stick. Luckily I remembered my lines after only a pause, and I don't think anyone realized how nervous I was. It only made me better, actually, because I'd done *Debts* so many times it felt sometimes as if I were saying my lines in a dream, and my nervousness woke me up. It was a good play; I'd forgotten how much I liked it, and suddenly I *was* the good and pious Margaret in a way I hadn't been in some time, and that made me remember the passion Sebastian DeWitt had said was still in me, and I thought maybe he was right. When it was over, I was proud of myself, which was another thing I hadn't felt for a long time.

The night was nearly as hot as the day had been—a week or more without rain, unusually warm—and with that and the stage lights and the close warmth of backstage, I was sweating as I hurried back to the dressing room after our bows. But once I was there, I was back to nerves again as I got ready to meet Nathan. I left on the costume—it was one of my best gowns, and my brown calico didn't go very well with the cloak and the hairpins I'd locked away in my trunk. When I followed Nathan's driver out, I glanced about for Sebastian DeWitt. I wanted to see his smile; I wanted to know he'd noticed tonight. But I didn't see him anywhere, and that was strange, you know, because lately he'd always been hovering about my dressing room, and his not being there left me feeling a little off balance.

That feeling only grew when I got to the carriage. The driver opened the door, and I saw the shadow of Nathan inside, and he moved into the light, his hair gleaming as if it had been freshly combed with macassar, and held out his hand. When I took it, he pulled me hard into his lap and kissed me until I was gasping for breath and I thought he meant to have me there in the carriage, which made me wonder why the hell I'd bothered to get dressed up.

Then he let me go. "So you've forgiven me," he said with a smug smile.

That smile annoyed me, but I didn't want him remembering that it was the other way around, that I'd needed *him* to forgive *me,* and so I said, "Yes. I'm sorry I lost my temper."

"Don't be sorry. It was . . . interesting." He gave me this leer that told me he was remembering what had happened after, and it shook me a little that he'd thought it was erotic, and I had to turn away to look out the window.

"Where are we going?"

"To the Queen City."

That surprised me. The Queen City Chop House was a better

restaurant than I was used to, and I was surprised he'd take me there, where someone might see us and recognize him. But either that didn't occur to him or he didn't care, and I supposed, now that his wife knew I was his mistress, it didn't matter.

The Queen City was large, but the cut-glass gasoliers were turned down low so it was very dim and hard to see anyone else, and the clouds of smoke from cigars and pipes only made everything fuzzier. It wasn't full; it was late for dinner. But there were a few people dressed in elegant clothing, people who had come from the theater, or maybe from one of the lyceums in town. I smelled something delicious, rich and beefy, that made my stomach grumble.

Nathan whispered something to the man standing just inside the door, and he whisked us through, seating us in a darkened corner, secluded, but not so much that we couldn't be seen, though he did seat me so my back was to the main. I whispered to Nathan, "Are you certain you like this table?"

He asked, "Why not? What's wrong with it?"

"I'd thought there might be a private room—"

"Are you ashamed to be seen with me?"

"I was thinking it might be the other way around."

He laughed. "My dear, if my wife can be seen having beer with Sebastian DeWitt, I can certainly bring a lady friend to dinner."

My stomach dropped. Suddenly I remembered that conversation he'd had with DeWitt in the carriage. "Your wife had a beer with Mr. DeWitt?"

"Didn't you hear? The rest of the world did." Nathan picked up his menu.

"I didn't realize they were such friends." And really, I should have stopped before I said it, because I remembered too what DeWitt had said about Nathan telling him to fuck his wife.

Nathan said, "Oh, I think they're much more than friends," in this nasty little way. My appetite fell away. I wanted nothing more than to go home, even though I knew how stupid it was. Sebastian DeWitt might see me as his muse, but he didn't belong to me, and I couldn't afford him that way anyway, so jealousy was just a waste of time. But still I wondered when he'd given in.

I wondered if that was where he was tonight, if he was with her. *Stupid, Bea. Stupid, stupid.*

Nathan ordered wine and a meal of beef in some kind of rich sauce and potatoes whipped and crusty brown and sweet glazed carrots, and when it came the smell was so good that I couldn't resist it after all. I'd never had a better meal, to tell the truth, and Nathan acted so besotted I thought he might crawl across the table and fuck me there in the chair. He cut my meat, poured me wine, and leaned close while I drank it, smiling and touching my hand until I laughed and said, "I'm not one of your helpless society ladies, you know."

He poured me another glass of wine. "No, you're something much better."

I'd had a little too much wine. I laughed again. "And what's that?"

"It's a relief to be with you after dealing with Ginny all day. You never pretend to be something you're not."

Which only made me think he was either stupid or deluded, because I was an *actress,* after all. My job was in pretending to be someone else, and besides, what was this dinner except pretense? He wanted to be in bed with me and I wanted to be away from him, and this all felt like some strange and confusing game. But I said, as if I were interested, "Really?"

"This acting nonsense . . . she has no real desire to be onstage, you know. She just likes the attention. She always has."

"I know actors like that too."

"The difference between them and my wife is that Ginny hasn't an ounce of talent."

He was so dismissive. It was insulting, the way he talked about her sometimes, and I didn't like it. But I didn't like her either, and I wasn't about to defend her.

Nathan smiled. "But then, no one in the company has your talent."

That surprised me. "You think I'm talented?"

"Of course you are. Why else would I have noticed you?"

"I'd thought . . . because I look like . . ."

"My wife?" Nathan laughed. "A coincidence, I assure you. I suppose I have a preference for dark-haired women. But no, it wasn't how you look that made me pick you out. It was your presence on the stage. You're quite charismatic, you know. There's a—what's the word?—oh . . . *feeling,* I suppose. One can see how you love being there. The eye is drawn to you."

The same thing Sebastian DeWitt had said, of a sort, and I'll admit it pleased me. "Well. Thank you."

"In fact, I had thought you might be well served by a good . . . ah, never mind."

"A good what?"

Nathan shrugged and toyed with the stem of his wineglass. "Nothing. What do I know about drama?"

"I don't know," I said honestly, but he'd piqued my curiosity and my vanity, and I couldn't help wanting to know what he'd been going to say, especially because he was echoing DeWitt, and I wondered how I managed to be so transparent when I worked so hard to make it otherwise. "Tell me what you were going to say."

He looked at me consideringly, his blue eyes glinting. "You need to grab the limelight, my dear, and to do that you need a part that grabs attention for you."

I couldn't resist a little jab. "That's what *Penelope Justis* was supposed to do."

"And it still will. When Ginny's gone, it will be yours again."

I sighed. "It will never be mine. Everyone will have seen her version first."

"Oh, I don't think so," he said with a thin smile. "But I was thinking of something else, something along the lines of . . . what was that play I saw recently? When I was in New York a year or so ago, I think. A French court, a woman with a scar . . . horribly disfigured . . ."

"From a bullet fired into her face," I said. "*L'Article 47.* Augustin Daly produced it in New York, though he stole it from Belot."

"The heroine was quite mad. It was stunning to watch. Greene should play it here."

"Well, it wouldn't bother Lucius to steal from Daly. You should suggest it to him."

Nathan leaned back in his chair, idly sipping his wine. "You know the part of the woman?"

"Cora. Yes, I know it. It's a good play."

"Say a few lines for me. I want to see how you do it."

I laughed and drank my own wine. I felt pleasantly full, a little drunk, and tonight Nathan had stroked my vanity in a way I wasn't used to. Perhaps he did truly feel sorry for giving his wife my part. In any case, I liked him this way, as charming as he'd been when I'd first met him, a charm I'd forgotten he had. So I put my elbows on the table, clasping my hands beneath my chin, taking on the persona of Cora, the mad mulatto. Dreamily, I said, "'Have you forgotten our first night? Our beautiful life in Louisiana! Do you not remember our room, opening on a garden full of fragrant flowers? In the distance, the Father of Water hurried down against the sea breeze and the rising tide! The birds that flitted by the window sang a chorus to our duet of kisses!'"

"Wonderful," Nathan said. "I'm entranced."

I smiled and went on. "'You swore by the myriad stars that glowed above us that you had never seen my like for beauty! That you could not tear yourself from me, and the morning star found us where Hesperus had last peeped in. Can our old-time bliss be never known again?'"

He leaned forward. "Amazing. You truly *are* her. That man she was in love with—"

"George."

"Had she looked at him the way you're looking at me now . . ."

Nathan's expression took on the ardency I'd never liked. I leaned away. "It's an excellent part."

"Can you do some of the mad lines? Act them out for me."

I glanced around. "Here?"

He shrugged. "Why not?"

"Nathan, there are people—"

"No one I know." He looked around as well. "No one I care about. Let's give them a start, shall we?"

I shook my head.

"What's wrong? You did it that night at the saloon. With Metairie and the others."

"That was for fun—"

"This will be fun for me," he said. "Go ahead. I want to see how they react. I'll warrant they've never seen anything like it. Amuse me, my dear. Be mad Cora."

There weren't very many people in the place, it was true, but still I was reluctant. And without my fellows . . .

Nathan said, "Don't tell me you're too shy. Come on. Show them what the famous Mrs. Wilkes can do."

His urging was pretty, and he was smiling, but there was something beneath it I didn't like, something that made me think of the way he'd looked when he'd slapped me, angry and not quite *there*. He was a little drunk too, and I knew how mean he could be, and it was stupid to be reluctant—I didn't care about these people, and he wanted it, and it was easy enough.

"Very well."

"I am your helpless audience," he said.

I took a deep breath and closed my eyes, remembering poor Cora, how desperate was her love for George, how well she'd been betrayed, and I said the first lines, " 'When I am alone, I see the amorous pictures glowing on the wall—I hear your ardent words—her sweet replies—I can even count your innumerable kisses!' " I let myself become her. My voice began to rise; I was aware of the growing attention of the other people in the restaurant, and as always, it fed me. " 'My blood boils!' " I rose from my chair, raising my voice, entering fully into the game now. " 'I stare until my eyeballs fit to burst!' " I fell to my knees, grasping his hand. " 'If you will not love me, kill me! Let me die by your hand!' "

"Please don't be so dramatic," he said—not the line, but close enough.

I sprang to my feet. " 'Then nothing will soften you. You call me mad! Mad? Mad—did you mean it? Yes, without your love I may go mad—I lose the thread of my thoughts sometimes—you know what I mean?' " Softer now, confused—I glanced about the restaurant, seeing the shock on the face of a thin aesthete of a man seated nearby, and I played to him. " 'That is not madness! I hear voices about me!' "

The waiter came forward, looking alarmed. He glanced at Nathan, and then to me. "Sir, are you—"

I grabbed his arm. " 'They come! Don't let them touch me!' "

The waiter looked horrified. Nathan said quickly, in the manner of a man both embarrassed and worried, "It's nothing. Leave us."

I released the waiter's arm. "'Police! I know, I know! He would denounce me—he would call me mad again! And the police would seize *me*! Oh, did you see that look he gave me!'" The waiter looked wildly about, as if hoping for rescue.

Nathan rose now, but he kept a small smile, and I saw his eyes urging me on. He was enjoying the game. "Come now, my dear—"

"'Ha ha ha! I have become a silly girl! Why am I frightened!'" I pulled away from him. "'But I have all my senses. Let me see—he sat there. I sat here. He said that he—that I—he told her—what is the matter with me?'" I passed my hand before my eyes. "'I don't know how it is, but there seems to be some presence in this room. I am alone though—quite alone! I'll ring—no! the servants must not see me in this state!'"

The thin man who'd been watching rose and approached us, glancing at Nathan and then saying soothingly to me, "Now, now, ma'am. I'm a doctor. Perhaps you should sit down—"

"'Who says that I am mad? I am not so'"—a whisper—"'mad.'" Then loudly again—"'How the echoes abound in this room!'"

"I think it best if we just leave," said Nathan to the man, who hovered solicitously near. Nathan looked to the waiter. "Send the bill to my home. For now, I think I should get my wife to bed."

Wife. It almost made me break character. I hid it by pressing my face into his chest, and he put his arm around me, and on cue, I pretended disorientation as he took up my cloak and led me from the restaurant. "'The secret police! They arrest men without noise or trouble! They are cunning. You think yourself secure! You go to rest one night and in the morning they are at your bedside—'" We were at the door. The doorman opened it with alacrity, Nathan led me out into the night, helping me into the carriage, turning back to whisper to the doorman, "Say nothing of this," and then he was in the carriage too, and the door was closed, and he fell into laughter that was so contagious that I laughed too.

"Oh, that was brilliant! Brilliant!" he crowed, his eyes

shining in the lamplight glancing through the windows. "Dear God, that was the best time I've had in months."

I smiled. "They won't let you back anytime soon, I think. At least not with me. Or your wife either. Why did you call me that?"

He wiped at his eyes. "I don't know. It was the first thing I thought of. It doesn't matter. Ginny dislikes the place."

I settled back into the seat.

"Did you hear that doctor? He truly believed. . . ." Nathan laughed again, letting it fall to a sigh. "Ah, my dear, you were born for the stage, that's clear enough."

"I'm glad you liked it. But you might want to go back and explain later."

"Of course," he said. "I'll tell them it was a command performance, and they should all rush to the Regal to take in the sublime Mrs. Wilkes. Would that please you?"

"Of course it would."

"It went very well." He looked smug, and I had the strangest feeling, just as I'd had the night he'd given me the cloak, as if I'd fallen into some little game running in his head, and you know, it spoiled my delight in it all. Suddenly I was uncomfortable, and I couldn't really say why, except that there was that . . . meanness . . . in him again, that deliberation, and I felt I'd been guyed. Which was stupid, because we'd played the joke together, but still I felt somehow I was the victim, and I didn't like it. In fact, I wanted nothing more than to be done with tonight, however the hell it was going to end.

Nathan said, "You deserve a reward."

I knew exactly what he thought my reward should be, and there at least was a game I knew how to play, and if it got me closer to being rid of him tonight, I was willing to play it. So I leaned forward and put my hand on his thigh and said, "Is that so?"

I crept my fingers toward his cock, but he caught my hand and gave a short shake of his head. "Not tonight, I'm afraid, my dear. There's someone I need to talk to."

"Tonight? So late?"

"Sorry to disappoint you. I'll take you to your hotel, but I'm afraid I must be off."

I pretended to be disappointed, when the truth was that I felt as if I'd been given a last-minute reprieve. Then I thought how strange it was that he'd gone to all the trouble to take me to dinner—and at the Queen City too—without expecting to get something in return for it. So I said, "Just take me to the Regal then," because I had this feeling that if I let him take me home, he might change his mind and decide to take a few minutes to "reward" me. Also, I was wearing the costume from *Debts*, and I needed to change again, and why not do it now, as I wasn't tired in the least bit. I felt the way I always did after a good performance—a little jittery and too awake—and Nathan was making me nervous besides.

"Not your hotel?" he asked.

"The theater's closer."

"As you wish." He pounded on the roof and told the driver where to go, and then he lapsed into thought, and those were the last words he said to me until we stopped. Then it was as if he came to himself. He smiled at me—a smile that didn't quite reach his eyes—and handed me down and said, "Everything should be done by tomorrow, but it may be a few days before I can get away again to see you."

I was confused. "Everything?"

Nathan only kissed my hand before he released it. "Not too long. Don't fret. You'll see me in the box."

"All right," I said. "Good night."

He closed the door. The carriage pulled away quickly, leaving me standing there in front of the darkened theater, and I breathed a sigh of relief and went to the side door. It was unlocked, as always—mostly because the set carpenter slept in a loft he'd built in the heavens above the stage, so there was always someone here. Lucius might even still be around, but I hoped he wasn't. I wasn't in the mood for any more pretense, and I couldn't rid myself of this uncomfortable feeling that I was going to come to regret what I'd done tonight at the Queen City.

I stepped into the darkness, felt my way to the stairs leading to the dressing rooms, and went down—they were familiar enough that even the soul-dark blackness didn't faze me. When I got to the bottom, I blinked, because there was a light coming from one of the dressing rooms—no, the greenroom. Dim, but it was there, slanting into the hall, and I was dismayed. I didn't want to talk to one of my fellows tonight; I just wanted to change and go home, and I wondered if I could sneak by the open doorway without anyone seeing me. Perhaps if I hurried, if I were very quiet—

But then, as I started to go past, I caught a movement out of the corner of my eye, and I stopped. Because it wasn't one of the other actors in the greenroom so late at night.

It was Sebastian DeWitt.

He'd pulled a table up to that old green armchair with all the stuffing coming out, and the table was covered with papers, as well as the floor around him, and he was writing as one possessed. His frock coat was thrown on the settee; he was in his shirtsleeves, which were stained with splotches of ink. Beside him on the table was an open bottle of what looked like whiskey.

I was so surprised to see him that I blurted, "What are you doing here?"

He jerked, spattering ink across the page, blinking, then squinting into the darkness beyond the light. "Mrs. Wilkes?"

I came fully into the room. "Yes. What are you doing here so late?"

He gestured to the papers. "Writing."

"I can see that. But why are you here, and not in your own rooms?"

"I could ask the same of you. I thought you went with Langley."

"Yes, we had dinner, and. . . ." I swallowed the urge to tell him how strange it had been. "He had an appointment. Or something. I asked him to leave me here to change. My costume, you see. . . ."

DeWitt's gaze swept me. "I see."

"He took me to a nice place, and. . . ." *Babbling, Bea.* "Well, it doesn't matter."

DeWitt leaned back in his chair. "The walls are thin at the Biltmore. My neighbor was snoring."

"Do you do this often? Come here to write, I mean?"

"No. But I was inspired. You were very affecting tonight."

There it was, the compliment I'd wanted earlier. I smiled like an idiot. "Truly?"

"Stunning, Mrs. Wilkes. So much so I had to buy whiskey." He pointed to the bottle. "Would you like some?"

I stepped over to the table. "No glass?"

"I'm afraid not," he said. "No doubt you'll think me uncouth."

"Oh, I think a great many things about you, but that you're uncouth isn't one of them." I took a great sip. The whiskey burned its way over my tongue, down my throat, leaving a raw, sweet taste after. "Why, it's not bad."

"Not the best, but I've stepped up in the world. No more rotgut for me."

"I'm gratified to hear it."

"You should be. You're the cause."

He was looking at me with that intent, too-warm gaze. I turned away. "Well, thank you for the drink. I'd better change now. It's late, and I—"

"Do you mean to go home?"

"Yes, but—"

"I'll walk you there."

"Oh. I don't want to take you from your work."

"I think I'm finished for tonight," he said, beginning to gather up the papers. "And I wouldn't be able to get much more done anyway."

I frowned. "Why not?"

"I'd be too worried that you might not get home in one piece. As you've already noted, it's very late. Only the debauched will be out on the streets."

I laughed. "You and me and the debauched. There's a nice thought."

He smiled. "Indeed. Perhaps we'll end up joining them."

"Speak for yourself. I don't think I even know how to be debauched."

"If you're very good, perhaps I could be persuaded to teach you." Again, that gaze.

I swallowed hard. "I'll go change."

"I'll be ready when you are."

And then I was hurrying toward my dressing room. My fingers were trembling when I lit the lamp—*what the hell is wrong with you?*—and I fumbled over the buttons of the costume. I couldn't make myself go slow, either, because I was half afraid he would leave without me even as I knew it would be better if he did. This was beyond idiocy. *It's just walking home. Nothing more than that. Don't be a fool.*

But when I was dressed again in the brown calico, I had to take a deep breath to calm myself. When I stepped from the dressing room, it was to find him standing there already, his coat on, his satchel over his shoulder. He had the whiskey in his hand, the bottle uncorked. He held it out to me. "Another drink?"

I took it and drank deeply and handed it back to him, and together we went back up the stairs and out of the theater, into the night, which was too warm for the cloak I still wore. My feet felt swollen in my boots. Once we were out in the dark, with hardly anyone on the streets, I was glad he was with me. We passed the bottle back and forth companionably as we walked, and the whiskey, along with the wine I'd had at dinner, set that deep warmth in my stomach that had nothing to do with the heat.

He asked, "Where did you go with Langley?"

"The Queen City."

I felt his surprise. "Really?"

"We were celebrating, apparently," I said.

"Celebrating what?"

I took the bottle from him. "My forgiveness."

"Ah."

"I'm happy for it, really. I was afraid he would lobby for his wife. Mrs. Langley wants me dismissed from the company as well as from *Penelope*."

"Perhaps you deserve that."

Another gulp of whiskey. "Please, none of your scolds tonight. It doesn't help."

"All right. But I can't convince her how brilliant you are if she hates you."

I laughed and looked up at the stars. "So you've said. But I doubt she would have liked me in any case. I'm her husband's mistress."

"Perhaps she might have forgiven you that. She said they'd been at odds lately."

"Well, that makes sense. Sometimes I think Nathan doesn't care for her at all. But if that's true, why pick me? She and I look so alike."

"Perhaps there's something to that." DeWitt's voice was quiet, musing.

"You think he loves her?"

He shrugged. "I don't know him well enough to say. She's an interesting woman. I'd say . . . easy to love."

That pricking jealousy again. "Don't tell me you've fallen for her."

He took a swig from the bottle and laughed. "If I had, would it trouble you?"

"Why should it?"

"I don't know. You sound as if it does."

We were at my hotel. It was time to say good night. His face was breathtakingly chiseled in the lamplight and the darkness, and I couldn't keep from staring. *Say good night. Tell him you'll see him tomorrow. Go inside.* But the whiskey had worked its magic; it had muted that energy I'd felt earlier, the excitement that a good night of acting left behind, and in its place put a loose, dreamlike sense that everything was safe, everything was good, everything was as it was meant to be.

Which was enough of a reason to send him on his way, and I knew it, because *this is dangerous, Bea. You're playing with fire.* Still, I heard myself say, "Will you come up for a bit? I have—I can give you an apricot."

"An apricot?" He seemed amused.

"It's candied. And French."

"Ah then. How could I refuse?"

"You can't."

"Then lead on," he said.

I was relieved; I felt this little joy, and I tried not to think of what I wanted from him, why the hell I'd asked him to come up, or how late it was, or the fact that I was a little drunk, or anything else. I was just glad he was here, and I was afraid to ask myself why that was, so I didn't. He followed me inside and up the flights of stairs. While I fumbled for the key, he motioned to the patterns made by the moonlight on the floor.

"Beautiful."

I glanced at them. Funny how I'd never noticed them before, but he was right.

I opened the door and gestured for him to go inside. The room was dark, and hot, but I'd left the window open, not that it helped. I took off the cloak and closed the door behind us and lit the oil lamp, and then I took another sip of whiskey and handed him the bottle. There was something about him that took up space, that just lodged there in my chest, and in an effort to escape it, I went to the bed and sat down, bending to unlace my boots. "So, what were you working on tonight? More revisions for *Penelope*?"

He shook his head and leaned against the bureau. "I was tired of ghosts tonight."

"Real or imagined?"

He took a sip of whiskey. "Both. I was working on something new."

"The play Nathan commissioned?"

He nodded.

I eased off one boot and let it fall to the floor, wiggling my toes in relief. "Well, with any luck I'll actually get to play it. Unless his wife decides she wants that part too."

"She won't want it."

I sent the other boot to join its partner. "Why not?"

"Because the main character will be worse than Penelope. I mean for her to be an out-and-out villain."

I stared at him in surprise. "A villain? But I thought you were supposed to write it for me."

"I am."

I made a face. "I thought you *liked* me."

"I do like you. Most of the time. But you seem well suited to villainy."

I laughed. It was the whiskey. "So you keep saying. Well, villains are more interesting, aren't they?"

He took another swig from the bottle. "Sometimes."

I was sweating. Without thinking, I pulled up my skirt and undid my garter, rolling my stocking down my leg and then letting it fall to the floor, and I'll admit that once I realized what I was doing, I did it a little to bait him too. A little punishment for what he'd said about my villainy. I felt him watching me. "If I'm such a villain, aren't you afraid to be alone with me?"

"Should I be?"

"I don't know. You can never tell with villains. Perhaps I might stab you through the heart."

"Already done."

I dropped the other stocking to the floor and glanced up at him. His hand was clenched hard around the bottle; I felt his desire clear into my toes, and I liked it, and that and the whiskey made me want more of it, made me want to torment him just a little. I could stop it whenever I wanted, after all. I got up, a bit unbalanced, and went barefoot to where he stood, taking the bottle from him, drinking—I was feeling the whiskey very well now. I gave it back. "Mr. DeWitt—"

"Call me Sebastian."

I laughed. "Sebastian DeWitt. That cannot possibly be your real name."

"Why not?"

"Too improbable. Sebastian—he was a saint of some kind, wasn't he?"

He looked surprised. "You're Catholic?"

"Oh no. We did a play once. 'Slay me not with words but with your arrows—' "

" 'And to my true heaven my soul will fly.' I know it."

"And then, of course, there's the DeWitt. What a name for a writer. Are you witty, Mr. DeWitt?"

"I like to think so."

"So you see: improbable."

"Perhaps. But my mother tells me it's mine."

"Did she mean for you to be a writer, then?"

He laughed shortly. "I think she would have preferred a safer occupation. A grocer, perhaps."

"Then she should have been more careful about the name she chose for you."

He said nothing, and we lapsed into silence, and I was suddenly nervous. I felt his desire as if he'd cloaked me in it. Uncomfortably, I said to break the silence, "I promised you an apricot, didn't I?"

"You did."

I nudged him aside, clumsy now from the drink, grabbing one of the candy boxes from the bureau, taking off the lid. "There're figs and cherries too, but the apricots are the best." I picked one up and held it out to him.

But he didn't take it as I expected. Instead he wrapped his hand about my wrist to keep me there, and then he leaned down and ate the apricot from my fingers, one bite, and then another, the whole thing, and I was startled to stillness. His gaze caught mine; I could not look away as he slowly and quite deliberately licked the syrup from my fingers. His mouth was warm and wet, and I felt as if something had dropped right through me. Damn, I was much drunker than I'd thought.

He released me and straightened, and I saw the movement of his tongue as he chewed. "Delicious."

I could hardly find my voice. "I'm not going to fuck you, Mr. DeWitt."

I meant to offend him, to back him off, but he seemed completely unmoved. He swallowed the apricot and took a sip of whiskey. Then he handed the bottle to me, saying mildly, "Is that so? Why is that, Mrs. Wilkes?"

"L—look at you. Have you even a penny to your name?"

"One hundred dollars. Thanks to our Mr. Langley."

"One hundred? He paid you that much?"

"Fifty for the play he commissioned for you. The other fifty for *Penelope Justis.*"

"It must be more than you've made in years."

"It's been a good month."

I gulped the whiskey. It went down hard. "Well, you can't expect to do better, can you?"

He took the bottle. "I'm like everyone else, Mrs. Wilkes. I hope to make a living."

"You don't look as if you've done very well. That coat—"

"You don't like it? It was the latest style once."

"You know what I mean. I can't . . . I mean, I won't . . . I mean. . . ." I was flustered; it was hard to think. He had not taken his gaze from me even a moment. I curled the fingers he'd licked into my palm. "I don't want to be poor," I burst out.

He set the bottle on the bureau and stepped closer. "I don't recall asking you to be poor with me."

"No, but . . ."

His hand came to my waist. I was very drunk; that was the only reason that came to me as to why I didn't step away, why I didn't dodge his kiss. I didn't mean to kiss him back. But the way he grazed his lips against mine, and then the way he kissed me, slow and easy, as if he had all the time in the world to do it . . . well, it seemed strange and rather fine and so different from the way I'd been kissed before, and I was dizzy from the whiskey too, and that must have been why I didn't notice how he got me to the bed. I didn't notice until I was there, and he was still kissing me and bringing me down upon it, and I felt his hand drawing up my skirt, the smooth heat of his hand against my skin, running up my bare leg—because it *was* bare, and I was the one who had bared it, and *you are a stupid fool, Beatrice Wilkes.* God, yes, I was. I meant to say no. What was I doing here with him? And then, when he drew away, I was going to say it. I truly was.

Except that what he did then startled me into silence. Except that before I knew what he was about, he was undoing the tie of my drawers and sliding them down, and I raised up to help him, though I hardly meant to. Then he knelt between my legs, and I had this moment where I knew he was going to fuck me and I wasn't going to stop it, but that wasn't what he did. He lowered his head, and lifted my knees over his shoulders and it was . . . he was . . . I felt the soft brush of his hair against my inner thigh, and then his tongue. . . . I heard a sound, a rush of breath, a moan, and I didn't realize it was me, not until I was lifting my hips to bring his mouth closer and I tangled my hands in his hair to keep him there. I was sweating and jerking and making these little sounds I could not keep myself from making, and there was something building in me until I thought I would go mad with it.

In the end I let him fuck me after all. I even begged him to.

It was the sound of a wagon overturning that woke me. I heard the clatter of the wheels, the driver's curse, the thudding, splintering crash, and an avalanche of bouncing thuds scattering over the road. I rolled over, thinking to scoot out of bed and go to the window to see when I realized two things: first, my head was pounding in a sick way, and second, Sebastian DeWitt was in bed beside me.

How stupid could one person be?

The chaos from the street below was loud, a horse's whinny, the driver still cursing better than I'd heard in some time, but DeWitt slept on. I wondered if I could creep out without waking him, and then wondered where the hell I would go, and it was my room besides, and I knew I was a coward and hated myself for it, but I did not want to see his face this morning and know what I'd done with him last night—nearly all through the night, I amended with a silent groan. I mean, he'd been half in love with me before we'd started, and I did not want to hurt him and knew that now there was no way I wouldn't. Because I had not struggled for thirteen years only to hitch my wagon to a spavined horse, and how the hell could I say to him that talent wasn't enough? That I liked being his muse and I wanted him to admire me and write plays for me, but he couldn't expect me to give up anything I'd gained, which meant Nathan Langley. What had happened last night was exactly what I'd meant to guard against.

I glanced at his back again, and then away, quickly, because even just that—his back, for God's sake—brought a quick stab of desire. And I found myself wondering if it was so bad to want just a little more before I let him go. Maybe just one more time . . .

Stupid, Bea. I pushed back the sheet very carefully and made to get out of bed without rousing him. There was a restaurant around the corner. I would go there and wait until he was gone. I wasn't going to the theater this morning, now that Lucius had taken me off *Penelope,* and so it would be hours before DeWitt would know where to find me. By then I would have thought of what to say to him. By then I would have a hold on whatever it was that made me want him.

I snaked a leg out, sliding to the edge—

"Not so fast." He pulled me back onto his chest. His hand tangled in my hair, holding me in place as he kissed me. All my good intentions got tangled up in that kiss, and suddenly I was straddling him, and his hands were hard on my hips, and we were both panting and straining and every sore muscle I had was screaming, but my desire was as strong as his, and I couldn't banish it. When we finally collapsed, and he kissed me lingeringly and well, I wouldn't have said no to doing it again. Which was so strange I couldn't fathom it. I'd never wanted to do it again. I'd hardly ever wanted to do it the first time.

Sebastian DeWitt was like those damned apricots. I never ate one that I didn't want another. Which was why, when he tried to bring me down so he could kiss me again, I skirted away from him and said, "It must be late. You'd better go. You've got rehearsal. Lucius will demand a forfeit if you're not on time."

He gave me a lazy look. "I'm not under contract to him. He can't fine me."

"They'll be waiting for you."

"I imagine they can get along without me for a day."

"Trust me, you don't want to make Lucius angry."

He traced from my shoulder to my elbow. "I don't give a damn about that."

"Sebastian, please," I said desperately, pushing at him. He was solid as stone. "Lucius took me off the play. If you're not there, what do you suppose they'll think?"

"That I'm protesting. I am."

"No. They've seen the way you look at me. It's too much coincidence that we're gone at the same time. They'll think you're with me."

A pause. "Ah. Langley."

I swallowed and nodded, preparing myself for his anger, for

all that stupid male possessiveness. "I don't want him to know. It could ruin everything."

But all he did was sigh and sit up, pushing the threadbare sheets aside. "Very well."

Very well? "You don't . . . you don't mind?"

He glanced at me over his shoulder. "Would it matter if I did?"

"No."

"Then what else am I to do?"

I was disconcerted. How well he was taking this. "I expected you to be . . . jealous."

He rose, going to where his trousers lay abandoned on the floor, picking up the underwear tossed beside them. "Langley's not only your patron, he's mine. Unless I care to give him up, which I don't, or you, which I won't, I imagine we're better off keeping this secret."

It was just what I wanted, wasn't it? Yes, of course it was, but you know, this little disappointment lodged in me and wouldn't quite get loose, which was the most stupid thing about this whole business.

I watched him pull on his underwear, and then his trousers. "You know . . . we shouldn't . . . this can't happen again. If Nathan were to find out—"

His smile cut my words dead. He stepped over to the bed and leaned down, whispering against my mouth, "He won't find out."

"When he sees you staring at me like some moonstruck calf—"

"He already sees that. Nothing's changed."

"I need to keep him from favoring his spoiled wife over me, and I can't do that if I'm constantly thinking of you—"

"Will you be?" He smiled. "How encouraging."

I slapped his chest in frustration. "You know what I mean!"

He backed away, that irritating smile still curving his lips as he picked up his shirt and shrugged into it. "You're an actress, aren't you? It should be nothing for you to fool a man like Langley, who's so taken with his own importance he's blind to all else."

He was right, of course. Sebastian made it all seem so damn easy, and you know, I was suddenly afraid. I wished he would demand that I choose between him and Nathan so I had a reason to tell him to go to hell and leave me alone.

But instead he trapped me with that gray gaze, and said, "You never see Langley in the afternoons. Those hours between rehearsal and the performance . . . those belong to me. He'll never know."

And suddenly I was thinking about having him again while the sun blazed through my west-facing windows, both of us sweating, and I couldn't even speak.

He finished buttoning his shirt and shoved on his boots, and then he grabbed his frock coat from the settee. And I couldn't keep from saying, "And you probably want to keep this a secret from Mrs. Langley as well, don't you?"

"She already suspects it."

"She does?"

"She knows you're my muse—what else should she think?"

"I thought muses were exalted beings. You know, like angels or something. Beyond common . . . fucking."

He laughed. "Oh, I think the best ones are wrestling in the mud with man, so to speak. You know. Debauched." He gave me a look that made me blush, and then he stepped over and kissed me, and I found myself leaning into him and wanting him, so he laughed when he pulled away. "Don't go anywhere. I want to think of you waiting for me just like this."

Then he picked up his satchel and slung the strap over his head, and he was gone, and I was still sitting naked on the bed and feeling as if something I'd wanted badly had just slipped through my fingers, and wasn't that brilliant? If I felt this way after one night, how the hell would I feel after two? Sebastian DeWitt frightened me more than I wanted to admit, and that was the truth I needed to remember.

That was when I decided there wouldn't be another night. I might be stupid once, but not twice. I would tell him that today, the moment rehearsal was over. I got out of bed. I went to the basin and poured lukewarm water into it and plunged my whole face in.

Chapter Nineteen

Geneva

I dreamed that night about my lunch with Sebastian DeWitt. That lunch, which had lasted longer than an hour, moving into two, had been filled with laughter and talk and a little more wine than had been wise. It had made me forget Nathan's betrayal for a while. Though there had been people in the restaurant I recognized, I'd made no attempt to quiet my laughter. I'd felt them watching us, and I knew that Sebastian DeWitt was right when he'd said there would be talk. But I no longer cared, not for Nathan's sake or my own. When I'd arrived home to Nathan's note that he wouldn't be home for dinner, I was glad.

That next morning, I deliberately kept from thinking about Beatrice Wilkes and her relationships with both Sebastian DeWitt and my husband. But at least I had managed things so that I would not have to see her, and that was some consolation. I had no idea whether or not Nathan would be angry at what I'd done in removing her from *Penelope,* and I tried not to think of the consequences of that, nor about the fact that it looked increasingly as if, despite my hopes, neither Seattle nor my good behavior could return my marriage to what it had been.

I had just finished breakfast when Bonnie came in. "Pardon me, ma'am, but it's Thursday."

I glanced up at her blankly. "Yes?"

"Tonight is my night off, ma'am."

"Yes, of course."

She hovered, shoving her hands in the pockets of her apron. "Well, ma'am, Mr. Langley usually leaves me my weekly pay in the kitchen, and it ain't there."

"I'm certain he'll provide it later."

Hesitation, a slight flush. "If you don't mind, ma'am, I can't wait. He won't be back until after I'm gone, and I was to go to a dance tonight, and—"

I held up my hand to stop her. "There's no need to tell me. Very well, I'll get it for you."

A quick curtsey, a smile of relief. "Thank you so much, ma'am."

I rose with a sigh and made my way down the hall to Nathan's study, where he kept the safe with money for the household accounts. The room smelled of him, of cigar smoke and the verbena of his custom-made shaving soap, and I felt a twinge of both anger and despair, which I pushed aside as I went to the cigar stand by one of the leather upholstered chairs at the fireplace. I flipped the latch, taking out the box of cigars, feeling along the bottom for the safe key.

There it was. I picked it up and put the cigars back. At the other end of the room was Nathan's large mahogany desk, littered with papers. Behind it were bookcases, one full shelf of ledgers. The safe was there, below the ledgers, but Nathan's chair was blocking it, and as I moved it, the key slipped from my hand, bouncing on the desk and falling into the partially opened, long, top drawer.

The drawer held Nathan's letterhead, creamy white, his monogram in swirled black at the very top, envelopes, and the key was not immediately evident. It must have fallen beneath them. I pushed the stationery aside to get at it.

And I saw the newspaper article.

I would not have noted it except for two things: first, it was cut neatly from the paper, which would not have been so odd if not for the second thing, which was the fact that it was the society column from the *Post-Intelligencer*, and part of it had been underlined in ink, with a handwritten exclamation point scrawled in the margin beside.

I picked it up. The column was from two days ago, I saw, and the item that had been underlined said:

> What notorious matron has been seen sharing smiles (and more?) with the Regal Theater's newest resident playwright? Little birds have spotted the two of them huddling together in the most unsavory locales, and lately they seem thick as thieves. These sightings, along with Mrs. L's latest foray into treading the boards, have all of society in an uproar, and many of our city's finest have declared her beyond hope or help. Dear Readers, can we be far wrong in anticipating another *Andromeda*—but this time writ in ink rather than stone?

I stared at it in dismay. Nathan had said not a word of it to me, yet he'd found it noteworthy enough to cut it out. To underline it. To set an exclamation point beside it.

I puzzled over it for a moment, and set it back where I had found it, pulling a sheet of letterhead to half hide it as it had been before, and as I did so, I revealed another sheet, handwriting I recognized, and I paused, arrested by the sight of my father's fancily looped *G. Gen—*

I pushed it to reveal the rest. *Geneva.*

Frowning, I pulled the letter loose.

> *My dear Nathan,*
>
> *Regarding operations for Stratford & Brown, you must know that I agree with you and trust your decisions in all aspects. Please proceed as discussed.*
>
> *As for Geneva . . . this is what I have feared for some time. As you say, it would have been best to insist on Bloomfield Estates in November, and I am sorry now I did not, and more sorry than I can say that you are now left to deal with the results of this lamentable decision. I think we had both hoped for so much better. From her letters to me, I know the removal to Seattle has seemingly made things worse. I am appalled at her most recent fancy, and*

her grandmother is beside herself at the thought of Geneva on a stage! And this relationship with the playwright, and how you say he has replaced Marat in her imaginings . . . I am beyond concerned. I would board the next train if I weren't in the middle of such delicate negotiations.

I laud you for your patience in such trying circumstances. Your letter regarding the doctor's findings was most revelatory. If he thinks she may go further into delusion if she is not checked, then there is no reason to hesitate.

It is long past time for us to do what must be done. I worry about her health most of all, and I will not contest your decision to have her committed, and in fact will aid you in any way I can.

You must let me know what the second doctor says, and if you feel the local asylum will house her appropriately. I understand your desire to have her housed in an institution near enough that you can see she is getting the proper treatment, and I defer to your judgment. Money is, of course, no concern; all of my financial resources are at your disposal. I have also immediately transferred Geneva's accounts to your control.

Your father-in-law,
Maynard Stratford

I could only stare at the letter, at my father's handwriting. *I will not contest your decision to have her committed. . . . I have also immediately transferred Geneva's accounts to your control. . . .* It was impossible. I could not be reading it correctly. But reading it again revealed no mistake, and my hands were trembling when I was done. They could not mean to do this. Not to me. I didn't understand—this talk about the theater, about Sebastian DeWitt—hadn't Nathan and I agreed to those things? Hadn't he urged me to them?

Then, suddenly, it all fell into place. Nathan's willingness to put Sebastian DeWitt in my path. The quickness with which my husband had acquiesced to my acting on the Regal's stage. The doctor's visit for an inconsequential cough.

I glanced again at the society piece, underlined for my father's benefit. I understood now, and saw how perfectly I'd played into their hands. How every single thing I'd done since I arrived in this town had done so.

An asylum. And I knew that once I was there, they would never let me out. Nathan would have control of my trust. Seattle society already loved him—I had seen that for myself, and the visit of Mrs. Brown and Mrs. Porter only confirmed it. They would fall over themselves in sympathy. The political career he wanted would be his for the taking. I would be out of the way, and my father would still love him.

I felt I would be sick. It was all I could do to put things back the way I'd found them, to close the drawer again, to put the key away, to go into the hallway. Bonnie was standing at the doorway to the parlor. She frowned when she saw me, saying, "Are you all right, ma'am?"

And I remembered why I'd been in the study to begin with. "I'm sorry, Bonnie," I managed. "I could not find the key. You'll have to wait for Mr. Langley after all." And then I went past her and up the stairs, one at a time, feeling as if I moved in a daze, to my bedroom.

Once inside, I closed the door and leaned against it. I could not think; I could hardly move. I felt my father's betrayal and my husband's malice like a poison. And there was no denying my own stupidity. I'd forgotten how completely Nathan had fooled me once before. I had been too willing to ignore my suspicions, so determined to restore my marriage that I hadn't remembered what a lie it had been to begin with. I thought of the night of the exhibition, how quickly Nathan had brought up Bloomfield Estates, as if he and my father had been considering it for some time, and I was afraid. How well I'd forgotten the choice I'd been given in Chicago, how foolish not to realize that they had never put it aside.

Dear God, what was I to do now?

The answer came to me in a surge of desperate panic.

Run.

But where to? And how? I tried to remember: Nathan would need a second doctor to commit me without my consent, and I remembered his asking if Mr. Edwards had come to watch rehearsals, and I realized who Mr. Edwards must be. A second doctor, the one who would see me upon the stage and say I was mad, because what sane woman of my status would do such a thing? Oh, how well Nathan had planned it! But Edwards had not yet attended rehearsal, and so there was some time . . . probably not much. I would need to plan it well, to go where they could not find me, at least until I had time to decide what else to do. If they found me, there would be no escaping.

I forced myself to think logically. First, I must not raise suspicion; I must allow Nathan to believe his plan was proceeding as he meant it to. If he suspected I knew, he would move more quickly. Better to go about my days as I usually did. To gather my resources, to pack, to find a place to go.

I would need money. A steamer ticket out of this godforsaken town. And I could not be seen getting those things; I could leave no trace, no trail to follow. I needed help, a friend to procure the ticket, but what friends did I have but for—

Sebastian DeWitt.

He would help me, I knew. And this morning, he would be at rehearsal, just as always.

Although it was now the last thing I wanted to do, I knew that I must go to rehearsal, pretend nothing had changed, hope Dr. Edwards was not in the audience, and plan. Panicking would only help Nathan.

I took a deep breath. The thought of seeing Mr. DeWitt gave me strength of mind and purpose as I readied to go. At least Mrs. Wilkes would not be there—how unimportant that seemed now, compared to only an hour ago. But with her gone, I would be assured of Mr. DeWitt's full attention.

Some of the others were already at the theater when I arrived: Mr. Metairie, for one, and Mrs. Chace, who lolled on a settee, fanning herself vigorously. Behind them, the painters worked steadily on the drop that had begun to take on color and shape: a painted cast-iron fence, marble statuary, a pretty gazebo bordered by pink rhododendrons. I glanced to the parquet—no one sitting in the seats, no visitor, expected or otherwise, and I was relieved until I realized that, while Mr. Geary sat at the prompting table, there was no sign of Mr. DeWitt, which was strange, as I had never arrived before him.

Mr. Geary glanced up as I came onto the stage and gave me a curt nod of greeting, which I took no offense to, having already seen that he greeted everyone the same way. But Mr. Metairie crossed to give me a little bow.

"I wish you good morning, Mrs. Langley."

His voice was so deep and smooth, his smile so genuine, that I told him the truth. "I do hope it gets better, Mr. Metairie."

The others had arrived as we spoke, all except for Mrs. Wilkes, whom I was not of course expecting, and Mr. DeWitt, whom I was. Mr. Greene asked irritably, "Where is DeWitt?"

No one answered; Mr. Greene sighed and spoke in a low voice to Mr. Geary.

Mr. Metairie said thoughtfully to me, "Perhaps our playwright is not so evenhanded as I'd supposed."

I had not thought of this. "You mean he's protesting . . . her removal?"

Mr. Metairie stroked his dark beard. "Precisely."

I felt a little stab of panic. "Oh. But . . . you don't really think he'd stay away?"

"Perhaps. He can't have liked her being removed from the play he wrote for her. Regardless, he'll achieve nothing by his absence."

"What do you mean?"

"Our Bea has a pragmatic soul. She won't look upon him the more favorably for it."

It hardly surprised me; I was not inclined to believe Mrs. Wilkes was possessed of anything but the most prosaic nature, and if Mr. DeWitt was protesting on her behalf, it was a gesture of such romance that I could not imagine she could appreciate it. And it only gave me one more reason to dislike her. Still, I could not quite believe Mr. DeWitt wouldn't make an appearance. But when Mr. Greene called for us all to take our places, Mr. DeWitt had still not arrived, and I was distracted and short waiting for him. But at least Nathan's "visitor" had not made an appearance either.

Rehearsal went long. Everyone seemed tired and irritable; we had to repeat scenes three and four times. The stage grew hot from bodies and the footlights, and we were all sweating. Mrs. Chace had ceased moving completely and was lying prostrate upon the proscenium, too hot even to fan herself.

As the hours went by, it seemed clear that Mr. DeWitt would not show, and my temper bloomed with everyone else's. I would have to go to Mr. DeWitt's rooms after rehearsal—I tried to remember if he'd ever told me where they were and realized he had not. But surely Mr. Greene would know. I resolved to ask him the moment rehearsal was over—which, at this point, looked to be never.

We were at the edge of the "pool" now, its boundaries marked by a circle of rope, and Mr. Wheeler had his arms about me, as I was supposed to be looking up at him in adoration, though it was too hot to do more than wish we were standing apart from each other, when Brody Townshend—who was supposed to come running to take a final try at killing Keefe—tripped over a bucket and sent it flying. Blue paint spattered across the stage, and he went skidding into it, falling flat on his back, cursing at the top of his lungs. The whole company erupted in chaos. Mr. Galloway swore as a bit of flying paint hit him squarely in the chest. Mrs. Chace yelped and clambered to her feet as if afraid it might touch her.

Mr. Wheeler dropped his arms from me and said in exasperation. "For God's sake, this is ridiculous!"

"Fire! Fire!" yelled a stagehand, racing onto the stage.

Mr. Wheeler sighed. "Not fire, boy. Paint. And you're a bit late. We already know it's spilled. Townshend's covered with it, as you can plainly see."

"It's true!" the boy insisted. "The Opera House is on fire!"

"Frye's Opera House?" I asked.

"Really?" Mr. Greene said with interest. "I suppose it's too much to hope it'll burn down."

"Good God, Lucius, why would you say such a thing?" Mr. Metairie asked.

"It would take months to rebuild. In the meantime, where would everyone go? Why, here, of course."

"You've all got to get out afore it spreads," the stagehand said.

"It's blocks from here," Mr. Greene said dismissively. "The fire department will have it well in hand. Now go on, boy. We've a rehearsal to tend to."

"But, sir, it's the block—"

"Go *on*."

Mr. Wheeler groaned. "Do you really mean to make this the longest rehearsal in history, Lucius? It's already after three. We've got to be back in an hour for *Old Debts*."

Mr. Greene took his watch from his pocket and glanced at it. "Ah, just so. Very well, my children, finish this scene, and then we'll be off."

Mr. Wheeler sighed and held out his arms for me to step obediently into, which I did, though I felt as he did; I wanted only for rehearsal to be over, so I could find Mr. DeWitt. I was also faintly concerned for the Opera House as well. Other than the Territorial University, Frye's was the most opulent building in Seattle.

"Do you think they'll save it?" I asked him.

"The Opera House?" He shrugged. "It depends on whether they can get water. Is the tide in or out?"

When the scene was finally done, the theater was so stifling and hot that it felt like an oven, and it was after four and already time for the actors to be at the theater to prepare for tonight's performance. No one made a move to go downstairs, however. Mr. Greene and Mr. Geary sat at the prompt table, haggling over a scene and complaining that Mr. DeWitt was not there to rewrite it. Mrs. Chace and Mr. Galloway sent a prop boy to the bakery down the street for "sustenance" and settled to wait. Brody Townshend wiped at his paint-soaked clothes with a rag and tried to avoid Miss Jenks's tender ministrations.

Mr. Metairie sat with a sigh upon the settee one of the stagehands had pulled out for a scene in *A New Way to Pay Old Debts*. "By God, no doubt it's hot as Hades downstairs. I'm taking a short nap right here. Someone wake me in twenty minutes."

The painters were raising the paint frame up and out of the

way so they could lower the drop for tonight's play in front of the newly painted one. It shrieked and creaked like a dying thing. Mr. Wheeler jumped off the proscenium into the parquet. "A perfect plan. Though I'll do it here, out of the way of the preparations."

I went to the table and waited until Mr. Greene looked up. "Yes, Mrs. Langley?"

"Mr. DeWitt was not here today," I said.

Mr. Greene said, "Yes indeed. I am aware."

"I had something . . . important . . . to discuss with him. Could you tell me where he keeps his rooms?"

"Rooms?" Mr. Greene laughed. "I doubt it's as grand as all that. I believe he stays at the Biltmore. But, Mrs. Langley, that part of town is no place for a lady."

"What street is it on?" I asked.

Mr. Greene frowned. "You cannot mean—"

"What *street,* Mr. Greene?"

"Washington."

"Thank you." I grabbed my purse and headed into the wings, toward the short flight of stairs that led down to the backstage door. It was even hotter there, in the darkness of backstage, and the air was hazy with dust. There was a strange acrid scent that burned my nose—some newly noxious potion of the set builders, I guessed.

I had just reached the landing before the door when someone came barreling up the stairs from the dressing rooms below.

Beatrice Wilkes. She paused when she saw me.

"I thought you'd be gone by now," she said.

"Good afternoon to you too, Mrs. Wilkes," I said stiffly. "As it happens, rehearsal ran late."

She gave a quick nod. "Is Sebas—Mr. DeWitt still here?"

"Mr. DeWitt declined to appear this morning."

Mrs. Wilkes frowned. "What?"

"Shall I speak more simply for you? He wasn't here."

"Why not?"

"I'm hardly privy to Mr. DeWitt's thoughts, Mrs. Wilkes. Now, if you don't mind—"

"FIRE!" Someone shouted from above. "Fire coming from the north! Get the hell out! Everyone get out NOW!"

Something dropped hard; I heard shouting, scraping, a cacophony of confusion.

"Fire! Fire!" The voice echoed down the stairwell. "Get out! Get out!"

"Fire?" Beatrice Wilkes said. "God *damn* it!" She spun on her heel, racing back down the stairs, and I stared after her in surprise as she disappeared into the gloom below stage. I had no idea where she thought she was going. The door was right here, for God's sake—

I reached for the handle. It was burning hot. I jerked back in pain. It was then I noticed the smoke seeping from beneath the walls. The acrid scent. The haze in the air wasn't dust but smoke. *From the north,* the boy had said. This was the north door. Dear God, the fire was just outside; it was already here.

Something crashed behind me. The floor shook. I forgot Sebastian DeWitt and everything else as clouds of smoke billowed from the stage. Mrs. Wilkes had raced down the stairs. She must know another exit. She knew the theater so much better than I. I tripped over my skirts in my haste to follow her, stumbling down the bottom few.

"Mrs. Wilkes! Mrs. Wilkes!"

There was no answer. The hallway was dim as always, but now it was like trying to see through a fog. Something else crashed above me. The struts of the stage quaked. There was a roar from above like a rush of air. "Mrs. Wilkes!" I heard the panic in my voice.

But there was no answer. No one was down here. Everyone else had been onstage. No doubt they were gone already. I knew where the doors were upstairs. I should not have come down here. I should turn around and go back to where I knew.

I spun around; my bustle caught a piece of scenery, dislodging it. It slid, cracking to the floor before me, splintering, blocking my way, and I started to step over it before I saw the clouds of smoke rushing down the stairway I'd just descended. Boiling, black, poisonous clouds. That way was gone. And if I could not find another way out—

Don't panic. Now is not the time to panic. But the smoke swirled around me, heavy, caustic. My eyes teared up so I could hardly see, and I stumbled forward, more from instinct than anything else. Just ahead, there was a light glowing through the darkness to the left, an open door. Gratefully, I stumbled to it, nearly falling against the doorjamb in relief.

But it was no door outside. It was a dressing room, and Beatrice Wilkes knelt on the floor before a large, open trunk, jerking out bundles of what looked like clothing.

"What are you doing?" I screamed at her.

She turned with a little jump and frowned when she saw me, but she didn't pause. She pulled out gown after gown, bundling them in her arms, and then she got to her feet. "Take these."

I stared at her in dumb astonishment. "What are they?"

"Costumes," she said grimly. She shoved them at me, and I took them because I could do nothing else, and she turned back to the trunk and grabbed up another armful.

"We have to get out of here!" I said. "You'll get us both killed."

"You didn't have to follow me," she said.

"I thought you knew another way out."

She slammed the trunk shut and hurried past me into the hall. In one glance she took in the billowing smoke, and her mouth set in a thin line as she shoved the clothes beneath her arm. "Christ. We'll have to use the parquet door."

"The parquet door? But that's upstairs, and the fire's blocked—"

"We'll take the stairs by Lucius's office." She moved swiftly down the hall, and I stumbled after, afraid I would lose her in the smoke. I dropped a gauzy scarf. The roaring sound grew louder. Smoke seared my lungs; my eyes watered so badly now I could see nothing, and I grabbed her skirt as she dodged before me, fisting the fabric hard so as not to lose her.

Something exploded behind us. She jerked around, her face white in the near darkness, and I glanced back to see flames leaping from the struts beneath the stage.

"This way!"

She ran, and I tripped and stumbled after her, dropping other scarves and a skirt and corset and letting them lie. The smoke was so thick now I wouldn't have known she was before me but for my desperate lock on her skirt. I coughed and choked, blind with stinging tears. I brought the bundle of clothes to my nose to try to filter the air. But she didn't hesitate, and suddenly we were plunging into a darkness that seemed less foggy; the smoke was not so heavy here, and I fell hard on the first step because I couldn't see it. I dropped my hold on her skirt, and all the costumes, and screamed, "Wait!" and impatiently she turned around and grabbed my arm, jerking me to my feet, pulling me after her.

And then, suddenly, we were at the top of the stairs, and the air grew lighter, though smoke boiled up from below, and the roar filled my ears. She pulled me with her from the wings onto the stage before she let me go. She held her armful of clothes in a death grip, though I had dropped the ones I'd carried.

She started across. Flames danced up the wall on the far side, leaping about the ropes and rolled canvas drops in the heavens, shimmying down the border curtains. A rain of ash fluttered to the stage floor. Firebrands smashed down, shattering and skittering everywhere. I stumbled to a stop, overwhelmed, horrified.

She yelled over her shoulder. "Come *on*!"

I heard a terrible crack. A frame swung down from the heavens, a mass of flame, crashing upon the stage, splintering, sending fire shooting in every direction. Something exploded behind me, and I screamed and jerked around to look.

When I looked back again, Beatrice Wilkes had disappeared.

Chapter Twenty

Beatrice

One moment the floor was beneath me, the next it was gone and I was falling. I screamed and slammed into the ground so hard it burst the breath from my lungs. Pain shattered into my spine and my skull and one elbow, and I was pelted with broken boards. The costumes I'd been holding floated around me like spirits. The dressing gown caught fire in the air, bursting into floating, live flame, and I rolled to escape it as it spiraled down.

Above me was the hole I'd fallen through. I was below stage again, and there was flame everywhere, a wall of flame where there had once been struts. I could not see beyond it to the hallway I knew was there. Smaller flames licked along the beam above my head. What remained of the trap was shattered all around me, nothing but little torches now, the rope that ran its pulley a line of flame to where it anchored on the winch. I'd fallen through the grave trap—an irony I didn't want to think of just then. A brand fell on the carriage just beyond me, and the papier-mâché went up before I could blink. Pieces of fire fell; it became a hellish game of tag as I rolled to escape them, and my whole body hurt so damn bad. Beside me, my satin gown suddenly exploded in a burst of flame.

I jerked up hard, scrambling back from it, screaming, "Help!" But the roar of the fire was loud, and even if she was up there, even if she were still alive, I doubted she would hear me.

I was going to die.

Then I heard, "Mrs. Wilkes!"

Her voice was a little squeak through the noise; I wouldn't have heard her if I hadn't looked up just at that moment. Mrs. Langley peered over the edge of the hole.

"Stay back!" I screamed up at her. "For God's sake, don't fall in! Can you get me out of here!"

She didn't move. She looked as if she were in shock, and I understood that, but just now if she didn't do something we were both going to die. "Mrs. Langley!" I shouted. "Help me!"

She seemed to jerk awake then. She stepped back from the hole, disappearing.

There was a crash; a beam to the left cracked and slammed onto the floor, boards splintered, a settee fell from the stage above, its legs shattering, its upholstery a mass of flame, barely missing me. Two counterweights smashed down, the burlap bags exploded, sand skittered out like water. I could hardly breathe through my coughing. The skirt of the calico I wore began to smoke. I was going to die here. I was going to die, and it was going to be so damned painful, and *dear God, save me, save me, save me. . . .*

The metal bar that crashed down missed me only by inches. I stared dumbly at it until I saw the rod coming up from it, the leather belt dangling. It was the hoe, the bar we used to ascend an actor to the heavens.

"Mrs. Wilkes! Mrs. Wilkes!"

The voice of an angel. I looked up and saw Mrs. Langley there at the edge of the hole, and I was so damned relieved and grateful that she hadn't gone my knees went weak.

"Hurry!" she screamed. "Get on the bar! Get on the bar!"

That was when I realized the bar still had a rope attached to it. A rope that snaked up into the flies, still strong, though it was singed in places. I stepped onto it, grabbing onto the rod, and Mrs. Langley disappeared again, and in a moment the rope went taut, squeaking. I clutched that rod so hard my knuckles went white, even though it was hot as an iron. To my left, the floor went up, a sheet of flame, and I felt its heat like a burst of wind, and *thank God* the hoe began to rise. Slowly, swinging madly, and I heard myself murmuring words I hardly recognized as she turned that winch and brought me inch by inch out of hell, and then, finally, I was suspended there above the flames already closing in over where I'd been, and she came rushing across what was left of the stage, screaming, "Jump!"

I launched myself to the edge of that hole with every bit of strength I had. I hit the floor flat, on my stomach, jerking hard away from the boards collapsing at my feet. She grabbed my wrists, hauling me from the edge, screaming into my face, "We've got to get out!"

I don't remember getting to my feet. I don't remember running. All I knew was that suddenly we were at the edge of the apron, and I saw the flames licking up from the orchestra pit and I felt the whole stage shudder and I screamed at her to jump and then we were both on the floor of the parquet, dodging down the aisles as the curtain and the boxes erupted into flame above and therc was this terrible crash and scream as the stage collapsed behind us, a scream like it was dying. Flames boiled out, clouds of smoke, and the two of us raced up that aisle with the monster chasing, and it was too much to hope that the door was clear, but it was our only chance. We rushed into the tiny lobby at the bottom of the narrow stairs leading to the boxes, and then suddenly, unbelievably, there was the door. I slammed up against it and she slammed into me, and then we were outside, half falling into the street, falling from one hell into another, into terrible heat and noise: alarm bells, steamship whistles piercing the roar of the fire, great crashes of collapsing buildings, explosions *rat-a-tat-tat* like gunfire, huge blasts, men shouting as the boardwalk blew up into flame and they scattered like ants. All around us was fire and ash and smoke.

We lurched out, choking and gasping, and a man black with soot grabbed my arm and shouted, "Get out of here!" as if I wasn't trying to do exactly that, but where the hell to go? It wasn't just the Regal; the whole city was in flames around us. Nothing but fire wherever I looked, and I started toward the harbor, thinking *water,* but that man jerked on my arm again and pointed and shouted though I couldn't hear him through the roar, only that his lips made the word "Run" and he was pointing east, away from the water, toward the hills, and I didn't question, I just grabbed Mrs. Langley's hand and ran the way he pointed.

Pyres of salvaged goods burned in the middle of the street; the sky rained flaming brands and sparks, falling signs and bricks and shattered glass. Telegraph and telephone wires snapped and melted. Clouds of smoke purpled in the sunlight. An explosion behind us made me jerk around in fear, but all I saw were flames shooting a hundred feet into the air, and the boiling smoke, and after that I didn't look behind anymore. I pulled Mrs. Langley with me to Second Street, where the brick building of the Boston block stood steaming and two bucket brigades of filthy men with sooty faces passed water from one to the other, sloshing it over their trousered legs, shouting at us to get out of the way, to get somewhere safe. I didn't see a single fire engine.

I kept running, my face stinging as if it had been burned. There were other people too, women and children mostly, running in the same direction. We didn't stop until we were on Third Street, and the fire was behind us, though the smoke was heavy and stinging both my lungs and my eyes and I couldn't stop coughing.

We stumbled into someone's yard, which was already crowded with people staring vacant eyed, watching the fire burn below, clinging to whatever they'd managed to save. I let go of Mrs. Langley and fell onto the grass, my lungs burning, and she collapsed beside me in a flurry of charred silk and exhaustion, both of us choking with every breath.

Another explosion, a fusillade of gunfire. There was nothing left of the block the Regal had stood on but fire; we were just in time to see the theater collapse in a big ball of flame. Sparks swirled through the smoky air; flaming brands landed on rooftops, and men beat them out with wet blankets. Someone yelled, "The hotel!" and I turned to see the fire leap toward the Occidental and thought how impossible it was that the hotel should burn. It was brick, and there was an excavation just before it. The fire would stop there.

But the building across on Second went up as if the devil were feeding it, and I saw the smoke come from the fourth floor of the Occidental when everyone else did, and there was an explosion, and suddenly the roof burst into flame.

It was then I realized where the fire was heading.

"My hotel," I gasped, lurching to my feet, but before I could run, Mrs. Langley grabbed my arm, jerking me back.

"There's nothing you can do," she croaked.

I knew she was right. And in any case I could not bring myself to run back into that fire. I could not make myself do it. Everything was gone. Everything I'd saved, everything I'd hoped for. All gone.

She released me as if she felt the same despair I did, and together we sank back again onto the grass, wordlessly watching the world erupt in flame.

I turned to look at her. She was unrecognizable, her hair falling and charred in places, her face so black with ash and soot she looked like she belonged in a minstrel show, and I knew I must look the same. There was a burnt hole in the shoulder of her gown; the fine lace at her throat looked half-melted and filthy. I would never have known her for Geneva Langley—even now, I didn't quite believe she was.

A burning coal fell to the grass near her booted foot; wearily she kicked it into the street, where it smoldered and died, and I watched numbly as the fire raced up toward the County Courthouse, while down on the waterfront the wind came up and Yesler's Mill went up like fireworks—flames shooting like geysers and terrible explosions and black clouds swirling to hide the sun. The wharves with their warehouses collapsed into the bay and burned and smoked on the mud as the tide came slowly in—too late to save us or put water in the hoses of the fire engines. Useless now. Only bucket brigades and men shouting orders and then running to catch up as the fire outran them. Then the coal bunkers caught, and those flames lit up the horizon like the biggest hearth I'd ever seen.

Hot air pummeled us so it was hard to breathe. When I rubbed my face, my eyelashes broke off in little stubs of soot. It seemed it would never end, that the fire would burn a swath clear to Tacoma, and Mrs. Langley and I would just sit there, unmoving, forever, while the sky turned this sickly purple and the smoke cloud grew bigger and bigger into twilight, while the setting sun shone bloodred through it.

As the night came on, it was eerie, a night that wasn't night.

The fire reflected on the underside of the smoke cloud, shifting and playing like the northern lights, and those coal bunkers burned steadily.

The lawn was crowded, stony-eyed men and women holding their frightened children with heaps of their belongings beside them; firemen with scalded faces and burned hands fallen into exhausted sleep. I wondered if anyone I knew had died. I wondered where Lucius was, and Jackson and Brody and Aloysius and all the others. But mostly I wondered why Sebastian had not gone to the theater, and where he was, and it was hard to think it had only been this morning that I'd awakened beside him. It seemed so long ago it might have happened to another person.

Beside me people curled up to sleep on the grass, and I realized that was what I would do too, and I didn't care. Where else would I go, after all? I'd lost everything. All my costumes. Everything I owned. Little as it was, it had been something.

I turned to Mrs. Langley. "Don't you want to see if your house survived?"

She looked north. I looked with her. It was impossible to see past the nimbus of the smoke. "The fire came from the north," she said thoughtfully. "That's what the boy said. He said it came from the north."

"Yes."

"Do you think it could possibly have survived this?"

"I don't know," I said. "Maybe. Where is it?"

"First Hill," she said.

Well, yes, of course it was. "Well, there's no fire here on Third. If it didn't cross uptown, you'd be all right."

She nodded and drew up her knees, settling her chin into them.

I glanced south, seeing nothing but smoke. The weight of what I knew I had to say settled hard, nudging, and I cleared my throat and said, "Thank you. You know, for not leaving me in there. For saving my life."

"You're welcome," she said softly. "But I think we're even. You saved mine as well."

"All I did was show the way."

"I would have been hopelessly lost." She wiped her hands on

her skirt as if it mattered that they were dirty when she was so filthy with soot and ash it would probably take three baths to get her clean again.

"I suppose your husband's probably looking for you."

She went quiet, too still. "Perhaps he's dead."

"Rich men don't die in fires like this," I said, meaning to reassure her. "He would have been out the moment anyone smelled smoke."

She nodded, her expression gone thoughtful. "What if he didn't get out?"

"Mrs. Langley—"

"Or what if I was the one who died?"

"But you didn't. You're right here beside me."

"It would be so easy now to just . . . be lost."

"Did something fall on you back there? Are you all right?"

Impatiently, she said, "I'm perfectly fine."

We'd been through hell, and I was almost too tired to think. She had to be the same. "I think you should go home," I said as gently as I could. "We're both tired. Go home. Sleep in your comfortable bed. Kiss your husband. No doubt he'll be glad you're alive."

Her head jerked up as if I'd hit her. "The very last thing I want is to see Nathan."

That surprised me.

"I'll leave him to you. You'd like that, wouldn't you? To have him all to yourself?"

I laughed; there was so much smoke in my lungs it turned into a rasping cough that went deep; it was a while before I caught my breath.

She asked harshly, "What's wrong with you?"

"What's wrong with *me*? I nearly died in a fire and I've lost everything I own, and now you're telling me you don't want to see your husband, and by the way, take him if you want. Frankly, Mrs. Langley, the question is: What's wrong with you?"

Calmly, she said, "Mrs. Wilkes, I would like you to do something for me."

I frowned at her. "What?"

"I want you to find out if my husband is alive."

"Wouldn't it be easier for you to find out? All you have to do is go home and—"

"I don't want him to know I've survived. Not yet. This is why I need *you* to ask about him. And why I need you to say that you haven't seen me since before the fire."

The way she said this . . . just so flatly, as if she were discussing the weather. It made me shiver. I was growing to hate that I knew the Langley name at all. I knew already that whatever this was, I did not want to be involved in it.

She went on, "I suppose someone from the troupe might know if Nathan survived."

"If they survived it themselves," I said—and damn if the smoke in my lungs didn't catch, so I couldn't help but choke a little. "I suppose I'll look for them in the morning."

"Can I count on your help, then?"

"No, you can't," I said sharply. "Whatever it is you're thinking, I don't want any part of it."

Her expression went hard as stone. "Mrs. Wilkes, I am in a position to reward you quite handsomely for your cooperation."

You know, there were times when I hated that I cared so much about money, and this was one of them, because suddenly I was all attention, and I knew better. "How much?"

Oh, that look of haughty distaste! So perfect—I memorized it for the future, for the next time I played an arrogant, bossy, supercilious character. "Would two hundred dollars be sufficient?"

Would it be sufficient? I would have walked naked through the streets for that kind of money, and she must have known it. "Two hundred dollars? And all I have to do is find out if Nathan is alive and pretend I haven't seen you?"

"That's all. Does it meet your mercenary standards, Mrs. Wilkes?"

"I prefer to call it pragmatic. And yes, it does."

She took a deep, obviously relieved breath. "Do you think you can find the company?"

I lay back on the grass, jerking a little in pain when my elbow hit the ground. I thought of my fellow actors. I thought of Sebastian. I stared up at the eerie northern lights. "If they're still alive, I'll find them. In the morning."

"Perfect," she said.

Around me I heard the mutterings of other people, someone sobbing, a dog barking. Her sigh. "No stars tonight," I said softly, more to myself than anything.

"But it's beautiful, isn't it?" she answered.

In the morning, I was stiff all over, my lungs tight from smoke, tasting ash on my lips. It was barely dawn, and hot, what was left of the city hazy through a lingering fog of smoke. Charred telegraph poles sheared of their stanchions poked through the haze like long black fingers. Beside me, Mrs. Langley was curled on her side, her face buried in her arms. Her bustle poked into my hip.

I peered at two uniformed figures who emerged through the haze, the Washington National Guard, their rifles over their shoulders, brass buttons glinting in the filtered sunlight. They crossed the street and came up to me as I sat, and the young and handsome one said, "Good morning, miss. Are you all right? Are you hurt?"

"I'm fine," I said. "Hungry and thirsty, but all right."

Mrs. Langley stirred beside me. The militiaman nodded to her and said, "She a friend of yours? Is she all right?"

"We're both fine," I said.

"You got somewhere to go?"

"I don't know. Is there any part of the city left?"

The young man frowned. "Nothing to the south, and most of the piers are gone or damaged. To the north it got to University. Most of the business area looks like this." He gestured vaguely. "Most of the houses are all right."

"And . . . did anyone die?"

The militiaman glanced at his partner, who shrugged and said, "We don't know. A few people missing, but other than that, it's too early to tell. They're planning to open relief tents in the next day or so." And then hesitantly, as if he felt guilty for having to leave us unprotected, "They should be able to help you and your friend out then."

"Thank you, sir," I said.

When they left, I looked down at Mrs. Langley. "They're gone."

She groaned and sat up, pushing at her bustle. It was riding lopsided and bent, and I said, "I think your bustle's ruined."

She rubbed her face, streaking the soot on her skin. Her dark hair was mostly fallen from its pins, tangled in a mass over her shoulder. She peered into the fog, frowning. "I don't recognize anything."

"The Regal was there." I pointed to a block of nothing but ash piles and the charred and leaning telegraph poles, and—very strange—a streetlamp that looked untouched except that its glass globes were gone. Yesterday morning if I'd been sitting here, I wouldn't have been able to see past the buildings across the street. Today, I could see clear to the harbor. I rose. "I'm going to see if I can find Lucius and the others."

She sat there like a statue.

I found myself offering, "You still want me to see about Nathan?"

"I would like nothing better." She was almost violent when she said it. Something else to wonder about, if I wanted to wonder, which I didn't.

I nodded shortly. "Very well. I'll see what I can find. I'll be back in . . . I don't know. However long it takes me to find someone in this mess."

"Thank you, Mrs. Wilkes." She was stiff as a dowager, as if she wasn't used to thanking anyone for anything, and I admit I liked her discomfort. Or maybe it was only that she disliked being grateful to me. If so, that was even better.

But best of all, I liked leaving her.

I walked away from her and that yard, into the city, and it was worse than I'd thought, worse than I could ever have imagined. The city I knew, nearly every building, was gone. Just . . . gone. The streets were lined with ash and piles of brick, smoldering ruins; here and there a wall looking ready to tumble down, and militia everywhere, and I didn't know how anyone could have survived it. Someone I knew had to be dead; I was certain of it, and that certainty grew with every step I took until my dread choked me along with the smoke that burned my eyes and made it impossible to breathe, and all I could think was *please not Sebastian. Please not him.*

I stared at everyone I passed, looking for someone familiar, and when they looked back at me, I saw my desperation reflected on their faces, the pause, the stare, trying to look through soot and dirt, then the disappointment, the sigh, the moving on. Twice someone came up to me holding a photograph. "Have you seen this woman?" "Have you seen this boy?" and I shook my head both times and asked, "Have you seen any of the actors from the Regal Theater?" and got confused looks and sorrowful no's. I had no way to even ask about Sebastian, because what would I say? *Have you seen the playwright from the Regal?* when no one even knew there *was* a playwright, much less what the hell he looked like. I would have given almost anything for one of our posters to show people, to be able to point to Jack or Aloys or anyone else. In the pictures, we were all in costume as characters, but it would be easier than what I did now, trying to describe an elaborate waxed mustache, a Vandyke beard, a handsome blond. . . . There was nothing to say that made them different from anyone else. But the only paper I saw was the proclamation from Mayor Moran that was nailed to every charred telegraph pole:

ALL PERSONS found on the streets of this city after eight o'clock without the countersign will be arrested and imprisoned. All persons found stealing property or otherwise violating the laws will be promptly arrested and if resisting arrest will be summarily dealt with.

ALL SALOONS in this city are hereby ordered to close and remain closed until further order, under penalty of a forfeiture of their licenses and arrest. No person will be allowed to sell or dispose of any liquor until further orders, and any person doing so will be immediately arrested and imprisoned.

OFFICERS AND MEMBERS of the militia and all policemen are strictly enjoined to enforce the foregoing orders.

At least there wouldn't be drunks making everything worse, which I supposed was a good thing, though it seemed to me there would be plenty of people needing the solace of a good drink. There were soldiers everywhere, watching, waiting.

The landmarks I did recognize were so ruined I couldn't quite countenance the fact that they had once belonged to anything I knew. What brick buildings remained were gutted: only brick walls and arched doorways were left of the Post Building, of a nearby bank there was nothing but a shell and a safe and a man guarding it, and that became a familiar sight too, big black boxes sitting in the middle of nothing, with men angling their chairs back against them as if they were sitting on a porch enjoying the morning sun.

I'd hoped to find Lucius or someone else near the ruins of the Regal, but there was only Mr. Hesse, who owned the saloon on the corner, spraying the smoking ashes of his building with a hose hooked to a fire hydrant. There was plenty of water now, it seemed. When I went up to him, he stared at me for a moment and then said, "Mrs. Wilkes," in that dead tone I was beginning to hear too often. It brought my worry into a lump in my throat, and I said, "Have you seen Mr. Greene? Or . . . or anyone else?"

He shook his head. "Not yet," and then, "They'll be fine, Mrs. Wilkes," but it was a hollow platitude and I didn't believe him, and that lump just stayed as I walked on, my eyes stinging as I tried to peer through the smoke. The horsecar tracks were twisted and melted as if some giant had squeezed and knotted them in his hand and then thrown them down again. There was nothing left of the docks but for hundreds of pier logs, only a few still with crossbeams, blackened and sticking out of the water like broken teeth. The train tracks crisscrossing them sagged and warped, and great cogs lay about the mess of wood and metal, still too hot to go near.

I'd been walking for an hour before I saw the tent. Some business had sprayed down the ashes and erected canvas on the gritty mud, and I stopped, startled, because in spite of the fact that it was just a tent, it looked so damn *normal*. A big sign out front, written on a board burned on one side, announced it to be a hardware store, and it was crowded, people going in and out as if everyone in the city had been drawn to it, and I felt that draw too, because it was such an everyday thing to do when you felt so helpless and upended.

There were barrels out front, and big coils of rope, and a man stood there calling people in: "Builder's Hardware! Still alive! Still selling! Come on in and see what we got!"

And there, leaning against one of the barrels in front, was someone I recognized.

I screamed, "Brody!" and he looked up and we ran into each other's arms so quickly we both stumbled at the impact. I kissed him hard and said, "Am I glad to see you!"

He hugged me until I thought my ribs would crack. "Damn, Bea! Where've you been? We've been looking and looking—I was scared to death you'd been caught in the fire. We all were."

"We? You've seen the others?"

He stepped away. His clothes were stained with what looked like blue paint, and I realized his hands were wrapped with dirty bandages. "Yeah. Aloys is fine. So're Jack and Mrs. Chace and Susan, though Jack's hands are burned too." He held up his hands wryly. "That's what comes of being a good samaritan. I'll know better next time."

"A good samaritan?"

"Well, I had to help, didn't I? And Galloway nearly got crushed by a beam, so me and Jack had to pull him out. He's burnt up pretty bad, and his back is all messed up, but the doctor's got his eye on him." Brody's grin widened. "You were the missing one. And Mrs. Langley. And DeWitt."

I swallowed hard. "Mr. DeWitt is missing?"

"No one's seen him. But he wasn't at the theater when the fire broke out, so I guess he's probably all right."

"It wasn't just the theater that burned."

Brody laughed. "No kidding. Damn, you ever seen anything like this?"

I shook my head. "How did it start?"

"Hell if I know." Brody shrugged. "Maybe a cow and a lantern like Chicago. Or maybe Celestials setting off fireworks—that's what Jack thinks. Where were you?"

"Downstairs in the greenroom. Getting ready for the performance." Part of the truth, but not all of it. But it was none of Brody's business why I'd arrived early, or that the heat and my near-sleepless night had conspired against me, and I'd fallen asleep in the greenroom and had only just woke up when I ran into Mrs. Langley coming down the stairs. "I nearly died in there. But for—" I remembered the promise I'd made to Mrs. Langley just in time. "But I made it out."

"You didn't see Mrs. Langley, did you?"

"No," I lied, maybe a little too quickly, but Brody didn't seem to notice.

"Lucius thought maybe she was still in the Regal when the fire hit, but I swear I saw her go when rehearsal was over. I guess she'll turn up eventually. Her husband's looking for her."

"So he's alive?"

"Hell yes." A grin split Brody's dirty face. "Lucius was on his knees praying for it."

He took me with him down the street, turning up what had once been Madison. A crowd of people gathered at the top of the hill, all ragged and dirty and haggard-looking, hovering around their belongings while the militia walked the border. It was only moments before I saw the company. Aloys and Mrs. Chace, Jack and Mr. Geary, and as Brody and I emerged from the crowd, Mrs. Chace caught sight of me and screeched out "Bea!" in a voice so loud it seemed to cut right through the people, and suddenly someone came running at me, and I was pulled into long, strong arms—Jack's—my nose pressed deep into his smoke-scented chest. I heard the rumble of my name in his throat, and then he released me so that the others had their turn, and I realized how glad I was to have found them. When I was finally released to stand on my own, I was crying from sheer relief and joy.

Brody handed me a filthy gray handkerchief, and when I wiped my eyes, I left big stripes of black soot on it, and Jack laughed and said I looked like a zebra.

"She hasn't seen Mrs. Langley either," said Brody to the others. "Or DeWitt."

Lucius rubbed his mustache thoughtfully. "Well, that is unfortunate. Let us hope they both turn up soon for our sake. And for Mrs. Langley's husband's, of course."

My stomach growled, reminding me that I hadn't eaten in twenty-four hours. "Is there any food?"

He shook his head. "Not a dry goods store or grocery left in the city, and only three restaurants, and they're already out of food."

"Did you manage to save anything?"

"Ah, only my skin, my dear Bea. But fortunately we've the whole of the company to continue on with. The Regal will rise again!"

"How? There's no theater."

"A situation I am trying to remedy. The show must go on, you know! These poor wretches will need our entertainment in the days to come. Your Mr. Langley is appealing to the city council now for a permit for us to continue in a tent. I've decided we shall call it the Phoenix!"

"I'm surprised he's not looking for his wife."

Lucius said, "I believe he has been. It doesn't bear thinking about, of course, a terrible tragedy, but . . . if the most unfortunate of events occurs, we will dedicate our first show to her. That should have the gossips buying tickets."

"What an opportunist you are."

He gave me a grim smile. "And it's lucky for you I am, eh, Bea? Else you would not have a job on top of having no place to live."

"Then perhaps you could find your way clear to advance me next week's salary?"

"Ah, would that I could, my sweet flower. Would that I could! Last night's receipts went up in flames, and much to my dismay, the banks have not yet opened for business. But rest assured that others share our dilemma. Of course, when I have the tent, I will insist the entire company stay there. Free of charge, of course."

Not out of any charitable feeling, I knew. If we were all staying in the tent, we would be at his beck and call.

When Lucius turned away to speak to a passing militiaman, I walked over to Jack, who was adjusting the bandage on his hand. "Let me," I said, securing the knot more tightly. "Do they hurt very much?"

"Only when I attempt to use them," he said with a smile. "My stomach complains far more, I fear."

"I heard they were setting up relief tents tomorrow."

"If they can find a way to get the supplies in. There are steamers waiting in the harbor now, but there's no place to dock."

I frowned. "What do you mean?"

"The wharves are burned to the ground, or haven't you noticed? One or two are only damaged, but I hear it will take days to repair them enough to unload a ship."

Jackson gave me a quick kiss before he walked off, and I stood there and thought about Nathan Langley being alive and Mrs. Langley saying she didn't want him to know she'd survived, and that made me think of his anger and the things he'd said about her. I didn't want to contemplate any of it. If I thought about it, I would care, and I didn't want to care. I just wanted her out of my life, the sooner the better.

So when Aloys came up to me and said, "Brody said you were in the theater when the fire broke out. You didn't see Mrs. Langley, did you?" I snapped, "No, I did not see her. I don't know where the hell she is." When he looked taken aback, I forced a calmer tone. "She'll land on her feet, Aloys. Rich people always do. I'm more concerned for Mr. DeWitt, to tell the truth."

He nodded and stroked his beard, and the thoughtful way he looked at me made me nervous. "We all are, my dear. We all are."

Chapter Twenty-one

Geneva

During the hours she was gone, it was easy to lose myself in the crowd, though I kept to myself and spoke to no one. The displaced people were not of my class, and I was a stranger to them. When the woman of the house—who I didn't know—came out with bread and butter and cool water to offer to those of us camped in her yard, I pulled out the few remaining pins in my hair and let it fall to cover half my face, and went like a beggar with the others, too hungry to care about dignity.

I could not wait for Mrs. Wilkes to return to tell me what she'd learned, whether Nathan was still alive. Everything depended on it. If he were dead, there would be no need to leave and go into hiding. There would still be my father to consider, but he was far from here, and that distance could give me the time I needed to convince him that Nathan had lied and slanted the truth, that I was not mad.

But if Nathan were alive, he would continue to lie about me, and I would need to run to save myself. My father would only see that as one more manifestation of insanity. Even if I could manage to convince him otherwise, it would take so much longer. Years perhaps. And what would I do for money, now that control of my accounts had been given to Nathan? There was the cash in the safe in Nathan's study, assuming I could get to it, but it wouldn't be enough to keep me for long, especially once I paid Mrs. Wilkes her two hundred dollars. Where was I to go?

There was a part of me that marveled at the suddenness

with which every bit of affection I'd felt for my husband had died, how quickly he had become my enemy. But then again, I was not surprised. After all, I had known already that my marriage was over. It was my attempt to end it that had brought us here. These last months, telling myself I could love him again, had been the lie. There was no point in berating myself for that; Nathan had made my father and society his accomplices, and I'd had no choice but to try to find contentment in the only life left to me. But that I had walked so trustingly the path he'd laid for me, that I had been so willingly blind—that was hard to forgive.

I stared at the smoking ashes, so deep in contemplation that when I saw the woman on the block before me, stepping gracefully through the wreckage, it seemed I was watching myself, as if it were my spirit that sat here on the hill, watching my body move through the world, and when the body stepped from the smoke, it took me a moment to realize it was Mrs. Wilkes.

She sat down beside me with a great sigh. "He's alive."

My dismay was so profound I had to close my eyes against the sudden press of tears.

"Dear God. What will I do now? Where will I go?" I whispered. I turned to Mrs. Wilkes. Her expression was more than faintly hostile. Desperately I said, "I need to find Mr. DeWitt."

She gave me a look I couldn't decipher. "Mr. DeWitt? Why?"

"It doesn't matter. If you could bring him to me—"

"That might be difficult, seeing as no one knows where the hell he is."

I looked at her in surprise. "Didn't you find the company?"

"Yes. But not him. He's missing."

Missing. "No. He can't be. That's not possible—"

"Believe me, it is."

"But where was he when it started?"

"No one knows."

"Do you think . . . no, he can't have been caught in the fire."

Mrs. Wilkes turned abruptly away. "I don't know, all right? I don't know where he is or where he was or anything else."

Her dismay was obvious. I thought of the things he'd said about her; I had thought his admiration only one-sided, given how she treated him at rehearsals. Apparently it wasn't. I wasn't certain how I felt about that, but now was not the time to wonder.

"I can't do this alone," I said to her. "I thought perhaps he would . . . but if he's gone . . . well, I can't wait until he's found."

She swiped a hand across her eyes. "You're talking in riddles."

I grabbed her arm so hard she started. "You don't understand. I need to get out of this city before Nathan finds me. I was going to ask Mr. DeWitt for help, but now I don't have any other choice. I need you to help me."

She jerked her arm away. "I only promised to see if Nathan was alive."

I could only promise her more of what I already had too little of. "Then I'll pay you more. Just . . . you must help me."

"You're right, I don't understand, Mrs. Langley. You've got a rich husband, servants, a fine house. Why would you give it all up?"

I barely heard her. "I'll need a steamer ticket—"

"A steamer ticket won't help you."

"—and after that a ship from San Francisco—"

"The steamers can't land to take you out of here," she persisted. "The wharves are all gone or damaged. It will be days before they repair one enough that a ship can dock."

"Days?" I asked in dismay. "How can that be possible?"

"Well, let me see. There was a fire. Wharves are made of wood. They burned."

I went hot at her condescension. "Surely the boats can land somewhere else?"

"Certainly they can. Just not anywhere in Seattle. Half the city is burned to the ground, Mrs. Langley. Nowhere I saw looked any better than this."

"Do you think it possible to pay someone to take me out of town?"

She shrugged. "You can pay someone to do most anything. Especially now, I'd guess. But it doesn't matter. Unless you have a fortune in your pockets, there's no money. The banks are closed. And even if they were open, you said you didn't want Nathan to know you were alive. How do you mean to get this money you keep talking about without his finding out?"

Quietly, I said, "I don't need a bank. There's a safe in Nathan's study where he keeps the funds to pay the servants and household accounts. There should be several hundred dollars in it."

"Several hundred dollars. For paying the household accounts and the servants." Mrs. Wilkes laughed.

"If I had it, I could hire someone to take me where I could catch a train. Or another steamer."

"If you had it, I imagine you could get most anything you wanted in this town just now," she said. "But why leave? Your husband is looking for you. Why don't you forget all this and go home?"

"You saw him?"

She shook her head, then shoved a lank tress of hair behind her ear. Some of the hair was melted; it broke off in her hand, and she threw the bits to the ground with a sound of disgust. "No. The others in the company said they'd seen him. He was in some city council meeting."

"A council meeting? God forbid he should search for me instead."

She turned to look at me. "Lucius said he *had* been searching for you."

Tightly, I asked, "And what did you tell them?"

"What we agreed. That I hadn't seen you. Aloys half doesn't believe me."

"Why?"

She laughed a little. "Because he knows me, and he knows how much I dislike you, and he's not quite sure I wouldn't have left you there to die. Complimentary, isn't it?"

"But he *will* believe you?"

"Yes. But it would be better if you showed up. Everyone would be relieved."

Stonily, I said, "I told you. I can't do that. I have to go."

"Suppose you give me a reason why."

I didn't trust her. Who knew how well she could keep a secret, or if she would even try? She was Nathan's mistress, after all. "I don't owe you a reason."

"No, but it would help. It's not easy to lie to Aloys. He's no fool, and neither are any of the others."

"Don't tell me you're not a good enough actress to handle a few suspicions."

"You're not nobody, Mrs. Langley. People will ask questions."

"I feel certain of your ability to manage it. And you'll have your reward too. I'm certain that if you play it well enough, you could even continue your sordid little affair with my husband once I'm gone."

"I could continue it even if you were here," she retorted. "But there's no point in it now."

"Why not?"

"Lucius says he's going to get a tent and—you'll enjoy this, I think—our first show will be a tribute to you if it turns out you're dead after all. Isn't that moving?" She smiled thinly. "Lucius never misses an angle. And if it's true that you mean to leave"—she glanced at me as if for confirmation, and I nodded—"Everything will go back to the way it was. I'll have the lead line. There's still *Penelope Justis,* and—" She bit back the words she'd been about to say. "I won't need Nathan."

"You had an affair with my husband simply for what he could do for you?"

"You thought there was some higher feeling?" Mrs. Wilkes laughed. "The higher feeling was this: I needed his influence and he liked to fuck me. That was all."

I recoiled a little at her crudity.

"What's wrong, Mrs. Langley? Have I offended your delicate sensibilities? Sex has nothing to do with love, you know."

I turned away from her. Before us, a man cursed as the wagon he drove bounced hard over a twisted horsecar rail, nearly turning onto its side before two militiamen ran over to help him right it. I stared down at the harbor, at the steamers and schooners anchored out there, so close, so impossible to reach. No docks. No way to get to San Francisco or anywhere else. The thought filled me with such despair I could not breathe through it.

"How much will your help cost me?" I asked.

She didn't flinch. "You already owe me two hundred dollars."

"There would be more, of course."

"How much more?"

"I'll need money for travel. And for expenses for a few weeks.

Until I can settle things. The rest would be yours. Let's say . . . a third of the money in the safe."

She was silent for a moment. "Half, and you've got an agreement."

I took a deep breath. "Very well. I'll need you to find out Nathan's whereabouts before I attempt it. I don't want him coming home while I'm there. Is that acceptable to you? Or will that cost me more?"

"That's easy enough. I'll include it in the price."

"How kind." I stared out at the desolation, thinking. "Once I know where Nathan is, I'll decide when to sneak in. Afterward, I'll meet you back here."

"How can I be sure you won't just take the money and disappear?"

"You have my word."

"It's not enough. What if you decide you've promised me too much, and you lie to me about what was in the safe?"

"You have a suspicious mind."

"A hazard of my profession. I suppose I'll need to come with you."

"I hardly think so."

"I don't trust you. As you don't trust me either, that should be easy for you to understand. I'll go with you. I can even help. I'll stand guard. I suppose you keep a good pantry too." She slanted me a glance. "Unless you're opposed to stealing food from your own kitchen."

I leaned my head back, looking out at the sunset, orange and fiery red against the horizon. I didn't want to admit that her suggestion eased my trepidation. With her standing guard, there to distract the servants if need be, everything would be much easier. "Very well."

Her smile was irritatingly self-satisfied. "Lucius will know Nathan's whereabouts. I'll ask him in the morning."

"The sooner, the better."

"There's something we're agreed on."

The smoke was lifting a bit now, clearing with the slight breeze coming off the Sound. Lights began twinkling on the boats in the harbor, and men picked among the piers, bending to retrieve one thing or another, little black figures against the reflection of the sunset on the water.

There was a commotion down the way, a group of men crowding around something—a cask. One man fell to his knees, cupping his hands beneath the whiskey pouring out, dousing his face to the delight of onlookers. A great cheer went up.

"We should find someplace else to go," said Mrs. Wilkes uneasily. "Nothing good comes from drunken men."

Just then a group of militiamen came up the street, their rifles at the ready. I felt Mrs. Wilkes relax. The men groaned and protested as the militia ordered them away, and one or two of the revelers staggered by, looking at us with glances that made me uncomfortable. The three soldiers kicked in the cask until the whiskey spilled over the grass. The scent of it drifted with the smoke on the air.

One of them came over to us. "There's an eight o'clock curfew. You people had best be moving on."

I looked at the others in the yard, most groaning at his words and climbing to their feet.

"Where are we supposed to go?" Mrs. Wilkes asked.

"Don't matter to me, miss. Away from here's all I know."

"Are there relief tents yet?"

"Tomorrow, I hear."

"How does that help any of us tonight?"

Smoothly, I said, "Officer, this is where we spent last night. We've nowhere else to go."

"I'm sorry for that, ma'am, truly I am. But there's a curfew tonight and I'm ordered to get everyone off the streets."

"And if we don't go?" Mrs. Wilkes asked.

He looked uncomfortable. "I'll be forced to arrest you."

I thought of what Nathan and my father would do with that and said quickly, "We'll be moving along."

He touched his finger to his cap and said, "Good night, ladies," and went down the street.

"Well." Mrs. Wilkes put her hands on her hips and sighed. "I've no idea where he expects us to go."

"There must be somewhere," I said.

"Oh yes. There's the St. Charles Hotel—right over there."

She pointed down the street to an ash pile. "Oh, that's right, it's gone. I suppose we might try the Occidental—"

"You may be the least charming woman I've ever known. How Nathan stood you, I've no idea."

"Oh, he found me charming enough," she said nastily. "Though I can't always say the same for him."

The comment surprised me enough that I had nothing to say in return. When she began to walk down the street, I followed her wordlessly, trailing behind like a duckling following its mother. She knew the area better than I did; she would know better where to go.

The heat of the day and the fire began to ease, and before we'd gone many blocks, we came to the part of the city the fire hadn't reached. On one side of the street were untouched houses and yards, trees with scorched trunks whose leaves had curled into themselves, showing their pale underbellies to the heat, but otherwise unchanged, dogs barking joyously in yards, tethered cows chewing their cud.

But on the other side there was only desolation, where heat rose from the smoldering ashes and a heavy cloud of smoke and ash obscured everything beyond a few feet. The streetlamps weren't lit—when I began to see oil lamps and candles in windows usually glowing with gaslight, I remembered that the gas and electric works was directly in the path of the fire. It had no doubt been destroyed along with everything else.

My lips were dry and parched; my lungs still burned. I felt as if I might never take a deep breath again. My feet blistered in my thin boots, which were not meant for walking, and there was another blister on my shoulder where something had burned a hole in the silk. I would have given a thousand dollars to be rid of my bustle and my corset. As the darkness grew, I moved closer to Mrs. Wilkes; there were too many homeless about, I did not like the shadows.

She paused when we came to a house with a stable off to the side. "What about here?"

"A stable?"

"Have you seen anything better?"

I had to admit I hadn't. "Do you know who lives here?"

"No."

"I can't take the chance that they might recognize me. You'll have to ask them if we might stay."

She rolled her eyes. "I don't plan to ask them. They'll just say no. We look like a couple of whores. Hell, *I'd* turn us down."

"Then I don't understand what you mean to do."

"We'll just go in there. Quietly."

"You can't mean to . . . sneak in?"

"Unless you want to spend the next hour explaining that we're respectable women, which they won't believe because we don't have a place to go, nor any family or friends to help. That is, *you* don't have friends to help. I'd guess Lucius might have his tent by now. We could just go there—"

"Absolutely not."

She sighed. "Then we'll have to sneak in, as you say, and hope to God they don't have a dog."

I followed her around the corner. There was no gate, no cow. Only an old wagon up against the stable wall. The door was half opened, warped, and caught against the dirt, and she slipped inside. My bustle, which was bent and sitting awkwardly, caught as I tried to do the same, and she whispered, "You might want to get rid of that."

It took a moment for my eyes to adjust to the darkness. Beyond was a horse, who stomped a little at us, but then went quiet again. There was a little crash, something scraped along the floor, and Mrs. Wilkes cursed beneath her breath. "Damn sawhorse."

"Ssshh," I said, and we both froze, waiting.

When we moved again, she stopped only a few feet on. "There's a pile of hay here," she whispered. "We'll be comfortable enough."

She sat down. I heard the rustle of hay, her sigh, and I made my way through the darkness until I felt the hay sliding beneath my feet. "Will you help me take off this bustle?"

I turned my back to her and undid the buttons on the bodice, peeling myself out of the tight-fitting silk. She undid the tapes holding the bustle in place as easily and expertly as any maid might do, though she was not the least bit gentle. She jerked the bustle loose, and it bounced against my petticoats and thudded to the floor beneath my skirts.

I stepped from it, kicking it aside. "I suppose it's best to leave it here."

"Maybe the lady of the house will be able to use it."

I pulled up my sleeves and rebuttoned myself and sat beside her. It was prickly and uncomfortable, but better than the hill where we'd slept last night. I stared up at the shadows of the rafters, listening to the rustling and shuffling of the horse beyond, freezing at the quick scamper of some creature I didn't wish to identify.

"I don't imagine you've ever spent the night in a barn before."

"Thus far it's something I've managed to avoid," I said. "I suppose you have."

"Once or twice. When I was with a touring company. Sometimes it was the best an advance man could do. And I've never known a manager who wasn't willing to save a dollar."

"That doesn't seem true of Mr. Greene."

"Lucius is better than some. Still, if his idea to open the Regal in a tent doesn't work, he'll send us on tour quickly enough until it's rebuilt." Another sigh. "I thought I was done with that."

"You needn't go, I'd think. Once I open the safe, you'll have money enough."

"It's not just the money that matters," she said. "I'll follow the stage, wherever it is."

I was surprised. I had thought her purely pragmatic, even mercenary. But suddenly I remembered her performance in *Black Jack*. I heard Sebastian DeWitt's voice in my ear: "*You could learn from her. . . .*"

How clearly I heard him. Suddenly his presence was so strong, I could not bear it. "He must be around somewhere. He can't have died."

"No doubt."

Not even a question as to who I'd been talking about. She'd been thinking of him too, which disturbed me more than I wanted to admit.

We lapsed into quiet again. I closed my eyes, trying not to think of him, breathing deeply of the hay, which smelled sweet and new, and the musky scent of the horse, along with that of manure and sweat and scorched hair and smoke, and I felt her relax beside me. I heard the swish of the horse's tail, the rise and fall of her breath, and I felt weariness invade my every muscle.

I ignored it. Instead I forced myself to think of a plan to break into my own house. I thought of the French doors into the parlor with their terra-cotta urns of flowers outside, the china and statuary and clothes I would be leaving behind.

And I was startled at the extent of my relief.

Chapter Twenty-two

Beatrice

I woke before she did. My stomach felt so hollow and empty all I could think of was how hungry I was. It wasn't quite dawn, but it was growing lighter, and now I saw what I hadn't seen last night: a wheelbarrow and a burlap bag of oats, a harness hanging on a stud, a driver's whip. The scorched scent of the air lingered in my nose.

I glanced down at my boots, dusty with gritty ash, and my skirt, which had holes burned in it and a great scorched spot blackening the calico. I had no trouble thinking of what to do with the money I'd get from Mrs. Langley, given that the only things I owned were on my back, and in no good shape either.

I shook her awake. "It's nearly dawn. We have to get out of here before someone comes."

She sat up, blinking. I went over to the watering barrel by the oats and plunged my face into it. It tasted and felt so good. When

I raised my dripping face, it was to find her beside me, waiting her turn anxiously, and when I stepped aside and she did just what I had, I thought how strange it was to see the well-born Geneva Langley washing her face in a watering barrel.

I took a handful of oats from the burlap bag. The horse made a little snort of disapproval. The oats were chewy and dusty and flavorless, but they made my mouth water anyway, and my stomach knew better than I did; I was swallowing before I had it fully chewed.

Mrs. Langley wrinkled her nose. "Raw oats?"

She hesitated, then reached into the bag and took her own handful, and I'll admit I liked to see the way her face screwed up as she chewed it, as if it were a punishment.

She followed me out the door, her skirt trailing in the dirt, now that there was no bustle. I moved quickly around the corner of the stable and then into the street and back down into the burned district. There was almost no one about, but here and there a soldier, half-asleep, some sitting at their posts, heads hanging, rifles braced upon their knees. A few dogs nosing through the ashes. I couldn't smell the tideflats or anything else. All I smelled was smoke, and I wondered for a moment if the fire had burned my nose, if I was destined to smell the fire forever, or if it was simply the way the city smelled now. It seemed permanent, somehow. When I looked about at the ash and the skeletons of buildings, it seemed it had always been that way; I could not remember what the street had looked like before.

I led her to where a still-standing building on the brick Boston block loomed like a mountain above the ruins, and dodged behind it, where a small group of people—three men and one other woman, all as roughly dressed as I was—were curled up and sleeping.

"This will do," I said, turning to Mrs. Langley, who looked at me in horror. "Wait here until I get back."

"Not with them," she said.

I sighed. "They're hungry and tired, Mrs. Langley. They won't know you from Adam. I'll go to the relief tents and get us both something to eat, and then I'll see if Lucius knows where your husband is. Do me a favor and don't get lost. I won't scour the whole city looking for you."

I walked away without a second look.

I meant to eat first, and then find Lucius. The oats had only stirred my appetite, and I could hardly think for hunger. But after that, the more quickly I could find where Nathan was and get back to Mrs. Langley, the better. If I was lucky and all went well, I might even be able to be rid of her by tonight. What she would do then was her trouble, and none of mine.

I made my way up Third Street toward University, and I saw the relief tent a block before I reached it. It was huge and white. Above it, strung between two poles, was a banner reading TACOMA RELIEF BUREAU in big block letters. Stretched as long as the tent and to the end of the block was a line of people—men mostly—waiting to be fed.

My heart sank; it would take hours to get something if I stood at the end of that line, and for a moment I paused, thinking there must be another way. But I was too hungry, and impatience couldn't trump it, and so I walked wearily toward the end of the line, passing men as dirty as I was, all wearing a lean, hungry expression, but at least it wasn't focused on me. They tipped their hats or bowed their heads as I passed, and then I heard someone call out, "Mrs. Wilkes! Mrs. Wilkes, right here!"

It was a man I didn't recognize, but when I approached him he bowed his head shyly and said, "I saw you in *The Last Days of Pompeii,* ma'am. You were very fine."

"Thank you," I said.

"I heard they was going to open up the Regal again."

"That's what Mr. Greene intends."

He stepped back. "I'd be pleased if you'd come into line in front of me, Mrs. Wilkes. It's the least I can do for all the hours of pleasure you've given me."

I was happy enough to take him up on it, and glad actually for his talk about the plays he'd seen and his commentary on each. It kept me from thinking about how hungry I was, or hearing the clattering of spoons and pans and knives that came from inside the tent, or smelling something salty and yeasty that managed to eke past the scorched scent in my nose.

From plays, we moved to gossip. He told me all the rumors about the fire's start, and that the Ladies Relief Society was also serving food and assistance out of the Armory, and that there would be cots here at the relief tent tonight and the army had sent 150 tents besides and wasn't it a blessing that the fire had got rid of the vermin—not just the damn rats (*"Excuse my language, ma'am"*) but the vagrants and the debauched down on the sawdust as well.

The debauched. I heard Sebastian DeWitt's voice in my ear. *"Perhaps we'll end up joining them."*

When the man paused, I asked, "Did you hear how many died?"

He frowned, rubbing his long chin. "Some rich woman maybe. And a passel of Chinamen—I heard about ten. They found a bunch of bones at Wa Chong's."

The man behind him offered, "Fire marshal says three men died rushing into the San Francisco Store. I heard tale of four others."

"Do you know their names?" I asked.

"No. You missing someone?"

I hesitated, and then I shook my head. "I just wondered."

But I couldn't stop thinking of him, watching for him. There were men in old suits and ash-dusted shirtsleeves and vests with limp neckties that spoke of how they'd dashed out of their offices to avoid the fire and seen their hotels burned just as I had. But nowhere did I see an old brown frock coat, or a walk I recognized, and the time I'd spent with him began to feel like a faraway dream.

I reached the front of the line. There were long, waist-high tables at which dozens of men stood, while aproned men and women stirred huge pots of soup at the big wood-fired stoves beyond, and dishwashers wet to the elbows scrubbed dishes in big metal tubs. Waiters bustled about bearing soup in small white crockery bowls and thick slices of bread, and men shoveled the food into their mouths. The air smelled of soup and sweat, coffee and sun-warmed canvas. As I went to the tables, men moved aside politely, and when a man wearing an apron and a large white badge saying TACOMA RELIEF brought me a bowl and a plate I asked for something to be wrapped for a friend too ill to come, and he eyed me as if to determine whether I told the truth, and then brought me a parcel of bread wrapped in butcher paper.

I was relieved, because I was afraid that once I started eating I would be unable to stop and save enough for her. I was like the men hemmed in around me, too hungry for talk now that food was set before us. I wolfed down that bread and soup so quickly I barely tasted them, gulping the coffee so it burned my mouth. I felt I could eat all day long and not be full, but the bread was a heavy lump in my stomach by the time I got to the last bite, and I was starting to feel alive again, and ready to do what I could toward Mrs. Langley's plan.

I wove my way through the crowd toward the exit, the parcel of Mrs. Langley's breakfast in my hand. The tent flap was tied back; I stepped from the hot, noisy tent into the open air.

And saw Sebastian DeWitt as if I'd somehow conjured him.

He had his back turned to me, and he was talking to some other man, but I recognized that coat, as dirty and streaked with soot as it was, and the satchel slung over his shoulder, and I stopped short, frozen by a quick leap of joy. *It doesn't matter if it is him, does it? It doesn't change anything.* But before I could think better of it, I called out, "Sebastian!"

He jerked around. "Bea!" He said my name like an explosion of sound, and we hurried toward each other like some silly reunited couple in a mellie. Then it was as if we both remembered where we were at the same moment; we stopped only a few inches apart, but he looked me over as if he couldn't believe I stood before him, as if he wanted to touch me but was holding himself back. "You're all right. Thank God. Thank God, you're all right."

I tried not to smile, but I couldn't help myself. "Yes. Well, a little burned here and there, but other than that. . . . Everyone's looking for you. Lucius, everyone."

"Everyone escaped then? Everyone's all right?"

"Except for Mr. Galloway, who's injured, and Brody and Jack both burned their hands. But everyone else is fine. Lucius is trying to get a tent to set up where the Regal was—the Phoenix, he's calling it now."

"The name *du jour,*" he said. "We'll be lucky if every business doesn't end up called that."

I laughed—a little too loudly, and he smiled as if he realized it too, and I went hot. It was only that it was such a relief to see him, I told myself. He was really such a talented playwright. *And lovely too. Even streaked with soot and filthy and dear God what a fool you are.*

I took a deep breath and stepped back. "Well. I'm glad you're all right. I was worried. But now I—I'd best be off. I meant to see Lucius and—"

"Where are you staying?"

"I—nowhere. I heard they planned to set up cots in here tonight, so I thought perhaps I'd come back."

"Only for men," he told me.

"Oh. Of course. God forbid they should end up housing a whore by mistake. Where the hell are the women staying?"

"Wherever they can."

"Well, I suppose Lucius has his tent—"

"I've a tent from the army. At Eleventh and Lane. Fort Spokane, they're calling it." A small smile. "I'm supposed to be sharing it with another fellow, but he can find somewhere else to sleep. There's room for you, if you like."

He said the words so casually, as if it mattered little to him whether I took him up on the offer, and I was calling myself sixty ways a fool for being tempted. What the hell did I want from him anyway? I had no intention of setting up with him; the fire had not changed that, in fact, it only made things worse, because who knew what I might have to do to survive now? Uncomfortably I thought of Mrs. Langley waiting behind the Boston block.

"I can't. Thank you, but . . . no."

"There are a few families there. No one's paying much attention to anyone else. They're too busy with their own situations to ask questions, if it's your reputation you're worried about."

"I can't, Sebastian."

He eyed me thoughtfully. "What's Langley doing for you?"

I dodged his glance. "Nothing. I haven't seen him."

"He hasn't even brought you a box of apricots? Not very gentlemanly of him, is it?"

I glared at him. "I doubt he's thought of me a single moment. I think he's more concerned for his wife."

"His wife?" Sebastian's tone sharpened. "Why is he concerned for her? Is she hurt?"

"She's missing. Haven't you heard?"

"No, I haven't. Missing? Are you certain?"

I was stung by the worry I saw in his expression. Too sharply, I said, "As certain as anyone can be."

"She was at the theater, wasn't she? Didn't she escape with the others?"

"I don't know what happened."

"Are they searching for her?"

"Of course they are."

"Where have they looked?"

"I don't *know*, Sebastian," I said, more snappishly than I'd meant. "Why don't you join the damn search party yourself if you're so concerned."

He gave me a look that shamed me, though I was damned if I'd show it. I turned away. "I should be going. To find Lucius—"

He fell into step beside me. "I'll come with you."

"There's no need."

"For me there is. Now that I've found you, I'm reluctant to lose sight of you again. And I still hope to persuade you to stay with me. At least for a while. The city's in chaos. Langley will be too busy to know or care."

"Sebastian—"

"Where did you sleep last night?"

"In . . . in a stable."

"And the night before?"

"In someone's yard."

His eyes looked blue today. "Both better than a tent and a bedroll, I'm certain."

The paper parcel in my hand felt suddenly like a lead weight. "You're very kind, but—"

"I'm not kind at all. I've purely selfish motives. I've spent two days searching for you. When the fire started and it looked like it might spread, I went back to your hotel to warn you, but you weren't there."

"I'd already gone to the Regal."

He frowned. "You should have heard the warnings by then. It was out of control by three-thirty."

"I was there before noon."

"You were? Why? I thought Greene told you to stay away."

I hesitated, trying to remember exactly what I'd meant to tell him, how I'd had it worded. I still needed him, after all. I could not afford to lose a playwright who found in me a muse, whether or not I meant to keep him as a lover. "I thought it was where you'd gone, and I"—*just blurt it out, Bea*—"I meant to tell you that I don't mean to . . . do what we . . . did . . . again."

"I thought we agreed we could keep it hidden from Langley."

Langley. The perfect excuse, just handed to me. It was easier than explaining the truth, which was that I was afraid of him, especially because I could hardly even explain that to myself. With relief, I said, "It's too big a risk. I can't afford it, and neither can you. We both have to keep him happy."

"I would have thought you'd want to keep me happy as well. After all, there's the new play to consider. The one I'm supposed to be writing for you." His voice was quiet. He put his hand to my elbow as we crossed the street as if I were a lady, and he didn't take his hand away when we reached the other side. That touch stirred a memory that I swallowed hard.

I said as casually as I could, "I do mean to keep you happy. But . . . as a friend. We could still be friends, couldn't we?"

He laughed. "Hmmm. Friends. Now there's a thought."

I felt myself flush and wished I knew why the hell he flustered me so.

He said, "Do you know what would make me truly happy, Bea?"

"I can't imagine." Though I could, of course. Too damn well.

"Stay with me. Just until things settle. It would help me write if I could see my muse whenever I wished."

"Very pretty, Mr. DeWitt, but I fear I must decline. It's better . . . for both of us. You'll thank me for it later, I promise you."

He leaned close, whispering, "Was it so bad that you prefer a stable to me?"

He smiled this knowing smile that sent the heat rushing into my face *again,* and I looked away, unsettled and embarrassed, *you stupid girl,* relieved when I saw that we were nearly to the lot where I'd left Lucius and the others. Even from a distance, I spotted Lucius—his hair spiking on his head as if he'd molded it that way, Jack's tall, lean figure hovering about him. "There they are," I said, quickening my step, nearly racing through the crowd to where they were. I saw Jack look up as we neared and wave us over.

Brody called out as we approached, "A glue pot, Bea! It was a glue pot that done it!"

"That did what?" Sebastian asked.

"Started the fire, I think." I called back, "Not Chinamen?"

"No." Brody smiled. "Though that's the better story. Some glue pot boiled over in a carpenter's shop on Front and Madison."

"The whole city destroyed for want of a chair." Jack shook his head. "Though I liked the rumor that Madame Minerva caught her fortune-telling cards in a candle flame myself."

"Here she is, sweet Bea back to her hive!" Lucius strolled over. "And with our playwright too! Ah, my dear, I should have trusted that he would find you—he is a kind of burr, eh? He shall stick." He clapped his hand on Sebastian's shoulder. "But thank God, thank God you're well, man. We shall have much need of you in the next days."

"Lucius has procured a tent. And a permit," Jack said.

"'Once more unto the breach, my friends, once more!'" Lucius smiled heartily.

"So you do plan to perform?" Sebastian asked.

"Well, what else is an actor made for? We shall enter into rehearsals tomorrow. The people ache for entertainment, a way to ease their weary cares, and we shall provide it. For a small fee, of course."

"Of course," I said.

"You can't mean to do *Penelope,*" said Sebastian. "Not with Mrs. Langley missing."

Lucius clasped his hands. "Oh dear no. In deference to our concern, we must wait on that a bit. At least until a new waterfall can be built. We shall start with a little Shakespeare, I believe. A comedy." He gestured to the gray and bony city beyond. "Here's enough tragedy for a year, I'll warrant. 'Tis best to make people laugh. Have you *Much Ado About Nothing* in your repertoire, my dear?"

I glanced to Jack. "Jack and I both. And I know Aloys does as well."

"Excellent! I shall need you, Mr. DeWitt, to refine the play for us. Cut out the extraneous parts. Find a spot for a song or two. I would do it myself, but there is so much to be done I haven't the time."

"Yes, of course," Sebastian said.

"It has the added benefit of keeping you near our Bea, eh?" Lucius gave me a ribald smile.

I said quickly, "Where do you mean to put your tent, Lucius?"

"Why, my dear, atop the ashes of the Regal. Where else?" He sighed. "I'd have it there already, but for Mr. Langley's insistence on searching for his wife's body."

"He thinks she's *dead*?" Sebastian asked—and there was a shock and dismay in his voice that pricked at me.

Lucius shrugged. "Who knows? I think Langley is simply ruling out all the possibilities."

"Perhaps she hit her head and don't remember where she is," Brody put in.

"Ah, the amnesia plot," Jack said with a wry grin. "A classic, with good reason. Nothing better than a bump on the head to explain the mysterious. Perhaps we should advance that theory to her husband."

I remembered why I was there to begin with. "Does Nathan intend to search with them?"

Jack shrugged. "Oh, I doubt he'll get his hands dirty, but I expect he means to supervise. Leave no ash unturned, as it were."

"When does he mean to search?"

Jack leaned back against the pile of stakes and canvas, crossing his arms over his chest. "Today, I believe."

"When will they be there? What time?"

Jack glanced at Sebastian and then raised his eyebrows at me. "What a greedy little thing you sound, my sweet. With one hand already full, you think to fill the other. Women are trying things, don't you agree, DeWitt?"

"Men are more trying," I said sharply. "Particularly when they concern themselves with affairs that are not their own."

"True. True. 'Tis not my affair."

"What *time*, Jack?"

He shrugged. "He may be there already. He was going after breakfast, he said. However it is that rich men can eat when the city starves around them."

"The relief tents are just up the hill," I said stonily, clutching Mrs. Langley's packet of bread. "There's no need for anyone to starve today."

"We mean to go up there when Aloys and Mrs. Chace return," Jack told me. "So someone can watch the tent."

I nodded. "Then I'll see you at rehearsal tomorrow." I was anxious to leave now, to get to Mrs. Langley and tell her Nathan's plans. I started off, and suddenly Sebastian was beside me.

"Where are you off to in such a hurry?"

"Nathan's at the Regal site," I said.

"You mean to talk to him there?" Sebastian looked surprised.

"I haven't seen him since the fire."

"He won't thank you for hunting him down, you know. Not in public. Not while he's looking for his wife."

"Perhaps not."

"Then why go now? Why not wait until he seeks you out?"

I kept my expression as even as I could. "What if he doesn't?"

Sebastian regarded me thoughtfully, and I had the uncomfortable sense that he saw right through me, that he would call me a liar, but he only said, "He'd be a fool if he didn't."

"I just want to be certain."

"Then what will you do?"

"I don't know. Come back here, I suppose."

"Come to my tent instead," he said in a low voice. "Spend the night with me."

I sighed. "Sebastian, please. Don't be a fool."

"Ah, if you'd only warned me sooner than this," he said with a smile. "'Answer a fool according to his folly,' isn't that what they say? You're my folly, Bea. Come to my tent. I'll find you apricots. I know they're your favorite."

I couldn't help myself; I laughed. "Do you never surrender?"

"Not until you do," he said. "But then I think I can guarantee a most enjoyable captivity."

I made the mistake of catching his gaze, and it went like a jolt clear through me. I had to admit it to myself; I still wanted him. And why shouldn't I have him, at least for a time? Just one more night. He was still writing my play; I *did* want to keep him happy. And things were moving even more quickly than I'd hoped. Unless I missed my guess, Mrs. Langley would be gone by tonight, and I would need a place to sleep. It wasn't as if I was committing to him, after all. I could leave whenever I chose.

"Where did you say the tent was?"

He looked so surprised that I laughed.

"Eleventh and Lane," he said quickly.

"I'll be there later," I promised him. Then I gave him a smile and set off alone, heading south a block or so as if I were going toward the pile of ashes that was the Regal, but when I knew they could no longer see me, I turned back to the Boston block, and Mrs. Langley.

Chapter Twenty-three

Geneva

I was starving, and bored, and apprehensive, with nothing to do but worry and watch the city come alive. Smoke rose from the ashes like a fog, curling and wisping, then settling like a miasma over the landscape. The Boston block loomed over everything like a great ogre; all the rest was spires and outcroppings like eroded rock in the middle of the desert, the formations

I'd seen from a distance through the windows of a train, there and gone and yet leaving a lasting impression. Lonely. Desolate. And weirdly beautiful.

There were men about now, spraying down the ashes of their buildings, militiamen poking about, watching, shooing away dogs who had yet to find their masters. I eased to the back wall again, farther out of sight, and wished Mrs. Wilkes would return. I was anxious to get on with things, to leave this place. I knew just how to get into the house, the paned doors that opened from the parlor onto the side yard. I would have to find a way to creep down the hall to Nathan's study unseen, but there was only Bonnie and the scullery maid and the cook, and I did not think it would be so difficult to evade them. With any luck, I could be in a wagon on the way to the nearest steamer dock tonight, and then on to San Francisco. And from there . . . I'd thought perhaps the Continent. Somewhere far enough that Papa's reach, and Nathan's, did not quite extend, somewhere to contemplate my next step. I had no hope of reconciling with any of the friends I'd known there—who were my father's as well, of course. The rumors of *Andromeda* and Marat would have reached them; they would be no more accepting of my behavior than had been my friends in Chicago. But some of the artists I'd known—perhaps one or two—were in Europe now, and they would welcome and harbor me until I could be assured of my father's support. That was my only hope. To win Papa—because Nathan and I were done, and there was nothing for it. I would not put myself in my husband's hands again.

Still, the task I'd set before myself was daunting, and I could not predict its outcome with any certainty. Papa would be difficult. The letters he'd written me had bristled with hurt and disappointment. I knew what I had not realized in Chicago, that my behavior since my marriage had tried him past all patience.

No, I wasn't hopeful. I was desperate, and becoming more so with each passing moment.

The others who'd been huddled behind the building near me rose and left, one of them—a whore, I assumed—informing me that the relief tents were open. A kindness, but I only nodded curtly and a bit rudely, and they left without troubling me.

When Mrs. Wilkes finally showed again, she looked tired and cross, her hair hanging loose as mine. Still, I was relieved to see her. She held a small parcel in her hand.

She handed it to me without a greeting. "Here's your breakfast."

I tore it open. Thick slices of bread, slightly compressed from being carried, and at the sight of them I was suddenly so hungry I could not contain myself. I only just refrained from shoving the entire package into my mouth.

"We haven't got much time," she said. "Nathan's at the Regal now, searching for your body. I guess he'll probably be there for a while."

I nearly choked on the last bite of bread. "My body?"

"He's afraid you're dead. Everyone thinks you must be dead."

I crumpled the butcher paper and threw it onto the ground. "Did you speak to him?"

She shook her head. "Jack told me. But I don't know how long they'll dig or how many men he has—"

"Let's go then," I said. "It may be our only opportunity."

I began to walk, and she fell into step beside me as we left the Boston block and moved away from the burned district, that strange journey into a world unchanged, where the only evidence of fire was an acrid fog that curled and hovered as it rose.

"What else did you discover?" I asked her.

"Lucius got his tent. We're performing *Much Ado About Nothing* as soon as he can raise it. No one's allowed to sell liquor. There're only three restaurants left in town and no groceries. The army's giving away tents to whoever needs one. And Mr. DeWitt showed up."

How casually she said it. As if he didn't matter in the least. I glanced at her. "Unhurt?"

"Unhurt. Unscathed. Lucius has set him to revising *Much Ado.*"

I was more relieved than I wanted her to know. "That's . . . thank God. Perhaps he'll be willing to help after all."

She gave me a quick look. "Why involve him? I said I'd get you out of town."

I could not explain, not to her, though I wanted to. I wanted to say: *I want to see him one last time before I leave. I want to reassure him that what I feel for him is no pretense, and to see that he feels the same for me. I want to tell him I will help him when I can, that I won't forget my promises to him.*

But I felt too how explaining this to her would cheapen my relationship with him, and so I only said, "I just feel I should explain things to him before I go."

"You haven't explained them to *me*," she complained. "Do you want to get out of town quickly or not?"

"Quickly, yes."

"Then we haven't time for Sebastian. I'll be happy to deliver a message for you when we're done."

I took a deep breath. "I suppose that will have to serve."

"I hope you've thought of a plan for getting in."

"The side doors to the parlor," I said, my breath coming shorter as we climbed the hill. "They open onto the yard. We can go in through there. I'll have to get down the hall to Nathan's study, but it should be simple enough."

"You know where the key to the safe is?"

I nodded. "It should only take a few moments. And then we can hire a wagon and I'll be off." Just saying the words was a relief.

"After you give me my portion."

"Yes, of course. I promised it, didn't I?"

"Just making sure you didn't change your mind."

"I'm not in the habit of going back on my word."

After that, we toiled on in silence. Up one block and then another. Trees gave some shade, though their leaves too were dusty. The closer to my house we got, the more I began to cling to the shade, to let my hair fall forward to hide my face. I daren't look at any windows, or at the carriages that went by, and luckily most of the men in town were preoccupied with the fire—and the women too, I assumed. The Ladies Relief Society must be in full force, and no doubt plenty of women had gone to help. No one paid any attention to us. I was glad she was with me; I was uncertain I could have gone this far without being recognized if

I'd been alone. But anyone looking for me would not be looking for two women—Geneva Langley had few friends, after all, and none of them female.

I stopped when we were two houses away, pointing out my home to Mrs. Wilkes, and then I took her down the street instead of into the alley behind, where the stables were and the stableboy and the driver, and the kitchen where the maids did most of their work. Past the rhododendrons flanking the porch that grew so tall they hid the side yard from view. I dodged behind one, and she followed, and then I crept to the edge of the parlor doors, angling myself to see inside without being seen. The parlor was empty, the doors to the hall shut.

"There's no one there," I told her, quickly twisting the handle of the door, easing it open. It creaked slightly, and I froze. Mrs. Wilkes went still behind me. Nothing. We slipped inside.

The house was quiet, as it always was. From this parlor I could not hear the sounds in the kitchen. How many hours had I spent here, completely alone, cocooned in silence and boredom? I realized suddenly and forcefully how much I despised this room.

I moved to the hallway doors, glancing behind me at Mrs. Wilkes, who was looking around as if she'd come into a foreign land. I mouthed *quickly,* and she came up beside me as I leaned against the door, listening. I was just turning the knob when I heard footsteps coming down the stairs, and I went still, holding my breath, Mrs. Wilkes frozen beside me as we waited to see if the steps would stop at these doors, but they only paused a little.

I heard a call, "Anna! Come help me with this rug if you please!" and a louder, "I'm coming," as Anna hurried down the hallway.

Everything was silent again.

I glanced at Mrs. Wilkes. "Are you ready?" I whispered, and she nodded, and I opened the door just enough to peer out, to be certain. The hall was empty. As we went into it, the floor creaked beneath our footsteps; it seemed as if the sound echoed up the stairs and down to the kitchen. I rushed to the door of Nathan's study; Mrs. Wilkes was so close behind me she stumbled on the hem of my dress. It was not until we were safely within that I could breathe again. The last time I'd been in this room I'd discovered Nathan's plan, and the memory of it hit me hard again; I had to work to contain my fury.

Mrs. Wilkes stood by the door as I went to the cigar stand. I flipped the latch and took out the box of cigars, the fragrance of tobacco easing through the smoke that seemed to have seared my nostrils. The key was where I'd left it, slid to the back, and I grabbed it and replaced the cigars, closing the small door again with a little click.

I went behind the desk, kneeling in a billow of filthy skirts, opening the cabinet to reveal the face of the safe.

Mrs. Wilkes said, "Are those real jewels in that clock?"

I glanced over my shoulder. She was staring at the small hanging desk clock on Nathan's desk, a gift from me on our third wedding anniversary. Irritably, I said, "Keep your voice down."

She whispered, "Are they real?"

"Yes, of course." I was nervous. I dropped the key. It clattered on the wood at the edge of the carpet and skittered.

"There are a lot of beautiful things in this house," Mrs. Wilkes murmured.

I felt anxiously for the key. "I suppose so." I could not find it. Not where it should be. Not along the wall.

"You're richer than I thought."

There. In the corner. I felt the rod with relief. "You've heard of Stratford Mining? That's my father." The key was in my hand. I set it into the lock.

"Your father is the Stratford in Stratford Mining?" Her voice was flat with disbelief.

"Yes." I twisted the key.

"Are you—"

The slam of the front door cut her dead. I heard the quick footsteps of the maid, her higher voice, then lower tones. Tones I recognized. I glanced with horror at Mrs. Wilkes, who had gone suddenly pale. *Nathan.*

"Christ," she said.

I pulled the key from the lock, shutting the cabinet door. Nathan's footsteps were coming down the hall. In a panic, I said, "You can't let him see me."

"What the hell am I supposed to do?"

"Whatever you have to. You said you'd stand guard."

"I didn't think—"

"Please." I didn't try to hide my fear. "Distract him until I can find a way out of here."

"Distract him?" Her own voice was nervous and fast. "How?"

"I don't know. Tell him you've come to see him."

"But then he'll think I—"

I squeezed the key so hard the pins bit into my palm. "You're his mistress, aren't you? *Do it.* Meet me after . . . at the Boston block."

Nathan's voice came closer. "I'll have dinner later," he was telling Bonnie. "Don't disturb me. I'll call for it when I'm ready." He was coming to his study; there was no doubt.

I crawled beneath the desk, curling in as small a ball as I could, pulling my skirt in tight around me. She cursed and seated herself on the edge of the desk. The hem of her skirt blocked whatever he could see of me.

The door opened. Nathan stepped inside. I heard him pause; my breathing came so fast and hard I thought he must surely hear it. When he said, "Ginny," in a rough and startled voice, I thought he'd seen me. Panicked, I glanced around to see what was showing—

"Not Ginny," Mrs. Wilkes said, low and smooth, the voice I'd only ever heard onstage. "It's me. Bea."

"Dear God." He sounded choked. "For a moment, I thought. . . . What the hell are you doing here? Bonnie didn't tell me—"

"She didn't know." Her foot came down. "I snuck in. I was afraid your maid wouldn't let me in. But I . . . I've been waiting for you."

"For God's sake, I don't have time for this now." His voice was tight with exasperation. "Please go. I've been all day in the ruins looking for my wife. I've business—" He moved toward the desk. She stepped in front of him.

"I had to know you were all right," she said.

"Yes, of course I am. Didn't your manager tell you?"

"Yes, but I had to see for myself. Don't be angry. Please, Nathan."

An irritated sigh. Another step. Another forestalling. "I'm not angry. But this is a devil of a time—"

"I'm sorry, I just. . . ." Her voice trailed off.

I heard the catch of Nathan's breath and wondered what she was doing to him. I could see nothing but their feet. She stepped forward, her foot between his, her skirt wrapping about his ankle, and Nathan made a little sound deep in his throat, a sound I knew, and I shut my eyes with loathing and resentment and gripped the key harder.

She whispered something; I could not make out the words. He hesitated. Then quick steps. They were at the door, and then they were out, and the door closed behind them, and I was undiscovered.

I let out my breath in relief. How close I'd come to being found, too close. Thank God she'd been here to distract him. Now that they were gone, I didn't linger. Who knew how long she could manage to keep him? I crawled from beneath the desk and went to the safe again, my hands steady now. I inserted the key and twisted it, pulling the safe door open, reaching inside to find—

Nothing.

I frowned and felt around again. There was nothing. Disbelieving, I bent to look inside. The safe was completely empty. The household money was gone.

I swept my fingers over every surface, cursing beneath my breath when it didn't suddenly appear. I'd counted on that money. Everything I'd risked to get here . . . Now what was I to do?

I locked the safe again, closing the cabinet, rising. I leaned against Nathan's desk, staring unseeingly down at the papers there, trying to think of any other place in the house where cash was kept. There was none that I knew. I would have to come up with another plan. Perhaps I could sell one of my jewels. Surely there would be a pawnbroker somewhere? I couldn't be the only one needing money. Perhaps I would have to wait a few days longer, hidden away, but it was better than nothing. And it would take time for Nathan to discover what I'd done. Long enough for me to get to San Francisco and perhaps farther.

But then I remembered Mrs. Wilkes, upstairs with my husband. I could not go up there now. The risk was too great.

I glanced at the clock on the desk. At the sapphires and rubies glinting in a Turkish-styled design. I couldn't retrieve my jewels, not yet, but there was this, winking as if to say *Take me.*

I reached for the clock, shoving the stand a little in my haste, and then I heard Bonnie's footsteps in the hall, her voice—"I'll do the study next then. Just let me get the polish." And her footsteps faded away again, and I knew I had no time. I had to get out of here. I shoved the clock into my pocket, and made myself move. I put the key back and somehow managed to avoid running into Bonnie as I made my way surreptitiously back down the hall, into the parlor. And once I was in the yard again, I ran. I did not stop until I was two blocks away.

Then I concentrated on staying in the shadows, on turning away from passing carriages and wagons. I did not slow until I was past the houses and back into the desolate, alien landscape, until I found refuge at the back of the Boston block, and there I leaned back against the wall and waited for her to return.

Chapter Twenty-four

Beatrice

I knew what Nathan liked, of course, and so it took almost nothing to seduce him, though I would have done almost anything else had I the choice. But I knew by the way he looked at me—once he'd got over his shock that I wasn't her—that I wouldn't get out of this house without fucking him, and I resented her for putting me in the position, for her assumption that I would do it to save her, and *here you are, Bea, doing it, just as she wanted,* and I was angry for that too.

But I was also relieved when he took me out of that study, because there was a moment there where I thought maybe he'd have me on the floor in front of her, though he wouldn't know it. And when he took me upstairs I was glad that I'd given her the opportunity to get the money and escape, and I told myself I was doing it not just for her, but for myself too.

He opened a door and nearly pushed me inside. I'd assumed it would be his bedroom, but I knew in a moment that it was hers instead. Chintz curtains and a bedcover in a pale green. A dressing table set with crystal bottles, a rosewood jewel box, silver-backed hairbrushes. Beautiful, expensive things, just as downstairs was littered with beautiful, expensive things. I remembered what she'd said about being the daughter of Stratford Mining, and that stirred something in my head, some thought that I couldn't gain hold of right away, because I was distracted by her scent, which I hadn't realized I'd noticed before. Something like almond. She was in every inch of this room, and I turned to Nathan in dismay and said, "This is your wife's bedroom."

He didn't answer. Instead he cupped my chin between his fingers hard and jerked me close, and then he was all over me, pulling off his clothes and mine until I wore only my boots and stockings—nothing but holes and runs now—and the smell of the fire on my skin rose through her almond perfume when he pushed me onto the bed and climbed on top of me. I wished he hadn't come home. I wished the money she'd promised me was in my hands, and I was on my way to paying someone to take her out of town, on my way to Sebastian's tent—

I closed my eyes, forcing that thought away.

Nathan grunted hard, an expulsion of breath against my skin, a hard little thrust of his hips, and then he was done. He pushed himself off and said nastily, "My God, you stink of smoke."

"Living through a fire will do that to a person." I raised myself onto my elbows. "I nearly died in that theater, you know."

He said, "Did you see her there? Did you see my wife when the fire broke out?"

He stared at me so intently, as if he could wring the truth from me if he stared hard enough, but I wasn't an actress for nothing. I met his gaze and said, "I was in the greenroom. Brody said she left before the others."

"No one's seen her."

"She must be around somewhere."

He laughed, this hard, short sound, and put his face in his hand as if he were too weary to think. "Goddammit, this was supposed to be over by now. Trust Ginny to ruin it."

"Ruin what?" I was confused. "What was supposed to be over?"

He shook his head a little and then looked back at me, his gaze burning, reminding me of the way Aloys looked when he played Macbeth, which was not a comforting thought. "I went to the ruins today. To search for her body."

I winced. "Yes. Lucius told me. Did you find anything?"

"Not in the ashes, but . . . I thought I saw her."

There was not one other thing he could have said that would have surprised me more. He'd seen her, and she'd said nothing of it to me. This whole drama had been unnecessary. I had been right not to trust her. "You saw her?"

"I chased after her, but she disappeared."

Carefully, I said, "Maybe it wasn't her you saw."

"Don't you think I know my own wife?"

"Then why would she run from you?"

"A good question," he said. "Why would she run from her own husband? It doesn't make sense, does it? I'd thought . . . ah, never mind. It can't be true."

"What can't be true?"

He sighed. "Before the fire, she was acting strangely. Lately I've been wondering if perhaps she was . . . ill."

I frowned. "Ill? With what?"

"Insanity," he said shortly. "Surely you saw signs of it too. Do you think acting in the theater the mark of a sane woman?"

"Well, yes. That's what I do, after all."

He waved that away. "Even you must see the difference between a cheap actress and my wife. You can't think I actually approved of her taking to the stage? She's a Stratford, for God's sake."

I chose to ignore his insult. "Then why didn't you stop her?"

"One doesn't stop Geneva Langley. One simply endures. She's become more and more unbalanced over the last few months. I'm not the only one who's noticed it. Our entire social circle has. The truth is that she hasn't been herself for some time, and now this . . . How else to explain why she hasn't come home? She's either dead or deranged."

Hold your tongue, Beatrice. But I heard myself saying, "Maybe she doesn't want to come home."

His gaze sharpened, and I wished I'd kept quiet after all. "What are you saying?"

"I mean . . . was she happy?"

"She had everything. She should have been happy. But Ginny was—*is*—hard to satisfy. She's always . . . tilting at windmills." He laughed softly, as if at some small joke. "I think she no longer has any sense of what is real. Since that debacle in Chicago—"

"What happened in Chicago?"

"Surely you know. Everyone knows. It's why we came here. She had an affair with Jean-Claude Marat."

"Who is that?"

"Dear God, how ignorant you are."

"I don't move in your circles. How would I know him?"

"He's a famous sculptor," Nathan said. "Perhaps the most famous of the last ten years. Perhaps you should read a newspaper, my dear, and learn something besides the lines in a melodrama."

"I wasn't aware that reading was one of your requirements," I said, no longer trying to keep my temper. I thought of Mrs. Langley escaping, money in hand. I thought of how little I needed her husband now. I started to get off the bed, but he grabbed my arm to stop me.

"Fortunately, you have other attributes," he said.

I glared at him. "I saw your wife every day at rehearsal. She didn't seem mad to me."

"No offense, my dear, but how would you know? Those actors you work with . . . the entire company borders on insanity."

I couldn't argue with him there. But despite what he said, I did know the difference, and while Mrs. Langley was infuriating, she wasn't insane. And I thought of the things Sebastian had said about her. Surely he would have noted if she'd been as mad as Nathan seemed to think.

I said, "She knew about us, you know. Perhaps that's why she stays away. Maybe she's angry."

"It's hardly unusual for husbands of our class to have mistresses. And if she's angry about it, it's her own fault."

"Her fault?"

"She did it first." He smiled meanly and rose. "It's what she deserves, don't you think?"

"What a wonderful marriage you have," I said.

"You have no idea." He went to the armoire in the corner, opening the door while I watched him. He reached inside, grabbing something, throwing it to me. A deep blue silk embroidered with butterflies in gold and red. It may have been the most beautiful gown I'd ever seen. "Here's a little present."

"Why?" I asked suspiciously.

"I can't give my mistress a gift?"

"Of course you can. But why her dress?"

"Because it's beautiful, and I want to see you in it. And I want to reward you."

"For what?"

"I'd like you to do me a favor. If you see her, if she tries to return to the company, I want you to tell me. Before you do anything else. Immediately. Will you do that for me?"

The silk was smooth and cool against my hands. I wanted to say I couldn't be bought with a pretty piece of fabric, but you know, the truth is that only people with money can afford to have scruples, and I wasn't one of them. How easy it would be to just say: *she's waiting behind the Boston block.* Six words, and she would be back in his hands and out of mine.

But then I thought of her saying, *"I need to get out of the city before Nathan finds me,"* as if she'd never meant anything so much. Uneasily I wondered just what had been Nathan's relationship with his wife. I didn't understand any of this, and the truth was that I wasn't ready to hand her over to him, and it didn't have anything to do with the money she was holding for me. There was something more here, something I didn't trust, something strange.

I gripped the gown in my hands and said hesitantly, "If she's not dead, she won't like this going missing."

"If she's not dead, a missing gown will be the last thing Ginny has to worry about," he said. "Put it on."

I did not refuse him. I knew that strange look in his eyes. So I put on my sweat-stained chemise, grayed with ash and stinking of smoke, and my corset, and he watched every movement. When I reached for my drawers, he shook his head. "Not those." In dismay I saw he was hard again and I knew what he meant for me to do and I didn't want to do it. I wanted to be out of this room, away from her smell, away from him.

But he played out the charade to the end, as I knew he would. He helped me with the many buttons up the back. The gown was made for a bustle, and all that fabric draped limply and heavily, so it didn't sit correctly at my hips. It was so low cut my chemise and corset showed—what kind of underwear did one need to wear this dress? She was slightly bigger than I was; the neckline gaped because my breasts did not fill out the bodice as hers did, but either he didn't notice or didn't care. When I had it on, he told me to get on my hands and knees, which I did, and I was trembling and angry and humiliated. But mostly I was afraid of him. And when he came up behind me, pushing up all that skirt so it billowed over my shoulders, I closed my eyes and bore it as he grasped my hips and punished her through me.

I was sore and angry as I left that house. The sun was setting, fiery gold and red, gilding the Olympics across the Sound, bruising what clouds there were, matching my temper. I had washed before I'd changed back into my calico, rubbing away every bit of Nathan Langley, but I carried the blue silk bundled in my arms. *"Your reward,"* Nathan had said mockingly, and I was damned if I'd give it back in any case. I deserved it, and I'd lost all my other costumes in the fire, and once I got another trunk, I'd put this gown away to wear when I played someone like Lady Macbeth. Someone bitter and angry.

I was anxious to get away from these well-kept homes and yards that seemed to hide some deeper discontent, and back among my own people—which would have made me laugh if I'd thought about it, because there wasn't anyone there I trusted either—with the possible exception of one. But the thought of him filled me with shame and regret; I could not go to him tonight as I'd promised, not after spending the afternoon with Nathan Langley. Once again Mrs. Langley had tangled my life and I had no way to get loose. I was so angry when I approached the burned district that I knew if she wasn't behind the Boston block I would hunt her down and deposit her on her husband's doorstep myself.

That afternoon, the burned district had been full of men digging through the ruins, and the sounds of hammering and sawing and pounding. There had been militiamen everywhere, but now the day was shifting into evening, and most of those men had gone. There were still a few people about, soldiers mostly, getting ready to enforce the curfew, but it wasn't eight o'clock yet, so I got to the Boston block without any trouble. The anger I'd been feeling since I'd gone into her bedroom with Nathan twisted like a live thing. I'd known not to trust her even as I'd gone up those stairs, and I'd done it anyway—

Someone came around the corner of the opposite wall. It was a moment before I realized it was her.

"Mrs. Wilkes," she said breathlessly, rushing up to me, and then she stopped. Her glance went to the blue silk bundled in my arms, the golden embroidery of a butterfly glinting in the sun, and I saw shock in her eyes. And then, incredibly, she began to laugh.

It was the last straw. My temper surged; I slapped her as hard as I could, hard enough that she stumbled back, putting out a hand to the brick wall to keep from falling. When she caught her balance again, she touched her cheek where I'd left an angry red mark. Her eyes watered. I did not feel the least bit sorry.

"What was that for?" she gasped.

"For everything," I snapped. "For making me fuck your husband, for being a goddamn Stratford, for involving me in . . . in any of this. Now if you don't mind, I'll take my money. If we're both lucky, I can still find someone to take you out of here tonight."

Her expression hardened. "There is no money."

"Don't lie to me."

"I'm not lying. The safe was empty."

Now I laughed. "You can't expect me to believe that."

"Whether you believe it or not, it's true."

"You said there would be several hundred dollars in there."

"I thought there would be."

"Where is it then?"

"I don't know." She leaned back against the wall, looking up at the sky. "I don't know. Nathan must have taken it for some reason. You said none of the banks were open. Perhaps he needed it."

I peered at her, not wanting to believe her, searching for any lie. But either Mrs. Langley was a superb liar or she was telling the truth.

She said, "You can't possibly think I'm happy about it. This ruins my plans as well."

There was no money in the safe. The idea sank into me, along with a kind of desperation that was starting to feel a little too familiar. I sagged back against the wall beside her. "So I fucked him for nothing," I said bitterly.

She glanced to the dress I held. "Not for nothing, I'd say. Apparently you have a new gown."

"My reward." And then, because I was angry, and I wanted to hurt her, I said, "He made me put it on. He wanted to pretend I was you."

But once I said it, I was sorry. I took no satisfaction from her flush or her embarrassment.

"He chose that dress for it? Dear God. How . . . wretched."

Now I felt worse. "What's wrong with this dress?"

She shook her head. "Nothing. I . . . it's nothing. I suppose I should thank you. For diverting him."

"Yes, you should," I said.

"It was best that he not discover me."

"Then why did you go to the Regal today?"

She frowned. "I don't know what you mean."

"Nathan said he saw you there. What the hell were you doing? Why didn't you tell me?"

"Because I wasn't there. I don't know what you're talking about. I never left here, as you commanded. Whatever Nathan thought he saw, it wasn't me."

I believed her. Her bewilderment was no act, and to be honest, I couldn't think what would have made her go down to the ruins. She was serious about wanting to stay hidden, and she wasn't stupid.

But suddenly I was more than tired of all of it. "Listen, Mrs. Langley, there was no money in the safe. It looks to me as if you're not going anywhere. I'll tell you what: pay me my two hundred dollars and we'll call it good."

"Where am I to get two hundred dollars?"

"From your bank account," I said sweetly. "The banks will open in another day or so."

"I can't do that. I told you, I can't be seen. And I . . . I don't think I can get the money in any case. Not from the bank."

I frowned. "Why not?"

She didn't answer. Instead, she reached into her pocket and pulled out that clock I'd seen on Nathan's desk. "I did get this. If you know where we can pawn it—"

"Nowhere," I said shortly. "The shops are burned. Maybe in a day or two."

"I don't have a day or two."

I sighed. "Look, your plan didn't work. There's no money, and I want to get on with my life. You've got a comfortable bed, and I've been offered two places to sleep and I'm in no mood to turn them down to spend another night in a haystack. And I'm starving. That soup at the relief tent was good."

"You've found a place to sleep? Where?"

"Lucius has a place for me."

"You said two."

Reluctantly, I said, "Mr. DeWitt has an army tent."

"I see," she said.

I didn't like the way she said the words, or what she thought she knew about me. Angrily, I said, "Go on back to your society parties and your money. Leave me alone. Your husband's right. You've got everything; why the hell can't you be happy?"

She jerked to look at me. "Nathan said that?"

"Among other things."

Her face hardened. "What other things?"

"Oh, that you're half mad and everyone knows it and I should take you to him the moment I see you. Believe me, I considered it. You're lucky I didn't. Now if you'll excuse me—"

I took a step, but before I could take another, she held out her hand to stop me. "Please. Don't go. Please. I need your help."

"I think you'll do just fine on your own."

"Please."

Her voice was calm and firm. She was used to giving orders, and before I knew it, I was obeying them. I stopped and turned to look at her.

Her face was strangely pale, her dark eyes glittering, her mouth set. "I need to tell you something: Nathan means to put me in an asylum."

"I can't say I blame him."

"This isn't a joke. You don't understand. He and my father . . . I saw a letter the morning of the fire. Together they've been planning to have me committed. My father has already transferred control of my funds to Nathan. They've been"—she looked away, as if blinking back tears—"it's all part of it. Everything. The stage. Mr. DeWitt. All of it. And I never suspected. I just followed the path they laid for me like some . . . dumb animal."

She trembled as she spoke. All the supercilious posture was gone. If there'd been any chance that I would turn her in to Nathan—and there hadn't been, not really—it would have disappeared then. Suddenly she was just a woman, helpless as we all were, as I was, and I felt sorry for her.

"What do you mean? What path?"

"I tried so hard to be what they wanted, but I just . . . couldn't." She gave me a look of pleading desperation. "No one in this city wanted to know me. My reputation . . . well, they'd made up their minds about me before we even arrived. I tried—I did. But I was lonely. And then I met the Readings, and Nathan introduced me to Mr. DeWitt, and—"

"Who are the Readings?" I demanded. "And what has Sebastian to do with any of it?"

"James Reading is part of what passes for high society here. But he paid the troupe at the Palace to act with him in *Julius Caesar*. He'd said it was always a dream of his, and when I saw it, I realized it was a dream of mine too." She looked off into the distance, and I saw a wistfulness in her expression that made her seem even more . . . well, human. "Nathan said he would consider it, and I should have known then. But I wanted it so much. And it was Nathan who brought Mr. DeWitt to dinner. He was the one who suggested that Mr. DeWitt escort me to the theater. He . . . encouraged our . . . friendship." She made a sound, a little sob. "How stupid I was. I thought Nathan was becoming again the man I'd married, but he was only . . . he only meant to—"

"Show everyone how mad you were, so that when he put you in the asylum no one would ask questions. He's still doing it too. He's telling everyone you've disappeared because you're unbalanced—at least that's what he told me." I laughed wryly. "Did he read *Penelope Justis*? Because it's as if he stole the plot."

"Without the ghost," she said softly.

"There didn't need to be a ghost. Not when you were so obliging."

"Well, you can be certain Nathan didn't read it. That was his reason for bringing me Mr. DeWitt in the first place. I was to read the play, because Nathan didn't have the time or the inclination. I was the one to decide whether it was worth investing in. And I was so excited about it. I hardly questioned it."

"He bought the play because of me," I found myself saying.

"Ah yes. I'd forgotten. Mr. DeWitt went to Nathan for you, didn't he?"

I didn't want to think of that. Not of Sebastian, nor the fact that I was supposed to be with him now. I swallowed and said, "Yes. But it doesn't matter. What I want to know is how Nathan meant to get you into the asylum. Making everyone believe you were insane is one thing. Actually *committing* you—"

Her smile was very small. "I had a cough, you see, and Nathan brought a doctor to examine me, but I don't think the cough was really the reason he was there. And Nathan said he had a friend who meant to come watch the rehearsal. I think it was to be another doctor. But he never showed."

And suddenly I remembered the night at the Queen City Chop House. The way Nathan had urged me into performing. The man grabbing my arm. *"I'm a doctor. . . ."*

I sagged against the brick wall. It was a coincidence, wasn't it? It had to be. But then I remembered how the whole thing had felt like some game I didn't know how to play, and I knew—I just *knew*—it had something to do with her. "There was a doctor. I think."

Mrs. Langley frowned. "One who came to watch the rehearsal? When?"

I shook my head. "Not then. The night before the fire, Nathan took me to the Queen City. He had me . . . act out the mad scene from *L'Article 47.* I thought it was strange, you know, but he was insistent. And there was a doctor there. Everyone was watching. And . . . Nathan called me his *wife.*"

She went pale. "But surely no one would have mistaken you for me."

"Have you looked in a mirror lately?" I asked sharply. "It was dark in that restaurant too. And I wasn't dressed like this. Nathan asked me to wear a cloak he'd given me, and these jeweled hairpins."

She glanced at the gown in my arms. "I had hairpins made to match that gown. In the shape of butterflies. I lost them."

I felt sick. "No, you didn't. They were gold, weren't they? With rubies and sapphires?"

She nodded, and we both went quiet for a moment before she said, "Dear God, what a fool I've been."

"He said it was supposed to be over," I whispered. "Nathan said that. Today, when I was with him, he said it should have been over by now, and that you'd ruined it."

"By disappearing," she said with a pathetic little laugh. "How inconvenient of me. No doubt he had them waiting to take me away when I returned from rehearsal. But I'd discovered the letter, you see. I'd meant to run away that morning, with Mr. DeWitt's help."

"Did you mention any of this to Sebastian?"

She shook her head. "He wasn't at rehearsal. There was no time."

"I don't understand. It seems like such a lot of trouble. Why go to such lengths? If Nathan wants to be rid of you, why not just walk away?"

"Nathan would never leave me. He wouldn't give up my money."

"Your money? Hasn't he any of his own?"

"Nathan comes from a very old family, but they lost everything when Cooke and Company went bankrupt. His father committed suicide. His mother went mad and died within a year. They left him nothing but debt."

"So the money is all yours."

"Yes. A trust from my mother. My father's largesse. All mine."

"I see," I said, and I did. Even if I'd never heard of Stratford Mining, I would have known there was a great deal of money; I'd seen it all through that house.

"An asylum is the perfect solution for Nathan, don't you see? He wants a political career. I've been a . . . liability. This way, he's rid of me, and our social circle would fall over themselves in sympathy. Half of them would say they weren't surprised. They would embrace him, and he would have control of my money. If they managed to commit me . . . I would never escape. Together, he and my father would keep me in an asylum forever."

"Why are you a liability? Except for that affair with the artist, what have you done?"

She gave me a sideways glance. "There wasn't an affair. But Nathan . . . everyone thought there was."

"So they thought there was. Affairs happen all the time. Half the plays we do are about them."

"In those plays, does the wife pose from life for a statue of a woman waiting for her lover? Is it displayed to all of society in a special exhibition?"

I was stunned. I would never have expected it of her. "*You* did that?"

She looked away again. "Yes. Foolish, I know."

I didn't miss that despair in her voice—one more thing to surprise. And again I found myself feeling sorry for her.

"What do you intend to do?" I asked quietly.

"I don't know," she answered, equally quiet. "I must admit . . . I am sorely ill equipped to be anything other than what I am. But I can't go back to Nathan. You must see that."

I sighed. "Yes. I can see that."

"I'd thought to gain some time. Perhaps go to the Continent until I could convince my father that things aren't as he believes."

"You'll need money for that."

"I suppose once the pawnshops reopen—"

"That clock? It'd buy you six months maybe. What would you do then?" The moment I said the words, the thought that had nagged at me returned. How rich she was. So much money. What I could do with even a fraction of it. Start my own company, build my own theater. No more relying on untrustworthy managers or patrons or keeping anyone happy but myself. . . .

I met her gaze. "There must be a way for you to keep your money. Without Nathan."

"Without him? You don't mean . . . kill him?"

I was startled. That had never occurred to me, but she said it so matter-of-factly it was disturbing. And what was more disturbing was how the thought gathered like a little knot in my chest, a possibility now that she'd mentioned it. "No. I'm no Iago, Mrs. Langley."

"Then how?"

We both fell silent, thinking, but I was hungry, and the day had been long, and my mind did not want to untangle a knot, not this one, not mine, *but it is now, Bea, why not just admit it? You could walk away, and you aren't.*

And on the tails of that thought came Nathan's voice, as if

it had just been waiting for me to come around to it. *"I thought I saw her,"* and my own words: *"Did he read* Penelope Justis*? Because it's as if he stole the plot."*

Suddenly I knew how we could have the money and be rid of Nathan at the same time.

"He said he saw you," I said slowly.

"Yes, you told me that. I tell you he didn't."

"I believe you. But what if he does? What if we make *Penelope Justis* real?"

She gave me a puzzled look.

"A ghost who drives a man mad. Penny pretends to be a ghost to drive Barnabus mad. It's fitting, don't you think? Nathan meant to commit you. What if we turn it about and have him committed instead?"

She went very still. "That's preposterous."

"Yes, but what if we could do it? What if I could make him believe you were dead, and that it was your *spirit* he saw? What if he *keeps* seeing it?"

"No one would believe it."

"We don't need everyone to believe it. We only need Nathan to."

"He won't. He's too rational."

"Nathan's angry as hell," I corrected. "And ambitious. And desperate enough to do what he did. Ambition, anger, and desperation . . . look what it did to Macbeth."

She hesitated. "That's a *play.* Things like that don't really happen."

"You think not? Truth is stranger than fiction, isn't that what they say? God knows I've seen strange things. And we don't need to actually turn Nathan insane, anyway. All we must do is make people believe he is. It's what he was doing to you. And once he's safely in an asylum, you'll have all the time you need. It should be easy to prove to your father that Nathan was lying—hell, he's in an *asylum.* And you'll have all your money. Except for what you give to me, of course."

"Such a thing could take months. I would need to stay hidden for months."

"Wouldn't it be worth it? A life without him, Mrs. Langley—if you end up with that, what's a few months? And maybe it would be quicker. Sometimes he already seems half mad. And you said his mother was. Maybe blood runs true."

"I've tried to manipulate Nathan before," she said quietly. "It was . . . disastrous. The way he thinks . . . he never does what one expects."

"But you never had *me* before. Together we can do this. You'll have to do some acting, but I think you have enough talent to fool him."

She glanced at me in surprise.

"Enough for that, anyway," I said—and pretty generously too, given everything.

"It's easy enough to say we could turn him mad, but the doing of it is something else."

"Sebastian's already thought of how to do it. We simply follow his play."

"But it changes by the hour. And we haven't rehearsed it in order. I don't *know* what happens well enough to follow it. Unless"—said hopefully—"you've been privy to the whole revision?"

I shook my head. "No one has. He hasn't finished writing it. When I last saw the full play, there truly was a ghost. Before Penelope became a villain and decided to invent one."

"Then there is no plan to follow," Mrs. Langley said.

"But there will be," I assured her. "He's revising it—all I have to do is read it."

"How do you intend to do that?"

"Well, he's invited me to stay with him, hasn't he? I suppose I'll have to now."

She went quiet, and her glance was thoughtful, and it made me remember her *friendship* with him, the way he defended her, and there it was, a jealousy that shook me.

Mrs. Langley said—a little irritably, I thought—"Yes, I suppose you shall. Where then will I be?"

"We'll find a place," I said. "It shouldn't be too difficult."

She nodded, and then she said, "Thank you."

"For what?"

"For helping me."

That gentle voice again, that voice she had like a wounded dove, so sweet and trusting, and I didn't like the way it wiggled into me, the way it sat there, the way it pleaded.

So I said roughly, "It's a lot of money. I'll expect a piece of it."

She said, "Believe me, I didn't expect it to be free."

Chapter Twenty-five

Geneva

In the end, she did sleep in a haystack again, despite her protests. I was grateful; I did not want to be alone to think of everything that could go wrong. Her plan had not required a great deal of contemplation. There was so much at stake. And I was desperate. My money was in Nathan's hands. My father was on his side. One step out of hiding and I would be locked away, with no chance to protest and no pardon, and I was more afraid than I had revealed to Mrs. Wilkes. So much depended on her, and I didn't trust her, but for now she was my only hope. If this should not work . . . But it *had* to work. What else was I to do?

She stirred beside me, rustling the hay, raising the scent of sun-warmed grass and smoke. "Tomorrow I'll go to the relief tent and get you something to eat. But I've got rehearsal after that. And then . . . I don't know how long it will take, but I'll have to leave you alone. I've been thinking about where we can keep you hidden."

"I can't stay here."

"No. If they add another tent for women up at the Tacoma Relief, could you go there? Would you know anyone?"

"Probably. I hardly know. There were balls . . . suppers. . . ."

She snorted softly. "So not there, I guess." She went quiet. Then she said, "Mr. DeWitt said there were families where he is, that they'd hardly notice me. We could get you a tent. At least for now. There might be people there who recognize me, but maybe . . . if people thought I was you, surely they would think you were me if they didn't see us together. You can't keep hiding out behind the Boston block. The militia won't let you stay."

"I don't want to stay there in any case," I said.

"We'll have to think of somewhere for you to go until I can get a tent. Perhaps . . . I don't know. I can't think of everything. Just stay around here tomorrow. Stay out of sight. Do you think you can manage that?"

"I suppose I'll have to." I took the clock from my pocket and set it on the floor. "What will we do with this?"

"Hold on to it. We might need it. But I wouldn't carry it around. I suppose you should give it to me. I'll hide it."

"Oh no," I said. "How do I know you won't walk off with it?"

"How do I know *you* won't?"

"Because I can't be seen. Not if I'm supposed to be dead."

She was quiet for a moment. "All right. Keep it then."

We lapsed into silence. I thought she'd drifted to sleep, but then she said, "How long have you been married to him?"

The question surprised me enough that I answered her. "Six years now. We married when I was twenty-three. But . . . Nathan was different then."

"Did you love him?"

"Oh yes. We were very . . . passionate. Then we were married and . . . things changed."

"Because of that sculptor?"

Such private things she wanted to know, questions I would have considered insolent only a few days ago. But I wanted to tell her my reasons, to justify myself, so I said, "Claude was the final thing, but it all started before then. I'd thought Nathan was the perfect man for me. He loved theater and art—we used to talk for hours. I thought he understood who I was. But . . . he became different. I thought at first it was because he was so busy working for my father. But then I began to realize he'd only pretended to be the man I wanted. He'd used me. As you said, he's ambitious, and I was only a step on the ladder. I was lonely, and angry. I felt trapped. And then Claude came along, and he was everything I'd thought Nathan was. When he asked me to pose, I thought it was the perfect way to end my marriage." I sighed. "I thought I would be free."

"How spoiled you are," she said.

I felt as if she'd slapped me. How had I ever expected her to be sympathetic? "Of course, how beyond reproach is your life! How sanctimonious you sound."

"I wouldn't have expected any man to understand me or any other woman," she said calmly. "If you weren't so used to getting your own way, you would never have made such a mistake."

Her words startled me; my anger fled. They were true, I realized, and was surprised at it. I had been wrong again: she *did* understand. I found myself asking, "Your own husband—?"

"The Mrs. is only a sign of respect," she said drily. "Haven't you ever noticed? Most actresses use it if they've been around enough. Lucius started putting it on the program two years ago. I've earned it too, believe me."

"You never married?"

"No." Short and to the point.

"Have you ever wanted to be?"

She said, "Managers pay a married actress less on the theory that their husbands will provide. I've never met anyone I liked enough to take a pay cut for."

"How . . . practical."

"I've lived on my own a long time, Mrs. Langley. If I don't watch out for myself, no one else will."

And in spite of everything I thought about her, those words sounded oddly lonely.

She rolled onto her side with a sigh. The hay gave beneath her; some of it was dislodged, poking into my arm. "I'm tired," she said. "Good night, Mrs. Langley."

I hesitated, but in the end there was nothing more to say. "Good night," I answered.

Beatrice

By the time I got back from the relief tent the next morning, Mrs. Langley was huddled outside the far wall of the stable behind a pile of straw and horse manure. She took the parcel of bread I gave her gratefully.

"It's all there is," I said. "Unless you can think of a way for me to carry soup."

"This will do." She opened the paper and tore off a piece of the bread. "Where's the gown?"

"I didn't want to carry it around, but it's safe enough."

I'd buried it that morning in the pile of hay, deep enough that none of those who lived here would find it for a few days if I had to leave it that long. I didn't quite trust her—who knew but that I might return to find her gone and the clock and the dress with her? Which might have been a relief, you know, but that dress was the only currency I had just now, and I didn't want to lose it.

"I'd best be off again," I told her, and she nodded and said she would wait for me there. I headed off toward the ruins of the theater, glad to be away from her and worried about her in the same breath. I'd dreamed last night of murder and Penelope and Macbeth all twisted up together, which left me tired and irritable.

It wasn't just that making me nervous as I made my way to rehearsal. I'd half hoped that I would see Sebastian DeWitt at the relief tent this morning, but he never showed. I'd been more disappointed than I'd expected at that, especially because I was fairly sure he would be angry with me for not coming to his tent as I'd promised. Or he would be hurt, which would be worse, and I didn't really want to face that in front of everyone else. It was none of their business, for one thing, and for another . . . I didn't want it getting out that he did anything more than just admire me, at least not until I knew what the hell I was doing.

The city looked alive again in a strange way. Even more foreign than it had yesterday: the harbor without its wharves and without the trestles that crisscrossed it, but with boats gathered in the water like ants waiting for a picnic to end; the colliers still burning; tents going up amid telegraph poles sticking bare and charred into the air and the remnants of brick walls and gnarled horsecar rails; the sounds of hammering and pounding and the spray of water from great fire hoses constant and loud. Now and then there was an explosion that made me flinch, the crash of brick as men brought down weakened walls and raised clouds of dust. The streets were hazy with it. Men coughed as they hammered together makeshift frames, sneezing as the flapping canvas duck caused little tornados of ash. One or two places were already open again. I passed a doctor's tent, and two that advertised lawyers, but I hadn't seen a store since the one where I found Brody; there was no clothing to be had and no steamer had been able to land supplies enough to start up a grocery or a dry goods store or a restaurant.

When I got to what had been the Regal it was to see something so astonishing that I stopped short. I recognized three of the set carpenters hammering together a frame of charred wood studded with nails, but beyond them were Jack and Brody and Aloysius, wearing only their shirtsleeves as they hammered alongside them. Next to them was Lucius doing the same, calling out orders to the others as he straddled a beam. Susan sat on a trunk off to the side, laughing as she watched them, and Mrs. Chace reclined on a wagon in the street, shielding her eyes from the sun with her hand.

I laughed as I came over. "Why, I never thought to see you do an honest day's work, Jackson!"

He flashed me a quick smile. "You'd best get an eyeful then, as it won't be happening again."

"And I had no idea Lucius was so handy with a hammer."

Lucius paused, wiping his forehead with the back of his sleeve. "You wound me, my dear! I was building sets when you were little more than a weanling."

I sat on the trunk next to Susan. Affecting as casual a tone as I could, I asked, "Where's Mr. DeWitt? I thought Lucius told him to be here today for rehearsal."

"He's been here and gone."

"Gone? Where?"

Susan gave me a sly look. "Don't worry, Bea, he'll be back any minute. Lucius sent him off to get breakfast. He looked ready to swoon for the lack of it. He was so eager to see you I guess he forgot to eat."

I felt myself go hot, and I looked away from her to hide it, and as I did, I saw him coming down the street, his frock coat flapping, his hand curled around the leather strap of the satchel over his shoulder. I went nervous as a schoolgirl. When he approached I looked away, suddenly wishing he wasn't yet here, when all I'd wanted the whole damn morning was to see him.

He came up to the trunk where we sat, ignoring the fact that I meant to ignore him, and said in a very cool voice, "There you are, Mrs. Wilkes. What happened to you last night?"

I refused to meet his eye. "What do you mean?"

"I thought we were to meet. To"—he glanced at Susan, who was watching us both avidly—"to go over the new scenes."

I made the mistake of looking at him just then, and he was staring at me as if he couldn't decide whether to hit me or kiss me. "I'm sorry. I was . . . delayed."

"Delayed?" His gaze sharpened.

"Yes." I looked at Susan, who was not even pretending not to listen. "By our mutual patron."

"Is that so?" There was not a trace of jealousy in his voice. "I would have thought him too preoccupied."

"With what?"

"Why, with his wife's disappearance. There was a search party up at the camp this morning. The rumor was that he'd sent it."

"I take it they didn't find her. Or her body."

Sebastian shook his head.

"The only bodies they found so far were some bones in Wa Chong's," Susan put in. "And those Celestials were already dead and waiting to be shipped back to China."

"I hope they *don't* find her," Sebastian said softly. "I hope she somehow escaped it."

"Then why hasn't she shown up?" Susan asked. "I think she's dead, Mr. DeWitt."

He sighed. "I wish I could disagree with you. I'd give my entire fortune to see her alive."

My stomach tightened. "Your entire fortune? I had no idea you cared for her so much."

"We were friends, as you know. And I wouldn't wish that kind of death on my worst enemy. Certainly not a friend."

"I bet Bea's glad enough of it," Susan teased. "Ain't you, Bea? Now that she's gone, you got Penelope back."

I looked away, back to Jack and the others, feeling more than a little sick.

"Oh, I doubt Mrs. Wilkes is so spiteful as that," Sebastian said—and damn if he didn't sound as if he thought exactly the opposite.

"Of course I'm not," I snapped.

Lucius cursed once more and rose, kicking at the framing, so that Jack called out, "Steady, dammit! I can't hammer a wiggling board!"

Lucius strode toward us. "Ah, back again, DeWitt."

Sebastian began to take his bag from his shoulder. "I'll come help."

"No, no." Lucius held up his hand to stop him. "No need. We can finish it well enough on our own, and you need your fingers, I think. I'll require the first act of *Much Ado* by tomorrow."

Sebastian nodded and settled the bag again. "As you wish."

"I thought you called a rehearsal this morning," I said. "Where are we to rehearse?"

"I had thought we would be further along than this by now. Ah, 'delays have dangerous ends,' but in this case, I think them inevitable." Lucius glanced ruefully at a swollen finger. "Rehearsal will be tomorrow instead. You are excused for today. Off with you now, or stay and be amused, as you wish." He strode back to the frame, picking up his hammer.

Susan wiggled off the trunk. "As funny as this is to watch, I got a whole morning off and a miner to see to. Tomorrow then!"

In the wagon beyond, Mrs. Chace settled back and lowered her hat over her eyes as if readying to take a nap.

Sebastian stepped closer. "Come with me."

"Really? You care to be with someone as spiteful as I am?"

"I already know what a villain you are, remember?" he said with a smile that whipped away my irritation.

"To where?"

"My tent. It's quiet there, now the search party's gone."

It was what I'd meant to do, of course, but now I was nervous. *Stupid, stupid girl.* I was already feeling guilty. I thought of the secrets I kept: Mrs. Langley alive and our plan and the fact that I needed to see what happened in the new version of *Penelope Justis,* and that was half the reason I would go with him. The way he looked at me was so damned disconcerting. "I thought Lucius wanted you to work on the play. Won't I be a distraction?"

His gaze riveted to mine. "I'm hoping so."

That gaze, those words, stole my voice.

He went quiet, watching me as if he could somehow read my thoughts. To tell the truth, I wasn't sure he couldn't. He readjusted the satchel over his shoulder and said, "Well. Let's go, shall we?"

I followed him down the street, and I was afraid and excited at the same time, as if the thing I most dreaded was also the thing I wished most to do, which wasn't such a bad way to put it, I guess. I *did* dread Sebastian DeWitt; I had this feeling that he was too much for me, that I couldn't control him. But I wanted him too, and I'd never felt like that, and that feeling was so damned *new* that I didn't know what to do with it—except maybe to fuck him until it was gone.

He walked quickly; I kept taking these running little steps to keep up with him, but he showed no signs of slowing. My corset gripped until I couldn't catch my breath. It was impossible to speak; I didn't have enough breath to form a single word, but that was a relief too. I didn't want to talk to him. I was afraid of the things he might say.

I was sweating and panting by the time we reached the camp. Dozens of tents settled on the vacant lot, the smoke from small campfires drifting, dogs barking and dodging, people moving about, cooking or drawing water from four huge barrels along the camp's edge. Women and children mostly—I supposed most of the men were gone for the day, looking for work or food. A few militiamen patrolled it, but they had a laxer air than those down in the burned district; they laughed and joked with the children following them, and the whole place had a strangely homelike feel.

Sebastian slowed. He took my arm solicitously, a little possessively, and I didn't pull away. I liked it more than I should—I was not used to men treating me as if I mattered to them. No one did more than hazard a quick glance at us as he led me through the tents, most of them wide open at each end to show gathered bedrolls and clothing hanging from tent poles and salvaged belongings.

"It's this one," he said. Four rows back, at the edge.

The flaps had been tied up; as we entered, he loosened the ties and let them fall. The canvas duck seemed to glow; it smelled of sun-warmed fabric, heated rubber. Inside it was spartan: a ground cover spread almost to the edges; a bedroll on one side; an oil lamp with a cracked chimney next to an ink bottle, scattered pen nibs, all set upon a crate that read SINGERMANN & CO; a battered pail black with soot on the outside; a ragged towel. Even at the very center, the tent was too low for us to stand. Sebastian let go of my arm and lifted the satchel from his shoulder, letting it fall near the bedroll as he went to loose the flaps on the other side. They fell closed, blocking us from the world's view. I heard voices, the laughter of children, the hiss as someone put out a campfire, and here we were, alone, and it seemed too quiet.

I stood back, unsure, as he shrugged out of his frock coat. He hung it on a nail sticking out from the tent pole, and then he turned to look at me. "Home sweet home. Perhaps even a sight better than where I was before the fire."

I glanced toward the crate, trying for nonchalance. "You've managed a desk."

"I did a little looting of my own before the militia came."

"It looks as if you've been writing."

"Last night," he said. "When I was in the mood for villainy."

He came up to me, hunched, his head brushing against the low-slung canvas, sending the walls shivering. There was no room to back away; even had there been, I'm not sure I would have. He whispered, "I've thought of nothing but you. When I woke this morning, my lamp was still burning because I'd fallen asleep waiting for you like some lovesick fool."

"You shouldn't . . . talk that way," I managed.

"Why not? Isn't that what I am?" He reached for me, his fingers at my waist again, curling, pulling me closer, such an awkward position, both of us bent and cramped, him forward, me backward, arched against him like a cat. "Don't torment me, Bea. At least tell me you've thought of me too."

"Yes, of course," I whispered back. "Of course—"

He was kissing me before I'd said the last word, and I twisted my hands in his hair until it must have hurt, anchoring him, breathing into him, going with him when he pulled me onto the bedroll. I heard the muffled voices outside, the sounds of daytime, while in the tent there was only our quiet moans, the harsh gasp of our breathing, the rustle of cloth as we undressed each other, and then he was naked beneath my hands. He groaned and I shivered, and when he rolled me beneath him, I arched to meet him, clasping him with splayed hands, and his mouth was on mine as my pleasure spiraled and grew, and I forgot Mrs. Langley and the plan and Nathan and everything else.

I was drowsy, and the tent was very warm with the sun beating down upon it; there was a thin veil of sweat shimmering on my skin and on his where we both lay upon the bedroll. I thought idly that anyone could simply step inside or even peek as they walked by; the flaps were not tied shut, and there was a crack between them. Instead of making me shy that thought raised a little excitement. *How shameless you are.* But there it was, no doubt the reason I'd taken to acting to begin with.

Sebastian's eyes were closed; his breathing was rhythmic and deep, his lovely thick hair falling back from his face, and I thought about tiptoeing my fingers down his body, bringing him awake with my tongue and my hands, but I liked watching him too. I liked wondering what he dreamed of, imagining he dreamed of me.

Now who's lovesick? the little voice teased and jeered, and I smiled and stretched. My fingers brushed against his satchel, lying abandoned on the floor, and I paused, thinking of what was inside it, the play he was revising. I glanced at Sebastian again, and then I rolled onto my stomach, reaching for the bag, undoing the buckle that closed it, and if I felt guilty, well, it wasn't too much. A host of pencils and pens threatened to roll out; I pushed them back, instead pulling out a sheaf of papers. *Much Ado About Nothing* was on top, the play Lucius wished him to alter. I thumbed through the pages until I found where it ended and another began.

Penelope Justis. I pulled the papers toward me, rising on my elbows to read it better, shaking my hair back from my face. On top was the scene at the funeral, the one I already knew, and I shuffled through the pages, past the fireside scene with Marjory, the original and then the revision where Marjory's idea became instead Penelope's plan to pretend to be Florence's ghost, to haunt Barnabus to madness. In spots they were nearly illegible, so many crossings-out and blottings, streaks where his hand had dragged the ink over the paper.

Sebastian stirred, making a sound in his sleep, and I glanced over quickly. He settled; outside someone laughed as they walked by, kicking a stone that skidded and thudded gently against the tent stake. I turned back to the manuscript. I was caught by new lines, a speech I hadn't yet read that sent shivers down my spine.

> Ah, how I would like Barnabus Cadsworth to feel my sister's despair, to wrest from him free will and reason, to see him twist and writhe as his mind slips ever more quickly into a fog from which there is no returning. . . . But why not? Why could I not take his future from him as he took my sister's? Why could I not make him mad with fear and melancholy? Why not summon my sister's spirit,

dripping wet and pale? A ghost to wring from him confession and remorse even as it steals his mind away? Now there is an idea to warm me at last! No more shall my bones be cold.

What a role! For a moment I was so hungry for it I forgot all else. I found myself mouthing the words, rolling them on my tongue, finding Penelope in them—

"What are you doing?"

Sebastian's voice was a whisper; still I jerked in surprise. I glanced over my shoulder at him. "Reading your new revisions. I hope you don't mind."

"No." He rose on one elbow. "Where are you in it?"

"Only where Penny decides to drive Barnabus mad."

"You've seen that already."

"No, the soliloquy's new. I adore it. I can hardly wait to speak it. I hope you've made her a villain of Richard the Third's stripe. There's a part to savor."

"Oh, she will be. I mean it to be a tragedy. Like *King Lear*."

"A tragedy?" I laughed. "The only version of *King Lear* we ever do is the one where Edgar marries Cordelia and they all end happily ever after."

"Such a terrible corruption of genius." He leaned to kiss my shoulder.

"This from the man who's busy revising *Much Ado About Nothing*."

"I'll take a scalpel to it rather than a bone saw." He nuzzled the hollow between my shoulder and my neck. "Speak the words for me. The way you were doing. I want to hear them in the voice I wrote them for."

I smiled and looked back at the pages again and did as he asked, reveling in his listening, becoming for those bare moments the character I felt I'd been born to play. There was no stage here, and no audience but Sebastian, but I let myself fall into the part, submerging so completely that when I was done it took a moment to come back to myself.

"You're the perfect actress to play her." His voice was reverent enough to make me blush.

I disliked the embarrassment; it was easier to tease. "You think me so calculating?"

He smiled. "I only meant that you bring her alive. And now she's yours again."

I stiffened—that guilt again, and along with it jealousy and resentment. "The perfect actress? You don't think Mrs. Langley was better?"

"Don't be absurd. Why compare yourself to her?"

And in spite of the fact that I was naked beneath him, and his hands played upon my skin, and I knew better, I could not help myself. "Everyone thought she had talent."

"So she did."

"They all think I'm glad she's dead."

"Do they?"

"You heard Susan. The rest haven't said it, but I know they do."

His hot breath pulsed against my bare shoulder. "I think you're imagining things. They think nothing of the kind. They adore you, Bea. They're all on your side."

"Now who's being absurd? I was afraid she might be better in the role, I admit it."

"There was no chance of that. She didn't want to be anyway."

"She didn't?"

"It was never her intention to steal your part. She was unhappy and looking for something to do. And she was trying to help me."

"How well you know her." I could not keep the acid from my voice.

"She would have helped you too. Eventually."

"You had that much influence with her?"

"She would have seen your talent for herself. Even without me."

"Ah, the story of my life. Another missed opportunity."

"You never know. Perhaps she'll appear yet."

I kept my voice as casual as I could. "Perhaps." And then, because now that it was in my head as a possibility, I couldn't let it go, "You know, I'm thinking of starting my own company."

I heard his surprise in the silence before he said, "Your own company? How would you do that? Were you looting? Did you find a stash of money hidden somewhere?"

"No, of course not. I was just . . . I've been thinking about it lately."

"You'd leave Greene and the others?"

"I want to be my own manager for a change. Lucius is the best of them, but I'm tired of kowtowing to someone else."

"What about Metairie? Or Wheeler? Townshend especially won't like to see you go."

"I suppose they could come along, if they liked."

"I think you'd miss them if they didn't," he said. "They're your family, aren't they?"

I snorted. "Would you call those fish that eat their young a family?"

I felt him smile against my skin. "Ah, Bea, do you never get tired of being so guarded?"

The question surprised me, not the least because it brought sudden tears to my eyes, and I didn't know where they'd come from or why. I blinked them away. "Where would I be if I wasn't?"

"Perhaps you'd be happier," he whispered. "Because you aren't so alone as you think."

The words made me uncomfortable. But what was worse was the longing they raised in me, the urge to ask him if he would come with me if I left Lucius. *And you'd be a fool to ask it.* Of course I would, because what else did I want from him but a promise to stay, and that was stupidity, pure and simple. So instead, I said, "It's better if I am, Sebastian. I can't trust any of them really, and you know it."

"I think you're wrong," he said quietly.

"I'll remember that. But for now, I have to think practically, and that means Nathan—"

"*Ssshhh.*" Sebastian shook his head slightly. "Don't speak of him. Not now."

"Why not?"

"Because I don't want him here with us." He traced down my spine, a light, lingering touch that made me shiver.

I stared at him, feeling a disconcerting little joy. I looked away to disguise it, back to the manuscript, turning the pages without really seeing them, one after another. *No doubt about it, Bea, but you're tangled in deep.* And I was, and I hated it.

"Do you never get tired of being so guarded?"

I forced the words away and made myself remember what I was doing here, and not think about the way his hand had crept to the indent of my waist, nor the feel of his body pressed to my back, his hair tangling with mine. I made myself focus on the words. I was here to find the means to play out the plan I'd devised with Mrs. Langley. Without that, there'd be no company. No money. No possibility. It was all that mattered. But to do it, I needed the *how.*

Finally I recognized the words scrawled upon the page. The rewritten scene at the fireside with the servant Marjory. I turned it over. Nothing on the back. Nothing else.

I frowned. "Where's the rest of it?"

"That's all there is," Sebastian murmured against my skin. "It's all I've rewritten."

"But—" I twisted to face him, slipping from beneath his talented hands. "But what happens next? What does Penny do?"

He gave me a lazy look from beneath his lashes. "You're so afire to hear the rest?"

"Yes. Yes, I am."

He laughed and caught me about the waist, bearing me down, kissing my throat. "It will have to wait until I'm done with you."

I grabbed his hair and pulled his face up so I could look into his eyes. "Tell me what Penelope does."

"You'd rather I do that than this?" He shook my hands loose from his hair, bending to flick my nipple with his tongue.

"Don't tease me, Bastian. Tell me." But my voice broke when I meant for it to be strong, and he only looked up at me through lowered lids and gave me a wicked smile that threatened to steal my reason, and his hand slid between my legs, and once again I had to force myself to remember what it was I'd wanted. The key to getting rid of Nathan. The key to all that money, to my share of it, the share that would let me start my own company, that would let me have what I'd dreamed of and keep this man and his plays and the way he touched me.

I clamped my legs shut tight. "Tell me."

"How strong you are," he whispered; I heard his laughter in it. "A veritable fortress."

"No battering ram can get through. It's futile to attempt it. You need the password."

He kissed my stomach. "I think the password may be different than you think it is."

In my silkiest voice, I said, "Do you remember the night we spent together?"

He stilled and raised his head to give me a wary look. "Of course."

"Tell me what happens next, and I promise you: the things I'll do to you now will make that night seem like a chaste dream."

It worked as I knew it would. He swallowed convulsively, and then said quickly, as if he could not speak the words fast enough, "Penelope tells Barnabus that Florence's spirit haunts her each night. She asks him to help her be rid of the ghost. He refuses, but he falls half in love with her."

"And then?"

"It's all a ruse. She merely wants Barnabus to think Florence's spirit is abroad. She enlists Marjory to pose as Florence at one of the Cadsworth balls, but only to flit about the windows, to make Barnabus believe he's seeing a spirit."

"That's . . . how diabolical."

Impatiently, he said, "As I said, she's a villain."

"What happens next?"

He drew himself up so that his face was even with mine. "What happens next is that I make love to you. Because I haven't thought beyond the ball. That's all I have. Now . . . I believe you made me a promise?"

Well, so I had. What else was there to do but honor it?

Chapter Twenty-six

Geneva

I had grown heartily tired of waiting, of the infinitesimal movement of a sun that seemed perpetually suspended in a single position. I'd spent the day hiding behind the stable and dodging the couple who lived there, wondering where Mrs. Wilkes was and what she was doing that was taking so long. I had never liked inaction, and I was no more patient with it now.

It was twilight when she suddenly came around the edge of the stable, and in the moment before I recognized her I started from my bored, half-asleep state, thinking I was caught.

"Dear God, you frightened me," I said.

"I'm sorry," she said. "I only just got away."

From Sebastian DeWitt, no doubt. I noticed how clean she looked. Washed and *satisfied,* while I hovered behind a stable like some vagrant, stinking, with my hair tangled about my face. I almost hated her in that moment. I could not keep it from my voice. "I've been waiting for hours. I'd quite thought you'd decided to abandon me."

She ignored that. She glanced over her shoulder. "Are we safe here?"

"The husband fed the horse an hour ago. I don't expect to see them again tonight."

She sat beside me. "I came as soon as I could. I wasn't sure he would let me go."

"You mean Mr. DeWitt, I take it."

She nodded.

"How nice for you," I said snidely, unable to help myself.

"Much better than sitting next to a manure pile behind a stable, I'll warrant."

"I need to keep him happy, Mrs. Langley. Especially now."

She was spending time with him; *she* was the one he wanted. I managed—barely—to hide my jealousy. "Did you get a tent?"

"Not yet. It was all I could do to leave long enough to come here."

"How glad I am that you managed that."

She ignored my sarcasm. "We have a rehearsal in the morning. It should be no trouble for you to stay in Sebastian's tent until afternoon. There was a search party looking for you there this morning, so I doubt they'll be back, but be careful. I'll return at midday to get a tent for you, and no one will be the wiser."

"And what am I to do until then?"

"I suppose . . . stay here. I would stay with you if I could, but Sebastian. . . ."

"Of course," I said. "Very well. I'll go down to the little tent city in the morning."

"His is four rows back, at the very edge. You'll know it—he's got a writing desk made of a Singermann crate."

"Four rows back. I'll find it. What about our plan? Did you discover anything to help us?"

She smiled a little. "I've discovered our next step."

"Which is?"

"In the play, the first time Barnabus sees Florence's spirit is at a ball. It's Marjory disguised as her, but he only sees her from a distance. I know there won't be many balls just now, what with the fire—"

"Never underestimate the philanthropic impulse," I said drily. "There will be several balls. For charity. To help the fire victims. And all this talk of statehood won't stop. Politics will go on as usual. There will still be suppers and speeches. Plenty of opportunities, I'd say."

She drew up her knees. "Well, that makes it easier, doesn't it?"

"It's the only easy part," I agreed. "How will my spirit appear to Nathan without anyone else seeing it? Unfortunately, I am quite corporeal."

"We have an advantage, don't forget."

"What would that be?"

"First off, I'm an actress, and you've some talent too. Secondly . . . look at yourself, Mrs. Langley. Look at me. I always wondered why Nathan chose me instead of Susan or anyone else. It's obvious he was looking for someone who looked like you. He's been planning your downfall for some time."

"Yes, of course, but I fail to see—"

"Mrs. Langley, *think,* if you would. Nathan sees your ghost in the crowd. It's you—*he* knows it's you. But when others look, all they see is *me.*"

"We switch places."

She nodded. "Now you see."

I couldn't help laughing. "Dear God, Nathan *would* believe he was going mad. What then? Very well, so I flit by at a ball. After that, then what?"

"I don't know. Sebastian hasn't written that part yet."

I imagined it: Nathan's startled face, his confusion when it was revealed to be not me at all, but her.

"But we'll need to keep you out of sight the rest of the time. Anyone who sees you up at the camp will only think you're me, and I've seen no one I know well enough to say differently but for Sebastian."

"I'll need to stay well out of his way," I agreed. "Especially as I'm supposed to be dead." I hesitated, not wanting to ask the question that nudged at me, but I could not help myself. "He believes it too, doesn't he? Mr. DeWitt? He believes I'm dead?"

She didn't look at me. "He doesn't know for certain."

"Yes, but does he . . ." I could not bring myself to say the rest.

She turned to me, her expression hard in the half-light, her eyes like flint. "No one would be happy to find you dead, Mrs. Langley. Bastian's no exception."

Bastian. So intimate. And her words were not quite what I'd hoped for, though I could not say what else I'd wanted. Some expression of grief, perhaps. Something to let me know that I'd mattered to him. That he'd seen in me the same kindred spirit I'd seen in him.

But perhaps he had not. Perhaps he was too enraptured by Mrs. Wilkes's pragmatic little soul—or, no, I thought uncharitably, no doubt his fascination lay in her more *physical* charms. I could not help feeling another twinge of jealousy, and I wished for this plan of ours to be done, to return to my life again, where I could talk and drink wine with Sebastian DeWitt and have my salons and feel alive again. Suddenly the need to be rid of Nathan now, sooner rather than later, was a fire within me. I had wasted too much time already.

Sharply, I said, "Well, I hate for anyone to mourn needlessly. When do we begin?"

"As soon as we discover Nathan's plans for the next few days," she said. "Before long, Mrs. Langley, you'll be sleeping in your own bed."

"Thank God for that," I said.

The next morning, I woke early and went to the camp. I found it easily, dozens of tents spread over a vacant lot, though my heart sank at how coarse it was. Campfires, for God's sake. Like some old-fashioned Methodist camp meeting. There were vacant lots on either side, one half-cleared, one nothing but trees and brambles, and I went there and drew back into the shadow of a scraggly cedar and a vine maple, salal and blackberry vines tangling at my feet, catching at my skirt. I found a relatively clear spot and sat down, confident that I was hidden from any casual eye, and I watched and waited for the two of them to emerge.

The morning was warm already, my skin felt coated with an unpleasant mix of sweat and dust and ash, itching beneath the corset I had not removed in days. I would have given my soul to bathe; the moment I saw them come out of the tent, I wished them to be gone. Mrs. Wilkes glanced around as if she expected to see me standing there. I waited until they were well away, and then I left my hiding spot and crossed the street.

Others were awake and about; hardly anyone spared me a glance. Two men lifted their hats to me respectfully and walked on; children ran about without heed; a woman or two acknowledged me with a nod. No one I knew—of course not. The newly homeless in the city were none I would have had anything to do with. I went inside the tent. It smelled of camp smoke and rubberized canvas and a deeper, muskier scent that I knew. I tried to ignore the image that leaped into my head.

The bedroll was at one side, in the middle a crate with an oil lamp and a pail. A towel hung on a nail in the tent pole. I went to the pail, which was half full of brackish water that still felt cool and good against my hands, and I undressed. It was not easy; I could not stand fully, and I'd dressed the morning of the fire with the help of a maid. I took off everything until I stood naked in the middle of that tent, and then I washed every inch of myself. There was not enough water to wash my hair; instead I sat on the bedroll and used my fingers to get the tangles from it. Bits broke off in tiny splinters of soot. It would be easier to just cut it off, but even had I scissors, I knew I could not take the risk of altering my appearance so radically. I still had one more great part to play as the old Geneva Langley.

When I was clean, and my hair was braided and pinned loosely with the few pins I'd had in my pocket, I glanced at the pile of clothing I'd abandoned and did not think I could bear putting any of it back on. I smelled their stink from where I was. But I had no choice. When I was fully dressed again, I could not think of what to do. I'd had a sleepless night, and I was exhausted, but I was afraid to fall asleep here. I was afraid that I might sleep so deeply I would not wake in time to get out before they returned. I also had to visit the privy, but in spite of what Mrs. Wilkes had said about my being mistaken for her if I were noticed at all, and the little attention paid to me when I arrived, I was nervous about being seen.

Finally, I could wait no longer. I snuck out, warily, hesitant, until it became clear no one cared to notice me. Even so, I nearly ran to the privy, and I didn't relax until I was safely inside its odiferous confines.

But when I stepped out again, and a child waiting slipped past me to go inside without a word, I began to feel that perhaps Mrs. Wilkes had been right. No one would notice me here—

"Mrs. Wilkes!" someone called.

I jerked, panicked at the thought that she was back again so soon, twisting to look behind me, expecting to see her and Mr.

DeWitt striding into the camp, but instead I saw a man standing there, a man I didn't know. He tipped his hat to me and took a step backward.

"Oh, I am sorry that I startled you, ma'am. It's all right, I'm not going to. . . . It is you, isn't it? Mrs. Wilkes? The actress at the Regal?"

My first reaction was to deny that I was her, but I stopped myself in time. We'd both hoped for this. But it felt frankly disconcerting and a bit . . . insulting . . . that I had sunk so low I might be mistaken for her, despite the fact that it was necessary.

I managed to smile at the man and say, "Yes. Yes, of course I am."

"I thought so!" he said with satisfaction. "I saw you standing here, and I thought: that must be Mrs. Wilkes from the Regal. And then I thought I should come over and pay my respects. You are the best thing about that company, ma'am."

"Thank you, sir. You're very kind."

He was about my age, with a round face and a thin mustache and brown hair. "I had tickets to see *The Last Days of Pompeii* the day of the fire."

I tried to think of what she might say. I tried to remember what she'd said about the Regal, about Mr. Greene and his plans. "I'm sorry for that. But Mr. Greene means to set up the Regal again in a tent."

"I'll be sure to go." He paused, and I smiled and waited for him to take his leave, but then he asked, "Are you staying here at Fort Spokane?"

"Fort Spokane?"

"That's what they're calling this place."

"Oh. Yes. Well, that is, I hope to. If I can still get a tent."

"I believe they've still got a few at the army wagon." He pointed to a wagon I just now saw, parked at the edge of the lot. "Some bedrolls too. I . . . I'd be pleased to help you with it, if you'd allow me."

"I hate to impose."

"No imposition," he said with a very broad smile. "I'm happy to do it. *Black Jack* was some of the best hours I ever spent."

It felt very odd to thank him again, to let him assume I was the one who'd given him those happy hours, to pretend that I had been the one with the pretty voice who'd sung a ribald song and cursed Black Jack the bandit border lord. But it wasn't unpleasant. I found I enjoyed it. Three days ago, I would have laughed had anyone told me I would like becoming Beatrice Wilkes, but now I played her role as if I'd been born to it.

"I would appreciate that greatly, sir. Believe me, I feel quite helpless going about it myself."

That was all it took. Within moments he was across the camp, procuring a bundle of rubberized canvas and stakes and a bedroll. We found one of the only bare spots left, a place only a few tents away from Sebastian DeWitt's, but it was out of the way of both the privy and the barrels of water, and I doubted he would have reason to pass by it.

He worked very quickly, far more efficiently than I ever could have hoped of doing myself. "It must be hard to remember all those lines," he said as he worked.

"I've grown used to it by now," I said. I cocked my head the way I'd seen her do it, a little flirtatious, a little arrogant.

"Have you been in Seattle long?"

I remembered what she'd told me that night in the stable. "A few years. I toured a great deal before that."

"That must be hard too. Moving from town to town." He raised the tent pole, jamming it hard into the ground.

"Not if you don't mind sleeping in barns."

He grinned. "Well, this tent will be a sight better than that."

"A great deal better," I agreed. "Thank you so much, Mr.—"

"Reynolds," he said, stepping from the canvas. "Dr. David Reynolds."

"A doctor?" I felt a sudden trepidation—I wondered if I would ever again hear the word *doctor* with equanimity.

"I've a practice on Front Street. That is, I *did* have a practice there."

"You'll be rebuilding, I hope."

"So do I. As soon as I can."

"Well, you've been very kind, Dr. Reynolds," I said. "I shall ask Mr. Greene to hold a ticket for you when the Regal reopens again."

"Why, that would be wonderful." His eyes lit. "I appreciate that, Mrs. Wilkes."

He said good-bye and disappeared into the maze of tents, and I told myself to remember to tell her his name and my promise, and then I spread the bedroll inside, making the tent as much a home as I could, and strangely enough, I found myself comfortable within it. I took the jeweled clock from my pocket and set it in the corner and let the tent flaps fall closed and lay upon the bedroll, staring up at the gently sloping canvas only a few feet above my head. Here I was, in a dress tattered and burned and smelling of smoke, in a tent on an abandoned lot, and yet, strangely, I felt more myself than I had in some time.

While thinking that, I fell into dreams. Dreams where Claude and I lay together in bed, and then it changed, then it was Sebastian DeWitt, crying out as he spent himself in me, and then, even stranger, the arms around me were not his arms, but those of Beatrice Wilkes, cradling me close, reassuring me, whispering in that resonant voice she used only for the stage, "We are the same, you and I. You know it to be true," and then the dream faded and was gone.

Beatrice

It didn't take long for me to realize that keeping Mrs. Langley's existence from Sebastian was going to be nearly impossible. Even if we hadn't meant to keep her in a tent only a few yards away, there was the little problem of keeping her fed. At the Tacoma Relief, I had to ask him to get me more coffee so I could wrangle an extra ration of bread from the waiter for "my friend," and though I stuck it in my pocket, it wasn't in there very well and I thought it might fall out and I didn't relish the thought of having to explain it.

We left the relief tent and I took him to the stable so I could retrieve the gown. I told him it was the only costume I'd managed to save from the fire, and he didn't question it but waited outside as I asked him to. I was afraid she might still be there, but she was already gone. I hoped she was at the camp, safe in Sebastian's tent. The gown was still where I'd left it. When I came out with it bundled in my arms, the jeweled butterflies glinting in the sun, Sebastian eyed it and said, "You bought *that* in a secondhand shop?"

"A gift from Nathan," I said uncomfortably, because I couldn't help remembering just why he'd gifted it. Sebastian said nothing else, for which I was grateful.

When we got to the Regal, the tent was up, just as Sebastian had said it would be, and there was a sign hanging there that looked like a board torn from a packing crate, with THE PHOENIX written upon it in thick black charcoal. Two of the carpenters were putting together what looked like a scaffold from bits of wood obviously salvaged from the fire.

Inside, the tent was long and narrow, maybe thirty feet wide and sixty long, canvas spread over a skeleton of a roof, exposed crossbeams only a few feet above our heads. The floor was dirt, the ashes of the Regal tamped down or shoveled out, and at the far end was the platform of a simple stage. There were no footlights that I could see, only a bunch of oil lamps sitting about, and no seats, and the wings were only a four-foot space on either side of the stage. Someone had strung a length of rope across the front of it and hung a big swath of bunting instead of a velvet curtain—where they got that, I had no idea, but then Aloysius came walking up and saw what I was looking at and said, "It's something, isn't it? We were lucky to get it."

"Where *did* you get it? I thought there was nothing left from the fire."

"A steamer came in yesterday with some dry goods."

"A steamer? But Jack said the docks were no good."

"They've fixed some of the damage to Schwabacher's, and

it jammed itself in there, though they'd thought the wharf too small," Aloys said with a smile. "Ah well, as they say: 'needs must,' eh? Now all we require are benches. Lucius is hoping to procure some at the charity ball."

Sebastian asked, "What charity ball?"

"One to be given by Mrs. Wilcox," Aloysius said. "Two days from now. We're all to go. Didn't Lucius tell you?"

"I haven't seen him yet this morning," I said, but all I could think was that Mrs. Langley had been right about the balls. This was what we needed, and it was to be in two days, which was sooner than I'd expected.

"They need players, it seems. For a tableau." Aloys stroked his dark beard. "We're to do scenes from great American disasters, I understand."

"D'you think Johnstown too raw?" Jack stepped up from behind me. "I'd thought to stand at the side with a bucket of water and heave-to at the proper cue."

I smiled. "Oh, how perfect! A little splash to show a great flood. I've a better idea: let's do Noah's Ark instead. You could spit on us to mimic a downpour."

Jack snorted. "DeWitt, I see you've not yet managed to tame her wicked tongue."

"I take too much inspiration from it," Sebastian said, grinning. I went hot. Jack and Aloys laughed.

"Oh undoubtedly," Aloys said, chucking my chin. "We all wish for *inspiration* such as that, eh, darling?"

Jack said, "Well, at least Bea is the proper muse for the writing of scenes of destruction. Thank God for that, as Lucius intends you to author it, DeWitt. And I stand ready to deliver if the flood takes your fancy."

"Great American disasters," Sebastian said wryly. "Well, I shall have my work cut out for me."

"Oh, you needn't spend all your time reenacting the Chicago fire, if that's what you're thinking," Aloysius said. "They're more intent upon the 'heroes' who rebuild. You know, the rich Astors and Vanderbilts and their *purely* humanitarian efforts."

I smiled. "What a cynic you are, Aloys."

"It is pretty to see what money will do," he answered, grinning.

"Ah, there he is! The man of the hour, come at last!"

Sebastian and I both turned to see Lucius ducking through the open end of the tent.

"*Monsieur* DeWitt! I have great need of you."

"So I hear." Sebastian patted his bag. "I've the first scenes of *Much Ado* worked out."

"Oh brilliant boy! We shall practice it anon, but for now, I must have something more brilliant still." Lucius put one hand on Sebastian's shoulder, gesturing with the other. "Can you see it? A tableau of our greatest calls to arms! The moments when the communities of America lived up to their philanthropic promise. Man helping his fellow man—"

"In other words, a fantasy," Jack interjected.

I choked a laugh. Lucius glared at both of us. He took his hand from Sebastian's shoulder. "There is to be a charity ball in two days at the Wilcox ballroom—given that all our usual venues have sadly turned to ash."

Aloys folded his arms. "Mrs. Wilcox is opening her doors to the hoi polloi?"

"Good gracious, no," said Lucius. "Only to those disposed to help and with the resources to do so. But their names are to be published in the *Post-Intelligencer,* so I think we shall have a goodly number. There is to be a donation at the door, a pittance of which I have been assured is to be given to the entertainers, that is, you and me, good ladies and gentlemen."

"Who's assured it, Lucius?" Aloysius asked.

"Our good patron Mr. Langley, of course, who is one of the sponsors of the event."

Nathan. Perfect. It all fell into place as if we'd planned it.

"He's become quite the political darling, hasn't he?" Jack asked.

I turned to him. "What do you mean?"

"This charity ball he's helping organize, for one. And I hear he's to be onstage with the mayor later this evening."

"What stage?"

"Oh, not really a stage. A speech, on the site where the fire began. You know, that 'bear up, my good citizens, we have disaster well in hand' kind of thing. I had no idea Langley had an eye for politics."

"I believe he always has," Sebastian volunteered. "But his wife made things . . . difficult."

I looked at him, surprised he knew such a thing.

He shrugged. "It seemed a rather obvious bone of contention."

"Well, now she's gone, he can do as he likes. Until she shows up again," Jack said.

"Have you heard something that makes you think she will?" Sebastian asked, and I didn't think I was imagining the hope in his tone.

Jack said, "Nothing. But no one's found her body yet. That seems a good sign, don't you think?"

I said, before Sebastian could comment, "When did you say this speech was to be, Jack?"

"Dinner hour, I take it," Jack said.

Dinner hour. And I thought: What if Nathan saw her at the speech tonight? The spirit of his dead wife wavering on the edge of the crowd, something to prime him for the ball? It seemed too good an opportunity to waste.

Lucius clapped his hands. "Now, let's all to work, shall we? And you, Mr. DeWitt, shall put aside your labors on *Much Ado* for the time being to concentrate on writing a fine tableau for us, which we shall rehearse the moment it is finished."

The others disbanded, going toward the makeshift stage, and I started after them. Sebastian grabbed my arm. When I turned in surprise to look at him, he said in a low voice, "You look like a cat who got into the cream."

I frowned at him. "I don't know what you mean."

"Something's going on in that head of yours. What has you smiling so smugly about Langley and this speech?"

I was horrified that I'd been so transparent—and that he'd seen it. Quickly, I lied, "I wasn't smiling. I was only surprised Nathan didn't tell me about it."

Sebastian raised a brow. "Should he have?"

"I *am* his mistress."

"So you are." He stepped away, but not before giving me a

puzzled look that said he knew I wasn't telling the truth but wasn't sure why, and I forced a smile and followed the others to the stage.

But I had trouble concentrating on the rehearsal. The ball, the speech, the plan I had with Mrs. Langley, Sebastian . . . there were a hundred things to think about, and none of them were Beatrice's damn dialogue with Benedick.

Finally Lucius called for a break. "Two hours, children, and then we shall reconvene to start on our tableau. How are you progressing, DeWitt?"

Sebastian looked up from his papers. "I've a first part ready. There will be more in two hours."

"Excellent!" Lucius boomed. "Two hours, children! No more!"

"Perhaps that's enough time for Bea to get her head out of the clouds," Jack teased as we stepped down from the stage.

I ignored him. Two hours was long enough to get to the camp and back, to tell Mrs. Langley about the speech, perhaps even enough time to get her the tent I'd promised. Sebastian would be busy with the tableau, so there was no question of having to talk him into letting me go alone. I picked up the gown I'd put at the far corner of the stage, away from the dirt. I felt Sebastian watching me—those disconcertingly transparent eyes, gray today—and so I made myself go over to him.

"I'm taking this back to the camp before it gets ruined," I told him.

He said, "I'd go with you, but—"

"Yes, I know. Write away." I leaned close, brushing my lips against his ear. "I'll think of you while I'm gone."

He looked a little stunned—it was an expression I liked, and I left him looking that way. Once I was on the street, I put Sebastian out of my mind. He was going to make things more difficult, but I would deal with that later.

When I stepped into Sebastian's tent, it was empty. I saw no sign that she'd even been there. It was after noon, which was when I'd told her we were likely to be back, so I thought she must be in the woods in the lot next door. I bent to put the gown beneath the crate.

"He isn't with you, is he? I didn't see him."

Her voice startled me so I dropped the gown and jerked up hard into the canvas ceiling. Mrs. Langley stood at the far end of the tent, peeking warily between the flaps.

"Is he here?" she asked.

I shook my head. "He's down at the theater." I reached into my pocket and pulled out the bread, handing it to her. "I'll go see about getting a tent. But then I need to talk to you."

"I have a tent," she said as she opened the packet and bit into the bread.

"You do?"

"I am capable of simple tasks, Mrs. Wilkes," she said snottily.

I ignored that. "You went out of hiding?"

"It was as you said. No one noticed me. Except for one very nice man who thought I was you. He was most complimentary about your work in *Black Jack*. He even put up the tent for you. By the way, you promised him tickets to the next performance. His name is David Reynolds. He's a doctor, with a practice on Front Street."

I stared at her in disbelief. "You pretended to be me?"

"It worked quite beautifully."

I didn't know what to say. The thought that she was pretending to be me . . . it bothered me quite a bit, actually, but what was I to do about that, given that I was the one who'd suggested it? And hadn't I done the same to her? Unknowingly, of course, but still . . .

She asked, "Shall we go there?"

I nodded, shoving the gown beneath the crate that served as Sebastian's desk, following her out. I was nervous; it was better if people didn't see there were two of us, as long as we were going to be playing this game, but there was no one around, and those who were didn't seem to notice us.

Mrs. Langley stopped at a tent only a short distance away. "This one."

I glanced back at Sebastian's tent. "Do you think it far enough?"

"I didn't have much choice."

She ducked inside, and I followed her, letting the flap fall closed behind me. There was a bedroll laid out, and the jeweled clock in the corner, and nothing else.

She said, "It's spartan, I know, but . . . I suppose I shall have to find a lamp and a pail of my own."

"I'll see what I can find when I go back to the theater."

"You're going back?"

"We've another rehearsal this afternoon. I came to tell you that there's a charity ball at Mrs. Wilcox's house in two nights. The company's to do a tableau."

She sat on the bedroll. "At Mrs. Wilcox's house?"

She said it in a funny little voice, as if something was wrong, or not what she expected. I sat as well. "Is she important?"

"A founder's wife," she said. "She didn't like me. She gave me the cut direct, in fact."

"Well, she seems to like Nathan fine. Lucius said he's one of the sponsors of the ball."

She laughed. "Well, of course. How he's moved up in the world already." Then her eyes darkened. "How soon before we bring him down again?"

Her expression made me nervous—a Macbeth look that made me remember what she'd said about murder. But I said, "We'll do something at the ball, of course. I have to be there anyway for this tableau, and it's as close as I'm going to get to any society party. But there's another thing too: Nathan's going to be with the mayor when he gives a speech later today. At the site of the fire's start. I thought you could appear there."

"Where is it?"

"Front and Madison."

"And where will you be?"

"Waiting to talk to him after," I said. "To convince him he's seeing a ghost."

She smiled, and it was a mean little smile that made me wonder what was going on in her head, at the same time that I didn't really want to know. "Perfect. It couldn't be more perfect."

Chapter Twenty-seven

The plan was easy enough. Mrs. Langley was going to go to where the speech was to be given, and stay at the very back of the crowd. We'd determined that anyone from her social circle would be up front, if they were there at all, which she doubted. "They're too busy with relief efforts to attend speeches," she said. But Nathan would be onstage, and he would see her. It was only supposed to be a moment, just an instant where she caught his eye, and then she was to disappear again, and I was to take her place. It was risky, I knew, but we had to start somewhere. And if Nathan searched me out after, I was to convince him he'd seen a ghost. Which was the most difficult part of the whole thing, and I admit I was nervous about it. She was right, this was all preposterous, and we were mad to try it. But if it worked . . . well, that was the lure, wasn't it?

When I went back to rehearsal, everyone was already there. It went quickly; Sebastian had managed to write only a few scenes for the tableau in that two hours, and the lines were pretty much given to Jack and Aloysius, as women didn't do much speech making in the aftermath of disasters, and most of what I had to do was to scream in terror and look mournful. Which was fine, you know, because I was distracted enough without having to learn new lines on top of it.

When rehearsal was over, I told Sebastian I was going to see Nathan at the mayor's speech, and though he gave me this puzzled and rather amused look that I couldn't quite understand, he shrugged and told me he'd see me at the tent later. I watched him leave and tried not to think of how much I wished I were going with him, and then I made my way to Front and Madison.

The crowd there wasn't large; most everyone was actually working to rebuild their businesses instead of just talking about it, but it was enough of one that she would have time to escape if he decided to come after her. They'd put down a wooden pallet to stand on, and there were police at attention on either side and an American flag hanging from a pole above. The mayor was already speaking, Nathan and someone else I didn't know were nodding somberly.

". . . in tents," the mayor was saying. "We will widen the streets and, at long last, rid ourselves of the deadly corner of Commercial and Front, that menace known as 'the throat,' where so many accidents have taken lives and property—"

I hung back in the shadow of a tent, where I could see but not be seen, and looked around, wondering where she was. The mayor kept speaking, now about the charity ball planned to raise money for the dispossessed, and Nathan kept nodding, the sun glancing off his fair hair. Every now and then, he looked out at the crowd. "Come on," I murmured to myself. "Come on, Mrs. Langley—"

And then I saw her. Moving quickly, her too-long, bustleless skirt swishing about her legs and dragging on the dust. She glanced around—looking for me, no doubt, but at this point I didn't dare try to catch her attention. Instead I watched Nathan, waiting for him to spot her, my heart pounding hard. I saw her move to the back of the crowd, and she was looking at him too, waiting, and his gaze cast out, roving, roving, and then. . . .

He went so still it was as if someone had turned him to stone.

It was a moment, maybe two. I could see his shock from where I stood. He mouthed something—her name, I thought. *Get out of there now. Now. Go now,* and she didn't go. She didn't go, and Nathan looked away to say something to that man who stood beside him, and it was all I could do to keep from screaming at her to get out of there.

Then, as if she read my mind, she turned, lifting her skirts, hurrying away, past a semi-erected tent, and then she was gone, and I raced forward to take her place at the edge of the crowd, looking up to see the man Nathan had spoken to glancing through the crowd. I saw when he noted me, when he whispered something back to Nathan, who frowned in confusion, shaking his head.

"—and soon, Seattle will be not just the city she was, but our queen city, the jewel of the Northwest, and of our soon-to-be state of Washington!"

The crowd erupted in applause. Nathan's gaze riveted to me. I gave him a stupid little wave.

The mayor stepped down. The crowd began to disperse. Now it was time to play my part. I stood there waiting, because, you know, I couldn't just walk up to *him* there. But he didn't come to me. Instead he stepped up to the mayor, speaking intently and quickly, and the mayor frowned and motioned for the police. When they approached, he spoke to them as well, and two of them fanned out. Searching for her, I knew, and I hoped she'd got a good distance away.

Nathan came off the makeshift stage, pushing his way through the dwindling crowd until he got to me. "How long have you been here?"

"It's wonderful to see you as well," I said.

His frown grew deeper. "How long?"

"A few moments. I only heard the end of his speech. Very well done."

"Did you see her? Did you see Ginny?"

"Your wife? You mean you found her?"

"No. But I thought I saw her. Standing just where you are. A few moments ago."

"Are you quite certain?"

"I know my own wife," he snapped, but he looked disturbed. "You didn't see her?"

"No one's seen her," I said softly. "There's not even the rumor of it. It's been four days, Nathan. Perhaps you might want to consider that she might . . . that she must have been caught in the fire."

He was hardly listening. He looked beyond me. "I saw her. I know I did. She was as real as you are standing there now."

I put my hand on his arm and made my voice as soothing as I could. "Perhaps you did see her. But perhaps she wasn't . . ."

His gaze riveted to mine. "Wasn't what?"

"Alive," I said.

He looked taken aback. "What the hell is that supposed to mean?"

I shrugged. "We do a lot of plays with ghosts in them. You

know, *Hamlet*. Or even *Penelope Justis*. The dead are always coming back to haunt the living."

"This is not a *play*," he said.

"Of course not."

"Are you telling me that you think I saw a ghost?"

"I don't know. I'm only saying it might be a possibility."

He laughed. "You can't possibly believe that."

"I don't discount it. I know a great many spiritualists."

"Oh for God's sake. Mumbo jumbo stupidity."

"Of course you're right." I stepped away. "I'm sorry I mentioned it. No doubt you saw her, and she's running around the city like a madwoman."

"You don't believe me."

"It's only that it seems strange that no one else has seen her, and I've heard no rumors of anyone suffering amnesia."

Nathan sighed and put his hand to his eyes. "Dear God. I know it's . . . Everyone seems to agree that she must be dead. Perhaps I was . . . imagining things."

I nodded, trying to keep from smiling. "I suggest you go home and lie down. Take a headache powder. It must be very stressful, all these meetings."

"Yes," he said. "I think you're right. I should lie down."

"Well . . . I should be going. Rehearsals, you know."

Nathan looked up. "So late?"

"Lucius is a slave driver." I turned to go. "Good night."

He grabbed my arm, stopping me. "You'll be at the ball?"

I nodded. "Mr. DeWitt is writing the tableau even as we speak. I think you'll be happy with it."

"You'll stay with me after," he said, and it was no question, which irritated me, you know, but there wasn't anything I could do about that.

"All right," I said.

His finger traced softly up the inside of my arm, and his eyes grew warm with that ardor I'd come to dread. "I'm sorry to neglect you. I've been very busy."

"Of course," I said, drawing gently away. "You've a city to rebuild."

"Yes. And . . . Ginny's absence has things quite . . . chaotic. Her father is beside himself and—" He shook his head a little, as if to clear his thoughts, or as if he only just realized that it was inappropriate to talk of his wife's father with his mistress.

"Mr. Langley!" one of the police officers called.

Nathan glanced over his shoulder and then back to me. "I must go." And then he was off, and I was glad.

I hurried away before he could think better of it and call me back, hoping that the things I'd said to him sank into him tonight when he was lying in his cold bed in the dark, with nothing to think about but his wife and what he'd been willing to do to her, and I let myself smile at last.

Chapter Twenty-eight

Geneva

She came to my tent that evening, bearing another packet of bread, which I ate just as rapidly as always—I had never been so hungry; my stomach seemed to rumble constantly.

"I can't stay long." She glanced over her shoulder at the closed tent flap. "I don't want him to grow suspicious."

"Where does he think you've gone?"

"To the privy."

"Then we must be quick," I agreed. "How did it go with Nathan today?"

"You got away all right? The police never saw you?"

"What police?"

She smiled. "The ones the mayor sent after you."

I didn't understand her smile; the idea filled me with dread. "He did? What if they come here? What if they—"

"They won't. They've already been here, remember? And no one believes Nathan saw you. They think it was me."

"How do you know that?"

"I saw their faces. And the police—well, that was halfhearted at best. Nathan said himself that everyone believes you're dead."

I didn't know what to make of that. How quickly they'd all come to that conclusion. But then, how little they'd cared for me. What a relief it must be to them all, to have me gone. "Well, that makes it easier then, doesn't it?"

"To convince him you're a ghost? Oh yes. He doesn't believe it yet, but he will, I promise it."

"How confident you are."

"Mrs. Langley, there was a reason Nathan had me act out madness in front of a doctor in a restaurant."

"Of course there was. To commit me."

She shook her head. "Because he knew I could be convincing."

I sighed. "I will say that you were the one I remembered from *Black Jack*. I'd thought then that you had the most talent of all of them. I couldn't even tell you who played the heroine."

She laughed shortly. "Stella Bernardi. Treacherous as a snake, by the way. We were friends once, until she stole the leading line from me. She didn't have much talent, but she was very good at finding rich patrons."

"It seems to be epidemic among your kind," I said drily.

"It wasn't what I wanted." Her voice was quiet. "But when Stella . . . well, it was the last straw. I had to do something."

"Why?"

"I'm nearly twenty-nine, Mrs. Langley. That's old for an actress, especially one who hasn't yet won the lead. I couldn't wait much longer. When Stella stole it . . . let's just say I had to take desperate measures."

"Then how providential that Nathan and I came to see *Black Jack* that night."

I had spoken sarcastically, but she sighed. "Yes. Though I wish you hadn't."

That surprised me. And puzzled me. "It turned out for the best, didn't it?"

She met my gaze. "It was the first time I'd done it. Taken a patron, I mean. I don't mean to sound self-righteous, because I played the same tricks everyone else did—except that one. I guess . . . there was a part of me that wanted my talent to be what mattered." She laughed a little, shaking her head. "And now I'll always be like Stella, won't I? People will always be able to say I won the line because of Nathan Langley and not because of my acting."

"I would never have supposed you so . . . idealistic."

Another sigh. "It's stupid, I know. Believe me, it's not something I'm proud of."

"I don't think it's stupid at all."

"You don't?"

"No," I said. "In fact, I think it rather wonderful."

She laughed. "You and Bastian . . . how the hell do the two of you survive in the world? You're like little lambs just asking to be slaughtered."

"I prefer to think that God smiles upon us instead. The meek shall inherit the earth, after all."

She snorted, not unpleasantly, and rose. "I suppose. I'd best get back. We'll talk about the ball tomorrow, when I bring you food."

I made a face. "I'd say I was tired of bread, but I'm too hungry to disdain it."

"I know. If I had any money, or there was any food to buy—"

"It's easy enough to bear when there's an end in sight," I said.

"Yes," she agreed. "Most things are."

Beatrice

The night before the ball, I told Sebastian I was going to the privy and I went to Mrs. Langley's tent to bring her food and to go over our plan one last time. I had it as memorized as Penelope Justis's soliloquy, where the words intruded even in my dreams. But I was anxious all the same. There were too many things I couldn't control. A hundred things could go wrong, and I'd had enough performances where flies dropped from the heavens without warning and traps opened up beneath an unsuspecting foot to believe something wouldn't.

She was to meet me at the Wilcox house that night, and in the meantime she was on her own. I wouldn't have time to talk to her before, or to bring her any food—and that was something that was going to have to be solved and soon, because she'd eaten nothing but bread for four days and not much of that either. I had rehearsal for *Much Ado* in the morning, and then the tableau to rehearse after, and then the ball itself, so I was just going to have to trust that Mrs. Langley would do what she was supposed to do.

The next morning, I gathered up the butterfly silk gown I meant to wear at the ball, and Sebastian glanced at me as he put on his shirt and said, "No one will steal it. You can keep it under the crate."

"I'll need it." I motioned to the scorched and filthy calico I was heartily sick of. "I can hardly wear this to a party, now can I?"

"I thought Greene meant to wrap you all in bunting."

"I think he means for us to mingle beforehand."

He made a noncommittal sound and buttoned his shirt. "Are you certain you feel up to this?"

"Why wouldn't I?"

He shrugged. "I thought perhaps you were ill. You've been a long time at the privy lately."

I didn't miss his quick glance, the question in it, how it slid away. Last night, especially, I *had* been gone a long time, but when I'd come back to the tent, he'd been half-asleep, and I thought he hadn't noticed. When I'd crawled into the bedroll beside him, he'd wrapped his arms around me and pulled me close against his chest, kissing my temple before he fell back to sleep, and I'd felt . . . *safe,* I suppose it was. Foolish, and don't think I didn't know it. I was beginning to have this sense that if I didn't get myself under control soon, I would end up doing something damned stupid because of him.

And now, on top of everything else, my fear that Sebastian would prove a problem when it came to my plans with Mrs. Langley was proving out. He was so damned observant. "There was a line last night."

"So late?"

"Yes, so late. Really, Bastian, what else could have delayed me?"

He met my gaze, considering, a little too thoughtful. "Nothing, I suppose."

I stepped up to him, running my finger down his shirtfront, meaning to distract him. "Nothing."

He caught my finger and kissed it. "You'll come back here when it's over? Or should I meet you there?"

Sebastian would not be going to the ball. He'd written the tableau, but he wasn't one of the players, after all. "There's no need to meet me there. Don't wait up."

"Ah yes. I suppose there's Langley to consider, isn't there?" He made a face and sighed. "I suppose it's a good opportunity to get some writing done."

I hated how disconcerting it was that he never did what I expected. I hated that I half wanted him to be jealous. But I was damned if I would show him that. "Good. I'm afire to know what happens next."

"I tremble at the thought of disappointing you." He dropped

my hand and pulled me close, kissing my cheekbone, my jaw, tangling his hand in my hair, which still hung loose, as I hadn't yet found hairpins.

I put my hand to his chest, gently pushing him away. "If you don't stop, we'll be late for rehearsal."

"Does it matter?"

"I can't afford the forfeit, especially now. And Lucius has never forgiven one in his life. Except for Mrs. Langley's, of course."

"How bitter you still sound."

"Why shouldn't I?"

"Because she's gone, perhaps? She can't take anything from you now, Bea. Why begrudge her the past?"

How quickly he leaped to her defense. It made me think of the way she talked about him, her possessiveness even as she forced herself to admit his admiration for me, and the way I understood why he'd liked her, which was more than I could say for why he liked me. I couldn't keep myself from saying, "Of course. Take her side as you always do."

"She's dead, Bea."

"But you would give your entire fortune to see her alive again. Isn't that what you said? What *good* friends you must have been."

"I enjoyed talking with her."

"Just talking? Or did you end up fucking her after all?"

He made a sound of exasperation. "No, I didn't fuck her. She didn't need a lover, she needed a friend."

I felt chastised and foolish, but I didn't take it back. "So if she *had* needed a lover, you would have obliged?"

He only smiled. "Is that jealousy I hear? Shall I throw you to the bedroll and show you just how little you have to fear?"

"I can hardly be jealous of a dead woman," I said, marching toward the tent flaps. "We'd best be going."

Sebastian sighed, but he followed me. "If we must."

The ballroom at the Wilcox home was on the top, T-shaped floor, at the end of a long hall that held rooms for changing, just as Mrs. Langley had predicted. Once we all arrived, Susan and Mrs. Chace and I went into one while Brody and Jack and Aloysius went into the other. Ours was small, with dormer windows that looked south over the city—a perfect view of the burned district and its crumbling walls of brick. I'd changed into Mrs. Langley's silk gown before we arrived, though I'd needed Susan to help me pin it in spots to make it fit, and since my only bustle had burned in the fire, there was all this fabric pooling in a train and dragging so the pins that held up the bodice bit into my shoulder. The moment I could find a needle and thread, I would be altering the gown; at the moment it was the most uncomfortable one I'd ever worn, though lovely. I didn't mean to wear it for the tableau, but I needed Nathan to see me in it before, which was not going to be that difficult, because Lucius had informed us that we were to circulate among the guests and make ourselves suitably charming. Just now, I guess, we were the only luminaries in town but for the Sells Brothers Circus, which had been scheduled to perform before the fire, but the mayor had refused them a permit and the city council was arguing about whether or not a circus was appropriate in light of the destruction, and no one would invite a clown or a trapeze artist to a drawing room ball in any case, so we were all there was.

And the damned room was full. Everyone who had any money at all must have been jammed into that ballroom. I was half surprised people weren't hanging from the decorative ivy twined around the pillars, because *up* was the only place left to stand. There were servants bearing trays with sherry, and others with oysters, but they weren't moving through the crowd so much as being pushed and jostled through. The talking and laughing was so loud it drowned out the quartet jammed up into one corner.

"Nothing like publicity to foster philanthropy," Aloys whispered to me as we stepped into the crush. "Everyone wants to be a hero when it's reported in the newspaper."

It could be that he was right. Or it could be that Mrs. Wilcox just had a small ballroom, and all these people might have fit in the salon at Frye's if it were something more than a pile of ash. But it did seem to be more people than I thought existed in Seattle society, and I found myself wondering what Mrs. Langley would say about it, and then I remembered that she was no doubt making her way here even now, and what we were about to do came back to me in a rush, and I was nervous again.

Except for the tableau, I had only one task tonight that I cared about, and that was to make sure Nathan saw me in this dress both before and after the performance. So I quelled my nerves. This was nothing more than another show, a part I meant to play. I followed Aloysius into the crowd and searched for Nathan.

It took me a while to find him. I was stopped by one man after another—I was surprised at how many of them seemed to know who I was, though I suppose I shouldn't have been. I'd seen society in their boxes night after night. But none of them had ever acknowledged seeing *me* before, so it was strange to be told by an aging, bespectacled gentleman whose suitcoat was made of the finest wool I'd ever seen that "your antics onstage are always one of my chief delights, Mrs. Wilkes," and, by another man, younger this time, with a dark mustache, "I saw you in *School for Scandal.* Truly no one has such superb comic delivery."

I admit it was heady. I was feeling quite the star before an hour passed, and the sherry pressed into my hands didn't hurt either. By the time I saw Nathan standing at the far wall, talking to some man who looked officiously important, I couldn't even remember that I'd been nervous. I made my way toward him through the crowd, past some woman with dark hair who stared at me as if I were one of those curiosities in Barnum's museum, and nudged the blonde who stood beside her so she could stare too. The train of the damned skirt was so long and bulky that people kept stepping on it, pulling me up short, and finally I draped it over my arm, and the bodice slipped lower and lower until I had to jerk it up as surreptitiously as I could, and I wondered how the hell Mrs. Langley had got about in this thing.

But when I got to Nathan, he stared at me as if he were stunned, and that made it all worth it. "Mrs. Wilkes," he said, when he'd recovered his breath. He took a great gulp of his sherry and then introduced me to the man beside him whose name I didn't remember the moment after he excused himself and left us.

"The dress becomes you," Nathan said to me when he was

gone. He put the empty glass on the tray of a passing servant and grabbed another.

I tried not to think of what he'd done the last time I'd worn it. "You were kind to invite us tonight. Lucius is beside himself with glee."

Nathan sipped at his sherry. "It was my pleasure. As I'm providing funds to rebuild the theater, it seemed prudent to pique the potential audience's interest."

"We're all very grateful."

He leaned close, watching the crowd as he did so. In a low voice, he said, "I look forward to seeing how much so tonight."

"As do I," I lied, trying to ignore that sick feeling in my stomach.

"After the ball then." He stepped back again, meaning to leave me, I knew.

I said quickly, "Have you seen your wife again?"

He glanced away. "I don't know."

I was startled. "You don't know?"

"My dreams . . ." He shook his head and then attempted a smile. It was a failure, and I saw a little fear in his eyes. "Well, let's just say I begin to wonder if you might be right."

"About the spirit, you mean?"

"Sssh, not so loud," he admonished. He finished his drink. Then, it seemed, someone caught his eye from another part of the room, and his expression went blandly polite. He said, "I look forward to seeing you in the tableau, Mrs. Wilkes. Now if you'll excuse me . . ."

"Of course." I stepped back to let him go. Jack came up behind me, touching my shoulder, saying, "It's time to change, Bea," and I nodded in relief and went with him to the changing rooms, to trade silk for bunting, to take my turn onstage. It was time to put our plan into motion.

Chapter Twenty-nine

Geneva

I knew it was time to go when I saw Mr. DeWitt return to his tent. He was the signal, Mrs. Wilkes and I agreed, because she'd said I should take his return to mean she'd gone on to the Wilcox house and the charity ball. I watched him surreptitiously from between the tent flaps, his weary stride, his head bowed so his hair came forward to hide his face, and for a moment I missed him so intently it was like a physical pain. But I forced myself to remember what I must do, and when he disappeared inside, I was out the back of my tent quickly, dodging among the others to the road as speedily as I could, glancing over my shoulder to be certain he didn't emerge again to see me.

I knew where the Wilcox house was, of course. I had no idea when the tableau was scheduled, but Mrs. Wilkes had told me that the actors were to socialize with the guests beforehand, and I knew that sometimes the entertainment did not take place until late in the evening. Still, I did not dally. To mistime it would be disaster. I was tired of waiting; if tonight did not come off as we'd planned, I thought I might truly go mad with impatience and frustration.

Even if I hadn't already known the Wilcox home, I would not have been able to mistake it tonight. Carriages lined the road before the three-storied, elegant house, their drivers leaning idly against the wheels, smoking or talking while they waited. The windows glowed from the light of dozens of candelabra, the romantic light I preferred, a necessity now, with the gas and electric works destroyed. The dormer windows on the top floor were open; I heard the music of a quartet, talking, laughing, and I felt a sudden rush of yearning for the balls I'd once known.

I would have them again, and on my terms, I vowed, going determinedly to the back of the house, to the servants' door.

I'd told Mrs. Wilkes that the servants would be too busy to notice another among their number, and that Mrs. Wilcox would have had to hire extra staff, so half of them wouldn't know one another in any case. I knew the moment I crept around to the door that I was right. It was open to let in the air, because the kitchen was sweltering, bustling as it was with activity, two girls shucking oysters over a tub already mounded with shells, the cook reddened and sweating as she yelled at a man stirring a steaming pot, waiters moving in and out, reloading their trays.

I swept up a few loose strands of hair and took a deep breath, stepping into the kitchen, keeping my head down. No one noticed as I grabbed an apron from the hook and tied it on, except one waiter who caught sight of me and said brusquely, "You girl. Come here and help me set this tray."

Obediently, I went over and helped him, loading oysters on the half-shell and trying to keep my mouth from watering and my stomach from growling. When the tray was full, he went off again, and I followed him as if I'd been ordered to, hesitating at the base of the narrow servants' stairs until he had gone up—I did not want to take the risk that he would order me down again. Another servant was descending; he hardly glanced at me as I passed him, affecting my best servant pose—or at least as close to one as I could imagine.

I paused at the top of the stairs, where the sounds of the ball grew louder, and peeked around the corner and down the hallway, ready to pull back again if I saw anyone I knew, looking for the dressing rooms I'd told Mrs. Wilkes must be there. I spotted them immediately, two of them, one on each side of the hallway just before the entrances to the ballroom.

"What are you doing, girl?"

The voice startled me; I had not heard the servant coming up the stairs behind me carrying a tray loaded with little glasses of sherry. I jerked around, trying a smile. "Waiting for an empty tray. He told me to stay here."

The man sighed and rolled his eyes. "Well, get out of the way then."

"Has the entertainment started yet?" I asked.

He shook his head. "The actors're all in there drinking with the rest of 'em. Watch that blond one. He's got a roving hand."

"I'll remember that." I drew back to let him by, smiling again to hide how quickly my heart was racing. Then I followed him, staying safely behind, bowing my head so that any guest coming into the hall would not notice me. When I reached the closed door of one of the dressing rooms, I slipped inside. I was lucky; it happened to be the one for the women. I could tell by the costumes hanging there, bunting draped in loose gowns, one single-shouldered.

There was no blue silk gown waiting for me, which meant I was early; she had not yet come in to change, and the tableau had not started. I glanced around the room, looking for someplace to hide until then. There was an armoire with a mirrored door, a dressing table, also with a mirror, as well as a settee and two chairs. Nothing else, nowhere to hide but the armoire, and so reluctantly I opened the door and climbed inside, pushing my way awkwardly past winter coats smelling of camphor, curling myself into a corner. It was cramped and dark and stinking, but given the coats, I doubted anyone would open it—at least not until winter came again, and so I made myself as comfortable as I could, and settled to wait.

It was a shorter time than I'd expected when I heard the door creak open, footsteps, a muffled laugh, "Well, who would've thought I'd ever say a word to Mrs. Denny? And there I was, slurping oysters right alongside her!"

"Good Lord, at least I can breathe now," grumbled a voice I recognized as belonging to Mrs. Chace. "I vow it was hot as a steam bath in there."

The door closed. "Will you help me out of this dress again, Susan? I think my shoulder's bleeding. Damn pins."

Mrs. Wilkes. I was relieved to hear her voice. It comforted me to know we were together in this.

But hearing her also reminded me that it was nearly time for my debut as my own spirit. I listened to them as they changed, my nervousness growing with every passing moment, and then, finally, they were done, and Mrs. Wilkes said loudly, as if she knew I hid in the armoire, as if she meant for me to hear, "The music's changed; it's time to go out," and the door opened and closed again, and it was silent.

I opened the squeaking door of the armoire. The room was a mess now, clothing abandoned on every surface, but the shapeless bunting gowns were gone, and there, draped over the settee, was the blue silk, the gold of the embroidery glistening. In the time I'd waited, night had truly descended; it was dark, the glow of the party from the windows lit the yard below in squares of light. I took a deep breath and went over to the gown, which still held her warmth, a little damp from her sweat. I stripped off the gown I wore and hid it in the armoire, and then I drew on the blue silk. It buttoned up the back, of course, and there was no maid, but I did the best I could. I took the pins from my hair and let it fall to hide the buttons I could not reach that were still undone—after all, Mrs. Wilkes was wearing her hair down tonight. For lack of pins, of course, but it gave her an alluringly bohemian air, and I meant to look as much like her as I could.

I glanced at myself in the mirror, shoving down the lace of my chemise that showed above the low-cut décolletage—I'd had chemises especially made for the Worth gowns, and I was not wearing one now. It was strange to see myself in the gown after so many months, and I felt myself to be Ginny Langley again, the woman I wanted to be.

How badly I needed that confidence now. I went to the door and opened it. The music had stopped; I heard voices, loud and projected—Mr. Wheeler and Mr. Metairie—coming from the ballroom, along with the sound of a storm, a shaken box of pebbles for rain, the crackling of a tin sheet to sound like thunder. I crept into the hallway, deserted now, as everyone had gathered in the ballroom to watch the show. Even servants had paused in their tasks. The laughter and talk had quieted. Only a muffled cough, the shifting of booted feet.

I reached the T—here the hallway split, each side going to a ballroom entrance. Before me was the wall on the other side of which the tableau was progressing. I had not thought exactly how to do this—I could not go into the ballroom, obviously, and I could not be trapped, which meant I had somehow to lure Nathan into the hall. Not usually difficult; he had always disliked the hastily assembled entertainments at affairs like these. I had expected that he would excuse himself for a cigar or a drink. But there had been drinking all night—the profusion of empty sherry and wineglasses showed that—and because his mistress was in the tableau, he might linger to watch it. And that was half of our plan in any case, that Nathan should see her and me at the same time, while no one else did.

I heard her voice: "We are all destroyed!" and a great crash of thunder, and I took my opportunity. I turned down one hallway, went the few steps to the ballroom entrance, and glanced carefully around the corner. Everyone was rapt, watching the actors. Quickly I looked for Nathan. When I saw him I knew he would not stay long to watch. He seemed restless; he watched her with a kind of impatience. Then she stepped offstage, and whatever small bit of Nathan's attention she'd held disappeared completely. He shifted; he glanced toward the window, and then the doorway—

I stepped fully out.

Whether anyone else saw me I didn't know, and it didn't matter. It was her job to convince them they had seen only her. My job was to capture Nathan's attention, and I did. I looked right at him; I caught his glance and held it. He froze. Even from this distance I saw the disbelief come into his eyes, and then I retreated.

I nearly ran down the hallway, grabbing up the train of the skirt so I didn't trip upon it. He would come after me, I knew, and I knew also that I could not be caught, and he had the whole of the ballroom to cross, people to dodge. I fled to the end of the hallway, to the head of the servants' stairs, just as I heard his racing footsteps behind me. I saw him as he turned the corner. I heard his anguished cry: "Ginny!" and I fled down those stairs, past the servants' pantry at the bottom with its sideboard holding dishes and candlesticks and piles of napkins. I raced past the kitchen, past two servants who startled and called, "Ma'am!" and into the main of the house. No one was there, of course, not with the party going on. I dodged through the first door I saw and into a darkened study. I heard him calling to the servants I'd passed: "Did you see her? Where did she go?" and the servants calling after him, "Sir! Please! The party is upstairs."

I ran to the drape, slipping behind it, pressing myself up against the paned windows of a door it covered, trying to gain my breath, trying to be still.

"Ginny!" he called from down the hallway, and "Ginny!" again, and then he was at the door of the study, pausing, no doubt trying to stare down the darkness, and I held my breath and closed my eyes and prayed he would not choose to investigate.

"Did you see where she went?" he asked, such a plaintive voice. He sounded overcome, so much so that even I almost believed he was grief-stricken at the loss of me.

But I knew better. I knew it was only fear of his position that made him so, the thought that all my money could disappear, that he could not control what I would do next unless I was safely under his thumb, put away as long as he needed.

"Sir, please," a servant's voice, quiet now, cajoling. "Wherever she went, she's gone now."

"But you . . . you *did* see her?"

"No, sir," the servant said. "But she's probably already gone back to the ballroom. The main stairs, you know."

"Yes, of course." Nathan exhaled deeply. "The main stairs. Yes. I shall go back up."

"It would be best, sir."

There was a pause, then slow steps away, down the hall, and I let out my breath—too loud, but I couldn't help it, and in any case, Nathan was gone. The servant closed the door to the study; the light from the hallway was cut, the darkness complete, and I stood there and waited, listening to a loudly ticking clock, counting the seconds, the minutes. It seemed I waited forever. Finally I crept from behind the drape. I did not want to go back into the hall; who knew what Nathan had taken into his head to do? So I opened the door I stood against and stepped out into the yard, breathing deep of the night, which smelled of smoke and the tideflats, and then I went around, back to the kitchen door again, still open, still with the hustle and bustle of the servants inside.

The dress was no maid's disguise, but I went up to the door

anyway, and when one of the girls who'd been shucking oysters saw me, she said, "Oh, ma'am, can I help you?"

I smiled at her and fanned myself. "It was so hot up there—"

"Yes, ma'am."

"—but I've caught my breath now. I think I'll return." I stepped into the kitchen, and the servants glanced at me and away except for one of them, who said, as I approached the servants' stairs, "Are you all right, ma'am? I saw you running from that man—"

"A misunderstanding," I said, attempting a smile. "I felt a little ill. But I'm fine now."

He gave me a shy smile. "I saw you at the Regal once. In that play—I don't remember the name. About the divorce?"

"Yes, of course."

"Well, it was good. You were good."

This was what we'd hoped for. Ginny Langley blending into Beatrice Wilkes, with only one seeing the difference. I smiled back at him. "Why, thank you. You're very kind."

"You won't want to go up them stairs, ma'am. They're for the servants."

"Oh, but I don't want to go clear around," I said. "And I'm no fine lady. Just an actress. I've seen worse stairs than these."

He ducked his head in reply, and said nothing more as I went up, pausing again at the top, listening. There was no sign of Nathan, and the crowd was clapping, Lucius Greene was saying something about the Phoenix, and I hurried down the hallway and back into the dressing room, nearly tearing off the gown in my haste, laying it back over the settee, crawling into the armoire, clad only in my corset and chemise. I'd no sooner closed the armoire door than the one to the dressing room opened, and the chatter of Mrs. Chace and Miss Jenks followed it. Then Mrs. Wilkes said, "That went well, didn't it?"

I sagged back against the wall of the armoire, putting my head in my hands, breathing deep. And suddenly I was trembling. I thought of Nathan racing down those stairs behind me, how big a risk I'd taken, how easily he might have caught me. Now that it was over, I was shaken at how dangerous it had been.

The chattering went on. Finally, I heard Mrs. Chace say, "I'm going back out."

Miss Jenks said, "Are you coming, Bea?"

"In a minute," Mrs. Wilkes said. "These damn pins. Go on. I'll be there shortly."

The door closed. There was silence. Then a tap on the armoire door. It creaked open, just a bit. She whispered, "Are you in there?"

"Yes," I said.

"What happened? I know he saw you. I saw him leave."

"He didn't catch me," I said.

"So it went as we planned?"

"Yes indeed. He was quite distressed."

"I hope so." She paused. "Well, then . . . good night."

She closed the armoire door. I waited for her to leave. Then I came out of the armoire and dressed in my old gown, putting up my hair again, tying the apron about my waist, and in my guise as a servant, I left the Wilcox house.

Chapter Thirty

Beatrice

The moment I returned to the ballroom after changing back into the blue silk, Nathan grabbed my arm and shoved me into a corner. He smelled of liquor as he breathed into my face, "Where were you?"

"Changing," I said, drawing back, though I couldn't go far

because the wall was right there. I pulled my arm from his grasp. "And if you don't mind—"

"Have you left this room at all?"

"Just to go to the dressing room," I said.

"You didn't go downstairs? You didn't run from me?"

"Why would I do that?"

"Are you telling me the truth?"

"Yes. Yes, I'm telling you the truth. Why wouldn't I? What are you talking about?"

He sighed and closed his eyes briefly. "Then it *was* her I saw."

"Who?" I feigned confusion when all I wanted to do was laugh at how well things had gone.

"Ginny. She was wearing that dress, the one you have on." He ran his finger from my collarbone to the swelling of my breast, which was nearly falling out of that low bodice. "The servant said it was you, but it was her. You promise me you weren't downstairs?"

"I've already told you I wasn't. How could I have been? I was in the tableau."

He shook his head, as if shaking off confusion. "I wouldn't have mistaken her. I saw her, I tell you. It was Ginny."

"Did anyone else see her?"

"No. They all look at me as if I'm mad. But I'm not mad, am I, Bea?"

I saw how badly he wanted reassurance, and you know, I could almost have felt sorry for him right then, except he had that strange look in his eyes, and I thought that if he'd managed to get hold of his wife, he might have strangled her. I knew already that feeling sorry for Nathan Langley was a waste of time, and I had a role to play. The role Sebastian had written for me. Penelope Justis. I felt her inhabit me the way the best roles did, her righteous anger, her determination, and I took hold of her hard and feigned sympathy as I touched Nathan's cheek. "I believe you've seen her."

His eyes widened. "You believe me?"

"Well, not that you've seen *her* exactly, but her spirit."

Uncertainly, he said, "I don't know. . . ."

"What else could it be?"

Nathan seemed to slump. He ran his hand through his hair and tossed off the rest of his drink. "No. That can't be true."

"No one else saw her. Not here or at the mayor's speech. It's clear she's appearing only to you."

"I don't believe it." But his tone said otherwise. "I've never believed in such things."

"It seems to me that you might want to start believing now. Really, Nathan, it would be one thing if you'd only seen her in the city. Then perhaps I'd think she might be alive. I mean, I suppose there's a possibility no one's spotted her. But to see her *here*—how could she have done it? Are you saying she snuck in? How?"

His jaw went tight. "I suppose not. Not here. She was never welcome here."

"There are a hundred people in this room at least. And servants too."

"Impossible," he agreed quietly.

I said again, "What else could it be but her spirit?"

"I don't know. I don't *know*!" He spoke the last so loudly I saw people turn to look. He lowered his voice as if he'd noted it too. "Dear God . . . what if it is? Why does she appear?"

"She must want something."

"Want something? Why would you say that?"

"It's what the spiritualists say. That spirits return because they've left something unfinished, because they want something. What could she want from you?"

He frowned. "Nothing. She had everything."

"She's left something undone then," I suggested.

"Undone? Like what?"

"I suppose there might be any number of things. Is there a reason she might be angry? Could she want vengeance for something?"

"Vengeance? What would she want vengeance for?"

"I don't know. You knew her best, didn't you?"

Beneath cheeks flushed from drink, he paled. "There's nothing," he whispered. "Of course not."

"Perhaps you should think on it."

"Yes," he said, nodding. "Yes, of course. I shall think on it."

I saw more than a few curious glances. I looked to where Jack and Lucius and Brody were packing the props we'd used for the tableau. "The others are leaving," I said softly. "You wanted me to stay?"

He blinked, looking at me as if he'd forgotten who I was or what he was doing talking to me. "I—perhaps not tonight. I find I'm . . ." He let the words trail off, and that was such good luck I could hardly believe it. It was all I could do not to dance off in relief. *But this isn't over, Bea, and you know it. It's only delayed.* Yes, I knew that too.

"Then I'll go with Lucius." I touched Nathan's arm as if I cared. "You'll be all right?"

He passed his hand over his eyes. "Yes. Yes, I'll be fine. You go on."

I nearly ran over to Lucius and the others, and when Lucius saw me he said, "Are you ready to fly away, sweet Bea?"

He was smiling as if he'd just won some huge prize, which I guess was pretty much the case, because then he said that Mrs. Wilcox had paid him for our services, a percentage of the donations, and the crowd had been large and wealthy.

"It went well then?" I asked.

"Such spoils surpass my wildest hopes."

"I trust you mean to share," Jack said wryly.

Lucius said, "But of course! Have I not promised it? A few coins to my good players in the morning. At rehearsal. Ten o'clock, and not a moment later."

I had to admit I was looking forward to maybe buying a new dress if there was something to be found among whatever dry goods managed to get into town, and maybe some food for Mrs. Langley too. Something besides bread.

I glanced over my shoulder to see Nathan snag another drink from a passing waiter. "Well, let's go then. I don't know about the rest of you, but I'm for bed."

Jackson winked at me. "How anxious you seem, my love! No doubt you expect it warm and waiting for you! Who's it to be tonight? Our rich patron or our resident playwright?"

"You haven't insulted Langley, have you, Beatrice?" Lucius asked.

"I have not," I said indignantly. "But as it happens, he has other obligations tonight."

"He looks to be glued to the bottle," Jack noted.

"And likely to stay that way a good while," I told him. "Shall we leave before he changes his mind?"

Jack laughed, and Lucius shook his head and tsked at me, but neither of them said anything more as we gathered up the others and made our way out of the Wilcox mansion. The night was cooling, but there was still the faint scent of smoke in the air. Mrs. Chace grumbled at the lack of a wagon, and Lucius complained of dyspepsia, and Jack said, "You should have known not to eat so many oysters."

Aloysius sighed as he looked up at the stars. "Ah, I vow 'tis a relief again to be in the open air! 'Society is now one polished horde, formed of two mighty tribes, the Bores and Bored.'"

Brody laughed. "Ain't that true enough! But there was fun to be had if you knew where to look. Some of them women ain't so buttoned up as they pretend."

"Nor are some of the men," Aloys said with a smile.

Lucius grimaced. "My children, I do hope you left them with an appreciation of our talents rather than cursing our debaucheries."

"Who's to say they aren't the same thing?" Jack asked with a smile. "To hear the rumors, some of them prefer to play in dirtier fields. I vow I'd never suspected such things of our good Mr. Fulton, for example. Or Mrs. Bailey, for that matter."

"Not to mention Mrs. Langley," Brody said.

Aloysius said, "Yes—speaking of her: Did any of you see the way her husband dashed out during our tableau?"

I'd only been idly listening while we walked, but now I perked up.

"Oh dear, did we bore him?" Mrs. Chace asked.

"I hear it was more than boredom," Aloys went on. "They say he saw his wife."

Jack asked, "His wife? So she's been found?"

"She hasn't been found," Aloysius said. "But the rumor is that he's seen her about town. More than once."

Carefully, I put in, "How could that be? I thought she was dead."

"Ah, but that's the thing. We're talking ghosties, darling. And Langley drinking as if he means to chase her spirit away with . . . well, spirits."

"Who's saying this?" I asked.

I almost heard Aloys shrug in the darkness. "It was all the talk tonight. One or two of his fellows are quite concerned. They say he was raving when he came back from wherever he rushed off to tonight. And he asked the mayor to send the police after her yesterday, even though no one saw anything then either."

Lucius said, "Good God, I hope the man's not mad! Did he seem so to you, Bea?"

I didn't want to overplay it, so I said, "He seems . . . not quite himself since his wife disappeared."

Jack said, "There once was a man name of Langley, lost his wife in a fire and said 'Hang me! For the one I loved most is a richly jeweled ghost, and I do feel a pang or two, dang me!' "

I glared at him. "That may be the worst limerick I've ever heard."

"But appropriate, don't you think?" Jack mused. "He had his hands full with her, and no doubt."

"So you heard the rumor about her too," Brody said.

"Which one?" Jack asked. "There seemed to be a multitude. I must confess, I wish I'd known of them when she was among us. She might have been a tasty treat."

"Though I recall that when you held her in your arms, it was only to subject her to your disdain," Aloysius reminded him.

"Ah, but I would proceed differently, now that I know she has a penchant for our kind."

"It was *one* artist," I snapped. "Even if it were true, that's hardly a penchant."

I don't know who was more surprised by my words, me or Jack. He stared at me like a gaping fish, and I was stunned that I'd defended her. For a moment I didn't feel like myself; it was as if I'd put on this gown of hers and was suddenly inside her skin, and *that is the most stupid thought you've ever had.* But, you know, I couldn't help it. I was annoyed at the way Jack and Brody talked about her, as if the rumor that she'd had an affair meant she would have fucked either one of them if they'd only smiled at her right.

Jack frowned at me, and Brody said, "Well, it ain't just that, you know. To hear some of them tell it, she was a wild one. They say her daddy sent her to Seattle to learn how to behave."

"So what if he did?" I asked.

"Children," Lucius admonished, but not as if he cared overly much whether we stopped or not.

"I wonder how tightly her husband held the reins," Jack said thoughtfully, and I felt his gaze on me. "There was a time or two when she looked at DeWitt that—"

"That *what*?" I asked—too sharply, but I was irritated and I meant for him to hear it.

Jack shrugged. "Only that I thought there was a . . . flirtation . . . between them. I suppose it's a good thing she's gone, eh, Bea? Or you might have a rival for your playwright's affections. Ah well, perhaps the two of you could have traded off. One night her husband, the next DeWitt. . . ."

He said it casually, teasingly, but I heard his meanness beneath it, his little revenge for the way I'd snapped at him, and it only reminded me of the truth we all knew, the thing that lay just beneath the surface of our affection and civility—that we weren't the family we pretended to be; that loyalty to one another was a road we traveled only as long as it was going our way.

And, you know, that bothered me suddenly, for no reason I could say. It wasn't as if I hadn't always known it, or used it when I needed. It wasn't as if I wasn't planning to leave them all the first chance I got to start my own company. It wasn't as if I cared. So why did it trouble me now?

"It hardly matters now, does it?" Aloys soothed. "They say she was mad herself. Not that I saw it, you understand, but one wonders if her husband isn't following in her footsteps."

The others laughed, and the conversation changed, and when we reached the road I was to turn on to go back to the camp, they said good-bye and blew me kisses as if our pretenses hadn't cracked open, as if the mend we'd made was solid, and continued their way back to the tent that served as the Phoenix, and I went on alone.

But I was suddenly desperate for some company, for conversations that didn't have hidden meanings or ones whose sole purpose was to veil little barbs and hurts. And there was Sebastian's tent, the only one still lit from within, though it must be nearly 2:00 A.M. I knew he waited for me, and there at least was a way to lose myself, to keep from thinking about the things I wanted and conversations without pretense and what the hell was wrong with me that I felt so damned weary of a sudden?

I already knew the answer. I knew I had to go to Sebastian to discover the next part in the play he was revising, the next step in the plan. There was a part of me that was using him, and so it couldn't be simple fucking, or solace, or any of the things I wanted tonight. There were too many things I couldn't tell him, too many lies. . . .

And suddenly I wasn't moving toward his tent, but toward Mrs. Langley's. I slipped inside. And once I was there, I saw she'd been waiting for me too, just as he was, and she said in this tight, terse little voice, "What happened?"

My whole body went limp, as if I'd been waiting for just those words all night, and with a little start I realized that she—*Geneva Langley,* for God's sake—was the only person I knew who didn't require pretense, the only one I didn't need to lie to.

Geneva

Her response to my words was to sag onto the floor near my bedroll. "Nothing happened. At least nothing we hadn't planned. It worked. It all worked perfectly."

"If everything went well, then why do you seem . . . distraught?"

"Do I? I'm tired, that's all. It was a long night."

"Yes, it must have been," I said. "A party and a tableau and then Nathan's bed after. It's no wonder you're exhausted."

"I didn't go to Nathan's bed," she snapped. "He was overset. He didn't want me after all."

"Well, that's good, isn't it?"

"Yes. Perfect."

I wasn't imagining the sarcasm in her voice. "What's wrong, Mrs. Wilkes?"

"There's nothing wrong. Nothing that concerns you, in any case."

"I would say everything about you concerns me now. You must know that I don't wish that to be true. But I also realize that I am"—oh, I hated to say it—"dependent upon you."

"We're dependent upon each other," she said roughly. "Don't think I don't see it. Do you know, Mrs. Langley, it occurred to me tonight that you might be the only person in the world I can be honest with."

"That would be disturbing if it were true."

"What makes you think it's not?"

"We hardly know each other."

"Well, that's the sad part, isn't it? But who else can I trust? Not Lucius or Jack or Aloys. Not even Brody, really. No one in the company."

"I think perhaps you underestimate them."

"Don't believe it."

"Well, then . . . what about Mr. DeWitt?"

"I'm not telling him the truth about what we're doing, am I? Nathan is his patron too. I don't know that Sebastian wouldn't tell him what we're up to if he knew. Hell, I would. And . . . he thinks Penelope's a *villain.* He won't like our plans. He would hate what we mean to do. He might even decide. . . ." She made a sound like a laugh, half-aborted, humorless. "No, I can't trust him. Only you. I would hate it if it wasn't for the fact that I think it's the same for you."

"Don't be absurd. We only trust each other because we must. There are others I trust. Of course there are."

"Really? Have you told someone else you're alive?"

"No, but I *do* have friends—"

"Here in Seattle? Or perhaps you left them behind in Chicago? I suppose there are people there you still write to? Perhaps someone who might come visit you in exile?"

My throat tightened. I could say nothing.

She went on, "Well, I suppose that might be so. But I confess I didn't see any friends of yours among those at the ball tonight. At least, if they were your friends, you might want to think about getting new ones. You should have heard Jack and Brody talking about the rumors they'd heard. Now that you're missing, it seems you're quite the topic of conversation. And they're not speaking of you with admiration."

"I don't imagine so," I said quietly.

Her voice went equally quiet. "There's more to it than that sculpture, isn't there?"

I was like any other woman of my class, skilled at shutting doors I didn't want opened, at discouraging intimacies with condescension and hauteur. I could have done so now. But I didn't want to, and I didn't know why that should be. Perhaps it was because she was right; she *was* the only person I could trust—the fact that she was tied to me only by necessity didn't make that any less true. Perhaps it was because of what we'd put in motion tonight, what had left me too stirred to sleep, the risk, the danger. Or perhaps it was only that it was late, and the thrill of tonight had faded to a dull thrumming in my blood, and I wanted someone to share it with, to laugh with over what had been dared, and there hadn't been someone like that in so very, very long.

"Posing wasn't all of it," I admitted. "I had a . . . reputation in Chicago. I—I've never had much patience with convention. Or for doing what was . . . expected. I was a bit notorious, I'm afraid."

"Is that why your father sent you here?"

I took a deep breath and lay back, looking at the darkness above my head. The hurt was still there, no matter how I tried to erase it. "I thought my father admired my daring. I thought he was proud that I wasn't like everyone else."

"That must be the reason he wants to put you into an asylum."

"Perhaps I wasn't seeing things clearly."

"Perhaps not." There was compassion in her voice. "You wouldn't be the first."

"After I married, he expected me to be a respectable wife," I went on. "He told me so more than once, but I didn't allow myself to believe it. I should have known better. I think . . . I must have always known the truth, because when I think back on my girlhood, I realize I kept the worst of it from him."

"Like what?"

"Shall I tell you the whole list?"

"One or two things would be enough, I think."

"Well, let's see. At fifteen I wagered with a friend that I could sneak into the bedroom of a boy we knew."

"Did you?"

I smiled at the memory. "I masqueraded as a maid. And stole his shaving razor to prove I'd been there."

She laughed. "You've been slumming for a long time then."

"It was hardly the worst of it. The truth is that the risk was everything. I've always liked gambling. I won a hundred dollars on a race once. Papa didn't know about that either."

"You wouldn't be thc first woman to gamble."

"No. And I suppose Papa might have laughed that one away. Until he found out I was the one racing the carriage."

"You could drive?"

"I asked a friend of my father's to teach me—in return for . . . well, a few kisses was all it took."

"Really? I never would have expected it of you! How did your father not find out?"

She was impressed, and I basked in it. "I threatened to tell everyone he'd seduced me. My father would have destroyed him. I was only sixteen."

"I'd fucked two managers by then. Not that it helped."

"At eighteen, I lost my virtue to a writer visiting my father's house. But he was the only one I . . . well, until Nathan."

"But you loved them both."

"Yes. You never loved any of your managers?"

I felt her hesitation. "I regretted it mostly, especially when it didn't work out as I wanted. Which was often enough, I promise you. They're all bastards, you know. What you were doing and what I did—they were different things. I wasn't doing it because I liked them or because I liked fucking. Mostly I hated that they had power over me, and I had to do what they wanted. And then I felt like a fool when it didn't make any difference. When I have my own company . . ."

"Your own company?"

"It's what I mean to do when this is over. With the money. Start my own company where I'm not beholden to managers or other actors. And . . . I mean to ask Sebastian to be the playwright for it."

I was surprised, though I supposed I shouldn't have been, not now that I knew her passion for acting. The passion Sebastian DeWitt had once told me about, I remembered, the thing I hadn't believed, and now I found myself saying, "What if I helped you finance it?"

A pause. "Why would you want to?"

"Because it's what I do. It's . . . well, Mr. DeWitt called it my gift, and I suppose it is. In Chicago, I introduced artists to the society that would fund them and make them famous. I was good at it too." I tried to find the right words, to make her understand. "I had thought to do the same with Mr. DeWitt here, before all this with Nathan . . . and . . . well, it occurs to me that together, we could make him a star. You're his muse, and I'm his patron. You could act in his plays, and I would provide the money for production. With your talent, and mine, we could become a force, Mrs. Wilkes. Mr. DeWitt is the key, but what you and I could do with him. . . ."

My words trailed off in the darkness. I could not think of what else to say.

"This is no passing fancy, is it?"

I shook my head. "There have been many of those, I'll admit. But this isn't one of them. As much as you love acting, I love this. I always have. Mr. DeWitt knows it too." I hesitated. "So . . . do you think the idea has merit?"

"Yes," she said softly. "Yes."

I let out my breath in a little laugh.

She said, "You know, what we're doing . . . what we've been through . . . it seems strange to have you keep calling me Mrs. Wilkes. My name's Bea."

"And I'm Ginny," I told her.

"Ginny," she said, as if she were trying out the taste. "Well, I should get to Sebastian. He's waiting up."

"Don't worry. It won't be long until we both have what we want."

"Yes." Nearly a whisper. She rose. "Good night, Ginny."

"Good night, Bea," I said, closing my eyes. For the first time since I'd left the Wilcox house, I felt I could sleep.

Chapter Thirty-one

Beatrice

So there we were, making promises to each other, and the damn plan was as risky as ever. But now it was about more than money. It was about my company, about Sebastian, about the lives she and I meant to start, the lives we'd always wanted. I crept from the tent feeling as if I wasn't so alone. And maybe I didn't like her so much yet, but I was beginning to feel as if we were somehow . . . lashed together. That one of us couldn't run without the other stumbling after. It was reassuring somehow. And my weariness was gone; in its place was this whirring little energy.

When I reached Sebastian's tent, I lifted the flap and stepped in, and there he was, slumped over the papers on his makeshift desk, sleeping, his shirt open, his pen still in his hand, the oil lamp burning.

I glanced at the pages beneath his head—more of *Penelope Justis,* a new scene. It was all I could do not to read it right then. But there would be time enough for that later. What I wanted now was something else.

I lowered the flame until it was quiet and dim. Then I lifted the pen from his fingers, setting it aside. I pushed aside his hair and leaned close to whisper in his ear, "Bastian."

He stirred, licked his lips, blinked once, and then his eyes were open, blue tonight in the half-light. He straightened, raking his hair back. "You're here. What time is it?"

"I don't know. After two, I think."

"How was the party?"

"Boring."

"And the tableau?"

"The high point of the evening, of course. Everyone was very entertained. And inspired enough to donate." I pushed the crate aside and pulled up my skirt to straddle him. His hands went to my waist, pulling me close.

"Was Langley there?"

"Of course he was. Why do you ask?"

"Because you're not with him."

"No." I kissed his jaw. "He was drunk and grieving."

"And you couldn't comfort him?"

I kissed the corner of his mouth. "I'd no wish to try. I'd rather be here with you."

He laughed softly. " 'For ne'er was flattery lost on poet's ear.' "

"It isn't flattery. It happens to be true."

"What really happened tonight, Bea? I think it wasn't as boring as you pretend. You're practically vibrating. Besides, I know you'd never lose an opportunity to keep Langley close."

I pulled away, disconcerted. "How grasping you think me."

"How grasping you are," he said, pulling me back, tightening his hold on my waist. "Tell me what happened."

"Nothing. Nathan was too upset. He told me to go home."

"Upset over what?"

"As I said, he was grieving."

"With all his peers about, commending him for sponsoring such a charitable enterprise? I doubt it. And he's a politician."

"Which means he doesn't mourn?"

Impatiently, Sebastian said, "Langley's never shied from appeasing his vanity or his desires. And after such a self-congratulatory night, I'd think he would be looking for a reward. Which would be you. And given that you've never said no to anything that advanced you—"

"That's not true!" Though it was, of course it was, and I admit it bothered me that he knew it. Or perhaps it bothered me that he didn't seem to mind.

"Has he thrown you over then?"

"Of course not!"

"Then why did he turn you away? Come, come, out with it. I'll hear the gossip from someone else anyway. Why was Langley upset tonight? Was he so struck by the profundity of my tableau?"

"He barely stayed to watch it," I admitted sullenly. "He left just after Jack succumbed to the Indianola hurricane."

A deep sigh. "He's a philistine."

"We all can't be Ruskins," I said nastily.

He raised a brow.

"I do read, you know," I snapped. "In spite of what everyone thinks."

"Everyone?"

"Mrs. Langley, you . . ."

"You spoke with Mrs. Langley about reading?" He looked puzzled.

Oh, perfect, Bea. I bit off the curse that rose to my lips and said quickly, "I didn't have to. She made it abundantly clear what she thought every time she looked at me."

He frowned. "Bea—"

"I don't want to talk about her." I leaned close, easing my hands past his open shirt, running them up his bare chest, over his shoulders, shoving his sleeves down his arms until his shirt pooled on the ground. I pressed against him and heard his little intake of breath.

"You can't distract me," he whispered.

But I could, and we both knew it. I took his hands in mine, and he did not resist me as I guided them beneath my skirt, and then he moved of his own accord, easing beneath the ample folds, running up my thighs to my hips, undoing the ties of my drawers, and I rose to let them fall and kicked them aside, and he undid his trousers and then I was straddling him again, and he jerked my hips down and worked me until I was moaning. He never took his gaze from mine, and it felt as if he was teasing my thoughts loose, tangling them, pulling them out to read for himself until I put an end to it and bent to trace the strong muscles of his throat with my lips and my tongue. Then his breath came short and his fingers dug into my hips and he groaned, and I cried out a little because it was over, and I didn't want it to be. Nothing had abated, and I was afraid of that. I was afraid of what I wanted from him, of what he would demand.

He leaned his forehead against my breast. When he lifted his head again and said quietly, "Let's to bed," I saw with dismay that his questions hadn't gone, and I felt this little clutch in my stomach that I tried to ignore. He wasn't going to pursue it now, but he would, and what the hell was I to do then?

But I went with him to the bedroll, and we undressed and I let him hold me and when he was asleep I was still staring up at the canvas ceiling above, no closer to sleep than I'd been at the start, and so finally I eased away from him. I took his shirt from the floor and put it on, and then I sat down at the desk and picked up the newest pages of *Penelope Justis*.

I slept barely at all. After I'd read the new scenes Sebastian had written, it was all I could do to keep from rushing to Ginny's tent to tell her what we must do next. When Sebastian finally woke, I yawned and pretended to just be waking myself and crawled from the bedroll to dress. "I'm going to the privy," I told him when I finished buttoning my dress, and he nodded as he stumbled to the bucket to wash and I was out of the tent within moments. I had to force myself to remember to head off toward the privy, but the moment I made the turn I doubled back, hiding myself between the rows of tents. When I got to hers, I plunged in.

She was still wearing her chemise and sluicing her face with water. I said, "I haven't got much time. I know what we must do next."

She was very quick. "The play? You've read more?"

"Last night. Penelope tells Barnabus that her sister's spirit must be put to rest, and because he hopes to exorcise her, he agrees to host a séance. But it doesn't work. Instead, the séance only brings the spirit more fully into this world."

She frowned. "How are we to do that?"

"I don't know. But I have some ideas. And the first, unfortunately, means that I have to meet with Nathan to convince him to have a séance." I took a deep breath. "I played a medium once. Delphinia Beaumont in *Heaven's Awakening*."

"A character in a play. It's not the same thing as *being* a medium."

"No, of course not. But at least I know what to do. How hard could it be just to light a few candles and say things like: 'Can you hear me, Geneva Langley? Speak if you be with us.' "

She gave me a thin smile. "You have truly found your calling."

"I only need to convince Nathan." I sighed. "Lucius means to pay us something this morning for our efforts last night. Hopefully there will be something more than bread to buy with it. I'll see what I can find to bring back to you."

"Thank you, Bea," she said softly. "That's very kind."

Said so sweetly. I tried to shrug it off, but I felt the heat of a flush. I said brusquely, "I need you to play your part, don't I? I don't think spirits swoon from hunger."

She laughed. "I suppose not."

Her laughter stayed with me as I left the tent and crossed the camp to Sebastian's. Fearless. That's what she was, and I liked that about her, and envied her for it too, though I suppose it was easy to be fearless when you had plenty of money to catch you when you fell. But I didn't feel the resentment I usually felt at that thought. Instead I remembered the things she'd told me last night, and the promises we'd made each other, and it made me laugh to think of Seattle society once she was set loose upon it, once there wasn't Nathan or her father to contend with, once she was free.

Then I stopped thinking of her, because when I stepped inside Sebastian's tent, he was gone, along with his ancient frock coat and his bag. Gone to breakfast and rehearsal without waiting for me, and my heart started racing and all I could think was *how long was I gone?*

Whatever appetite I'd had disappeared. And then I grew angry at myself because—if I was going to admit it, which I wasn't—it was easier to be angry than to be afraid. I cursed myself silently all the way back down into the burned district, and then I spent the blocks until I reached the Phoenix trying to come up with some lie to tell him, and that only made me angry again.

By the time I got to the Phoenix—early, which must have been the first time—I was so touchy that even Mr. Geary's "Good morning, Mrs. Wilkes" made me bristle.

Lucius looked up from a script he was going over. "I sense a productive rehearsal," he said wryly.

Before long Jack and Aloysius arrived, joking with each other as they came inside, Brody and Susan behind them.

"Only four more rehearsals," Lucius called out. "Our first show, children, is scheduled for seven o'clock on Monday. I have already placed an advert in the *P-I.* So there is much to do, and little time for nonsense."

Mr. Geary rapped on the stage with some stick he'd found somewhere and called for the scene, and though I didn't feel any enthusiasm, I didn't need enthusiasm for rehearsal, and I followed the others to the stage.

Sebastian showed up fifteen minutes late. He glanced at me as he stepped inside, but I was in the middle of a line, and I couldn't tell by his expression what he was thinking. My stomach did a little lurch, and I stumbled over the line so Jack whispered, "Focus, my love." Sebastian sat at the makeshift table—a couple of scorched crates—with Lucius and Geary and bent his head to work, and I made myself concentrate on ignoring him, which became harder when, in the middle of the act, I glanced up to see Nathan Langley come inside. I expected him to call for me, but instead he went to where Sebastian sat. He said something in a low voice to Lucius and Mr. Geary, and then Sebastian nodded and straightened, and the two of them left the table and went to the corner.

I was so startled that once again I stuck, and Geary had to prod me twice with a cue line before I could continue. Even so, I could hardly take my eyes from Sebastian and Nathan. I couldn't hear anything, of course, but they were talking so intently I felt a little sick. What the hell could the two of them have to say to each other?

Nathan was Sebastian's patron, I told myself. It was nothing. No doubt something about the new play. Or about the revisions to *Penelope.* Or maybe even the tableau Nathan hadn't paused longer than a few minutes to watch. There were a hundred things the two of them might have to discuss. But that sick feeling didn't go away, and when they finally broke apart, and Sebastian went back to the table, I sent him a questioning glance. He ignored me. But Nathan stood watching, and when the act ended, he applauded.

"I've come to see how my investment progresses," he said, walking past the pile of benches the carpenters were cobbling together from whatever bits of wood they could find. Now that he was closer, I could see he looked tired; his eyes were red-rimmed and he was pale, almost gray. His bonhomie was only an act. "And to see the reason for my investment, of course."

I felt Sebastian watching us, but I ignored him. I'd meant to hunt down Nathan today, and whatever had brought him here, I wasn't about to waste the opportunity. So I stepped off the stage and went to Nathan with my hands outstretched, even though all I really wanted was to know what the hell he and Sebastian had spoken of.

"How lovely to see you."

Nathan took my hands, clutching my fingers hard, and said to Lucius, "Might I steal her away for a few moments? Is there some scene you can rehearse without her?"

"But of course," Lucius said with an obsequious little bow. "We are at your disposal, sir."

Nathan led me from the tent and around the corner, where one of the carpenters was tearing apart a scorched cask, and made a little imperious gesture that had the man scurrying off to give us privacy.

"What is it?" I asked, and I meant to ask him about Sebastian, but before I could, he kissed me, long and lingeringly, and that was so surprising I didn't know what to do but kiss him back. Nathan had never spent much time on such things; I always had the sense that he found kissing me to be more a task he meant to get through than any source of pleasure. His hands crept down to my ass, jerking me closer—which was much more like him—and then he lowered his mouth to my throat and whispered against my skin, "Is there somewhere we can go? I find I've much need of you."

"I can't leave for that long. We're in the middle of rehearsal. And Lucius has scheduled our first show for Monday."

He made a little sound of frustration. "I've missed you. I hardly slept last night."

"Not for want of me, surely," I said.

"Too many dreams," he murmured. "Nightmares. I think if you were there to exhaust me, I would sleep."

"Nightmares? About your wife? Did you see her again?"

He went still, and then he pulled away. "I dreamed about her. I can't seem to stop. I've hired crews to dig for her everywhere. Near the docks, at the jewelry store . . . I think everyone half believes I'm mad. But I'm determined to find her body."

Now was my opportunity. I put my hand on his shoulder. "Perhaps there's an easier way."

"What would that be?"

"Perhaps you could . . . ask her spirit."

"What?"

"Don't you want to know why she's haunting you, Nathan?"

He dragged his hand through his hair, which only showed how disconcerted he was because his hair was usually well slicked into place. "I don't see how—"

"A séance," I said.

He stared at me as if he didn't understand the words. "A séance? Are you mad? I can hardly be seen to indulge in such foolishness. There's no one I could ask who wouldn't . . . who didn't—"

"We don't need to ask anyone," I said calmly, though my blood was racing. "I know what to do. I played Delphinia Beaumont in *Heaven's Awakening.*"

"I doubt playing a medium onstage is the same thing."

The echo of his wife's words. I smiled grimly. "How much harder could it be? I remember it very well. There were candles, and holding hands, and calling the spirit. . . . Why not try, Nathan? The worst that could happen is that we fail to contact her."

He looked at me assessingly, but then, finally, he nodded. "Very well. If you truly think you can do this. I admit I don't understand how it works, but—"

"I've known many actors who are spiritualists," I told him, which wasn't a lie. Half the actors in New York City dabbled with spirits. I even knew one who claimed to have a spirit guide telling him how to deliver his lines. "And Delphinia Beaumont was very successful. I had spiritualists coming backstage for weeks thinking she must be real."

"I confess I . . . I cannot think what else to do. And her father . . . if I don't find her soon . . ." He looked at me with eyes so haunted I was taken aback. "I must lay this to rest once and for all."

"Then all it needs is to decide when," I said, putting my hand on his shoulder again, leaning close to reassure him because he looked so despairing.

He said, "Tonight. It must be tonight," just as someone came around the corner.

"Pardon me, but it seems they require Mrs. Wilkes back upon the stage."

Sebastian, of course. Who else could it be? I cursed Lucius inwardly for sending him, because I knew he'd done it deliberately—Lucius's particular kind of joke.

"Of course," Nathan said with a thin smile, and then, as if he too was part of Lucius's badly timed joke, he kissed me and said, "Twilight tonight, then. Shall I send a carriage for you?"

I shook my head mutely.

Nathan stepped back. "She's all yours, DeWitt."

I struggled to keep from wincing at the words. I didn't look at

Sebastian. Instead I watched Nathan walk away. But then when I went to pass Sebastian, he caught my arm. "Just what the hell are you up to, Bea?"

Now I did look at him, and I wished I hadn't. Because his eyes were hard, and I knew I wasn't going to be able to wiggle my way out of this one easily. Still, you know, you can't help trying, no matter how stupid the attempt. "I've no idea what you mean."

"Why does Langley think he's seeing his wife's spirit?"

I wondered what else he'd heard and tried not to panic. *Remember what you want, Bea.* I shrugged as nonchalantly as I could. "Maybe he's been reading his wife's copy of *Penelope.* How should I know? Why don't you ask the local spiritualist society?"

"My guess is that I could get a better answer from you."

"I'm not privy to Nathan's thoughts." I tried to pull away, but he held me fast.

"You said something about Delphinia Beaumont."

"I thought you above eavesdropping."

"What are you scheming, Bea?"

"I'm not scheming anything. Take your hand off me."

"What are you planning with him for tonight?"

I glared at him. "I'm planning to fuck him."

He flinched, but his grip tightened on my arm. "You're lying to me. Why?"

"Because it's none of your goddamned business."

"Where were you this morning?"

"At the privy."

"You weren't. You took so long I went to find you."

"What were you talking to Nathan about today?" I countered. "When he first came. What did he want?"

Sebastian's expression went guarded. "He asked me about his wife."

"What about her?"

"Whether I'd seen her the day of the fire. He'd heard a rumor that she was asking after my rooms. He wanted to know if she found them, if I might . . . be harboring her there."

I stared at him in dismay. "Why would he ask you such a thing? Why would he think *you* might be keeping her?"

He looked away uncomfortably.

"He asked you to have an affair with his wife," I remembered, and now I understood why. Another affair with another artist. The rumor mill had already been grinding over the mere fact that she'd had a beer with him. How much more unbalanced would she have seemed had Sebastian done what Nathan wanted—what *she* no doubt wanted as well, because I wasn't imagining the fascination Sebastian held for her, no matter how well she tried to cloak it. I couldn't blame her for that, could I? Not when I felt the same way?

Oh, clever, clever Nathan. So damn cruel, the way he'd played her, the temptation he'd dangled—how hard it must have been for her to refuse it, if she'd even tried.

"That's what he thinks, isn't it?" I asked Sebastian. "That you did as he asked."

He met my gaze. "Yes."

"What did you tell him?"

"That I hadn't, for God's sake! That I hadn't seen her the morning of the fire, or the goddamned night before. That I wasn't keeping her now. Damn Langley and his games."

"Was Nathan convinced?"

His gaze sharpened. "What webs are you spinning, Bea? You mean to get something from Nathan Langley. What was all that about Delphinia Beaumont and spirits? What are you doing to him?"

I'd had enough. I started to push past him again, and this time when he stepped in front of me, I said, "Get out of my way."

"Not until you tell me."

"I'm looking after our best interests. That's all you need to know."

"*Our* best interests? What are those?"

"The company, of course. Money."

"Whatever it is you're doing, you don't need Langley for it. There are other ways—"

"There is no other way," I snapped. "And it doesn't matter how much I love you, I'm not going to live like a pauper for you. One of us has to know how to make a living. Obviously it's going to have to be me."

I stepped around him, dodging his hand, marching to the tent without him, and I was so angry and afraid of his questions I was breathing hard. I marched into the tent like some fury from a romance, and it wasn't until then that I looked up and saw the rest of the company staring at me as if I'd grown an extra head, and I realized two things: first, that they'd heard every word Sebastian and I had shouted at each other, and second—and most troubling of all—I'd told him that I loved him.

Chapter Thirty-two

Geneva

I'd been without conversation or company all day, and I was as lonely as I'd been before I'd met her—lonelier, actually, because at least then I had novels to distract me, and now I did nothing but wait for her to return. I was anxious, wondering if she'd met with Nathan, if she'd convinced him to hold the séance. Three times that afternoon, I went to the lowered flaps and peeked out the crack between them, hoping for a glimpse of her.

The third time, I saw Sebastian DeWitt instead. Strangely, she was not with him, though it was late, and I expected the rehearsal was over—it had to be. He strode into camp, his bag bouncing against his side, and as I watched, he glanced at the tent, and it seemed our eyes met, though he could not have seen mine through the narrow opening, and the contact was like a little blow. Breathlessly, I dropped my hand, pulling shut the flaps, scooting back, my heart pounding. For a moment I was certain he would come here, and I berated myself for my foolishness. But he did not, and when I dared to look through the crack again, he was gone.

It was perhaps half an hour later that she swept inside, restless and agitated. "The séance is tonight," she said by way of greeting.

"Tonight?"

"At twilight, Nathan said." She grimaced. "I don't know where he got that. Perhaps he thinks he's in a mellie."

"It's too little time to plan."

"It doesn't need to be complicated. What do we need but a medium and a spirit? We have both. You'll have to tell me what room would be best. The parlor we went into before? You could come in those doors and hide behind the drapes until I call you."

"I suppose. I could escape easily enough if things got out of hand."

"And then . . ." She paused uncomfortably. "He'll no doubt want me to stay."

"I'll be safe walking back. There are militia everywhere if I need them." Then, when she said nothing more, I ventured, "What about Mr. DeWitt?"

"What about him?" Her voice was sharp—a sore point, obviously.

"I saw him return without you today."

"He's not my servant. I can't order him to wait for me."

"But he always has," I pointed out.

Her expression went grim. "We had an argument. He overheard me talking to Nathan."

I felt a flutter of nervousness. "Overheard? What did he overhear?"

"That Nathan was seeing your spirit. And that I meant to meet him tonight."

"Dear God. He didn't . . . he doesn't think—"

"Not yet. But he's clever, you know. Too clever."

"What did you tell him?"

"That I was playing the role of mistress tonight. I don't think he entirely believed me. He heard me mention Delphinia Beaumont to Nathan, and now he's suspicious. He's asking questions. He's a writer. He knows a plot when he sees one."

"You can't tell him anything." The thought of Sebastian DeWitt being privy to this plan . . . I could not bear to think of how it might change his perception of me. I was as afraid as she was of what he would think of our scheme. "Do you understand me? Nothing!"

"Don't think I don't know that. Unfortunately, he knows me a bit too well. And it doesn't help that questions about you keep coming up. He couldn't forget you if he tried. Even Nathan's asking him about you."

"About me? Why?"

"Apparently he thinks you and Bastian had an affair." She said the words casually, but I saw how tense she was. "Today he asked Sebastian if you'd been with him the morning of the fire."

I stared at her in surprise. "What did Mr. DeWitt tell him?"

"That you weren't—which I know to be a fact, because he was with me. But I don't know if Nathan believes him, and *I* certainly can't tell him the truth."

"My interest in Mr. DeWitt is purely platonic."

Bea's gaze was cool. "Is it? Nathan also asked Sebastian if he might be harboring you now."

Now I was both panicked and confused. "Why would he think that?"

"Because Nathan's afraid enough of what he thinks he's seeing that he's desperate to find you alive."

"What will we do?"

"What we planned. But the longer this gets played out, the more suspicious Sebastian will be, and the more questions he'll ask." Her gaze met mine. "This is your chance to really take the stage the way you wanted. You're going to need to act your heart out tonight, Ginny. We need this to proceed more quickly if it's going to work at all."

"I'll do my best."

"You're going to need to do better than that." Her expression was set and sober. "Nathan's not sleeping. He looks terrible. He said he dreams of you."

"Nightmares, I hope."

She smiled a little. "Oh, yes indeed."

"Much deserved," I said. "I hope to make them worse."

We spent the rest of the afternoon making plans. Then, when it was time, and when she determined that we would not happen upon Mr. DeWitt, we left the camp—one at a time, so as not to raise any suspicion. Once we were away, we walked quickly, and as we reached the house and I pulled into the shadow of a neighboring tree, she asked a little breathlessly, "Are you ready?"

I nodded. In truth, I had never felt so ready for anything. I was hardly nervous, only buoyed with determination and anticipation.

"Then I'll go," she said.

"Good lu—"

"Don't say it!" she whispered harshly, just short of panic. "It'll guarantee things to go wrong."

I looked at her in surprise. "I had no idea you were so superstitious."

"I'm an actress, aren't I? Now take it back."

"Very well, I take it back. But I can't quite make myself hope for bad luck instead."

She nodded without smiling, obviously tense. "I'll see you inside."

I watched her as she went to the door, knocked, and was ushered in. Then, quickly, I ran around to the side yard, to the French doors, waiting until I saw Bonnie bring her into the room and close the parlor door before I opened them.

Bea glanced over her shoulder and gave me a reassuring smile, and then I was inside, hiding myself behind the drapes veiling the door.

"The toe of your boot," she said quietly, and I pulled it back.

"Perfect," she whispered.

I waited, hardly daring to breathe, listening as she moved around the parlor, the clink as she picked up something here, another as she set it down. It seemed we waited a long time, but it was probably only a few moments before the parlor door opened and Nathan said, "Thank God you're here."

"You said twilight."

"So I did." The rapid pace of his footsteps; I imagined he was embracing her. "Do you really think this will work?"

"I think it won't hurt to try. You should have some bourbon, Nathan. Or some sherry. You're far too tense."

"I don't want any."

"No spirit will come when you're like this," she urged. I heard the clink of the decanter—gold-chased crystal. "Sherry? Or—what is this—scotch?"

"Scotch." His voice was barely there.

"Here. Drink that and have another. We'll start when you've relaxed."

There was a pause, then the decanter again, her approving "Much better." Two drinks, undoubtedly heavily poured. Perhaps three. He said, "We shall need a table, won't we? Will the dining room do?"

"The dining room?" How calm she sounded. "I suppose it depends. Where did your wife spend most of her time?"

"Her bedroom, I suppose—"

"Not there," she said quickly.

"Well . . . here, I suppose. That pile of novels was hers. I believe she spent a great deal of time reading. She told me once that her isolation"—a little laugh—"drove her mad."

Another little irony. I wasn't surprised he remembered it. No doubt it had fit perfectly in his plans. I dug my nails into the palm of my hand.

Bea said, "Then we will hold the séance here. There's only the two of us—that game table will suffice."

I heard the drag as he moved it. Night was falling, the blue-gray of twilight deepening. I heard the strike of a match, the hiss of a wick.

"There's no gas still," he was saying. "The oil lamp is all—"

"Do you have candles?" Bea asked. "I think the spirits prefer a calmer light."

I heard him moving, the setting of candlesticks on the tabletop—I knew just the ones. Large and ostentatious, red cameo glass. "Will these do?"

"Perfectly. One will be enough."

She was ordering it carefully. Dim light, enough to disguise that I was indeed corporeal. The curtains at the windows overlooking the front yard were drawn, the oil lamp extinguished.

For a moment, the room was plunged into darkness; that of the night outside seemed less. Then the soft light of the candle, very dim. I imagined it lit only the circle of them, that everything beyond was cast in shadows. I heard the drawing up of chairs, and I took a chance and peeked past the curtains to see the table at the other side of the room, Nathan's back to me. Bea's face looked strange in the candlelight, weirdly lit, shadows and gold and the reflection from the red glass of the candlestick. She had lowered her head and closed her eyes.

I knew *Heaven's Awakening*, of course. I had seen it at least twice in Chicago. But even though I knew this was only an elaborate fiction, Bea made me believe she *was* the medium. She grasped Nathan's hands and bade him close his eyes.

"Think only of her," she told him. "Concentrate on your wife's spirit. Call to her with your thoughts."

She let the silence grow in the room until it was almost unbearable. Five minutes, ten. There was no sound; the only clock I had in this room was well oiled, as Nathan was disturbed by little, repetitive noises. The clang of pots and pans did not reach from the kitchen. The maids had been schooled to soundlessness.

Fifteen minutes, twenty. Nathan shifted restlessly and then stilled.

Twenty-five. And then it seemed Bea's whole body seemed to thrum. A subtle vibration—how she did it, I had no idea. Sebastian DeWitt had been right about her potential.

She opened one eye, directing her gaze at me, and I shrank back into the curtains again, catching my breath, waiting.

She said, "I feel something."

"What?" Nathan's voice, too harsh.

"Quiet. Is there a spirit here? Can you not feel how cold it's grown? Spirit, if you be here, make yourself known."

I let a moment go past. Another. Then I rapped my knuckles against the wall.

"My God!" Nathan's voice squeaked.

"We are calling the spirit of Geneva Langley," Bea called, her voice eerily pitched, high and low at the same time, modulated like a song. "Are you that spirit?"

I rapped again.

"It's her." Nathan's voice. Hushed, reverent.

"If you be the spirit of Geneva Langley, can you show yourself to us?"

I took a deep breath and stepped from behind the curtain. Nathan did not see me. His back was to me, of course, and he was peering about the room as if trying to pierce the shadows with his gaze. I saw her head come up, her glance sharpen.

"She is come," she whispered.

Nathan twisted in his seat. He gasped when he saw me and tried to pull from her, but she anchored him with her hands. I didn't move. I was close enough to the curtain that it brushed my back, close to the doors. I could be out them in a moment.

"Do not go to her," Bea ordered. "She's a spirit, Nathan. Do you want her to flee?"

"Ginny," he said hoarsely. "Ginny, my God. Is it truly you?"

I pitched my own voice low, far lower than my usual tone. I held it to a whisper. "Who else should I be?"

"Ginny. My God. Dear God, where are you?"

"In the spirit realm," I said. "As you have known."

"You *did* die then. The fire—?"

"Painful and punishing. Does that please you?"

"No. Dear God, no. How could it?" He looked truly stricken, half shadow himself, his hair shimmering. The candlelight hid his excesses, the faint paunchiness of his jowls. He was handsome as he'd been when I'd first met him.

"Tell me where you died, where I can find your body," Nathan begged. "Is that what you want? Tell me, so I can lay you to rest."

"What *do* you want of us, spirit?" Bea asked. "Why have you come?"

"Vengeance," I said, dragging the word out, holding the sibilance, letting it slide through my teeth in a hiss, a serpent's voice, pleased when it sounded as eerie as I meant it, and Nathan drew back, visibly distressed.

"Vengeance?" he asked in a strangled voice. "For what?"

"You know. And I shall not rest until I have it, my husband."

He looked back at Bea; I slipped behind the curtain again.

"She's gone," Bea said. "She's gone."

I had my hand on the door behind me.

Nathan said, "For God's sake, light the lamp!" I heard the shriek of the chair across the floor.

I pushed. The door opened without a sound, and I stepped out, closing it again quickly and quietly, stepping into the shadows of the huge rhododendron just in time. I had not been there more than a breath before the curtains drew back; Nathan stared out the parlor doors into the darkness, his eyes black hollows in his face.

I heard her cry out, "Nathan!" and he turned again and let the curtains fall into place, and I let out my breath in relief, letting all my tension from the last hour dissolve away. It had worked. Dear God, it had worked just as we'd planned. Once again, my blood seemed to race through my veins; I could not keep still. I wanted to laugh.

Beatrice

Nathan," I said, relieved now that she was gone—what a clever girl she was, to have predicted him so well, to have gone before he could get at her—and when he turned to look at me with this wide-eyed, scared little-boy look, I said, "Well, do you believe she's dead now?"

"What did she mean? Vengeance—what does that mean?"

"I don't know." I sat back, sucking on my finger where, in my haste to light the lamp, I'd burned it. "You would know that better, I think. I couldn't hazard a guess."

"She never said anything to you?"

"About why she might want revenge on her husband?"

He stopped pacing and stared at me, but not as if he saw me.

I might as well have been the chair. "No, I suppose she wouldn't have."

He went back to pacing. I watched him go to the wall, stop, and turn, like an actor with a bit of business he couldn't lose. "Well, there must be something," I said finally. "It seems odd that she would want vengeance badly enough to keep her spirit from resting, yet you don't have any idea what she's talking about."

He stopped at the wall, pressing his forehead against it. I'd never seen him so distraught, and I had to suppress a smile, because, you know, this had worked better than I'd dared to hope. When he finally looked at me, his eyes were bigger than I'd ever seen them, and bright with fear.

"What do you think she'll do?"

"I'm not an expert in spirits. Perhaps you should ask one of your friends. There must be a spiritualist among them."

"No!"

His vehemence made me jump, and suddenly I didn't want to be there any longer. "Perhaps I should go."

He was across the room before I took another step. He grabbed my arm hard. "No. Don't leave me."

"Nathan, I'd rather not be around when the spirit decides to take her revenge. She doesn't like me very well, if you remember."

"She won't do it while you're here," he said, fingers tightening. "I'm certain of it."

I tried to pull away. "You're frightening me."

He dropped his hand. "I'm sorry. I'm just . . . it's been a difficult day. How the hell am I supposed to explain all this to Ginny's father?"

"Write him a letter."

"Too late. He's on his way here. I received a telegram just before you arrived. He'll be a few more days at most. Monday at the latest."

I tried to look uninterested, but my heart started pounding so loudly I was certain he could hear it.

Nathan squeezed the bridge of his nose. "Christ . . . it would all be bearable if only I could sleep."

"Perhaps you should consult a doctor," I suggested.

He laughed shortly. "And tell him what? That I'm seeing my wife's spirit? That I dream of her every night? No, I don't think so. What I need is you."

"It seems to me that laudanum might serve you better."

He pulled me to him, kissing me the way he had outside the Phoenix, as if he couldn't quite get enough, and there was nothing to do but kiss him back. And after that, he took me upstairs to his room, telling the servant waiting in the hall that he would have no more need of her tonight, and she looked at me as if she thought I were Ginny for just a moment before her expression cleared and went scandalized instead. Nathan didn't seem to notice or care. He led me to a room down the hall from the one I'd been in before, and I was relieved that it wasn't her bedroom again—of course it wasn't. His wife's spirit was swearing vengeance against him; Nathan wasn't so stupid he would fuck his mistress on her bed.

He opened the door to his room and stood back to let me go inside first, and it was just exactly as I might have imagined his bedroom to be. Heavy dark woods and deep blues, and it smelled like the citrus shaving soap he used, macassar and beeswax and leather, and he jerked me to that big bed, and I let him use me the way he wanted to, over and over again, because in spite of what he said about wanting me to exhaust him, it seemed as if he didn't want to be exhausted, as if he were afraid of sleep. And when he finally did succumb to it, he twitched like one of those dead frogs the lyceum lecturers were always bringing around to illustrate the miracles of electricity. I heard him murmuring her name, and it didn't sound as if he spoke it with love, or even liking.

I didn't bother to wake him but let him stew in it. I thought of the things he'd said about Ginny's father coming here, and the fact that I'd just spent an hour or so in his bed when I wanted to be in someone else's, and after that I couldn't sleep—not that I would have been able to anyway, not with his tossing and turning—and it wasn't yet dawn when I got up and dressed and left that house.

It was a long walk to the tent city, and the birds were starting to wake, their twittering loud and urgent, as if they meant to warn one another of the day ahead, and my own footsteps grew heavy with dread. It wasn't just because of what I'd learned about Ginny's father, either, but the fact that every step took me closer to Sebastian's tent, and now that the séance was over, I couldn't keep from thinking about what I'd said to him yesterday, and the truth I didn't want to look at.

Because what I'd told him wasn't a lie. I was in love with him. *Stupid girl.* I'd always somehow thought I was immune to love, as if it were some deadly disease a person ought to run from. Which it was, of course, because loving him meant I cared what he thought of me, and that was the most dangerous thing I knew. I did not want to cut off my own wings to have him. But I was feeling more and more as if that was what I should do, as if maybe the wings I had weren't the ones worth having. And I was more afraid of that than anything.

The only thing for it was to avoid him, at least until this whole thing with the Langleys was over—and how was I to do that when I also needed the newest scenes of *Penelope Justis* for the rest of the plan . . . well, there was a problem, wasn't there?

Unless you stop it all right now. Unless you abandon the plan. Because Ginny's father was on his way, and I didn't know what to do about him, or how we would go on with this when he was here. *Monday at the latest.* It was too little time to do what we needed. Given what I'd seen tonight, Nathan was on his way to where we wanted him to be. But how could we take him from nightmares to madness in only a few days?

You can't. Let it go, Bea. Let it all go. The company and the future I wanted. After all, I had the lead line now, didn't I? *Until someone new comes along to steal it away.* And that was a real possibility, given that Lucius was as faithless as a serpent. Which meant I would have to keep on with Nathan—and that thought was so exhausting I could not bear to think it.

And Ginny would have to return from the dead.

So there it was, really, the real reason for not stopping. Because nothing had changed when it came to her situation. Nathan still wanted her in an asylum, and the fact that she'd been missing for days meant no one would disagree that she needed to be put there, even without taking into account her father, who wanted it as much as Nathan did. There was no way she would escape it. And however irritating she was, she didn't deserve that. She deserved to be free from Nathan, free to tell her father to go to hell. I hated them both for what they'd done to her and what they planned to do. It was strange, you know, but the two of them got caught up in my head with every manager or actor who'd ever taken advantage of me, and her revenge felt like my own.

But Monday. *How would we do it by Monday?*

I didn't know. I was too exhausted to think. When I finally reached Fort Spokane, I went to her tent instead of Sebastian's. He would not be expecting me, given that he knew I was with Nathan, and that was a relief, one less thing to worry about. I pushed aside her tent flap, stepping inside. She was asleep; she didn't even stir. I lay down on the ground cover next to her bedroll.

The next thing I knew, I was waking to a whisper.

"Bea?" Her voice in my ear. In my sleep, I'd rolled closer to her, and I felt her at my back, nestled against me as if she'd gone searching for warmth in the early hours as well. My nose was full of her—fire smoke and sweat and unwashed hair. I bit back a moan and rose to one elbow.

"Sorry. I didn't mean to fall asleep." I sat up, twisting to look over my shoulder at her, and for a moment it was almost as if I looked into a mirror. Blinking, bleary dark eyes, skin pale and smudged with dirt, dark hair falling around white shoulders, a grayed chemise. It was disorienting. I had to blink to make it go away, to make myself see her again, instead of myself.

She said, "You're not with Mr. DeWitt. Or Nathan."

"No flies on you," I said, rubbing my eyes. "Sebastian thinks I'm with Nathan. And Nathan's too busy having nightmares to care where the hell I am. Terrible ones too, by the sound of it. Damn, I'm tired."

"Perhaps you should go back to sleep."

I shook my head. "I've got rehearsal."

"Let it wait."

"Lucius will fine me."

She laughed quietly; the sound was rough and deep. "What do you care for a two-dollar forfeit, Bea? You'll have so much more before long."

"Will I?"

Her amusement died in a quick frown. "Why do you say that? What happened last night after I was gone?"

"Your father telegraphed him," I said bluntly. "He's on his way here. Nathan said he'd be here by Monday."

"My father's coming here?" She said the words so plaintively, in this wistful voice that was hard at the same time, as if she both wanted to see him and was afraid of it, which I supposed was probably true. "Dear God. Are you certain?"

"Do you think Nathan would lie about it?"

"No." She shook her head, saying bitterly, "He wouldn't lie. There's no reason to. This changes everything."

I got to my feet and went to the lard pail in the corner, which held some tepid water. I knelt beside it and splashed my face, which felt good, but it didn't ease my bone-deep weariness.

"What are we going to do?" she asked.

"It's not enough time," I told her, drying my face on my filthy skirt—and no doubt streaking it once again with the ashy dust that covered everything like a fine scrim. "And *Much Ado* opens on Monday as well. I'll be too busy with the show."

"But we must. What did Mr. DeWitt say happens once the spirit appears in the séance?"

I turned to look at her. "I don't know. Yet."

"You said the spirit gains power, didn't you? That once Barnabus called her up, she doesn't go away."

"Well, yes, but—"

"Then I won't go away. I shall keep appearing to him. Where is he today?"

I felt a little panic. "I don't know. But you can't do that, Ginny. Not without me, and I can't be there. I've got rehearsal, and there's Sebastian to manage as well."

"You manage him. You go to rehearsal. I'll follow Nathan."

"It's too dangerous. What if you're seen?"

"I hope to be."

"Not by Nathan, you fool," I snapped. "By someone else?"

"What else am I to do? We've only a few days. It's hardly enough time."

"Damn it, Ginny, let me think—"

"There's no time to think." She was kneeling on her bedroll, and now she leaned forward, imploring me with her bare arms, pale as any spirit's. "I'll go to the house. I'll linger by the windows. He'll never catch me."

"But the maids—"

"Do you think I don't know the schedule I set for them? I can avoid them."

I shook my head. "It's too risky."

"What other choice is there?" She went still, studying me as if I'd suddenly become something strange, the same way those women at the charity ball had looked at me, and I felt this little shiver of fear. "Do you want to abandon this?"

And my decision was made, just that quickly. "No."

She gave me a short nod of satisfaction and rose, grabbing for the dress hanging from the tent post. "It's early yet. I have time to get to the house before he leaves."

"I don't like this," I said.

"You're afraid I can't do it? I thought you said I had talent?"

"It's not about that. It's—"

"It's my risk to take, Bea, and I'm willing to takc it," she said, a little coldly. "Please don't forget how much I have at stake. Or what you hope to gain."

"No, I don't."

"Good." She smiled. "Now all you must do is find Penelope's next step."

"Easier said than done," I said wryly.

"I have faith in you."

And I hated to admit it, but you know, the way she said it, so simply, as if there was no question I could do it, got into me like a splinter you keep worrying until it gets deeper and harder to dislodge, and my exhaustion suddenly disappeared. Suddenly I was ready to do what needed to be done.

"Be careful," I said.

She gave me this purely luminous smile. "It will be worth it, Bea. Think what a prize we'll have when it's done."

And I knew the prize she meant.

Sebastian.

Chapter Thirty-three

Geneva

I dressed and left the tent as quickly as possible, dodging among the other tents on the grounds, ignoring the people bustling with the morning, too busy with their own lives to trouble mine. I was so intent on the task at hand that I didn't feel the hunger that had become my constant companion. It didn't matter. Nothing mattered but Nathan.

Bea's news that my father was on his way both distressed and emboldened me. There was a beauty in it, actually, a wonderful irony in the fact that my father would soon have no choice but to admit that it was his son-in-law who belonged in an asylum instead of the daughter he had nearly committed. And then I would step forward, pleading amnesia—a plot right out of a melodrama, Bea would no doubt say—and take up my place in Papa's affections again. With my husband out of the way, I would be able to show my father how well he'd been lied to. I would be able to mount the defense I needed.

I was more determined than ever to see this plan through.

It took me longer than I'd thought to reach the house, and I was sweating when I reached the rhododendron in the side yard. I hid within its glossy green leaves and glanced at the sky—it must be nearly nine. Given the night Bea said Nathan had had, he would no doubt be only just rising. Bonnie would be serving breakfast, and then she would go upstairs to make beds and tend to the bedrooms. The cook and Anna, the scullery maid, would be cleaning the kitchen. The iceman would be coming around soon, to the back door, where the cook would meet him and complain about the price, and they would speak idly together for a few minutes. Now was the perfect time.

I crept around the side, past the parlor doors. I kept to the wall until I reached the single window of the dining room, measuring the distance I would have to run if Nathan decided to give chase—only a few yards.

Slowly, I peeked into the window.

He was there, as I'd predicted, the paper folded at his side, unopened. He was in his shirtsleeves, elbows on the table as he leaned over his coffee cup, stirring it like one half-dead, his hair unmacassared, falling forward into his face. He paid no attention to the window at all.

I withdrew again, safely out of sight, and then I called, "Nathan."

The windows were thin; I did not doubt he could hear me. I waited. Nothing. No sound, no discernable movement.

Again I said, "Nathan," and this time I drew it out, long and haunting, the kind of sound a ghost might make, turning his name into a dirge.

This time I heard something drop.

"Nathan," I said, and then I stepped into the window.

He was staring toward it, his face white, his eyes hugely round. At the sight of me, he jerked back so hard his chair screeched upon the floor. I saw him make a sound, his lips formed my name, but it must have been a whisper, because I couldn't hear it.

More than that, I didn't wait to see. I withdrew again, and this time I ran to the other side of the rhododendron, my heart racing, trying to quiet my nervous breathing. I waited for him to come racing out. I waited for the scream of my name.

There was nothing.

It was not what I'd expected, and that made me nervous. Cautiously, I peeked through the leaves of the rhododendron. He would have had to go to the parlor doors, the nearest ones, but I saw no movement there at all. I eased around the edge of the tree, holding my breath. I could not see the dining room window clearly—it was at too much of an angle, but what I did see made me scoot back into the protection of the leaves again. Nathan, his hands pressed against the glass, his posture tense with what could have been terror or anger or both; I could not tell.

But he had not tried to come after me. Why not? Because he truly thought I was dead? Because he was convinced I was a spirit? Or was there some other reason?

I didn't dare go to the dining room window again, but neither was I ready to leave this place. I glanced around, my gaze lighting again on the fence of our neighbor's house, the large maple there. If I could appear to him once more as he left . . . It was a risk, I knew, but one worth taking.

Quickly I dodged from our yard. The neighbor's fence was not tall, three feet only, but it was enough to hide me if I crouched very low. I glanced at the windows of that house—the drapes still drawn. The man who lived there owned one of the shipyards; he was rarely home, and I'd met him only once. Just now the house seemed still as a corpse and just as empty. I hurried down the path that broke the fence, to the right of the maple tree, jerking my too-long skirt after me when it caught, and then I knelt in the lee of the fence, waiting for the carriage to come around for my husband, glancing nervously to the house behind me, hoping I was right and that Mr. Anderson, who was so seldom home, was not so today either.

There was not even a rustle in the drapes, and so I turned my attention back to my house, and Nathan. It seemed to take a long time; long enough that I began to wonder if Nathan intended not to go into the city today. He hadn't slept well; his office was no longer. Perhaps he meant to stay at home—

But then I heard a carriage coming around the block, and I peeked to see—ours, with the emblem gold upon the door, coming from the back stables, and I breathed a sigh of relief. It stopped before the house.

My thighs were burning from the position I held, but I dared not move. Only a few more moments, and ah . . . there it was. The front door opening, the driver hastening to open the carriage door for my husband, who wore a suitcoat and a hat now, but who glanced about nervously, as if he expected to see a ghost.

He spoke something in a low voice to the driver, and then

climbed inside. The driver closed the door and went quickly to his seat, taking up the reins. I rose, clinging to the tree, and then, at the right moment, I came around, stepping into view, and I saw Nathan's face in the carriage window, the jerk of his head. Our gazes met. Deliberately, I filled mine with hatred and rage. I saw his pure fear in response, and then the carriage was past, and I melted back into my hiding place until it was out of sight.

It had worked. I had done it, and I had not mistaken the expression on his face. Nathan was afraid. Whatever Bea had said to him last night had worked. He truly thought I was a ghost, and he truly believed I was there for vengeance.

It was all I could do not to leap from the tree and run back to the tent, to tell her what had happened, how well it had gone. But I forced myself to wait, to be certain Nathan had not told the driver to turn around, and when I knew he had not, I went back to the road and hurried away from this neighborhood. No one was about other than one or two gardeners, a maid emptying chamber pots, the iceman on his wagon. They all glanced up at me and then away again, uninterested, as if I were below their notice. I could not blame them. My hair was loose, my gown burned and filthy beyond recognition; I was not the Ginny Langley I'd been, and yet how much more alive I felt now. I knew that was something Bea would understand, because I knew she felt it too, every night upon that stage, as she bowed to laughter and applause—and for a strange, disorienting moment, I felt her thirst for it, as if she were somehow inside of me, and I knew that was part of my giddiness now, the realization that she and I were together in this, that it was something we shared that we would always share. No matter what happened after today, whether this plan worked or did not, *Penelope Justis* belonged to us. We had not written it or devised it, but we had made it live, and I knew it would stay, something bright and luminescent and perfect. As if somehow, despite ourselves, we'd created our own star.

Beatrice

So . . . keeping Sebastian from asking questions. That was my first goal of the day, and don't think I didn't know how impossible it was going to be, because after what I'd said yesterday, and the fight we'd had, he was going to want to talk. It was inevitable, and any other time I would simply have avoided him. But that brought us to my second goal of the day, which was to discover the next step in our little plot. I suspected he'd spent last night—no doubt late into the night—revising *Penelope,* and I needed those scenes. Ginny had gone up to the house—a bad idea, no matter how you looked at it, and too damn risky—but that wasn't going to be enough. We needed more, and that *more* was in Sebastian's fertile brain.

Two more contradictory goals you couldn't find, and on the way down to rehearsal, I tried to think up some way to have them both. By the time I reached the Phoenix, I felt strung tight, which was never good, and worse still when it came to the troupe. They would sense it, and I would be in for no end of teasing, which I wasn't in the mood for, not the least bit.

I was early again, surprisingly enough. Lucius was there, and he and Mr. Geary and Sebastian were busy conferring over some scene while Jackson was lying on the stage, reading the newspaper. Jack glanced up when I came inside, and he must have sensed my mood straight off—and really it was amazing how good I was at predicting things like this—because he said, "Ah, my beauteous Bea! 'Where the bee sucks, there suck I; In a cowslip's bell I lie; There I couch when owls do cry—' "

"Shut up, Jack," I interrupted irritably.

"Ah, my sweet girl, why so snappish? Ah, I have it: 'The course of true love never did run smooth.' Am I not hit upon it?"

I opened my mouth to say something nasty, but before I could, Sebastian said, "Don't be an ass, Wheeler," which surprised all of us, and Jack especially, because his mouth snapped shut like a fish trapping a fly.

"My, my, aren't we all foul-tempered this morning," Jack said sullenly, turning back to his paper. And then, beneath his breath but still loud enough for us all to hear, "God save me from true lovers."

I glanced at Sebastian, who looked at me with a question in his eyes that I could read as if he'd said the words. *We need to talk, Bea.*

I turned away, uncomfortable, wondering again how I would manage, and just then, Aloys came in, his dark face darker than usual, as if some shadow had crossed it, his brow furrowed.

I said, "You look as if you swallowed a lemon, Aloys."

His frown grew. "Has Langley been here?"

I glanced at Sebastian, who was watching, and said, "Nathan? Why would he be?"

"He's all the talk this morning."

I thought of Ginny going up there alone, my feeling that it was a bad idea. I hadn't thought I could get strung much tighter, but I was wrong. "Why? Why happened?"

Aloys said, "Apparently, he's seeing ghosts again. Or that's the talk, in any case. When he went into the city council meeting this morning, he was off his head, shouting about how he had to find his wife's body, et cetera, et cetera. Quite a scene, I take it."

"How do you know this?" Sebastian asked.

"I was accosted on my way here by several people who'd witnessed it themselves. They know of our association with him, of course. I told them he must have been reading our new playwright's *Penelope.* Nothing like a little publicity, you know, and God knows the play's enough to give anyone nightmares."

"He hasn't read it." Sebastian glanced at me. "Has he?"

I felt his suspicion, but at least Aloys had said nothing of

Ginny, and that was a relief. "Has anyone? You haven't even finished the new version."

Lucius glanced up. "How does that go, by the way? I hope your efforts with *Much Ado* have not derailed it unduly."

Sebastian did not take his gaze from me. "No. I'm nearly finished. I've had plenty of time lately."

I felt a little flare of excitement. "Are you past the séance scene then?"

"Séance?" Lucius clapped his hands together. "Ah, excellent, excellent! Everyone loves a séance. I suppose, as a grave trap is impossible for the time being, we could set secret doors into the flats for the spirit to emerge through. There is a spirit that appears, isn't there?"

"Oh yes," Sebastian said with a grim smile. "A quite bold one. It even appears in Barnabus's bed."

I went still. *Impossible*. How the hell were we to effect that?

Jack rolled onto his side. "In his bed? Now that would give the bravest man nightmares."

"Well, let's hope Langley doesn't hear of it," Aloys said. "God knows he doesn't need more to imagine."

"Has he seemed off to you, Bea?" Jack asked me.

"Has who seemed off?" Brody asked as he came in.

"Langley's gone half mad," Jack informed him.

"Has he? Well, that don't surprise me, I guess. What with his wife going missing in the fire like that and the whole city burning down around him."

"It burned down around all of us," Aloys said. "And most of us remain quite sane."

Jack said idly, "Yes, well, you aren't missing a rich wife, are you? Well, Bea? Should we call the asylum men if he shows up here again?"

I felt them all looking at me, Sebastian's gaze most of all, and I avoided it as I said, "He was very distraught last night."

"No doubt it took all your skill to soothe him," Jack said with a little grin.

"I never did manage it. He isn't himself, that's true enough."

"As long as he keeps the money coming in, eh?" Lucius said.

"Enough talk, children. Go on now, and give me act two, scene one."

Obediently, we did as he directed, but I felt Sebastian's eyes on me throughout, and that unspoken question hanging in the air only adding to the other ones I knew he wanted to ask. At least I'd discovered the next part of the play—though how *that* was going to happen, I had no idea, and I didn't like the thought either, of her being close enough for Nathan to touch. But I also saw how the thing Jack had said was true. It would be enough to unbalance most men, and Nathan was on edge. A little more than I'd expected, but if Ginny and I could manage this . . .

My mind was spinning with *how*, so the end of rehearsal came as a surprise, and I was distracted enough that I didn't race out the way I should have done, and there was Sebastian waiting, and I was trapped.

Still, I tried. I hurried to the opening of the tent, dodging outside, into little clouds of dust that made me choke, but I didn't get far. I'd got only a few tents away before he was there, beside me. "Where are you off to so quickly?"

"To the relief tent," I lied, because the truth was that I didn't think I could swallow anything just now. "I know you have to write—"

"There's plenty of time for that latcr. There are things we should discuss first."

Like the fact that I'd told him I loved him. I swallowed. "Not now," I managed. "I've things to do."

"Like what?"

"I—"

"Come with me, Bea," he said softly. "Talk to me."

"There's no point," I said, a little meanly too, and I knew it. "Nothing's changed."

"Some things have," he disagreed. "Like the fact that Langley's dashing about like a madman and saying he's seeing his wife's spirit. Things like that don't happen overnight. Is that what your séance was about?"

"I don't know what you're talking about."

"What plan are you hatching? Why won't you tell me?"

He was looking at me so intently that the urge to tell him came over me like a fever. I bit it back.

"I don't want you to go to him again," he said.

"Don't be absurd, Bastian."

"He's unstable, if what Aloys said is true. He could be dangerous."

"It's nothing I can't handle."

"Bea, I mean it. Stay away from Langley."

I met his gaze. "I can't. You know I can't. I need him."

"You don't need the things you think you do. Your talent—"

"Was wasted until Nathan Langley came along," I said sharply. "I've already told you, I have to be practical."

"You said you loved me," he said. "Was that a lie?"

There it was, the thing I'd been waiting for. "No," I said, and it was a damn whisper; there was no strength to it, and I couldn't find any, and it would have been better to lie. Why the hell hadn't I? "But it doesn't matter, does it? Loving you doesn't put food on the table, and it doesn't protect me from Lucius's games. Only Nathan can do that."

"What if you're wrong?" he asked. "What if I can do those things for you?"

I laughed. "Then I'd say you're a damn magician."

"I've never written better or faster in my life. *Penelope*'s almost done, and I'll be able to devote myself to the new play. We could be a force together. I'd write the plays, you'd act in them. They'd form lines around the block. Eventually we could have the company you want."

He said it so damn ardently that I wanted to believe him. It was stupid how much I wanted it.

I glanced away. "It would take too long. Look at me, Bastian. I'm nearly thirty."

"You've just reached your prime."

"I can't keep the lead without Nathan."

"Lucius won't take it from you now."

"You don't know him the way I do."

A sigh of exasperation. "How can you be so damned blind? Why can't you see that he would do anything for you?"

"Because he won't," I snapped. "I'd like to live in your world,

Bastian, where everyone's good and their motives are pure, but it's a delusion."

"If *Penelope*'s a success, your position will be assured."

"I hope so," I said. "But I can't afford to count on it."

Sebastian swept his hand through his hair, obviously frustrated. "God, if only she hadn't died—"

Ginny Langley again. I snapped, "But she did, didn't she?"

He went still. He said softly, "We could do it. You know we could. Don't go back to him, Bea. Please."

And there it was, the jealousy I'd waited for, that I'd wanted. And, you know, the irony was that if he'd said these things to me even a few days ago, I might have done what he wanted. If I'd got Ginny on a wagon that night. If we hadn't snuck into her house and I hadn't seen how much money she had. If I hadn't made her cause my own. Now there was too much I wanted. And we were too damned close. It was too late. I was entangled with her in ways I couldn't see clear of, and more important, I didn't *want* to see clear of them. I would save Geneva Langley. I could save myself.

"Trust me, Bastian," I said quietly. "Can you do that? Just for a little while longer?"

He hesitated. I saw his struggle. I put my hand on his arm.

"Just a little while longer," I said again. "And it will all be over." I thought I had him. I truly did. But I was wrong.

"What will be over, Bea?"

I couldn't answer. And so he walked away.

Geneva

When she came to the tent that afternoon, bearing the usual half-smashed, moist, and doughy slices of bread, I was still elated over my success with Nathan. I ate the bread so quickly I nearly choked on it.

"You should have seen his face," I told her. "He was terrified."

She was sitting on the floor, her arms around her knees. "Aloys said there was talk. People are saying that Nathan is coming undone."

I smiled. "Well, then it went better than even I'd supposed, didn't it?"

"Yes." Distracted, barely audible.

I frowned. I noticed for the first time how quiet she seemed. "What's wrong? What is it?"

She shook her head. "Nothing. I have the next step. The next step in the plan."

That distracted me, as she must have known it would. "What is it?"

"I don't know how we can do it, but the spirit appears to Barnabus in his own bed."

I stared at her in disbelief. "His own bed?"

A little smile. "I told you I didn't know how to do it. But it's perfect, of course. Trust Sebastian to bend a plot."

There was a sarcasm there, and something else, something I would have questioned had I not been so caught by the plan. "Well, there's no other choice, is there? Unless you've a better idea?"

"It's dangerous," she said. "Nathan's not himself."

"Isn't that what we wanted?"

"We wanted him to appear to be mad, Ginny, not to actually . . . be mad."

"I doubt he's as far gone as all that."

"You haven't seen him the way I have."

"Don't tell me you're afraid."

Her chin came up, her dark eyes lit. "Of course not."

"And we don't have much time until my father is here."

She sighed. "Yes, I know."

"What other way is there?"

"None," she said. "None at all."

And I saw again her strange mood, a kind of bleakness that seemed to have settled over her. I didn't like it. "What happened today, Bea?"

"It was nothing. Another argument with Sebastian. His questions are becoming impossible."

"It's only for a few more days," I reassured her. "He'll be fine. When it's all over and I reemerge, I can help you to smooth his feathers."

"I'm certain he'd like nothing better."

Now I heard jealousy; I was not mistaking it, and I knew I should try to assuage it. But there was a part of me that liked the fact that she was uncertain of him, even as she shared his bed and owned his heart, because it meant that I had been important to him.

So I only said, "Remember what we intend for him."

"Yes. I remember." Then she sighed. "Damn. I suppose . . . I must spend the night with Nathan again. And you'll have to be waiting."

"I was rather hoping I never had to share his bed again."

"I'll try to have him tired enough—and drunk enough—that all you'll have to do is lie in it."

"Poor Bea," I said, meaning it. "I do sympathize."

She rubbed the back of her neck. "At least do me a favor. While you're waiting there, sneak into the pantry or something and have a decent meal. You aren't one of those who makes the cook sleep in the kitchen, are you?"

I laughed. "She has her own room at the bottom of the stairs."

"Is she a sound sleeper?"

"I don't know. Strangely enough, the question has never arisen."

"Well, I hope for both our sakes that she is." She closed her eyes and let her head fall back. "I don't want her waking up and raising an alarm."

"You can trust me to be certain of it," I said.

Her eyes opened. She met my gaze. "I do," she said, and there was a wondering in her voice. "I do trust you. Funny, isn't it, when you think of how we started? Remember that first rehearsal? Bastian told me I would regret it. And I do, you know. I regret it."

I told her, "I regret a great many things. I try not to think of them."

A half smile now, one that warmed me. "Neither do I."

Chapter Thirty-four

Beatrice

Another plan: Ginny said, *"Go to the Rainier Club. At least they'll know where to find him. Offer to soothe him. Offer to stay. Unless you come back here, I'll assume he's taken you up on it. I'll wait until midnight. Then just unlock the bedroom door."*

She made it all sound so damn easy, and I suppose I was glad for it too, in a way, because it meant I didn't have to spend the night with Sebastian. I'd stopped at his tent, feeling nervous as an ingenue, and I'd been both relieved and disappointed that he wasn't there. There were scraps of paper laying around, a pencil, and I wrote him a note telling him I was with Nathan and left it on the crate for him, and then I left. Sebastian felt like a little wound, a bruise deep in my chest that I couldn't lose and that wouldn't heal, and I hated that feeling. I hadn't shared it with her, either, and that was something I couldn't explain. Maybe because she had so much confidence now that this was all going to work, and that we'd be able to make it right. She'd made me believe it too, when I was with her, but now that we were apart, I wasn't so certain.

But I couldn't think of him now. I had to think of Nathan, of how to find him, of how to convince him he needed me tonight. The Rainier Club was my first step.

It was the bastion of men in this city, settled in the old McNaught mansion up on Fourth Street. Even before the fire, you could see its elaborate tower from almost any point in the city, and now that the whole business district was nothing but ash, it sat there like some king holding court, unharmed, its grassy yard untouched. I'd never before done more than walk by it, and so it felt strange to go up those long, sweeping stairs and ask the doorman if Nathan Langley was about. Truthfully, I didn't expect that he would help me. I mean, I looked like some flotsam dragged off the street, if not a vagrant then certainly a whore, and neither of those would be even close to welcome in this place, so it surprised me when the doorman tipped his hat and said, "He's not here, Mrs. Wilkes. They had meetings all day, but he went home for the evening. He was a bit under the weather." He smiled. "May I say I hope the Regal starts up again soon. I went to see you every week."

I was startled, and more than a little pleased. "We're doing *Much Ado About Nothing* starting Monday. At the tent where the Regal used to be, though we're calling it the Phoenix now."

His eyes lit, and that filled something inside of me, something I hadn't realized I'd been missing. That yearning for admiration, the things that fed my vanity and my pride.

"I'm surely happy to hear that," he said. "I'll be there. You can count on it."

It was growing late now, the cool breeze off the harbor settling into that stillness that came with the sunset. By the time

I got to the Langley house, it would be dark. I was tired; it had been a long day and meant to grow longer still, but I trudged my way up First Hill, wondering how I would get past the Langleys' maid. God knew if I were her, I'd kick me to the street quick enough. Although she'd seen me the other night, I supposed, so she already knew who I was.

By the time I made it to the path that led to Nathan's front door, it was as dark as I'd predicted. Still no streetlights, and still the dim yellow pulse of oil lamps in the windows. But the night was cooler, even a little chill once the breeze came up again, drying the sweat on my face and neck. I took a deep breath, gathering my courage, and went to knock upon the door.

It wasn't long before I heard footsteps. When the maid opened the door, I said politely, "I'm Beatrice Wilkes come to call on Mr. Langley."

Her expression collapsed into a scowl, and in one quick sweep her gaze took me in. "Yes, ma'am. He's been waiting for you." She said it in this tone that told me how little she thought of that, which didn't surprise me. What did surprise me was his knowing I would come. But before I had time to think about that, there was a flurry of footsteps behind her, racing down the stairs, and then Nathan was there, pushing her aside.

He looked terrible. Worse than last night, worse than I'd ever seen him. He was swaying, as if he'd been drinking, and his hair looked as if he'd raked his hands through it a dozen times. His face was almost gray, and there were great shadows beneath his eyes, and I remembered what Ginny had said about his mad mother. Suddenly I wanted nothing more than to be away from here, because his gaze seemed to gobble me up like a fox devouring a hen, and there was something desperate in it.

"Bea," he said, grabbing my arm, pulling me inside. He turned to the maid. "That will be all, Bonnie."

She gave me a disdainful glance and then she retreated, and Nathan closed the door. "Thank God you got my message."

"Your message?"

"I sent one to Greene this evening asking for you. Didn't you get it?"

"Oh yes. Yes, I did," I lied, because it made everything so

easy. I made a note to thank Lucius for so promptly searching me out, the bastard. Of course, there wasn't a message box now, and I didn't suppose he'd march himself to the tent city, but they all knew where I was, and he could have sent Brody to find me.

"I imagine you heard," Nathan said.

"Heard what?"

"That I saw her again." He walked distractedly toward the parlor, leaving me to follow him. He picked up a glass and splashed scotch into it—quite a bit of scotch—and he downed most of it in a gulp. At least I would be able to keep my promise to Ginny that he'd be drunk or exhausted tonight. He poured in more and gestured to it. "Would you like a drink?"

I shook my head. "You mean you saw your wife's spirit again?"

"This morning. Twice. And then once at the windows of the club."

She'd said nothing about going to the club, and I didn't believe she had. Nathan was fevered, talking fast. I had no doubt he was seeing things in every shadow.

"She said she wanted vengeance. I think she won't leave you until she has it."

"That's what I'm afraid of," Nathan said. He downed the drink completely and set the glass aside. "I was hoping, with you here, she would leave me be."

"I saw her last night too," I pointed out. "I don't think I'm much of a safe haven."

"Then you'll exhaust me so I can sleep. I . . . these damn nightmares . . ."

"What did you do to her, Nathan?" I asked him. "Why is she so bent on haunting you?"

He turned a bleak gaze to me. "I wish I had some idea."

He should have been an actor; he was that good a liar. I hated him for it, how damn innocent he appeared, as if he hadn't been scheming to put her away, as if he hadn't still been working all those angles even after the fire.

I had to look away, because I was afraid he would see my contempt if I didn't, and it took me a minute to compose myself. "Well, perhaps she'll tell you."

"Christ, don't say that!" He was across the room in no time, grabbing my arm. "Don't say that! Take it back!"

His fingers dug hard into my arm, bruising it. "All right. I take it back."

"I don't want to tempt fate." He glanced around the room as if he expected to see her in the gently flickering light of the oil lamp.

I didn't like Nathan anyway, but I really didn't like him this way, like a pocket watch wound too tight, one more turn and a click and you had a broken watch in your hands. And then I remembered that it was what we wanted, for him to be broken, for his mind to snap like that watch, and he looked near enough to it that I started to wonder what would happen to anyone standing too close. *And here you are, Bea, closer than anyone.*

I tried to pull away. "Christ, Nathan, you're hurting me."

His grip went slack. "I'm sorry. I . . . just . . . please don't go. I haven't slept. . . ." He put his hand to his eyes. "If I had a good night's sleep, I would be fine."

So of course I was going to make certain he didn't get much more than an hour or two. Just long enough for her to slip inside and show herself again. *Just one more turn.*

"As you like," I said. Then I smiled wickedly. "But I don't expect you'll get much sleep with me here."

He caught my gaze. "That's what I want. Exhaust me."

He grabbed my hand and pulled me with him up the stairs to his bedroom. He locked the door behind us, but he left the key there, and I told myself to remember to unlock it when he was asleep so she could get in.

He kissed me and said, "Promise me you'll stay," and I told him I would, and then he lit a lamp on the bedside table and turned it down low. He looked at me, slow and admiring, and you know, I'd never seen that in him before. It made my skin crawl. I preferred him impatient and distant, where I was just a body for him to use.

He came over to me and undressed me, and he was deliberate about it too, another strange thing. And then he undressed himself and pulled me to the bed, and though I didn't mean to feel anything and never had with him before, the way he touched me tonight . . . well, he knew what to do, and he was good at it too, though I'd never seen that before now. He wasn't the Nathan Langley I knew at all, not the selfish bastard who'd bribed me with money and candy, not the one who hurt me.

And though I was uneasy at the change, I had to do this, and I stretched beneath his hands and thought of her, and that made it easier. I remembered what she'd said about the passion between them, and I pretended to be her. I imagined her twisting beneath him, desiring him, and it was like a part I took on but not like that too, because I heard Sebastian's voice in my head saying, "You *became* her . . ." and suddenly I was. I was Ginny Langley. And then it was all right that I bucked like a wild thing beneath him. And it was all right too when he made me come the way no man but Sebastian had ever done, because in my head it was not Beatrice Wilkes he was making love to, but her.

It made it easier to do what I had promised I would do, to exhaust him. We were both sweating when we finally stopped, and he rolled off me and threw his hand over his eyes, and it wasn't more than a few moments before he whispered, "Ginny," as if he were half-asleep, and there was a moment where I accepted the name as mine, a moment before I remembered who I was and was ashamed. But there was no time for that now, and I pushed it away, and then his breathing became rhythmic and steady, and his hand slipped from his closed eyes.

I lay still, waiting for his sleep to deepen, wondering when I could risk moving. Finally, he began snoring lightly. When I was certain he wouldn't wake, I moved carefully from the bed. He shifted; his snore caught, and I froze until his breathing righted itself again. I went to the door—stark naked, but if I wanted it to seem as if her ghost had just replaced me, I couldn't do anything about it—and unlocked it, opening it a crack, which was the signal Ginny and I had agreed on.

The house was dark and there was no sound. The servants had gone to bed, everyone asleep but the two of us. She must have been waiting in the shadows down the hall, because she was there in moments, slipping inside, glancing at me in question and not even raising her brows at my undress. I gave her a quick little nod, and crept to the other side of the bed, Nathan's side, where the lamp was, and drew back against the wall, waiting while she went to where I'd just been lying.

She lay down beside him, fully clothed—the gown she'd died in, still burnt and filthy with ash and heavy with the smell of smoke. She turned onto her side, raising up on one elbow, and Nathan kept sleeping the sleep of the dead, not even snores now, and our eyes met across him and she smiled this beautiful smile, and I felt a shiver of excitement that raised gooseflesh. Then she touched his shoulder.

"Nathan," she whispered in the creepy hoarse voice she'd used in the parlor. "Nathan, my love."

He started awake, jerking, turning. "Wha—" and then the word broke into a scream when he saw her, and it was the most godawful sound I've ever heard. No man should scream that way. He scrambled away from her so hard he hit the headboard and the whole bed rocked and swayed, and he was still screaming, and in that moment I blew out the lamp and the room fell into darkness filled with that scream.

I ran around to the other side; I felt the brush of her skirt against my leg as we passed each other, and I took her place on the bed and said, as if I'd just woken from sleep, "Nathan! What's wrong? Nathan!"

I grabbed his shoulder and shook him, and he wrenched away from me so violently I heard the thud of him hitting the floor. Then his scream stopped, thank God, and I knew it would only be a moment before one of the servants rushed up here to see what was wrong and no doubt they were all thinking I was murdering him.

"Ginny," he gasped. "Ginny—"

"Not Ginny," I told him, pretending to be irritated. "It's Bea."

His breath was rasping and loud. I heard him fumble, then the lamp was lit again, and he stood there naked, staring at me as if he'd never seen me before.

"What is it?" I asked. "What's wrong?"

He was trembling. His eyes were so big they took up half his face—in the lamplight he almost looked like a ghost himself. He knelt on the bed, reaching out, grabbing my chin hard, turning my face as if trying to find her within it. "I saw her," he whispered. "She was there. Just where you are."

"Who?"

"Ginny." He released me and sat on the edge of the bed, burying his face in his hands. "Dear God. Ginny."

I heard the clatter of footsteps in the hall outside, an impatient knock, the servant calling, "Mr. Langley? Mr. Langley, are you all right?"

He didn't raise his head from his hands. "I'm fine, Bonnie. Just a nightmare. Go on. Leave me be."

She hesitated, and the footsteps left again, almost as hastily as they'd come, and I didn't blame her for not wanting to be anywhere near what had made that scream.

"It wasn't a nightmare," he said to me then. "She was there. Her spirit. I could have touched her. Didn't you see her? She was where you are now. It was you, and then it was her. . . ." A little gulp, like a half laugh or a sob. "Dear God, I'm going mad."

I bit back a smile.

"Dear God," he whispered, and then over and over again, like a meditation or something, so long it started to worry me, and I wondered if I was hearing that snap in his brain I'd wanted, if his mind had just left him. It was more unsettling than I'd thought.

I glanced at the door, wondering where she was, if she'd left already, if she was close enough to hear my screams if I made them.

I began to ease off the bed. "I should go—"

Nathan twisted fast enough to grab my arm before I could move. "You promised not to leave me. *Don't leave me.*"

He *looked* insane. Whatever was churning in his head wasn't something I wanted to know. But there was desperation on his face too, and in any case I wasn't going anywhere as long as he wanted me to stay, because I couldn't get across the room fast enough to keep him from stopping me, and I was naked besides.

"All right," I said softly. "I'll stay."

He released my wrist, but slowly, as if he were ready to grab me again if I bolted, and then he said, "I wanted to tame her. What was so wrong with that?" He turned completely, one fluid motion, on me before I had time to realize that he'd moved at all.

He leaned close, ardent, his breath hot in my face, pressing me back against the mattress. "I think she's jealous of you. It's why she's here, I know it. She was always so jealous."

He smiled, but his teeth glinted in the lamplight, very white, bared like an animal's. Once again, I thought I heard the snap. I saw something deep in his eyes, the seed of the madness we'd planted there, and I was suddenly afraid. I remembered his scream, the way it had sounded. I had been a fool to push him. I should not be here with him.

"But I'll protect you from her, Bea. I promise I'll protect you," he said, and then once again, chanting it, and I was reminded of the scene in *Macbeth* with the witches, and *something wicked this way comes* and *what will you do to escape him now?* In the lamplight it was easy to imagine him the monster he was. His hands tightened on my shoulders, and he was on top of me, and his arms wrapped around me as if he meant me to be a balm against the fear I saw in his eyes, and in pure defense, hoping it would make him stop, I said,

"Her spirit might be here even now, Nathan, watching us."

And then I wished I'd never said anything at all.

Chapter Thirty-five

Geneva

The night was well advanced, the moon already falling, as I made my slow way home. The streets were quiet and dark, the shadows of the wooded lots I passed seemed to eke onto the road, stretching out their long fingers. I looked at them and laughed, imagining they withdrew again when they realized they could not touch me.

The excitement of tonight beat its pulse beneath my skin; I remembered Nathan's fear and his scream, and I thought *soon.* I would be free soon, but my excitement came from more than that. Acting the part of my own spirit, watching him believe, I'd felt different. Not Ginny Langley but some *other,* more powerful yet still in some way me, as if everything I was had been distilled to some essence that was also bigger than myself.

As I approached the tent city—dark now, with the canvas shelters subtly glimmering with reflected moonlight—I did not think I would be able to sleep. There was no one about so late. Only one tent showed any signs of life, the one I knew was Sebastian DeWitt's, but the light was dim, as if his lamp were sputtering out. I could see no movement within, but it reminded me of what was at stake, what she'd said about his asking questions, and although the rest of the camp felt as if it were in the grip of a fairy tale, a sleeping spell, I crept as carefully to my tent as if it were midday. Neither of us could afford discovery now.

I pushed aside the lowered flaps and went inside. Once there, I sat upon the bedroll and took from my pocket one of the apples I'd stolen from my own pantry, biting into its sweet flesh, though my appetite—for once—had been sated by a hearty beef soup and potatoes withered in their jackets and shiny with butter, three gooseberry tarts I'd eaten while waiting for my turn to appear to my husband.

As a spirit. I laughed out loud—too loud. I covered my mouth with my hand to muffle it.

How addictive this was, how I could not wait to have my life again. And this time, it would be as I wanted it. No half measures. When Nathan was gone, I would not settle for little pieces—no, never again.

I woke at a sound, a little cry, and opened my eyes to see Bea standing there. Two thoughts chased themselves before I was fully awake. One, that she was here in this tent instead of with Sebastian DeWitt, and two, that she was white-faced with pain.

I came fully awake and sat up. "Bea?"

"I'm sorry," she said. "I didn't mean to wake you."

"What's wrong?"

"There's nothing wrong. Go back to sleep. It's early. I thought . . . if you wouldn't mind, I might sleep here for an hour or so before rehearsal. Did you get something to eat last night?"

I pushed back the blanket and rose. "Something's wrong; I can see it." I grabbed her shoulder, forcing her to face me, and she gasped as if my touch hurt her. "Why are you hurt?"

"Ginny, it's fine. It was worth it. Nathan's nearly—"

"You mean *Nathan* did this?"

A grimace. "Of course he did. Who else?"

Grimly, I demanded, "Show me."

Obediently she undid the buttons at her bodice and held out her arm. "Can you pull the sleeve, please?"

I did, taking the bodice from her, letting it fall to the floor when I saw the bruises on her arms where he'd grabbed and held her. She turned for me to undo the skirt, and when I did, and it crumpled to her feet, she lifted her chemise to show me a huge bruise, nearly black, that stretched from her hip to just below her ribs, curling a little to her back.

I lifted my gaze to hers. "Dear God. He's always had a temper, but this . . . how did he manage this?"

"I said something I shouldn't have," she said steadily, meeting my eyes without flinching. "He threw me against the dresser."

I stepped back, dismayed past bearing. "He's never hurt me. Never."

"He's not himself. I told you that."

"There must be another way, one where you needn't get so close."

She sighed and let her chemise fall. "It's all right. It hurt worse the time I fell from the mountain path in *Mazeppa*. And this will be over soon enough. I can bear anything until then."

"Bea—"

"I mean it. All this—" She gestured to her bruises. "He didn't know what he was doing. I tell you, he wasn't *there*. I don't even think he knew me. It will only take one more turn, I think."

"One more turn?"

"Like winding a watch," she said. "If you wind it too tight, it snaps. Nathan's wound very tight."

"I don't know if you can afford another turn. Look at you! You can't go to rehearsal like this."

She made a face. "I have to. We've the show in two days."

"You can hardly move."

"It will be worse tomorrow. At least he didn't hit my face. No one will even know." She hesitated. "But . . . this makes things difficult. There's Sebastian."

"He'll never allow you to go back to Nathan when he discovers this."

She made a little laugh, and then caught her breath at the pain. "He didn't want me to go back to Nathan anyway. I can't keep this from him if I'm sharing his tent."

"What will you do?"

"The only thing I can do. I'll have to . . . leave him. For now."

I felt a little moment of panic, as if it were somehow *me* leaving him. "He's not going to let you go so easily."

"I doubt it will be so difficult as you think." She closed her eyes. "God, I'm tired. I'd be glad of a rest from Nathan today. It's going to be all I can do to face Sebastian as it is."

"Then don't worry about Nathan. I've nothing to do while you're at rehearsal. Do you know where he means to be? I could appear to him."

She grabbed my arm so quickly and unexpectedly I let out a cry. "No! I don't want you near him! Do you hear me? You mustn't go near him!"

I stared at her in confusion.

"Last night, when he did this . . . it was you, not me, Ginny. He thought I was you. I think—Christ, it sounds like a mellie, I know, but I think he would kill you if he could."

"Nathan?"

"Promise you won't appear to him without me. Promise me."

"You sound so worried."

The concern I thought I'd seen in her dark eyes faded. Brutally, she said, "If he kills you, this whole plan fails, and where the hell would I be then?"

Not concern, at least not for me. I was surprised at the

disappointment I felt over it, by my sudden realization that I wanted her to be worried for me, that I wanted her to care. Who else did, after all?

"As you wish," I told her, stepping away. "I would hate to do anything to jeopardize our plan."

She gave me a careful look, as if she didn't quite believe me. "See that you don't."

Beatrice

Sebastian was gone already, so I was left to walk to the relief tent and rehearsal alone. I guessed he still hadn't decided what he meant to do with me, and that was fine. If he was distant today, it meant I could be distant back, though the thought of it left a tight little knot in my stomach that drove my hunger away, and I hurt too much to eat in any case.

Ginny didn't want me to go, but I wanted to be away from her too. I wanted some time to think about everything: last night with Nathan and what I'd seen in his eyes and how much it frightened me; what Sebastian had said to me and how it made what I meant to do so much easier.

I made my way to rehearsal, walking slowly because it hurt like hell to move, and that was going to be a pretty thing to explain to the others when I was hobbling across the stage. When I'd left Nathan that morning, he'd been sleeping, but restlessly. Last night I'd seen something that looked like murder in his eyes—or as near to it as I'd ever seen except those nights onstage when Aloysius was in good form. I hadn't lied to Ginny—I *was* afraid that if Nathan ever laid hands upon her "spirit," he would try to choke the life out of it for good. And it frightened me enough that I'd thought again about ending this.

But every time I did, I also remembered that when it was over, she would be free, and so would I.

And that was the rub, wasn't it? Because I knew how close we were, and that meant my future was about to change, and there was Sebastian DeWitt to consider, with his strange eyes and the stranger fact that I'd fallen in love with him. But some things you just couldn't have, and for now, he had to be one of them.

I felt like one big bruise, not just my body, but my emotions too, but by the time I went into the Phoenix, I didn't think anyone would have suspected I was hurt in any way at all.

The others were already onstage. Lucius and Mr. Geary watched from the makeshift benches; Sebastian was bent over the crate table. Lucius, who was sitting angled sideways, spotted me first. "Ah, there she is! You're late, my sweet. That's a two-dollar fine."

There was no point in arguing it. I had no excuse but for the one I couldn't tell them, so instead I just went to the stage. Sebastian looked over his shoulder at me, and just that one glance sent me into such confusion—desire and love and fear all tied up together—that I had to look away. And then I was mired in rehearsal, and I had to concentrate so hard on remembering my lines despite the pain that jarred up into my chest with every motion that I had no more time to think of what we would say to each other.

When the rehearsal was over, Lucius said, "Two more nights, my children, and then it's opening night at the Phoenix!" and we all clapped like dutiful little servants and I didn't feel the excitement I usually felt at the thought of opening night—and my first one as lead besides. As the others left, I stepped gingerly off the stage, slowly enough that Sebastian, who was gathering up his papers, could ignore me and hurry off if he liked. I was happy to play the coward today, even though there had to be a reckoning before evening.

But, of course, because I wanted him to flee, he waited. He buckled his leather bag and slung it over his shoulder and stood there watching me come toward him, and it was all I could do to straighten my shoulders and keep from clenching my teeth in pain.

When I got close enough to speak, he asked nastily, "Too busy with schemes this morning to be on time?"

My temper flared. "Go to hell."

"I'm already there," he said—which was such a fucking writerlike thing to say that I laughed out loud—and then regretted it for the pain.

But I don't think he saw it. I managed to say, "How clever. You must write mellies."

"It feels lately as if I've been living one." He sighed and gave me a wary look. "Let's go."

"I thought you were angry with me," I needled.

"I am. But I'm willing to try to understand."

And, you know, that would have been enough any other time. It was still more than I deserved, and don't think I didn't know that. I wanted to let him take me into his arms and back to the tent we shared. But then I thought of what he would see when he undressed me, and so I pushed past him and said, "That's not good enough, Bastian."

"Bea—"

He had taken my arm to slow me, a gentle touch, but it hurt so I had to work to keep from crying out in pain. I jerked away. "Don't touch me."

He frowned. "What is it? What's wrong?"

"I'll be getting my own tent this afternoon."

He went still. "You don't mean that. You can't mean it."

"Believe me, I do."

He looked so damned confused that I hated it. He glanced around—only Lucius and Mr. Geary remained, but Lucius was watching like a vulture while pretending not to. Sebastian bent close, whispering in my ear, "What are you so afraid of?"

"I'm not afraid."

"Then why are you running away from me?"

"Because you don't trust me."

"Then show me I can. I want to believe you, Bea. Explain things to me."

"There's nothing to explain."

He let out his breath in exasperation. "I know you're lying to me. I *know* it. What I don't understand is why."

I made myself think of Ginny. Of money. I made myself think of my own company. The future we'd planned. I made my voice as even as I could. "I think it's best if we—"

"Don't say it."

"—if we part. Until things settle."

His gaze riveted to mine. "Until things settle? What things?"

"I don't know, Sebastian. Please. Just . . . let me go. This has all been so . . . so much. I need some time."

They were the hardest damn words I'd ever said, and he did nothing to make it easier. He just looked at me in that way he had—as if I was suddenly illuminated to him.

"Very well," he said quietly. "You want time. I can give you that."

I didn't know what to say. I'd expected more of an argument. Once again, he'd managed to disconcert me. And when he looked away, I felt as terrible as I'd ever felt, and yet relieved too, that he was letting it be so easy.

But then he turned back to me again, taking my chin, tilting my face up so he could kiss me, and it was soft and lovely, like the first kiss we'd shared, and I thought of my room and the whiskey and the apricots and suddenly the taste of them was strong in my mouth and I couldn't bear it.

"Let me walk you back," he whispered when he pulled away.

I shook my head. "You go on. I think I'll just stay here for a while."

I didn't watch him leave me. I went to the table where Lucius and Mr. Geary were, and I sat down, putting my face in my hands, and told myself I'd done the right thing. I'd done what I had to do. It was only until this was over anyway. It wasn't forever.

But when I felt Lucius's hand on my shoulder and heard him say, "He'll come back, my sweet. I've never seen a man so besotted," it was all I could do to force back my tears.

Chapter Thirty-six

I didn't sleep well. The bruises hurt, and the ground was so damned hard, and I told myself it was that, and not the fact that I wasn't with Sebastian. But all that sleeplessness had a good effect, I suppose, because lying there in the darkness, I thought of *Penelope Justis* and how Barnabus had seen Florence's spirit in a crowd at a ball, just as Nathan had seen Ginny at Mrs. Wilcox's, and that made me think of a plan for the spirit to appear at *Much Ado,* where Nathan would surely be because it was the debut of the Phoenix, and Ginny's father too. I had to admit it was damned clever.

When she woke that morning, I told her what I'd come up with. She gave me a dubious look. "You're certain? What about the rest of the company? Surely they would recognize me?"

"You'll be wearing a mask. And they won't even look at you," I said—I was at least confident of that. I couldn't have told you what any of the supernumeraries we used looked like. They were faceless crowds, servants with no lines, strollers in a park, passers-by. "It's not as if you'll be onstage, is it? I'll steal a mask from one of the others. All you have to do is walk outside. Everyone will just assume you're one of the company. I'll lure Nathan outside, and you can appear to him and come back here."

She still seemed doubtful.

"Do you have a better plan?"

"No," she said. "We'll need a doctor. To commit Nathan."

I sighed. Another thing to do. "Yes, I suppose."

"David Reynolds."

I stared at her blankly. "Who?"

"The man who helped me put up this tent. The one who so admired you. I promised him tickets to the next show at the Regal."

"So?"

"He's a *doctor,* Bea. And one enamored enough with you that he might listen *very hard* to what you have to say."

"Why . . . that's a good idea."

"All you must do is talk to him. His practice is on Front Street. He must have a tent there himself by now. Tell him you're worried about a madman who's been following you, et cetera. Make certain he's at the show."

"We'll need two doctors, won't we? To commit him?"

"If Nathan is at the play, my father will be there too," she said, shaking her head. "Believe me, if he thinks Nathan's mad, we won't need another doctor. Papa will see that things are taken care of."

So it was set. All I needed was to find her a domino. The mask part was easy; Mrs. Chace was making them, and she was distracted at best, it would be easy to borrow one before the show started. No one would miss it until the cue to go onstage, and I'd have it back well before then. The plan wasn't perfect, but it was the best I could do.

Somehow I managed to get through rehearsal, though it wasn't easy, because Sebastian was there as usual, and how you feel about someone doesn't just stop because you want it to. I did my best to ignore him, and when rehearsal was over I watched him walk away and my throat closed up, and it was only by teasing Aloys about the filthy lace on his cuffs that I kept from crying.

"What ails our playwright this morning?" Jack asked, sitting down beside me and giving me this concerned look that I knew was all pretense. "He seems mightily struck dumb. Had I to guess, I would think him sick at heart. What have you done to him, my love?"

I rose. "Go to hell, Jack."

I went to the dry goods tent where Aloys said they'd got the bunting for the curtain. They had a bit of it left, along with a packet of needles, and the woman there gave me what thread she could spare. Then I went to look for David Reynolds, M.D.

As I made my way along Front Street, there were dozens of men working among the ruins, great piles of twisted railroad track and huge metal cogs and other piles of charred planks and pilings. Smoke still rose from the coal bunkers beyond, and the whole harbor was veiled by its haze, so the masts of schooners and steamer smokestacks seemed disembodied, floating in a fog like some Gothic stage set, while seagulls dipped and soared, disappearing and appearing like ghosts—the world seemed full of them, my mind stuck on spirits.

I didn't have to go far before I found Dr. Reynolds's tent, bordered on one side by piles of ash and on the other by a lawyer's tent. He'd painted DR. DAVID REYNOLDS above in black, and the tent flaps were wide open to show a cot and a table—which I supposed he'd been lucky to get. The man sitting on a crate before it looked just as Ginny had described, and when I stepped up, pasting a smile on my face, he leaped up so quickly from the crate that he dislodged it.

"Mrs. Wilkes!" he said, his smile so large I thought it might actually split his face. "How wonderful to see you! You look . . . well. Better than when I saw you last, I must confess."

I smiled. "A bit cleaner, no doubt."

"Please, sit down."

I shook my head. I thought perhaps I recognized him; there were many people who came to the theater night after night, and his face looked familiar. But now I was pretending I'd been the one he'd spoken to at Fort Spokane, and so I said, "I hope you're doing well, Dr. Reynolds. I haven't seen you about the camp."

"I've moved down here. It's better to stay with my equipment, such as it is."

"Well, I've been looking for you. To say thank you again, and also to tell you there will be tickets at the door for you when the Phoenix rises on Monday night."

His smile broadened, as impossible as that seemed. "I would be there in any case, Mrs. Wilkes. I am your most devoted admirer. It was an honor to help you."

I smiled again and motioned toward the cot. "No doubt you've been busy."

"Yes indeed, though things have slowed this afternoon, thankfully. Burns, broken arms, that sort of thing."

"I suppose it was lucky no one was killed."

"Very lucky," he said.

"I imagine some were quite"—I fumbled for the words—"undone by the tragedy."

"Undone? Oh, I'd say so."

"I have a friend . . . an admirer, like yourself. But since the fire, he's been strange. Almost as if it . . . unhinged him."

Dr. Reynolds clicked his tongue in sympathy. "It's been a strain for many. Some have lost everything."

"I've wondered, do you think . . . could it be a temporary illness?"

"In some, certainly. But I would have to see him to know for certain."

"Oh, yes, of course. It's only that he's been quite out of his head."

David Reynolds frowned. "In what way?"

"He's been seeing things. Ghosts and such. And he's been violent—"

"Has he threatened you in any way, Mrs. Wilkes? Do you think him a danger?"

I let out my breath in feigned relief and gave him my best strained smile. "I must admit I've been a little afraid. He's very ardent, you see. I think he might be mad."

"Who is he? Perhaps I can pay him a visit. To ascertain the extent of his condition."

"Oh, I couldn't ask it—"

"I'd be honored to serve. I don't like to think of you in any kind of distress. If I can in any way put your mind at ease—"

I hesitated. "Well, I doubt he'll like you paying him a visit, but I expect he'll be at the show. Perhaps you could watch him. Discreetly, of course—"

"Of course."

"—and tell me what you think I should do."

"What does he look like?"

"I think you must recognize him," I said. "His name is Nathan Langley."

Dr. Reynolds looked taken aback. "*The* Nathan Langley?"

"Yes, I know. It's very difficult, I'm sure you understand the situation. But"—here I wrung my hands in my skirt and tried to look distressed—"but I do think he might be dangerous, and I'm afraid."

Reynolds said quietly, "Has he hurt you, Mrs. Wilkes?"

It was perfect, how well he played his part. I could not have asked for better. Carefully, I pulled up my sleeve to show the edge of the bruise that covered nearly my whole arm now, and I was rewarded by his little gasp. "That's only the start of it," I confessed in a whisper.

"My dear Mrs. Wilkes." He looked absolutely shocked and horrified.

"It's all right." I shoved the sleeve down again. "He was out of his head when he did it. I—I'm hoping it's only that the fire, and the loss of his wife—"

"I think you should stay away from him. Until I have the chance to observe him for myself."

"Then you'll be at the performance?" I asked.

He nodded, his smile completely gone now, his mouth a tight line. "I would not miss it."

So that was done, and I was relieved as I made my way to the relief tent for a meal and then back to the tent city, carrying my pile of bunting and the needles. I didn't see Sebastian at either place—another relief, though I missed him, and that was not something I was used to.

Ginny was waiting in the tent, of course, lying on the bedroll and staring up at the ceiling, and I could tell the moment I came in that she'd been thinking, because what else did she have to do all day but that? I gave her the bread I'd brought, but she didn't open the packet, just stared down at it unseeingly.

I sat down opposite from her and pulled out the needles and the thread and began to sew the domino. "I spoke to the good Dr. Reynolds this afternoon. He's so ready to see Nathan as mad I think he might do so even without observation."

Her gaze came up to meet mine. "Do you think this might do it? Do you think this could be the end of it?"

"Perhaps. And Ginny, you've got to keep your distance from him. I mean it. Promise me you will."

Something came into her eyes then, some quick flash, and she thinned her lips the way she always did when she was readying to do something that mattered to her, and it shook me that I knew her well enough to know it. "My father will be there. Nathan wouldn't dare hurt me."

"I suppose not," I said reluctantly. "But promise me all the same."

She nodded. "I promise."

She said it quickly, and with enough emphasis that I should have been reassured. But there was something else there too, her delight in risk, that edge that made her impossible to predict, and it made me think once again of *Macbeth,* the forest marching on the castle, the unexpected turn, and I was suddenly afraid.

"Just follow the plan, Ginny," I told her.

She gave me a slow smile. "Of course I will. What else would I do?"

And it was stupid, I know, to be comforted, to bask in that smile of hers, but I was, and I did, and when I finally finished that domino, and we went to sleep, I'd forgotten all about that strange foreboding.

Chapter Thirty-seven

Usually dress rehearsals were just short of tragedy in the sheer scope of disaster that accompanied them. We'd never had a dress rehearsal where it didn't look like the show itself was doomed: people sticking, flats falling over and splintering, wrong backdrops, doors not opening as they were meant to . . . you name it, and it happened. But the one for *Much Ado* went off without a hitch, and that should have been my first clue that opening night itself would be a disaster.

Had it been any other performance, I would have known to expect it, and I had no excuse for ignoring it this time, because so much depended on it, and that alone should have raised an alarm. But the truth was that as nervous as I was that everything should go as it was supposed to, I was also excited—not only because of what Ginny and I meant to do tonight, but also because that was how I always was before a show, and it was hard to separate my excitement and dread from the nervousness I felt over our plan. This was my first performance as lead, besides, so there was that too. And it had been weeks since I'd been in front of an audience. I hadn't realized how much I'd missed it.

I'd sent a note to Nathan early that morning asking if I should save him tickets for the show, and he had sent the boy back with a yes. I hadn't seen him for two days, and I hoped it wasn't too long, that he hadn't somehow found his sanity again in that time.

So given all that, I suppose it's not too hard to imagine how much trouble I was having keeping a straight thought as I went down to the theater. Ginny was going to meet me there later, behind the tent, where the set carpenters had piled the crates and pieces of wood and barrels that they'd managed to collect. Easy for her to hide in and around. She had the rough domino I'd fashioned, and when I got to the Phoenix I saw the masks Mrs. Chace had made hanging from a nail in the tent post—not as elaborate as they would have been any other time, just painted papier-mâché on a stick, stuck with what looked like seagull feathers, which were never hard to find. Everything was as it was supposed to be. As I dressed in the butterfly gown and put on my makeup in the makeshift backstage space, my whole body seemed to hum; even my bruises didn't hurt.

No separate dressing rooms here; there was barely room to move. We were practically falling over one another. The others were laughing and talking in low voices; we could hear the audience arriving, Lucius's hearty voice as he welcomed them and collected the tickets. The tent could not hold even a quarter of the number of people we would usually have had on an opening night, and we were sold out within minutes. When I crossed the stage to peek through the curtain, I saw lumbermen and miners, one or two merchants I recognized. Dr. Reynolds about halfway. Sebastian standing at the back. I made myself look away, to find Nathan—ah, there he was, come just as we'd hoped, third row from the front. The oil lamps serving as footlights were lit, the reflection casting onto his face, but even allowing for that, he looked terrible, his eyes red-rimmed, the circles beneath them deep, shaded pockets. No macassar in his hair; in fact, it looked unbrushed, and his tie was so messy as to be nearly undone. He sat between two men who looked prosperous—one should have been Ginny's father, but neither looked old enough.

I backed away from the curtain. It was time to meet Ginny. I stepped off the stage, through the others—a few other supernumeraries standing about looking nervous, Brody and Susan snapping at each other as they always did, Aloys glancing up idly as he read the newspaper, Jack too busy trying to put on kohl by a tiny shaving mirror to pay attention. I grabbed one of the masks and slipped out the back. The sun had set, the shadows were growing. She was there, near the pile of salvaged wood.

She came from her hiding spot and glanced around nervously. "Is he here?" She was wearing the cape and had drawn the hood up over her hair.

I handed her the mask. "Yes. How old is your father?"

"Fifty-eight. Did you see him?"

"No. But I suppose he and Nathan might not be sitting together."

She frowned. "Of course they would. He must be there somewhere."

"I suppose you're right. I wouldn't know him anyway." I looked her over. "Are you ready?"

Again, that expression I was beginning to recognize. "More than ready."

"Then it's time."

I left her there and went back inside. One of the stagehands shouted, "Five minutes!"

I grabbed the prop boy, who was darting furiously about. "Peter, go tell Mr. Langley to meet me outside."

He gave me an impatient look. "Bea, it's five minutes, didn't you hear? I don't got time—"

"Just do it. I can't go on without seeing him."

Peter halted and sighed. No one checked an actor's obsession with good luck; he was used to stupid little requests, strange whims; we all had them.

"All right," he said sullenly and went to deliver my message.

I slipped out again, past the dark shadow of her huddling against the pile of wood pieces. She reached out a hand, and I grabbed it and squeezed, and then she released me and withdrew deeper into the shadows, and I went around the corner to the side of the tent, out of sight of any last-minute stragglers. The night was warm, the talk loud, the tent pulsing with lamplight and bodies. My mouth was dry with nerves.

It seemed I waited forever, but it could not have been more than a few moments before Nathan came around the corner. His eyes still looked haunted, which reassured me. Whatever the two days apart from me had given him, peace was not it.

"What is it?" he asked. "The boy said you needed me."

"You're my good luck charm," I said, drawing him close. "I wanted a kiss."

Obediently, distractedly, he kissed me.

I said, "How are you? It's been two days. I was worried."

He looked away. "No one believes me."

"About what?"

"That I keep seeing her. And my nightmares . . . they've grown worse."

I noticed then that his hands were trembling. "I'm certain they'll fade when her body is found. Has her father come? Is he here?"

Nathan shook his head. "His train was delayed. He won't arrive until tomorrow."

Not as we'd planned. I felt the change like a little jump. I tried to think . . . what to do? We needed him. There was no second doctor. Perhaps it would be better to postpone this, to tell Ginny to wait—

And just at that moment, with his usual impeccable timing, Sebastian came around the corner. "Bea, they're ready to—"

Ginny swept out.

Sebastian stopped short. Beside me, Nathan froze.

"No," I heard myself saying. "Oh no, no, no . . ."

Too late. Too late to change anything, to do anything. Nathan grasped my bruised arm so hard I cried out in pain, and I saw the way Sebastian's face paled, though he wasn't looking at me. He was staring at her, and she had lowered the mask so Nathan could see her face, and I saw her shock too, her horror at seeing Sebastian, and then, quickly, she turned and ran back behind the tent. Not fast enough.

Nathan gasped, "Ginny!" His voice was a stifled scream. "Ginny!"

I grabbed his arm to hold him. "Nathan, for God's sake—"

He jerked away. "Ginny!" He ran after her.

I shouted, "Nathan, don't!" Desperately I glanced back at Sebastian, who gave me a look of pure fury as he tore off after Nathan, and I followed.

I came around the corner just in time to see Sebastian ducking through the back flap leading to backstage. Inside was chaos. Supernumeraries muttering, Jack on his feet, the kohl brush still in his hand. "What the hell—"

Nathan lunged, wrecking the place as he looked for her. Masks fell to the floor. Capes. A prop chair. "Where is she! Where are you hiding her?"

I screamed, "Nathan!"

Lucius stepped from the wings. "What the hell is this commotion?"

Nathan lurched up the two steps to the stage, pushing Lucius out of the way hard, sending him crashing into the backdrop. "Where is she? Where are you hiding her?" A flat clattered to the floor, and then another, as Nathan tore the set apart. I heard Aloysius's deep voice shouting, "For God's sake, stop him!" The audience was on its feet, unhappy murmurs, chaos, shouting. Some clapped and laughed as if they thought it part of the show.

Sebastian leaped up the stairs, tackling Nathan where he stood on the stage, and Nathan struggled and fought his hold, shouting, "You saw her! You saw her too, I know you did!"

Lucius struggled to his feet, but it was Aloys who plunged toward them, grabbing Nathan's other arm to help Sebastian wrangle Nathan offstage, back into the wings. I stood at the bottom of the two stairs, and Nathan looked up at me, his face reddened, spittle flecking his lips.

And I froze, because that was the look I'd seen when he'd thrown me against that dresser. Pure murder, and I went cold with fear and grabbed Jack, who'd come up beside me, so he looked at me in confusion.

Lucius called out, "Calm down, Langley. For God's sake, calm down or we shall have to call the police."

But Nathan didn't calm down. He snarled at me, "It's you! It's your fault. She comes for you!" He looked wild—there was nothing human behind those eyes—and at that moment he jerked, throwing both Sebastian and Aloys loose, and I turned and ran, pushing past Jack, past the supernumeraries, toward the back flap, only a few steps, but there was Mrs. Chace standing there, blocking my way.

"Move!" I screamed, and I saw her look up and past me, and her mouth opened, and I knew Nathan was there, just steps away—

Something crashed. Someone screamed, and I twisted to see where he was, and Jack made this flying leap like some mellie hero and Nathan went down under him like a sack of potatoes, and then Sebastian was pulling me hard out of the way.

"I apologize, ladies and gentlemen, but we will have no show tonight after all!" Lucius's voice carried from the stage. "There will be another performance tomorrow night, hopefully with less disruption! Your tickets are still good!"

I thought: *there's Lucius for you. Never offer a refund.* And then everything hit me, the way Nathan looked, his shouting, his near attack and Ginny's escape and my fear, and I began to tremble. Jack was still sitting on Nathan and two soldiers with their rifles pushed through the crowd—thank God for the militia—along with Dr. Reynolds, who was saying, "Please. Please, I'm a doctor."

"Let's get you out of here," Sebastian said, taking me out the back of the tent, but not gently, and when we stepped outside I realized I was still shaking.

But he wasn't going to soothe me or comfort me; I saw that now. His eyes were blazing—black fury was a misnomer; it really should be called blue instead. He could set something afire with that heat. And then, you know, I realized that what he meant to set afire was me.

He strode fast, pulling me away from the Phoenix, down the street. No doubt he meant to walk that way every step, propelling me along, and I felt every bruise.

"Slow down," I complained. "He's not about to get loose from those soldiers."

"I thought he couldn't get loose from me and Metairie either," he said grimly, but he let go of me and slowed, glancing over his shoulder as he did so. "He was right, wasn't he? That was his wife, wasn't it?"

And though it was stupid to try, I did. "I don't know what you mean."

He gripped my arm so hard I yelped. "The woman in the cape," he said through clenched teeth. "It was Mrs. Langley. She's alive, and you've known it all this time, haven't you?"

"You're hurting me."

"What game are you two playing?"

I stopped short. "Damn you. Let go of me."

"It all makes sense to me now. She's alive and flitting about town, pretending to be her spirit. You've convinced Langley that she's dead, and that she's haunting him."

"I don't know what he thinks he's seeing."

"God *damn* you, Bea. It's *Penelope,* isn't it? Isn't it? That's what the two of you are doing. Christ, why didn't I see it before now? He's Barnabus. You mean to turn him mad."

I glared at him. "What an imagination you have."

He glared right back at me. "All the time, I thought I was writing it for you, and I was, but only so you could use it as a manual. My God, what have you been doing in the time you've spent with him?"

"Fucking him mostly," I said meanly.

He gave me a little shake. "Do you have any idea what you've done?"

There was no point in denying it any longer. "We had to do something! You don't know what he meant to do to her! He meant to put her in an asylum. That was the reason he let her do *Penelope* to begin with. Nathan and her father meant to have her committed."

"How do you know that?"

"She found a letter. Nathan wanted her money and her father wanted her out of the way. She was an embarrassment, and so they thought to put her in an asylum and Nathan meant to use me to do it. Haven't you noticed how much we look alike?"

"I've noticed," he said grimly.

"The things he did . . . he used me too, Bastian. That's why he wanted me. Because I could fool people into thinking I was her from a distance. We're only doing to him what he meant to do to her. We followed your play step by step. Well, except for tonight. Because I didn't have the last two scenes and—"

"Christ, Bea, do you know how *Penelope Justis* ends?"

"Barnabus goes insane, doesn't he? You haven't changed that?"

"Yes, he goes insane," he snapped.

"That's all we want. Just for Nathan to be committed so Ginny can be free—"

"Barnabus goes insane, yes, but he commits suicide, Bea. He kills himself. But not before he kills Penelope too."

I stared at him. "He commits suicide? He kills Penelope?"

Sebastian held my gaze. "Do you understand now?"

"But . . . why?"

"Because the spirit only appears when Penelope does. Barnabus kills Penny because he cannot kill the spirit, and then he kills himself because of what he's done."

"It's you! It's your fault. She comes for you!"

"My God," I whispered. "Why didn't you tell me?"

"I had no idea what you were doing, or I would have."

"Well, it doesn't have to end that way, does it? Those soldiers have Nathan. Everyone can see he's quite insane."

"He's Nathan Langley, Bea," Sebastian said steadily. "What do you think they'll do without a wife or relative to commit him?"

And suddenly I understood the great flaw in our plan. "They'll take him home," I said dully. "If he's still raving, they'll give him laudanum. And in the morning, everyone will pretend they saw nothing."

"Yes. And then what do you think he'll do?"

"He'll come after me."

Sebastian let out his breath and raked a hand through his hair. "Unfortunately, I think you're right."

I'd been frightened before; now I was terrified. I thought of how Nathan had thrown me against the dresser and his violence after, the wildness of his eyes back there in the theater. I thought of his scream when he'd seen her. And I thought of her alone in our tent, thinking everything had gone perfectly, and suddenly I was nearly running toward camp, too panicked to care that it hurt. Suddenly, I had to find her; I had to be sure she was safe.

Sebastian hurried after me, pulling me to a stop, and I said, "Ginny's alone."

"She's safe enough for now."

Of course he was right. There were soldiers with rifles holding Nathan. They would take him home, as Sebastian had said. They would dope him with laudanum. She was safe tonight.

But there was something else, some feeling I had, and I couldn't put it right. Some panic that snaked its way through me like a lit fuse, and I couldn't just leave it be. Something was wrong; I could *feel* it.

"I need to see for myself," I told him. "I want to be certain."

"Bea—"

I was moving before he could say anything else. In the end he had no choice but to follow. I walked so fast that even my panic couldn't keep me from gasping in pain, and I saw his little sideways glance and ignored it and kept ignoring it as we hurried the blocks, and it was still taking too long. Too damn long. Then finally we were at the camp, and it looked quiet and comforting as *The Western Home* made the prairie out to be, campfires and lamps glowing through tent walls in the darkness and someone laughing. No chaos at all, no screams of panic. But still I didn't believe it. Still, I went as quickly as I could to her tent.

I was saying her name even before I burst inside, into darkness. "Ginny?"

Silence.

I didn't believe it. Where the hell could she be if not here? "Ginny?"

Sebastian came in just behind me. "Perhaps she's gone to the privy," he said, and I dodged around him and was out again, scanning the darkness, searching for her, racing like some madwoman, thinking I could ask someone until I remembered that no one knew us to tell us apart. I was standing right before them; how could I ask if they'd seen *me*?

I ran to the privy, which was empty, and then to the water

barrels, but there was only a little girl there dipping water. Ginny was nowhere; she was gone completely. Where else would she go?

When I got back to the tent, I couldn't breathe for panic. Sebastian had lit a candle. He stood there, his head bowed beneath the canvas, staring at a paper in his hand. I recognized it as a page from the revision of *Much Ado*.

He looked up when I stepped inside, and held out the paper. "Read this." His voice was so grim it seemed to stop my heart. "Maybe you can make sense of it."

I took the paper. Geary had copied Sebastian's adaptation on both sides; but in the top margin, heavily written in ink that she'd no doubt pilfered from Sebastian's tent, it said:

> *Bea—*
>
> *One more turn, I think. I've gone to wind him. Back soon.*
>
> *G.*

Chapter Thirty-eight

Geneva

When I stepped from behind that tent and looked into my husband's eyes, I knew it was almost over. Not even in our most passionate moments had Nathan looked at me like that, and now, to see the fear that came along with it, how he seemed to almost spasm with it, filled me with a gruesome satisfaction. Bea had said she thought he was close to succumbing, that she felt it would take one more turn, and I knew the moment I heard his scream that it was true.

But I had not expected to see Sebastian DeWitt standing there, and the sight of him, the recognition I saw in his expression, sent me into a panic. All I could think of was escape. Mr. DeWitt wasn't supposed to be there—why was he there? Why hadn't she warned me?

I dodged to the other side of the tent and flew through the darkness. Perhaps we could still salvage something, though how that was possible if Sebastian DeWitt knew the truth, I didn't know. But I was certain that it had to end now, tonight. Now that Sebastian DeWitt knew, it had to end, and that was the fact that rang in my head, a thought of such brilliant clarity that I knew what I must do, how I must hurry. I was uncertain how long I had before Nathan returned home. I did not know whether they would take him there now or whether he was subdued. Whichever it was, it did nothing to change my plan. If there were people with him, I must only wait until they were gone. If he were dulled into a laudanum haze, so much the better. *One more turn,* she'd said, and I knew I could finish this tonight. I had seen the madness in his eyes, and I knew I could push it further. In any case, I had no choice. Mr. DeWitt's witness had made certain of it.

The camp was quiet and dark. I went into Mr. DeWitt's tent, stumbling against the shadow of a makeshift desk, grabbing up the first piece of paper I felt, then trying to find a pen or a nib. There was one, along with a bottle of ink. Quickly I uncapped it and dipped the nib and scrawled a note on the top of the page, and then I put the ink back and took the note to my tent. I laid it upon the bedroll before I started out again, on my way to my house, to finish things once and for all with my husband.

I had no real plan beyond that. To end it was all I thought. To appear to him, to send him screaming and terrified into the arms of Bonnie or the cook, to watch the police come to take him away. And then, *voilà*! I would be myself again. Geneva Stratford Langley returned from the dead, amnesia gone, restored to my life.

I reached the house. Lights—oil lamps, candles—blazed from

every window but that of my bedroom. The carriage stood outside; I pulled back into the shadows of the huge maple until I was certain the yard was empty, and then I hurried through the darkness to the side yard, to the parlor doors. The curtains were drawn; I pressed my ear to the glass and listened for any noise, but it was quiet. Not even the clink of the sherry decanter. Still, I waited; one minute, two. Still nothing. I opened the door carefully and slipped inside, shielding myself in the drapes.

It was then that I heard the footsteps in the hallway, the sound of quickly conferring voices, Bonnie's quick assent, the light tap of her heels as she hurried away. I froze, waiting, straining to listen. The voices were low—men's voices. I thought I heard the words *laudanum, needs sleep,* something about morning, and then there were Bonnie's footsteps again, and her pert voice, carrying beautifully, "We'll keep a close eye on him, Dr. Berry."

Berry. The doctor who had examined me. The thought made me furious again, and more determined than ever. Tonight I would see to it that Nathan never had such power over me again.

I heard the front door open, the sounds of farewell, the close. I heard their steps down the pathway to the street. The front drapes were drawn as well; I could not see the men get into the carriage, but I heard the close of the door, the rattling of wheels, and then they were off, and Bonnie went down the hall again, back toward the kitchen, and it was my chance.

I stepped from the drapes to the parlor door and opened it—just a crack at first, peeking through, and then, when I saw no one, I stepped into the hall. As quietly and quickly as I could, I went to the stairs, hurrying up them, down the hall, and there was Nathan's room, his door shut firmly. On the table outside was a brown bottle, a pitcher and a glass, a spoon. I touched the lip of the bottle and brought my finger to my lips, tasting laudanum. I wondered how much they'd given him, how deeply asleep he would be. Perhaps not much. Perhaps just enough for tranquility, that wonderful, drowsy languor where everything seemed a dream.

I turned the knob and stepped inside—the small oil lamp at the bedside burning, the flame dancing against the glass, illuminating Nathan's pale face, his hair. I closed the door behind me. His breathing was even; but he was tightly wound even in sleep, twitching lightly. Blessed laudanum. It would not be enough to save him tonight. I thought of the great bruise on Bea's body, her arms. I thought of what he had meant to do to me.

I stepped to the foot of the bed. I leaned down, pressing my hands into the mattress, near his feet. "Nathan," I whispered.

He stirred, whimpering a little.

I jarred the mattress. "Nathan, my love. Wake up. Wake up and see me. Your darling Ginny come to life."

A restless twitch.

"You *will* see me, darling," I said, but this time I went around to the side of the bed. This time I knelt beside it, leaning forward to whisper into his ear, "Wake and be damned, my love."

He started so suddenly I fell back, fully awake in a moment, blinking, rigid. "Bea!" he said, and then profound confusion. "Ginny?"

I rose, stepping back, smiling. "Do you not recognize your own wife?" I asked him, needling, nasty. "Or have you put me aside so quickly?"

He went white. "Ginny. Why? Why does your spirit torment me?"

"I'm in hell, my darling. And now I've come to take you with me."

He made a strangled sound, a half scream, pushing aside the blankets as if they pained him, his movements clumsy with laudanum. "Come, Bea, come to bed—"

"Bea isn't here, Nathan. Only me. Only the spirit of your *darling* wife. Come to me, my love." I stepped closer; I held out my arms. I gave him my nastiest smile. They had doped him so well he was swaying. His eyes round with horror, the pulse beat fast in his throat.

But I underestimated him, as I had always done.

"Bea," he spat, and then he lurched from the bed, too fast; I had no time to back away. I turned to flee, but he grabbed my arm, jerking me back hard. I fell into him, then onto the bed, him on top of me, his fist slamming hard into my face, my scream, sparks before my eyes.

I tried to roll away; it was useless, and he was a madman, and as he hit me again, I thought it was truly over; I could not escape him. He screamed, "I shall send you straight to hell!"

The door bounced open; someone came racing into the room, someone grabbing Nathan, pulling him off me. I heard him crash into the dresser; I heard him scream. I saw Bonnie hovering in the doorway, "I let them in, sir. They said—" Her gasp when she saw me. "Mrs. Langley?"

And then there was a face above mine—Bea's face, her dark eyes large and worried.

"Damn him," she said, and then her arm was behind my head, helping me sit up. "Are you all right, Ginny? Christ, why did you do such a stupid thing? Are you all right?"

I nodded, wiping the blood from my nose with a shaking hand.

"I told you he would kill you," she whispered, and she pulled me hard into her side.

There was Sebastian DeWitt standing beyond—the one who had dispatched Nathan—and now he strode over, as concerned as she was. "Thank God we got here as quickly as we did."

None of us were watching him. I should have known to watch him. He'd been clever all his life. My head was throbbing. I tasted blood. My left eye would not quite focus. When I saw a movement beyond DeWitt I thought it was the curtain blowing from the open window; it took me a moment to see that it wasn't that at all, but the white of Nathan's nightshirt, and by then it was too late. I heard the slide of the dresser drawer and Bonnie's scream. DeWitt spun around and went stock-still.

Nathan stood unsteadily, the gun he kept in that desk drawer in his hand, wavering from DeWitt to Bea, who knelt on the bed beside me, her arm around my shoulders, to me. He was full of laudanum; I wonder if he even knew who he meant to shoot.

He pointed the gun at me, smiling, skull-like, his lips drawn back over his teeth, feral. "Which is Ginny?" Singsong, and then pointed the gun at her. "Which one Bea? Or are you both spirits come to take me to hell?"

"Langley," DeWitt warned.

"You don't want to do this, Nathan," Bea said steadily, her

voice reverberating against my cheek. "We've come to help you—"

"To help me straight to hell," he said.

"No," she insisted. "Please, Nathan. Put the gun down."

"Which are you? Ginny? Bea? Or am I seeing double?" Nathan laughed; once again, he pointed the gun at me.

DeWitt stepped toward him slowly, hands outstretched. "She's right. You don't want to do this. Give me the gun, Langley—"

I heard the blast; I saw the flare of the gunpowder, blinding—it seared into my brain along with the pain, exploding through my shoulder, slamming me back into the bed.

I heard Bea's scream as if from far away. Then she was bending over me, pressing her hand to my shoulder, her hands red with blood—they should not be so red, should they?

My vision blurred, but I saw Nathan with a sharp clarity as he lifted the gun again, aiming at her. I opened my mouth, trying to warn her. So fast, too fast. And then a blur of movement, blocking my view of my husband, at the same time I heard the second shot, so loud it echoed in my ears.

Bea gasped and jerked.

Beyond her, Sebastian DeWitt sagged to his knees, swayed, and thudded to the floor.

Bea screamed, "Bastian! No!" and let go of me, flinging herself at him. He struggled to get to his elbows—still alive, thank God. Still alive. But . . . there was so much blood. His shirt . . . it had been so white and now . . . there shouldn't be so much blood, should there?

His hand went to his chest. "He . . . shot me," he said, this wondering voice. He brought his hand away again, fingers covered with blood, and stared at it, and then he said, "Bea?" and then he crumpled.

Bea cried out in anguish. She tore at his shirt, pressing on the wound, screaming at Bonnie, "Get a doctor! Send for a goddamned doctor!" Then, pleading, desperate, "Bastian, no. No, don't die. You can't. Bastian, please. Please, I love you. Don't leave me—"

"Dear God." Nathan's voice now. He was pale as death. His eyes were blank. His hands shook. "He shouldn't have stepped in the way! He shouldn't have!" And then, "What have I done? Ginny?"

Bea's sobs echoed. But Nathan wasn't looking at her or Sebastian DeWitt as he lifted the gun. He was looking at me.

The third blast reverberated through the room.

I felt the splatter against my face, warm and wet. Bonnie screamed, "Mr. Langley!"

But Nathan was already past hearing.

Chapter Thirty-nine

He'd been trying to save her, trying to save both of us. The scene played out in my mind like the worst nightmare, a tragedy in three acts, and my eyes were blurry with tears when I opened them. I hoped she would be there to tell me it wasn't true, that he had somehow survived.

But it wasn't Bea who met my gaze. It was my father.

I felt groggy and sick with pain, the aftertaste of laudanum heavy on my tongue, but even so, Papa looked aged almost beyond recognition, exhausted, shadowed circles beneath his eyes, worry lining his face, along with the ravages of grief. When he saw I was awake, he grabbed my uninjured hand, but the movement jostled the bandage and sling on my other arm, and I moaned.

"I'm sorry," he whispered, releasing my hand again quickly. "Did I hurt you? I'm sorry. Would you like more laudanum?"

"You're here," I said. And I knew it was something I should have been worried about, but I wasn't. I didn't care about him just now. "Where's Bea?"

My father frowned. "Bea? Do you mean that actress?"

"Where is she?"

"Gone home, I imagine. She was here, but some friends of hers arrived to take her away. She was quite exhausted. Apparently she'd been watching over you until I arrived last night."

"And . . . is he all right? Tell me he's all right."

My father's expression contorted. "I'm sorry to tell you that

Nathan's dead, my dear. In the end, I don't think he knew what he was about. Or perhaps he did and that was why . . . well, he's gone. I'm sorry."

"I didn't mean him. I meant . . . Mr. DeWitt."

Another frown. "That playwright? Oh yes. He's gone as well, regrettably. I'm told he got in the way. What was he doing here, Ginny?"

I was too tired, too hurt. I could not keep the tears from rolling down my cheeks. I looked away from my father, toward the windows with their chintz curtains. My longing swelled to tighten my throat. "He was our . . . future," I managed.

"My dear . . . I think you should have more laudanum." He reached for the bottle on the bedside table.

I raised my good hand to stop him. "I don't want that. I want Bea."

He frowned. "You're overset. Here now . . . take the medicine."

"I'm not overset. You don't know . . . you don't know anything."

"There's no need to explain now." His voice was soothing, cajoling, as if he spoke to a child, and I fought the fog of grief and pain and said the lie Bea and I had agreed upon. I could explain away questions later.

"I hit my head in the fire," I said dully. "I didn't remember . . . anything. And then . . . Nathan thought I was . . . a ghost."

"He meant to kill you, she said. That actress said he tried to kill the both of you."

"Yes. I don't remember very much. It was all very . . . confusing." Again, I turned away.

Papa sighed. Then he said, "There's time enough to sort it out. The police want to speak to you, but I've told them they must wait. In the meantime, I've made arrangements to take you home."

"Home?"

"Back to Chicago," he said gently. "I've been very worried about you, Geneva, but thankfully you seem . . . well, better than I'd been led to believe. Nathan thought . . . he implied . . ."

I met my father's gaze. "I wasn't going mad. It was Nathan."

Papa said grimly, "Yes, I see that now. I hear he made quite a stir these last few weeks. But it's all over now, Ginny. The doctor says you should be ready to travel within the week."

My resentment flooded back through my pain, the thing he'd been willing to do, the way he'd trusted my husband. And I knew what it would be like if I let him take me back to Chicago. I would be the widowed daughter, my behavior circumscribed, my every move scrutinized. Because there had been the possibility of commitment before, even without Nathan's lies, and that could not be undone. It would forever be the shadow between us.

No, it was time to become what I'd meant to become. Otherwise, Sebastian DeWitt's death meant nothing. And that was something I could not allow.

"I'm staying here," I said. "In Seattle."

"That's the laudanum talking," Papa said. "We'll speak of such things later. Now you should rest."

"It's not the laudanum. And I won't change my mind. I'm not going anywhere. I want to stay."

He looked so shocked I might have laughed any other time. "Ginny, you can't be serious."

"I'm very serious," I said, and I thought of Sebastian DeWitt, the flash of his white shirt as he took Nathan's bullet, the way he'd died in her arms. The pain in her voice as she'd called out his name. "There's . . . something I have to do."

"Something you have to do? What could that possibly be?"

I met his gaze evenly. "I have to make a star."

Chapter Forty

Beatrice

Now that it was over, it seemed inevitable that it would turn out as it had—like every damn tragedy I'd ever acted, where, had any one thing *not* happened, the whole thing could have been avoided. Romeo hesitating just a bit longer so that Friar Laurence's letter could get to him, Oedipus agreeing that Laius had the damn right of way at the crossroads, Penelope Justis deciding to get some sleep instead of sneaking through the dead of night to show the spirit to Barnabus one last time.

"I mean for it to be a tragedy," he'd said. And he had made it so. As brilliantly as he'd done everything else.

Ginny's father stayed until the day after Nathan's funeral, and the two of them seemed reconciled enough—at least he agreed to restore her funds. They buried Nathan Langley in a plot here in Seattle because Ginny meant for people to see the act of her grieving. She paid a fortune for an elaborate headstone and cried and beat her breast, and the fact that she was half-dead herself with pain and loss of blood only helped people to believe it—or at least, no one said otherwise in my hearing. There were plenty of tales going around about it. No one cared for the truth as she told it: how she'd hit her head in the fire and woke with no memory of who she was until that night, and how she'd enlisted Sebastian's help to take her to the house and Nathan had been so crazy he'd shot her and Sebastian both before he committed suicide. It was a good story, but people found the others better. There was the rumor about how she'd gone to San Francisco the morning of the fire and Nathan had known all about it and pretended she was dead so he could be rid of her. Or the one of how she'd fled Nathan's growing insanity and come back with Sebastian to find the two of us in bed together, and Sebastian had got in the way. A third about Nathan and Sebastian fighting a duel over me when Ginny returned unexpectedly.

All equally good. It would settle down to some truth sooner or later, but in the meantime, she and I were infamous, and I could see by the way Ginny's eyes sparkled that she liked that, and there were times when I didn't mind it either.

We all live with illusions, I guess. Even I had, though I'd never suspected it until we buried Sebastian. Lucius took all the receipts from that night and asked if anyone minded if he used it to buy a headstone for "our sadly lost genius," and though I expected most of the company to object, no one did, and they all came to the funeral. Aloys spoke some very nice words about beautiful fallen angels and Shakespeare's spirit taking Sebastian to his breast, and I could not keep from remembering the words I'd said that didn't help, the *I love you* that couldn't save him, and Aloys put his arm around me and let me cry into his shoulder and whispered in a rough voice, "You must let us comfort you, my dear. We are your family," and it was a shock to realize he meant it.

The others were the same. For weeks after, I felt as if I moved in a fog, and Jack hovered about me like a damn nurse, his eyes dark with worry, vying with Brody to see which of them could make me laugh. Mrs. Chace brought me a bag of hard candy because she said she knew I loved it and "sometimes little comforts help." Their obvious affection surprised me. I think it was even what saved me.

And then . . . Ginny. She was the only one who really knew what had happened, who knew what we'd done, though we never spoke of it, and sometimes it was hard to look at her and see myself in her eyes, and sometimes I couldn't look away, and the connection to her was so strong it felt as if we'd somehow been woven together, and I was surprised that it wasn't a feeling I wanted to go away.

Strange, isn't it, how things come back to haunt you? The

little ironies God or whoever keeps in store to abuse you with when you least expect it? Because I hadn't liked her and she hadn't liked me and yet here we were, and it was because of her that I had everything I'd wished for.

Well . . . didn't I?

Chapter Forty-one

Geneva

SEATTLE, WASHINGTON STATE, MARCH 1890

I could not take my eyes from her. Such pure perfection she was; such restrained sorrow and rage as she trod the boards of the rebuilt Phoenix, as she raised her dark eyes to the heavens and swore vengeance for her sister's death. Every gaze in the house was fixed upon her, rapt, captivated, there was hardly a breath that could be heard. Even the gallery gods were so quiet one barely remembered they were there, and someone hushed the lozenge boy before he could say the first words of his sales patter.

The audiences had been this way every night since *Penelope Justis, or Revenge of the Spirit* had opened, and I had not missed a single performance. I had helped her sew the deep blue gown she wore—the finest velvet we could find—and she had laughed at the gold embroidery I'd paid a dressmaker to embellish it with and said it was fit for a queen rather than the baker's daughter that was Penelope Justis. But she'd worn it, and I'd seen the lilt of pride that came into her face and was glad to have put it there.

The crowds came because of the notoriety; as they took their seats, I never failed to hear someone comment how closely the play was said to mirror reality, though of course they could not know how deep the resemblance truly went. They came for that, but they stayed because of her. Because she brought Penelope alive, and there was no one still caring about Nathan Langley when it was over, and I took as much satisfaction from that as she did.

I remembered the first time I'd seen her, playing Pure Polly's sister in *Black Jack, the Bandit King of the Border.* It was the night that had started all the others; the night Nathan had seen her and realized how she could be of use to him. But more than that, it was the night that I recognized her, the night I somehow knew to mark her, and that was what I could not forget. A year ago now, but it seemed a hundred years since I'd known her. I hardly remembered a time when she was not in my life, or when I did not spend the afternoons after rehearsal with her in quiet companionship, or watch her sparkle as she circulated among the friends who came nightly to our house—the company, of course, and whatever artist or writer or actor happened to be in town and one or two members of society—the Readings, of course, and, to my surprise, Mrs. Orion Denny, who'd been drawn by the genius of Sebastian DeWitt's play and turned out to be rather a kindred spirit. But these were not salons. What need had I of salons, when I had friends to talk and laugh with? When I had Bea?

Tonight, as always, when Barnabus shot Penelope and then himself—and Aloysius Metairie had never met a death scene he didn't love—the audience exploded in a riot of applause and *Bravos,* leaping to their feet, requiring curtain call after curtain call. I left my seat then, pushing past those still standing, making my way past the salon and down the steps and out into a night heavy with the smell of construction—dirt and brick and stone—even through the rain. I dodged in through the backstage door, pressing myself against the wall to stay out of the way of the stagehands, most of whom gave me a quick smile. I heard the applause still, reverberating to backstage, but there came Susan down the stairs, and then Brody, both sweating but looking supremely satisfied, and Mrs. Chace red-faced and waddling, and Mr. Galloway with his perpetual limp from the damage done to his back by the fire. Then Aloys, who stopped and smiled at me, raising a dark brow in question, and I said,

"More perfect than any night before. You do know how to die, sir."

"Did you like the twitch at the end? Or did you think it too much?"

"It could not have been better."

"You are the perfect patron, Ginny." He took my hand, bending over it with a deep bow. "Always complimentary."

"And never stinting on the money," I teased.

"For God's sake, move out of the way, Aloys," came Jack's voice. "You've garnered enough compliments. Now it's time for mine." And then he was pushing past Aloysius, swooping me into his arms. "Well, Ginny? Was I not perfection itself?"

"Your head's too big for me to get around, Jack," Bea said wryly from behind him. "Will you move or do I have to deflate it?"

He let me go with a smile. "Careful, Bea. You'll spoil our patroness's good opinion of me."

"You needn't worry over that, Jack, as she has no good opinion to spoil," she retorted.

I laughed. "We'll argue about it over absinthe. Where's Lucius?"

"In his office, I believe, going over receipts," Jack said.

"Tell him to come tonight, would you please? I'd like to discuss a set change with him."

The others went off, and Bea came to stand beside me, leaning against the wall. She went quiet, a little too thoughtful, that thoughtfulness I couldn't bear.

"It was wonderful tonight," I said fervently.

"You say that every night."

"It's always true. It's a lovely play. And you're perfect in it."

"Because it was written for me," she said, and then, among the chaos of stagehands and dressers and supernumeraries, she said quietly, "It reminds me."

She surprised me; we did not usually speak of it. "I know. But we've made him famous. There isn't anyone in Seattle who doesn't know his name."

She said nothing. Then a sigh, and she squeezed my hand and pushed from the wall. "You know, as much as I love this dress, I'm dying to be out of it. I won't be long. Don't let Jack talk you into going ahead. I don't care if he insists he'll leave some absinthe for me."

"I won't," I promised.

I watched her as she went down the hall to her dressing room, feeling the race of her heart as if it were my own. Once she was there, she paused, her hand on the door handle, and turned to look into the darkness beyond. I knew better than anyone the ghosts that lurked in this hallway, the ones who called to her, the truths they spoke. I'd heard them myself.

And I was relieved when she turned her head away.

Acknowledgments

As always, I owe a great debt to Suzanne O'Neill at Crown, who managed once again to find the heart of this story, and to Kristin Hannah, who never fails to remind me "it's about focus." Also many thanks to Kim Witherspoon and Julie Schilder, and the staff at Inkwell Management, for all their efforts on my behalf, and to Elizabeth DeMatteo, Jena MacPherson, Melinda McRae, Liz Osborne, and Sharon Thomas for their unwavering encouragement and support.

This book could not have been written without the online resources of the Seattle Public Library and the University of Washington Library—both a researcher's dream.

And of course, I owe the greatest debt of all to my husband, Kany, and to Maggie and Cleo, who put up with a great deal and still manage to love me anyway.